STAR'S END

ALSO BY CASSANDRA ROSE CLARKE

Our Lady of the Ice
The Mad Scientist's Daughter
Magic of Blood and Sea
Magic of Wind and Mist

STAR'S
END

CASSANDRA ROSE CLARKE

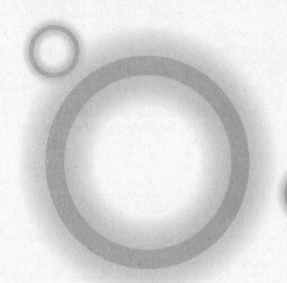

SAGA PRESS

LONDON SYDNEY **NEW YORK** TORONTO NEW DELHI

SAGA PRESS

AN IMPRINT OF SIMON & SCHUSTER, INC.

1230 AVENUE OF THE AMERICAS, NEW YORK, NEW YORK 10020

* Text copyright © 2017 by Cassandra Rose Clarke * Cover illustration copyright © 2017 by Darren Hopes * All rights reserved, including the right to reproduce this book or portions thereof in any form whatsoever. For information address Saga Press Subsidiary Rights Department, 1230 Avenue of the Americas, New York, NY 10020 * SAGA PRESS and colophon are trademarks of Simon & Schuster, Inc. * For information about special discounts for bulk purchases, please contact Simon & Schuster Special Sales at 1-866-506-1949 or business@simonandschuster.com. * The Simon & Schuster Speakers Bureau can bring authors to your live event. For more information or to book an event, contact the Simon & Schuster Speakers Bureau at 1-866-248-3049 or visit our website at www.simonspeakers.com. * Also available in a Saga Press hardcover edition * Interior design by Greg Stadnyk. * The text for this book was set in Sabon. * Manufactured in the United States of America * First Saga Press paperback edition November 2017 * 10 9 8 7 6 5 4 3 2 1 * Library of Congress Cataloging-in-Publication Data * Names: Clarke, Cassandra Rose, 1983– author. * Title: Star's end / Cassandra Rose Clarke. * Description: First edition. | New York : Saga Press, [2017] * Identifiers: LCCN 2016041030 | ISBN 9781481444293 (hardback) | ISBN 9781481444316 (eBook) | ISBN 9781481444309 (pbk) * Subjects: LCSH: Science fiction. | BISAC: FICTION / Science Fiction / General. | FICTION / Science Fiction / Adventure. | FICTION / Science Fiction / Space Opera. * Classification: LCC PS3603.L372 S73 2017 | DDC 813/.6—dc23 LC record available at https://lccn.loc.gov/2016041030

STAR'S END

NOW

He was dying.

The restaurant hummed, soft murmuring voices, the rattle of silverware, a cobwebbed overlay of music.

"What?" Esme said.

Miguel balanced his fork on the edge of his plate and made a show of wiping his hands on his napkin. He wouldn't look her in the eye. It was a tell she had warned him about when he first joined the company.

"He's *dying*?" Esme said.

Miguel nodded. "He went in for testing three days ago—"

"Three days?"

"Yes. It's galazamia."

The word was sharp-edged, like a knife. Galazamia. Aina Mitsuke's disease. Zamia. It had a hundred different names but the results were always the same: you wasted away until you were nothing. It was not a disease Esme would ever have associated with her father.

"I'm sorry he didn't tell you himself. He asked me not to, but—" Miguel twisted in his seat. "It didn't feel right, keeping it a secret from you."

Esme closed her eyes. Her body hummed like a live wire. She thought about the last time she had seen her father. It had been less than twenty-four hours before. He'd been sitting across the table from her at an investor's meeting up in the space station, lightscreen glowing while Steve Bajori rattled on about this season's financial reports. She hadn't paid much attention to him, having other things on her mind, but she did remember glancing at him halfway through the meeting to catch him staring out the window at Coromina I, at the fine-hewn golden-red swirls of its surface.

Her father wasn't one for looking out windows.

"Esme?"

Esme opened her eyes. Miguel was staring at her, leaning into the table, looking concerned.

"I'm sorry if this was an intrusion—" he began.

"An intrusion." Esme shook her head. "No, it's fine."

"I felt bad keeping it from you."

"I understand. It's fine." Esme looked down at her half-finished meal. She didn't have the appetite to finish. "He seemed healthy the last time I saw him." She said this more to herself than to Miguel.

"It's in the early stages."

Esme laughed, shaking her head. She didn't mean to but it slipped out anyway. "The early stages," she said. "What else do you know?" She looked up. Miguel looked away. "Come on, Miguel, it sounds like he really opened up to you." It came out more bitterly than she intended, but bitterness was impossible to avoid when Phillip Coromina was involved.

"Not much." Miguel sighed. "Just that that it's galazamia, that it's in the early stages, that he's already started treatments."

"How long?"

"How long what?"

Esme clenched her jaw, teeth grinding together.

"Oh. How long till he—" Miguel shook his head. "God, Esme, I don't know. He didn't tell me. I don't know why he told me about the zamia in the first place."

"He likes you."

Miguel blinked at her in surprise, his eyes big and dark. Her father did like Miguel. Esme liked Miguel too, which was why she had brought him on as her assistant almost fifteen years before. But it had been her father who'd been impressed with his work, who promoted him to senior vice president. Esme outranked him on the corporate ladder but not, apparently, on personal matters.

"Esme, I'm sorry," he said. "Let me get lunch."

The muscles in Esme's face tensed into something like a smile. She didn't know what Miguel was apologizing for—the fact that her father told him first, or the fact that her father was dying at all. Maybe both. Maybe it didn't matter.

"It's not your fault," she said, a response that would fit either circumstance.

Miguel smiled at her, a sad smile, tactful and appropriate. Esme poked at the salad on her plate, then dropped the fork and drained her glass of wine. Miguel watched her, his face blank. Nonjudgmental. That wasn't the reason she hired him, but it was the reason she went to lunch with him.

"I'll get the check now," he said, and lifted one hand in the air.

Esme clicked off the holo and stared at the bluish haze the image left behind as the light faded. Another call finished. This one had been with the lab out at Starspray City on Catequil, the heart of the Coromina Group's weapons manufacturing. She'd been on three such calls in the two hours since lunch, and with each one she'd smiled, she'd soothed, she'd promised her employees that the Coromina Group was looking into their concerns about the whispers of anti-corporate rebels hiding out in the system, about the possibility of a containment breach. She didn't let any of her colleagues know that her father was dying.

Esme pushed away from her desk and walked over to her window. Her office was on the seventy-fifth floor, high enough that she could almost make out the ocean sparkling in the distance, the water that bright emerald green that was one of Ekkeko's many trademarks. She crossed her arms over her chest. Her reflection moved in the glass. Her father was in a meeting; at least, that's what his assistant Lucia had told her when she rang her up on the holo, right after she had returned to her office. No telling when he'd be out.

Esme leaned against the glass. Wind whistled around the building but down on the ground the jacaranda trees and tall silvery-green sea grass were unmoving. This wasn't the first person she'd lost in her life—her mother had died in a war in the Iaon system a few years earlier, doing what she loved. And of course Esme's sisters were gone, a fact she had come to accept a long time ago. But her father was different. He was three hundred years old. He'd been taking rejuvenation treatments since before they were safe. He was the sort of person you wanted to die and so you knew never would.

The holo trilled on Esme's desk.

She pulled away from the window and sank down in the chair. She ran one hand over her hair before switching on the holo. It was a reflex. She hardly even knew she did it.

Lucia materialized in miniature on the top of Esme's desk. "Good afternoon, Ms. Coromina."

"Lucia." Esme said the name carefully, not wanting to give away any of the turbulence spilling around inside of her.

"Mr. Coromina is out of his meeting, if you'd still like to speak with him."

"Love to." Esme forced a smile. "I'll be right up."

"Very good." Lucia reached forward with one hand and then her image vanished. Esme took a deep breath. She'd told Lucia this was about the contract with the Spiro Xu Military Alliance. It was going to be a surprise when he found out it wasn't. As much of a surprise, perhaps, as Esme learning from Miguel Lee that her own father was dying.

Esme rode the elevator to the top floor. She wore a lightbox around her wrist to look official, but no one was in the elevator with her, so she just leaned against the cool, sleek metal and closed her eyes. Her heart fluttered. It was like she was a teenager again, an intern, afraid to look her father in the eye. She hadn't felt like this in years.

The doors slid open. The warm honeyed lights her father favored made Esme's eyes hurt, but she stepped off the elevator with graceful strides. Only she knew how hard her blood was pumping through her system, how hard she found it to breathe.

Lucia glanced at her. "You can go on in."

Esme nodded. The orchids flanking the big wooden door leading into his office were new, replaced since the last time Esme had been up there. White petals speckled with red. And as a little as Esme knew about galazamia, she knew the early symptoms involved coughing blood. Red on a white handkerchief.

For God's sake. Even his decor knew before she did.

She went in without knocking.

Her father sat at his desk, lightscreen up. From Esme's perspective the screen was nothing but a display of neo-minimalist red flowers (*more red, more blood*), transparent enough that she could see her father staring at whatever file he had pulled up.

He swiped his hand across the screen. "So, what's this about Spiro Xu? I thought we had that one in the bag." Another flick of his hand. The red flowers rippled.

"We do." Now that Esme was there, in his lush, golden-lit office, her words had drained away. The window behind his desk took up an entire wall. You could see the ocean from there, easily, but he kept the glass dark.

"So, what's the problem?" His focus stayed on the lightscreen. "Don't you usually have Will deal with these military guys? That's why we brought him on board, remember? You know how those assholes are; they think anybody who didn't—"

"It's not Spiro Xu," Esme said.

"Then what is it?" Her father finally looked up, staring at her through the lightscreen. The glow fell across his face, turning his eyes unnaturally blue.

"You're dying."

She hadn't meant to say it so directly; she'd meant to build to the moment, to massage him. She'd learned how to manipulate people from him, after all.

Her father went still.

"Excuse me?" he said.

Esme walked up to his desk, reached over, and switched off the lightscreen.

"I had lunch with Miguel this afternoon."

Nothing.

"You told him," Esme said, her voice tightening like a wire, "before you told *me*?"

No answer.

"I'm your *daughter*."

Her father sighed. He folded his hands across his desk. "He wasn't supposed to tell you."

"You couldn't expect him to keep a secret like that."

"I just wanted to—" Another sigh. "You've got a lot on your plate right now, especially with the potential breach issues."

Esme bristled. "I've been handling the breach issues just fine. That's no excuse for you to keep this a secret from me."

Her father rubbed his forehead, and Esme's anger lurched inside her. He was all she had left. Even Star's End was gone, burned away in the war that made them trillions. She should have known better. It was too much to expect him to even realize that. To even care.

But she didn't tell him any of this. Her father was not one for public displays of emotion.

"You weren't supposed to find out that way," her father said, as if that was all she needed to know.

Esme knotted her hands into fists. Even as spacious as the room was, the walls seemed too close, the ceiling too low. She wished the glass in the window was clear, wished she could see straight on through to the ocean.

"Then you should have told me."

He looked up at her then, and Esme felt herself falter. She expected him to be stern, forceful, the way he'd been her entire life. But there was a sadness in his features that caught her off guard. She didn't know what it meant.

"I'm telling you now," he said.

And like that, the moment was gone. He reached down and

switched the lightscreen back on. "Go back to work, Esme. Your first concern needs to be with the security breach. And don't worry about me."

Esme stared at him, her throat dry. Her eyes itched and she thought she might start crying. It seemed absurd, to cry over him.

"Go," he said, and she did.

The next morning, Esme rode to Hawley Laboratory, her head pressed against the window's glass. The car's engine hummed, a low soft song that flared when the driver directed the car out into the highway. The scenery blurred, like stars on a hypership. Esme's stomach roiled. She closed her eyes.

Today, her father's illness felt like a strange dream, something left over from her adolescence, when she still thought she might become someone else. But she hadn't dreamed last night. Her sleep had been deep, fathomless, the sleep of comas and sickness.

The car slowed as it wove through the woods surrounding the lab. Esme looked out at the greenery already curling up in the heat. They were coming into the dry season. Everything was dying.

"What entrance would you like to me to drop you at?" The driver spoke with the mechanical cadence all drivers did when they were hooked into a car, their mind and the car's engines twisting together into a dance really too complex and elaborate for chauffeuring Coromina Group executives around. But the technology hadn't been developed for cars.

"The main entrance is fine." Esme could see it up ahead; Will was waiting for her, standing in a soldier's stance, feet planted wide apart, arms crossed. It was a stance that had been engineered into him almost thirteen years before.

The car stopped, and Esme thanked the driver and stepped out into the bright morning heat. Will waved at her. She wondered if he knew about her father. Probably not. He was one of the R-Troops— part of that first batch, actually—and although he had been trained after the war to work alongside the upper tiers of the Coromina Group infrastructure, he was still a soldier to most of them. Still a bioengineered piece of weaponry.

"Morning," he said, giving her that drama-star grin of his. It faded quickly enough, though.

"Aw, come on, Esme," he said. "You know this is just the scientists worrying about nothing."

It took Esme a moment to realize that he was talking about the possible containment breach and not her father's illness. She sighed. "I had a bad night." They walked toward the entrance, the lab doors sliding silently open for them. Cold air billowed into the heat. "A bad afternoon, yesterday."

Will frowned, turned his dark eyes to her.

"I shouldn't talk about it here," she said.

"Later," he said. "Promise."

"Promise." Her father probably didn't want her telling Will—his rank was too low for personal matters—but she told Will things she wasn't supposed to all the time. Will was her only friend in a world full of colleagues and underlings.

They walked side by side down the narrow entrance hall. Invisible scanners washed over them, reading the microscopic chips embedded in both of their bloodstreams, ensuring that they were supposed to be there. Esme only knew the scanners were installed because she was ranked a Ninety-Nine, the highest rank you could have within the Coromina Group.

A lab assistant materialized up ahead, stepping out of one of the side rooms—Esme couldn't remember her name, only that she was a transfer from the lab on Catequil, that she came highly recommended by the program director there.

"Ms. Coromina, Mr. Woods," she said. "Right this way, please. The new recruits are set up in one of the meeting rooms, as you requested."

"Has there been any more trouble?" Will asked.

The lab assistant shook her head. "Not since the report we filed, no. And just between you and me"—she smiled sweetly at Will—"I don't think it's anything major. But Dr. Goetze was part of the team that had been affected by the last breach, so he can be paranoid about these things."

"He's conscientious," Esme said. "That's why I hired him. Let's just hope you're right about this being nothing."

Their shoes clicked across the slick tile of the laboratory hallway. The meeting room was set off from the main corridor. The windows hadn't been tinted and Esme could see the three soldiers she had read about yesterday morning. Before her world broke open. Before she found out about her father's illness.

They went inside. The soldiers stood to attention. None of them had Will's face. Five years ago, Esme had requested that it be phased out. She didn't like seeing a man who was Will and not Will at the same time.

"At ease," she said. "Have a seat." She slid into the chair at the head of the table. Will settled into the one on her right, and she surveyed the three soldiers, looking for outward signs of trouble. They were obedient, bright-eyed. One of them smiled nervously at her. She wondered how old he was. At least a year, but if they were new recruits, they wouldn't have been going through training for long.

"None of you are in trouble," she said in the calm, clear voice she used when she wanted control. "And none of you are at fault. This is simply an inquiry to ensure that the Radiance aren't attempting to break through the boundaries again."

"Yes, ma'am," murmured the soldier who smiled at her. The other two nodded.

"Good. I want you to know you can be forthright with me and Mr. Woods. Mr. Woods comes from your same background, so he'll be asking most of the questions."

More nods. Esme turned to Will. This routine came easy to her these days, even if this particular inquiry left her feeling anxious. The two of them had interviewed R-Troops on all four planets in the system, looking for defects, for problems, for solutions. The information they dealt with was too sensitive to trust to lower-ranked employees, so even though she held the title of Vice President of Genetics, she spoke to the R-Troops herself, with Will at her side. This was especially true when there was a chance that the Radiance might be trying to break through to the world again. They had last tried almost five years before, reaching out to a squadron of new recruits, manipulating the minds of the R-Troops, using them to work their way back to the world. The Coromina Group had caught it early, though, and now upper management all knew the signs. Dreams. Disloyalty. Insubordination. Two reports of suspicious behavior had come in recently: one here at Hawley, and another out on Catequil.

No, Esme told herself. *Don't start worrying until we have definitive proof.*

Will activated his lightbox, a curtain of light coming up between him and the three new recruits.

"Have you had any unusual dreams in the last week?" he asked, lifting his gaze toward them.

The recruits shifted in their seats, glanced at each other—they never expected this question, which was why Will and Esme had decided it was best to always lead with it. Just in case it was one of the R-Troops who was helping the Radiance.

"No, sir," the first one said, and the others agreed.

"Do you remember any of your dreams from this time period? Can you describe them to me?"

Another uncomfortable pause. Esme leaned back in her seat, trying to make herself as nonintrusive as possible. She needed to be there to hear the answers; it was her decision, ultimately, if further action needed to be taken. She might consult with Will, because he understood better than she did. But everything came to her in the end.

Two of the recruits shook their heads, but a third said, "I always remember my dreams, sir. I dream in tandem with the rest of our unit. Recycling the day's events, that's what they tell me dreams are."

"That's exactly what dreams are." Will smiled, gentle and fatherly. "And yes, you're all dreaming in tandem with your unit, even if you don't remember. Tell me"—he thumbed his lightscreen—"Private Woods-33, do you recall any dreams that featured any of the following?"

He coughed, cleared his throat. Private Woods-33 blinked expectantly.

"An unfamiliar language?"

"No, sir."

"Images of black feathers or scales?"

"No."

"Inhuman creatures?"

Private Woods-33 frowned. "You mean animals, sir? I think I dreamt of a cat one night, since there are cats all over—"

Will waved his hand dismissively. "Not a cat, no. By inhuman I meant"—here he glanced at Esme, and she nodded once, giving permission—"alien."

Private Woods-33 went very still. One of the other recruits turned pale and ashy. "A breach," he muttered. "This is about a breach."

"We're here to determine that," said Esme. Her voice seemed to startle him, and he jumped, glanced over at her suspiciously. "But so far, that doesn't appear to be the case."

"I agree," Will said. "Have any of you experienced daytime hallucinations?"

They all shook their heads no, much more fervently now. They understood the ramifications of what the questioning was about.

"Have you noticed any strange behavior among your unit?"

Here, though, was a hesitation. The R-Troops were designed to be loyal, both to each other and to the Coromina Group. Sometimes, these loyalties conflicted.

Esme leaned forward and folded her hands on the table. "If a soldier has been acting strangely," she said, "he will be treated with dignity and respect. A breach is not the fault of a soldier. It's the fault of the Radiance." Unless the soldier *was* helping the Radiance, of course, a possibility Esme dreaded dealing with a second time. But she didn't say this to the new recruits. "They're locked away in their dimension, and you are the most vulnerable point of entry." She smiled, having worked with new recruits long enough to know when it was necessary for her to become motherly, the way Will became fatherly. "Your greatest strength—your connection with each other—that's how the Radiance will find their way in. If we can stop it before it gets too far, it works out much better for everyone." She paused, and then said, with a dry tongue, "Radiance included."

This soothed them, the way it always did. She settled back in her chair. "That's good to know," said Private Woods-33, "but I haven't noticed anything strange. Truly."

"Me, neither," said one of the others, and the third nodded in agreement.

"No strange thoughts?" Will asked. "No whispers in an unfamiliar language?"

No, nothing.

Perhaps Dr. Goetze had overreacted after all. The R-Troops were safe, and the Radiance were still tucked away in the strange, poisonous dimension where they'd been contained thirteen years ago. The year of the attack at Star's End.

The year Isabel went away. Then Adrienne, a year later, disappearing when she went off to college. And then finally Daphne, a few months after that. All three of Esme's sisters scattering across the system, vanishing the way the Radiance had. Fading into an alternate reality.

"Thank you for your time," Esme said. "The Coromina Group appreciates your cooperation. If you ever noticed any of things Will mentioned, please don't hesitate to contact me. Dr. Goetze can give you my information." She smiled, one dazzling corporate smile, and the recruits returned it, nervously.

Will did his part, thanking them, shaking their hands as if they were war-brothers. Then Esme and Will filed out into the hallway. The lab assistant waited for them, wide-eyed.

"Everything appears fine," Esme said. "But keep an eye on the unit. Watch for sleeping troubles especially."

"Yes, ma'am." The assistant scurried into the meeting room to deal with the recruits, and Will and Esme showed themselves out, back into the thick heat of the forest.

"I told you, we're worrying about nothing," Will said.

"Well, I still have to investigate Catequil, so we'll see. Do you want to share a car back to the office?" Esme looked over at him. "I hope you're right, though." She thought about her lunch with Miguel. *Your father's dying.* Maybe this was her father's doing. What had happened with the Radiance had been his biggest fuck-up, even if he'd managed to turn it around in the end, with the cover-up, the containment, the R-Troops. She wouldn't put it past him to try a do-over. One more fight before his body gave out.

She shivered in the heat.

That night, Esme dreamt of the garden at Star's End. Rows of pineapples and acacia trees and a maze built of genetically engineered plumeria plants. The grass wet and soft beneath her bare feet.

Isabel, whispering into her ear: *Ms. Coromina. Ms. Coromina.*

"Ms. Coromina, you have a visitor."

Esme's eyes flew open. For one delirious moment, she thought she was in her childhood bedroom. But then the familiar walls of her apartment swam into view, stark and empty, and the voice of the apartment's AI system grounded her in the present.

"Ms. Coromina, you have a visitor."

"I heard you the first time." Esme pushed herself up and tossed her blankets aside. "Who is it?"

"Your father."

Esme's chest constricted. All the bleariness of sleep blinked away. "Are you sure?" She slid off the bed. "What time is it? Why is he here so late?"

"It's nearly midnight. I told him you were asleep, but he insisted I wake you."

This sounded like her father. It was a relief, really, to know that even dying couldn't change him completely. Esme ran her fingers through her hair, blinked the sleep out of her eyes. "Send him up, but put him in the parlor while I get ready."

"Very good, Ms. Coromina."

The apartment fell silent. Esme went into the bathroom and splashed cold water on her face. Her hair was mussed from sleep, and she brushed it out and pulled it into a knot at the back of her neck. Then she changed out of her sleeping clothes, pulling on an old Coromina Group uniform shirt, a pair of loose pants.

When she walked into the parlor, her father was waiting.

"Did I wake you?" he asked.

"You know you did." Esme perched on the edge of a chair, keeping her posture straight. They regarded each other in the silent emptiness of her apartment.

"Miguel wasn't supposed to tell you," her father said, after a time.

"Yeah, you mentioned that."

He sighed. "This is a complicated matter, Esme."

"It's really not," Esme said. "But I guess I shouldn't have expected better from you."

He didn't react. She hadn't expected him to.

"There are some things life prepares you for," he said. "And some things it doesn't. This is one of the latter."

Esme looked away, at the light painting hanging above the unused fireplace. An ugly thing, streaks of blue on a gray background. An old boyfriend had bought it for her. It was supposed to show the tumult of psychic connection. She got rid of the boyfriend but never bothered with the painting.

"I wanted to tell you myself," her father said.

"Then why didn't you?"

He stared at her, face blank. "I was waiting for the right time. When you weren't investigating Dr. Goetze's concerns. I told Miguel because, I don't know, I needed to tell *someone*. Some secrets are too . . ." His voice trailed away.

Esme didn't move. This was the closest to vulnerable she'd ever seen her father, and for a moment he was no longer Philip Coromina, prospector and visionary and billionaire, but a man who was dying.

"I need you to do something for me," he said, and the moment was lost. "Since you know anyway."

Esme glared at him. "You're not going to apologize."

"I only apologize to clients," he said, "and I never mean it."

Esme sighed. Of course.

"How much did Miguel tell you?" he asked.

"You mean you don't know?"

Her father shook his head. She choked back her surprise. Odd, that he didn't go intel-gathering before he showed up at her apartment.

"I wanted to hear it from you. Wanted to—to talk to you."

Esme gave him her iciest businesswoman glare, trying to mask the treacherous warmth that flared when he said he wanted to talk to her.

"How much did he tell you?"

She didn't want to answer. She wanted to answer. Nothing was ever cut and dried when it came to her father.

"Only that you've been diagnosed with galazamia." She crossed her arms over her chest. "That you got the test results back three days ago. That he didn't know how much time you had left."

"Yes," her father said. "I kept that information to myself."

Esme had never seen her father visibly unsettled. She had never seen him undone.

A coldness spread through her veins.

"How long?" she said.

Her father gave a brief, short laugh.

"How *long*?"

"Not much. Six months. A year at most."

"Six months!" Esme sprang to her feet, panic forcing her into movement. "Six fucking months! Most people with galazamia live six *years* from the time they're diagnosed, and you—"

"Most people are diagnosed early," her father said softly. "Then they take the medications and they undergo the treatments and they drag it out as long as they want."

"How could you—lord, Dad, how could you miss the symptoms? The coughing up blood and the dizziness and the—everyone fucking knows that, Dad! Everyone."

"I'm nearly three hundred years old, Esme. I thought it was just my time."

"Bullshit," said Esme. Her father had always seen dying as a form of giving up. Lots of people took youth treatments if they could afford them, but most didn't do it for three centuries. He had. He was that self-involved. That *controlling*. Three hundred years old so he didn't have to give up leadership of his company.

Her father watched her, taking in the situation, weighing the pros and cons like it was a business meeting. She stared right back. She'd been through this before.

"You always did know me the best," he said with a smile.

"Why the hell did you ignore the symptoms?"

A pause. A hesitation. Then he said, "I thought my youth treatments would counteract the worst of it. So, I set the zamia aside. Powered through."

There, that was the answer she expected. He despised weakness. In some ways, it was startling to hear him confess he was sick at all.

Her father shifted on the couch. He didn't look sick. Old, yes, the rejuvenation treatments could only do so much at three hundred, but not sick. Not dying.

"I don't regret it," he said. "I only wish I could have done it longer."

"What, pretended you didn't have fucking zamia?"

"That language, Esme, really isn't becoming."

She glared at him.

"There's no point in wallowing in self-pity. No one's found the cure for death yet." Her father laughed, hard and bitter. "As you well know."

Esme sighed. The Coromina Group's search for immortality had been the subject of rumors the last few years, mentions of a new high-clearance project popping up on the different news streams. She had spearheaded the project herself, although not for the reasons her father thought. She knew immortality was impossible. But medical advancements—that was something she wanted for the company. Make people better rather than killing them.

"It's a shame we weren't successful," he said. "You could move out of this penthouse to your own planet system. And I wouldn't have to die."

"You're not planning to shut the project down, are you?" She hoped not; otherwise she would have to go behind his back to get it up and running again. And that was not something she wanted to deal with, not when she needed to investigate these reports alerting the company to signs of a potential security breach.

"No, of course not. There just won't be anything for—for me." He looked down at his hands, and Esme felt a quiver of pity deep inside her chest. She hated it. She'd seen the damage his secret projects could do. It was fitting that he wouldn't benefit from this one.

"So, this is why you show up at my apartment in the middle of the night?" she snapped. "To tell me you failed at living forever?"

He stared at her, eyes dark and piercing. "I need a favor from you, Esme."

"What?" This, she hadn't expected. "A favor? Right now? I still have one more security breach report to investigate!"

"Yes." Her father took a deep breath, his slumped shoulders rising and falling. "The timing is bad, but you found out earlier than I intended."

Typical of him. One urgent assignment piled on top of another.

"I know you learned well from me, Esme. Never do a favor without expecting something in return. But this isn't business. This is family."

Esme looked at him. She was stunned into silence.

"I have to achieve my immortality the old-fashioned way." He smiled at her, although it was a cold, empty smile. "With you. And your sisters."

Esme didn't say anything. She'd never thought of children as a continuation of self. She'd never thought of children at all.

"A year from now, I'll be gone. And I want to—" He closed his eyes. In the parlor's thin white light, he was unsettlingly pale, like he'd already become a ghost. "I want to see them again. The others."

Silence rushed in. Esme couldn't move. She thought she might strangle on the shock of his words.

"All of them?" she said carefully.

Her father jerked his head up. "Yes." His voice was like stone. "All of them. Adrienne. Daphne." A pause. "Isabel."

They won't want to see you, Esme thought, but she couldn't bring herself to say it aloud. For all her attempts at it, she had never been as skilled at cruelty as her father.

"I know we parted on bad terms. I'm not an idiot. But it's been over a decade since I talked to—to any of them." Vulnerability flashed across his features again. The second time today. Esme found it disturbing. She found it sad. "I can't go tracking them down myself. I've got my affairs to attend to, and they wouldn't listen to me, anyway."

"You think they'll listen to me?"

He looked at her. "I don't know."

Esme sighed. It'd been years since she'd spoken to Daphne, and Daphne was the last sister she'd spoken to—over the holocomm, not even face to face. The connection had been bad, Daphne's face stretching out as if she were made of liquid. She was living on Catequil at the time, working at one of the cooperative wind farms. Four years ago, maybe. The Light Solstice. It had fallen during summer that year, at least on Ekkeko. Daphne hadn't said what season it was on Catequil. And what they'd talked about had been even more frivolous than the weather.

"I thought about hiring someone to track them down," he went on. "A PI, you know. But since you found out about it anyway, I decided I'd rather keep it in the family."

Esme sighed. He kept saying *family* as if it meant something.

"You disagree?"

"I'm not sure how much of a family we are."

For a moment, Esme thought she saw her father recoil. But she couldn't believe that was possible, that those particular words could hurt him that much.

"Am I to take that as a sign that you're not interested?"

Was she? The request was so absurd, after everything that had happened, and all the time that had passed. She wondered what he really wanted from them. There had to be another reason beyond hoping to simply talk to them, to see them again. There always was with her father. "It's not—I guess I just don't understand why you want to do this."

He looked almost confused and Esme didn't expand on what she meant, what she really wanted to say—that she understood why *someone* would want to do this, she just didn't understand why *he* would want to do this.

"They're my daughters," he said, his voice quiet. It was the same tone he used whenever he fired someone. "I want to see them again before I die."

The parlor was shrinking, drawing in closer and closer, sucking out the air.

"I still don't think they'd listen to me."

"They'll listen to you before they'd listen to me. And an investigator could only find them. He couldn't bring them home."

"I don't know why you think I could."

Her father looked away, toward the fireplace. Neither of them spoke for a long time. But eventually he said, "You were closer to them than I was." His gaze snapped back over to her. "You'll of course have access to as much money as required to track them down, as well as any diplomatic contacts that may prove necessary if they left the system."

"I didn't say I'd do it." But even as Esme spoke, she knew she couldn't say no. She was reeling from the idea that she and her sisters had been close—because they had, hadn't they, all those years ago? Sitting in the gardens at Star's End, eating formal dinners in the grand dining hall.

But more than that, she couldn't say no, because it was her father who asked her. He wasn't just her father; he was her boss. She was the one sister who stayed behind, because at the core of it, she'd spent her entire life trying to please him in a way the others hadn't. She'd done everything he'd ever told her to do. This request wasn't any different.

He knew it too. Maybe the promise of dying made him vulnerable, but it didn't make him stupid.

Esme toyed with her hair. It was already coming loose from of its bun. "How secret does this need to be?"

"Treat it like a Ninety-Nine-level project."

Of course. She sighed. "Can I at least get help from Will? We've worked together on sensitive projects before, and he might be useful . . ." Her voice trailed off. She didn't want to talk about her sisters like they were clients.

"Yes," her father said. "I agree that Will might be a help in all this. With his connections."

They sat for a moment, and Esme considered her options. She could contact Daphne, no doubt still windfarming on Catequil.

Daphne'd be the easiest to convince to come home. She was always the most easygoing, the most peaceable. And Esme needed to go to Catequil anyway as she followed the trail of security breaches across the Four Sisters.

"I'd like you to keep me informed of your progress," her father went on, although he was unfolding himself from the chair, a signal that the conversation—the *meeting*, because Esme knew damn well that's what this was—was coming to a close. "Weekly reports, let's say? And feel free to let me know if you uncover anything significant."

Esme murmured a note of acquiescence. Rubbed again at her aching head. Her father stood up.

"Thank you, Esme," he said, and he was staring down at her, and he meant it, he actually fucking meant it.

"Why don't you keep me informed," she said, "of your progress, too."

His mouth tightened into a slash of disapproval. "Very well."

They stared at each other for a moment longer, and then her father left the parlor. Esme dropped her head against the chair and listened to his footsteps echo against the tile in the foyer, listened to the chime of the apartment as it called the elevator for him.

After five minutes or so had passed, she asked, "Is he gone?"

"Yes, Ms. Coromina," the apartment answered.

Esme stood up and stumbled out of the parlor into the big empty space she called the living room. Night had fallen and the room was lit with the pale electric lights she'd had installed last spring. But even they seemed too bright, and the air in the apartment was stifling and hot. She went out onto her balcony. The wind whipping off the ocean was damp and unseasonably cool, which was exactly what Esme wanted.

She leaned against the railing, breathing in the scent of the sea. Lights twinkled down below, from the Coromina Group housing complex, from the village ringing around it. A few boats out on the water, bobbing like lanterns.

It was cloudy, too cloudy for stars. But all three moons were visible. Catequil, cleaved in half. Amana, a sideways smile. Quilla, a sideways frown. Esme had visited all three. They were company moons. The Coromina Group, under the direction of Esme's father, had terraformed them all, as well as Ekkeko, long before Esme was born, when her father was a young man through natural means and not artificial ones.

And her father was where Coromina I got its name, of course, the big gas giant the color of fire. There wasn't much of it tonight, only a sickle of burnished gold. Four satellites, four colonies. The Four Sisters, people called them. A name they'd been given before Phillip Coromina had four daughters.

Esme had never thought that was a coincidence.

TWENTY-SIX YEARS
EARLIER

When I was sixteen, my father called a family meeting. This was unprecedented; even after he'd married my stepmother, the first Isabel, I hadn't thought he cared enough to do such a thing.

It was raining that day, sheets of water pouring over the garden, and the curtains were pulled away from the windows so that gray light seeped in. I slunk into my father's office with a sweater draped over my shoulders. Isabel was already there, Daphne sitting in her lap, Adrienne on a blanket at her feet. For the longest time, I could only tell the twins apart because Isabel always dressed Daphne in reds and oranges and Adrienne in blues and greens, but in the last few months, I realized I didn't need the color-coding anymore. Daphne was the one always playing make-believe out in the yard. Adrienne was the serious one, always asking *Why*. The one destined for company work, the one that even at three years old made me nervous. It occurred to me that I had become used to the idea of having sisters, a fact I thought I'd always resent.

It was a good thing, too, because Isabel was pregnant again. You could already see her belly curving beneath her clothing.

I sat down in one of the big leather chairs and waited.

Dad wasn't there. Mr. Whittaker, his personal assistant, had materialized during my tutoring session to ask me to come to the office, and so I did. I wasn't surprised that he was making us wait.

Isabel giggled. When I glanced at her, she was smiling down at Daphne's face, toying with the ends of Daphne's black hair. She looked up at me. "Hello, Esme."

"Hi."

"How are your lessons going?"

"Fine."

Our conversations were always like this: short and polite, the bare minimum of what was expected of us. Isabel was only ten years older than me. She was graceful and elegant, like an actress from an Amanan drama. She was nothing like me, and nothing like my real mother.

"Phillip says he wants to see about getting you an internship in the fall." As she spoke to me, she brushed her hand over the curve of Daphne's head, a maternal gesture that always twinged the jealousy in me. "Has he told you that yet?"

I nodded. "He said something about setting me up in accounting, since I like math, but I'm most interested in planet maintenance."

"PM!" Her eyes widened in surprise. "That's an intriguing choice."

I shrugged. Planet Maintenance was the division of the Coromina Group that focused on the welfare of its citizen-employees—making sure that utilities were working, that cities and towns weren't falling apart. To me it seemed the best way to help my friends Laila and Paco in the village from my place in the citadel that was the CG main campus. I didn't want to tell Isabel all that, though.

Daphne squealed and tugged on a lock of Isabel's hair. Isabel laughed and tickled Daphne's stomach, and I looked away, over at the rainwater sluicing over the glass. Lightning flickered shadows across the room. Thunder rumbled off in the distance. Isabel sighed like she was happy.

An entire happy family, and me.

The office door banged open and Dad bustled in, his hair damp and the tops of his shoulder glistening with raindrops. "God," he muttered, dropping into his chair behind his desk. "I hate the rainy season."

Neither Isabel nor I said anything. A few seconds passed before Dad looked up at us, like he was just remembering we were in the room.

"Oh good, you're here," he said.

"We've never had a family meeting before," Isabel said, gazing at him with her usual sweet expression. "What's the occasion?"

"A family meeting, I like that." He laughed. He never laughed with me. "Although I'm afraid the occasion's not too joyous."

"Is it about the flu?"

Dad and Isabel both turned to me. I suppressed a smile, glad that I had ruined their banter.

"That isn't a flu," Dad said.

"Yeah, it's worse." I crossed my arms over my chest. "Laila told me her friend's third cousin caught it in Soxal, up north."

Dad didn't answer.

"She's dead now," I said, an unnecessary statement. If you caught the flu, you died. Thank God most people didn't catch it. "It's also popped up on Quilla."

Dad narrowed his eyes. "Where did you hear that?"

I shrugged. Isabel shifted in her chair and gave a nervous little sigh, one hand stroking distractedly at Daphne's hair. "Is that true, Philip?"

Dad was still glaring at me. "Where did you hear that, Esme?"

"Newsfeed."

"The Coromina Newsfeed has reported no such thing."

"Didn't hear it there."

"Enough!" Isabel hugged Daphne to her chest a little more closely than she had before. "Is this why you called us here? To talk about the flu?" She fixed Dad with a surprisingly steely gaze. "You don't have to listen to the illegal newsfeeds to know that there still isn't a cure. Everyone's been talking about it."

Dad glowered. "We've contracted out with Dobbin and Shook to help find a vaccine. You know that. The whole damn system knows that. But these things take time."

I sank back in my chair, arms crossed over my chest. Isabel fussed with Daphne, her expression dark. I'd spent enough time preparing for an internship with PM to know that the Coromina Group was responsible for the wellbeing of *all* the inhabitants of the Four Sisters. Every single citizen-employee, from the lowest to the highest. This was a responsibility, I'd learned over the last few years, that Dad frequently sent out to contractors.

"Well, I hope they develop something soon," Isabel said.

Dad cleared his throat and tapped his fingers against the desk. "There's no point in talking about the outbreak," he said. "It's a minor thing and it'll clear up eventually."

My stomach knotted up. *Liar.* I had been listening to Galactic Media Standard, to Amana Free, all the illegal newsfeeds. They were saying that once the flu got a stronghold, it could wipe out an entire town. People weren't even sure how it spread—not aerially, they knew that much, which meant it had to come from contact, from the exchange of human matter. Right now, the Ekkekon outbreaks were all far from here, up in the north, although they appeared in strange patterns. A cluster of deaths here, an isolated case five miles away in an old man who hadn't traveled and didn't receive visitors. And then there were the reports from Quilla—

This was not a minor thing.

Dad was staring at us, his fingers still rapping against the desk. Rain pinged against the windows, and the air had that steamed-up quality of the rainy season. We were all waiting for something. I knew what Isabel and I were waiting for, but I didn't know about Dad.

"If you're not here to give us word about the flu," Isabel said, one hand in Daphne's hair, the other wound around Adrienne's shoulder, "why did you call us into your office?"

"I had something unrelated to tell you." Dad leaned back in his chair. "I hired a military squad to stay with us for a while."

A stunned silence. The rain was like a metronome.

"*What?*" said Isabel. "Why? My God, Phillip, this is about the flu. Don't you dare lie to me."

"I told you, it's not a flu." Dad's voice was sharp with anger. "And this isn't about it either way. There are some security concerns—"

"Security concerns?" Isabel grabbed hold of Adrienne's hand, squeezing it tight.

"Mommy!" cried Adrienne.

"What sort of security concerns? I was thinking of inviting Marianne to stay sometime next month—will that be a problem?" Isabel's eyes were wide with fear, her skin pale against the dark curve of her hair. She looked even more beautiful when she was scared. Some sort of evolutionary tactic, I supposed, so that you'd want to take care of her. I certainly hadn't evolved that particular trait.

"No, not at all. The concerns are nothing major. We had a bit of trouble with protestors in the last year." He looked over at me. "You can thank those illegal newsfeeds for that. But really, dear, this is *nothing*. I'm just paranoid." He smiled, and that was how I knew he was lying. Whatever this was, it wasn't nothing.

Isabel stared at him. Adrienne squirmed against her grip.

"Which military?" I asked.

Dad glanced at me. "Alvatech," he said, before turning back to Isabel. "I just have our family's safety in mind. I would be distraught if anything happened to the kids or to you."

His attempts at consolation washed over me. Alvatech. Not the military my mother worked for. When Dad had said *military squad*, my thought had gone immediately to her, and I'd felt a tiny flicker of hope that I knew was fruitless. And I was right.

"They'll arrive in three days," Dad said, still speaking to Isabel. "You won't even notice they're here. They'll be casing the perimeter of the estate, monitoring the roads. We aren't concerned so much about the house itself."

"Then what are we concerned about?"

It struck me as strange that he hadn't told her. The way he'd gaze so adoringly at her when they were together, the fact that he came home for dinners more often than not these last four years, since they married, eloping in secret—I figured he told her everything. But right now, she was glaring at him, her shoulders trembling, spots of red decorating her pale cheeks.

He sighed. "It's a work matter, darling. I told you—"

"It is the flu, isn't it?" She smoothed down Daphne's hair, her hands shaking. "Esme was right. It is the flu."

Dad shot me a furious look, which I met with the impassive gaze I'd learned from him.

"It's worse than the Coromina Newsfeed is saying, isn't it? Has it spread offworld? You told me it was dying out in the north—"

"And I wasn't lying," Dad snapped. "It is dying out. The squad has nothing to do with the outbreak—and I keep telling you, it's not a flu."

"Everyone calls it a flu."

Dad scowled. "What does it matter? It's almost eradicated. It nearly kills itself out after every outbreak. The squad has nothing to do with the outbreak—I'm bringing in the military because there's been some minor concern about a security threat. Anti-corpocracy radicals. I doubt they would hurt you or the babies, but I want to *make sure*."

I noticed I wasn't included in the safe list.

Isabel's hands stopped shaking. "Radicals," she said.

"Oh, you know, they pop in from the Murtro system from time to time, whenever they can get a ship captain to take them on the jump, and set up Connectivity centers and spread lies around—it's nothing you need to worry about, dear."

"You keep saying that." Isabel closed her eyes and pressed her mouth against the top of Adrienne's head. "But if it were nothing to worry about, you wouldn't have hired soldiers to come to our home."

She stood up. Dad didn't say anything. I always took that as a sign that he truly loved her, the way he let her have the last word. He never did that with anyone else. Certainly not with me.

She murmured down to Daphne, "Come along, sweetness, let's go." Daphne tottered up, then called out to Dad, "Bye, Daddy!" before following Isabel and Adrienne out of the room.

The air sighed when she closed the door. Dad stared after her, fingers tapping against the desk. *Tap tap tap.* The sound of his fingers blended in with the sound of the rain, and I started to slide out of my chair.

"I suppose you have some questions too," he said. I stopped, looked at him, slid back into place.

"Not really."

He turned to me. He was made of stone now. His vulnerability, what little of it there was, only bubbled to the surface when he was with Isabel.

"If anything happens to me," he said, "you'll be given a place on the board of directors. Mr. Ortega will serve as temporary CEO until you're old enough to take control."

"Is something going to happen to you?"

"Don't be a smartass." Dad pinched the bridge of his nose. I didn't bother telling him I was genuinely curious. Genuinely concerned.

"I finally got Isabel to have a gender test done. On the baby."

I didn't say anything.

"She kept insisting she wanted to be surprised. Ridiculous." He shook his head. "Another daughter."

He exhaled when he said *daughter*, like the word had some unbearable weight to it. I looked down at my lap. I could have assumed that, this new baby being a girl. He wouldn't have told me I'd take over if anything happened to him otherwise.

We sat in silence. I was waiting for him to say something else, but he eventually just flicked his hand at me, gesturing toward the door. I left without saying goodbye.

After the meeting, I went up to my suite instead of back to tutoring. Mr. Garcia would come looking for me soon enough, but I wanted a few minutes alone. The rain fell harder now, pounding against my windows, so loud I could hardly think. I went into my closet and pulled down the little metal box I kept next to my shoes. I carried it over to my bed and sat down with it in my lap, and then I pressed my thumb against the lock. A tiny prickle passed through my skin as the lock tested my DNA, and then the box sprang open.

My mother.

The box was half-filled, mostly by the big, old-fashioned holocube my mother had given Dad when she left me at Star's End. There was also a handful of datachips, all of which contained the transmissions she sent me, once every five or six months, about her adventures across the system. *Adventures* was my word, not hers—she was professional military, and she just called all of it her job.

I pulled out the holocube and activated it. My mother appeared, shimmering with static. When I was younger, I'd played the message so often that it had started to wear out. Now I only played it when I really had to.

My mother's hologram smiled and it made her beautiful, even more beautiful than Isabel. She was muscular and broad and she wore her hair clipped short.

"Hey, sweetie," she said. Her voice distorted as she talked, stretching out into electronic feedback. "I guess you're old enough by now to know I left you with your father. Sure am sorry about that. But he's got money and he'll take good care of you down at that mansion of his. Figure gardens and the ocean would be better for you than the Corps." Another smile, although this one wavered, and I always wondered about that, why she wavered. If she almost changed her mind. "I ain't going away forever. I promise I'll write—Phillip says he'll save my transmissions for you till you're older. Funny how we still call it *writing*, eh?" She laughed, shook her head. "And promise you'll write me. It might be tough for me to get your messages right away, but I'll get them. Us Oxbow girls always keep our promises. I love you, sweetie. I'm sorry I couldn't raise you."

And then she kissed two fingers and pressed them out, like she was pressing them against the holorecorder. "How we keep our promises in the Andromeda Corps." Her image fizzed away.

My cheeks were damp. I set the holocube back in the box and stretched out on my bed. I thought about watching some of my mom's other transmissions, but I decided not to. I'd watched them all so many times, I had them memorized. I'd even started to notice that some of them had patterns thumping in the background, a weird static that I knew was probably nothing, although that hadn't stopped me from trying to break the patterns like a code when I was kid. I never found anything, though.

I wondered why Dad hadn't contracted with her military, why he hadn't brought her back to Star's End to work. I'd come to terms a long time ago with the fact that he wasn't going to marry her, that the affair that created me had been a fling and nothing more, but CG still did work with Andromeda Corps. It would have been such an easy gift for him to give me, and he hadn't bothered.

It shouldn't have surprised me, not by that point in my life. But it did anyway.

I walked down the Undirra highway. The rain had slowed to a hazy drizzle, but I'd always liked walking in the rain. I didn't even bother putting on a raincoat.

No one was out. I walked beneath the row of mango trees lining the road, and the air smelled like mangos, sweet and overly ripe. Every now and then, a car zipped by on the road, a gleaming, illuminated blur. Heading out of the village and into Undirra City.

It took me twenty minutes to reach the food stand where Laila worked. She was saving her money to buy the stand from its current owner, although there was nothing in the Coromina System that wasn't ultimately owned by the Coromina Group. The stand was built in the shape of a conch shell and had once been painted in vibrant pinks and yellows, although the colors were faded now. No one sat at the pair of picnic tables surrounding the stand, and Laila had the order window shut against the rain.

I rapped on it, to the tune of that Flying Trace song we'd been hearing all season. A moment's pause and then the window slid open.

"Good lord, Esme, you're soaked." Laila looked unfamiliar in her waitress outfit, the frilly little apron and the seashell pins holding back her hair. "Did you walk here?"

"Yeah." I pretended to read the menu—I came here often enough I had it memorized. "You think you can fry me up a shrimp plate?"

"Sure. You wanna come in? It's probably going to start raining again."

I nodded. I felt numb after the conversation with my father, and even seeing Laila didn't brighten my mood. She disappeared from the window and opened up the door hidden against the side of the shell. I stepped in. There was more room than you'd think from the facade, since the back extended out farther than the shell shape would allow. The fryers bubbled up against the wall, the lightbox's blue light gleamed across the tile floor, and the Coromina Group camera in the corner watched us with its unblinking eye.

"Here." Laila handed me a towel and I halfheartedly dried my face and hair before sitting down in the plastic fold-out chair next to a rickety table, empty except for a portable holocube. Laila pulled the ingredients for the shrimp batter off the shelf.

"So, what's up?" she asked, dumping corn flour and cheap beer into a metal bowl.

"Nothing."

"Liar." She looked at me over her shoulder. "You wouldn't have walked all the way out here if something wasn't going on."

I shrugged. Laila dropped the shrimp into the batter one at a time, swirling them with a fork. The rain picked up too, like she said it would, banging on the top of the conch shell.

"It's not Paco, is it?"

Paco had been a pearl diver for the last few years, but recently he'd turned vaguely radical, always spouting off against corpocracy. It gave him more of an air of danger than the pearl diving ever did. He was the one who told me about the illegal newsfeeds and showed me how to access them on my lightbox.

"No, it's not Paco."

Laila dropped the shrimp into the oil, where it splattered and hissed. She turned to me and crossed her arms over her chest. And waited.

"It has to do with—" I never liked talking about my family with Laila. She listened and nodded along, but I always got the sense that she didn't think my complaints were as real as hers. "Dad's hiring a military squad to stay at the estate."

Laila stared at me. Her hands dropped to her sides.

"The flu hasn't been contained," she said quietly.

"He says he didn't hire them because of the flu."

Laila turned back to the shrimp, fished them out, and dropped them in the biodegradable canisters all the shacks used. "Do you believe that?" she asked, staring down at the shrimp.

"I have no idea."

Laila sprinkled salt and pepper over the shrimp and then dropped in scoops of rice and macaroni salad. She handed the canister to me along with a fork and leaned up against the wall. She looked tired. And older than seventeen years.

"People are worried," she said, gazing over at the closed service window. Rain pummeled against the glass. I picked at the macaroni salad, waiting for my shrimp to cool. "I heard an entire fishing village up north got wiped out." She swished her hand through the air. "Like that. Everyone dead within a week."

"Dad's hired contractors to help find a vaccine." I didn't know how else to respond. My skin was itchy and hot, like I'd been caught doing something wrong.

"Yeah, the Coromina Newsfeed has been saying that for weeks. The GMS says that's a lie, though." She turned back to me, her eyes big and imploring. "God, Esme, you don't think it's going to make its way down here, do you?"

"If it did, I don't think a bunch of soldiers is going to keep it at bay."

Laila looked at me for a second longer, and then laughed. "I guess not."

We fell into silence, rain pattering around us. I bit into a shrimp, and it was perfectly cooked, the way Laila's always were. I ate, and Laila watched me eat, and neither of us uttered that unspoken truth: Soldiers might not keep a virus out, but they could stop a village from rising up against the man who didn't stop the virus in the first place.

My tutoring sessions were canceled the day the soldiers arrived. Rena showed up in my suite that morning with a breakfast tray and told me I needed to be downstairs by nine thirty. That was another change that I'd had to get used to when Isabel moved in—Rena had been my nanny, my surrogate mother, for so long. But when the twins were born, she transferred her attention to them. Not that I minded too much. I was too old for a nanny anyway.

I ate and showered and dressed and made my way to the sitting room by nine twenty-five. Isabel was already down there, wearing a floaty white dress and too much makeup. That didn't seem like her—she was nervous too. The twins sat together in the corner, playing with a children's lightbox, the pale impressions of fairies and dragons shimmering on the air.

Isabel glanced at me and smiled. "So, has he told you anything more about why he hired the squad?" she asked.

I managed to choke back a laugh, bitter and sarcastic. "He hasn't told me anything."

Another smile, although this one seemed more forced. Polite. "He gets so busy."

Music trilled from the lightbox and one of the twins laughed.

"Yeah," I said. "He does."

The door to the sitting room opened, and in walked Mr. Whittaker, and then Rena, and then Dad. "They're here," he said. "I wanted you both to meet them. Isabel, dear, leave the twins; I think they're too young for this."

Isabel didn't protest, although the skin around her mouth tightened.

"Come on," Dad said. "They're waiting out in the garden." He was sterner than usual. The thought of Dad's anxiety gave me a quiver of fear.

Rena knelt with the twins, and Isabel and I followed Dad and Mr. Whittaker into the hallway. The sun was out and the staff had opened the windows so that the sea breeze blew in, and as it ruffled my hair, I thought of invisible creatures riding on it as if it were a wave, bringing death into the house.

Beside me, Isabel wrapped her arms around herself and shivered, even though the breeze wasn't cold.

We stepped out on the patio. Mr. Whittaker closed the door behind us, disappearing back inside. The soldiers were on the lawn, five of them, all standing in a line. They wore fatigues and helmets and light rifles strapped across their chests. From the patio I couldn't tell how many were women and how many were men.

"Mr. Coromina! Is this your lovely wife?" A tall man in a blue Alvatech officer's uniform strode up on the patio, grinning. I'd studied Alvatech in tutoring, the way I'd studied all of the three primary militaries the Coromina Group contracted out to. They originated in the Alvaverra system, three or four jumps from here. My mother didn't serve with them. I should have known more, but I'd forgotten the rest of what I'd supposedly learned.

"It is indeed, Colonel Nahas." Dad beamed over at her. "Allow me to introduce Isabel May Coromina."

Colonel Nahas held out one hand in Isabel's direction, and she responded immediately, like a doll, smiling and saying her pleased-to-meet-yous.

"And this is my daughter Esme," Dad said, startling me into standing up straight. Colonel Nahas shook my hand like he cared. "She'll be taking over the company when I retire. Starting her first full internship next year."

"Noted," Colonel Nahas said, as if my father had just given him instructions. Then he grinned at me. "You're safe with us, Ms. Coromina."

I wasn't sure how to respond, as I didn't even know what I was supposed to be safe from. Colonel Nahas gestured at the soldiers. They snapped to attention, rifles clicking into place.

"Best of the best, as you requested," Colonel Nahas said. "Sergeant Rowe and I served together out on Tinin during the Sinn Initiative, and the rest of them have proved themselves on missions to Ulysses, Orane III, and Ychee. Private DuBois there earned a Medal of Valor." He nodded at one of the soldiers, whose mouth twitched like he was suppressing a smile. "I've seen all of them fight, sir, and I don't think you'll be disappointed."

Dad squinted at the soldiers like he was sizing up a new car. "I specifically requested men who'd fought guerrilla-style."

"And Orane III trained them well for it."

"All of them fought at Orane III?"

"Of course!" Colonel Nahas gave a satisfied nod. "Would you like a demonstration?"

"A demonstration?" Isabel muttered, quietly enough that Dad couldn't hear her. She was frowning, one hand held up to her eyes to block the sun.

Dad stepped off the patio and walked through the grass to the soldiers. They didn't move. Nothing about them seemed human. He wandered up and down the line, peering at them each in turn. The second-to-last soldier he studied longer than the others. Then he laughed.

"This is one of ours!" he said.

Colonel Nahas beamed. "Wanted to see if you'd notice."

"Of course I'd notice." Dad stepped back, his hands on his hips. "What's your name, soldier?"

"Private Steven Snow."

"Snow! Grown out on Quilla, eh?"

"Yes, sir."

Isabel shifted her weight and gave a soft murmur of disapproval.

"Well, I'm glad to have you on board." Dad turned from the soldiers and joined Colonel Nahas on the patio. "They look good. We'll give them a week as a test run, and if I have any problems, I'll let you know."

"You won't have any problems."

From there, Dad and Colonel Nahas launched into a drawn-out negotiation for payment, and I turned my attention to the soldiers standing motionless in the grass. They were out of place there on the lawn, hemmed in by flowering vines and the blue sky. I wondered how Dad was able to tell Private Snow from the others. He might have led the Coromina Group into the production and engineering of superhuman soldiers, but he certainly didn't have a hand in their actual development. Dad wasn't a scientist, not even close. And the engineered soldiers were supposed to be superficially identical to an ordinary human. There must be some tell, some particular feature molded into Private Snow's face, that I couldn't see.

I squinted at him in the sunlight. He didn't look at me; he didn't seem to be looking at anything. None of the soldiers did. It was hard to see what he looked like beneath this helmet. Ordinary. He just looked ordinary, like all the rest of them.

The soldiers must have met with Dad's approval, because a week later, they were still on the estate, prowling around the perimeter with their light rifles. According to Galactic Media Standard, there'd been another outbreak of the flu on Amana. But no one from the village had come beating down our door over it.

The soldiers became part of the landscape, like the pineapple garden and the plumeria maze and the bougainvillea cascading in waterfalls from the third-story balconies. But I couldn't get used to them. Their presence reminded me that being Dad's heir put me at risk, possibly from the village, from the people I called my friends. It was a risk Dad didn't see fit to explain to me, and the soldiers' presence was a reminder of that omission.

It was a reminder of my mother as well.

I had to change some aspects of my routine because of the soldiers. For nearly a month, I didn't sneak off to the public beach to see Paco and Laila, afraid one of the soldiers would mistake me for the phantom threat and shoot me. Instead, I started taking walks around the estate, following paths where I could see them patrolling in the distance. I figured out early on that they weren't living in the house with the rest of the staff but out in the guest houses on the edge of the property—but that was all my long walks told me.

Still, I kept watching. I was curious about them, about Private Snow in particular. He was—I wasn't sure how to put it. A part of Dad's company? My company, at some point in the future? He wasn't a part of the company the way the citizen-employees were, the people I'd be helping out if I got an internship in PM. He was—the only word for it was *product*, the thought of which made my stomach feel weird.

When I'd been ten years old, Dad had taken me to one of the labs where they grew the soldiers. The creatures in the vats had looked partially formed, and I hadn't totally understood at the time what I'd been looking at. My memories of that day didn't line up with the reality of Private Snow.

Laila thought I was being absurd, following the soldiers around during my free time.

"They're trained professionals," she said, her face flickering and transparent on the holo's projection. "You think they haven't seen you?"

"Probably," I said. "But they'll think I'm just, you know, milling around."

Laila rolled her eyes. "So, they know what you look like, is what I'm getting at."

I lifted my chin a little. "Maybe. Why do you care?"

She laughed. "Oh my God, Esme, I *miss* you. I'm off tonight and Vanda's throwing a beach bonfire, and if you don't come, I will literally die." She shook her head, long dark hair flying around her shoulders. "I mean that. I will *literally die.*"

There it was. She wanted me to sneak off the property.

"Me, too, if one of the soldiers shoots me."

"They won't shoot you!" Laila folded her hands like she was praying and said, "Pleeeease, Esme? You're my best friend and this flu thing has me freaked out and I just want to get drunk on the beach with you. Please."

She pulled an exaggerated sad face, like a melancholy clown. She'd said I was her best friend, which she'd never said before, even though I'd always thought of her as mine.

"Fine," I said. "I'll see what I can do."

She squealed and threw out her arms as if to embrace me. I did the same and encircled the empty air of her holo. Her laughter trickled out of the speakers. It sounded far away.

"Nine o'clock," she said. "My place."

She signed off—I could hear her mother shouting at her in the distance to come help hang the laundry—and I stretched out on my bed and stared up at the ceiling. Sneaking past the soldiers in the dark really did worry me. It wasn't exactly like half-following them from a distance during the day.

I rolled off the bed, struck with a plan.

It was raining again, and I pulled on my rain boots and grabbed an umbrella. I scurried out of the house and set off across the gardens toward the cluster of guesthouses. If I couldn't find anyone there, then I'd walk down to Beachway Road and wait until one of them marched past.

Rain sprinkled across the gardens, compelled not so much by gravity but by the gusts of wind blowing in from the sea. It sprayed across me sideways in a thick gray cloud. The gardens were lush but drowned-looking, the way they always were during the rainy season. Everything sparkled like it was covered in diamonds.

The guesthouses appeared at the top of the hill, white wooden siding with yellow trim. They were surrounded by banana trees. The first one, and the smallest, was shut tight, the shutters locked over the windows. I followed the gravel path around to the next one. The shutters were open and a pair of black boots sat next to the front door. My heart fluttered.

I walked up to the porch. The main door was open too, although the screen door was locked into place. I banged on the metal frame. "Hello!" I called out. "Is anyone there?"

Silence answered me at first, and then footsteps, soft and padded like a dog's. A man appeared in the foyer, dressed in a thin white T-shirt and green-gray fatigues. I didn't recognize him at first, not without his helmet. It was the engineered soldier. Private Snow.

"Can I help you?" He sounded formal, like one of the staff. He leaned up against the frame and studied me. "Ms. Coromina, right? The eldest daughter?"

He might have phrased it like a question but I could tell he already knew the answer. "Yeah. Can I talk to you?"

I was staring at him, fascinated, trying to figure out how Dad had known he was engineered. But he looked like anybody else.

"Yeah. Sure. You're not going to get me in trouble, are you?" A half-grin appeared, along with a dimple in his right cheek.

"I don't think so."

He laughed. "That's a yes." But he unlocked the screen door anyway and held it open. I pulled off my rain boots and dropped my umbrella on the porch and went in. I wasn't sure I'd ever been inside this particular guesthouse. The decor was unfamiliar: wooden blinds covering the windows and Quillian rugs on the floor. Maybe Isabel had redecorated it.

"You want a towel?" Private Snow asked.

I shook my head.

Private Snow led me into the living room. The furniture had been shoved off to the side. Exercise equipment littered the floor. "Sorry," he said.

I shrugged. He grabbed two armchairs, one in each hand, and dragged them into the center of the room, in front of the fire. It was weird to watch. The armchairs were made of dark wood and leather. Heavy materials. Too heavy for a normal man to pull across the room one-handed.

"Thought you might want to sit down," he said, not quite looking at me, like he was shy.

"I just had a quick question. Or a request, really."

He snapped to attention.

"You have to promise not to tell my dad, though. Or anyone at the house."

Private Snow shifted his weight and crossed his arms over his chest. "I can't promise that until I've heard what it is."

I sighed. "It's not a big deal. There's a party I want to go to, down at the public beach. But Dad won't let me go if I ask him, so—" I shrugged and grinned, hoping he would figure the rest of it out.

"Oh," he said, dropping his arms back to his sides. "You want to sneak out."

"But I don't want to get shot."

"We wouldn't have shot you."

I blushed. "It'll be after the sun set, so I didn't know."

Private Snow looked like he wanted to laugh. "We're trained," he said, "not to do that. And we aren't stumbling around in the dark. I've got night vision, and the others have goggles."

He tossed that off casually, *I've got night vision*, the way someone else might say *I can do a hundred pushups*. Not a confession so as much as a brag, like I could have night vision if I just put my mind to it.

"But if it makes you feel better," he continued, "I'll let the others know you might be slipping through the woods." He smiled again, more shyly this time. "We're always glad to be of service, Ms. Coromina."

"And you won't tell my dad?"

"My word as a soldier." He stuck out his hand. I wasn't sure what he wanted, but he said, "In Alvatech, we shake on it."

"Oh! Sorry."

I grabbed his hand and shook.

I slipped out to the party without trouble, taking my usual path through the gardens and down to the dirt road that led into the village. The rain clouds had cleared away during sunset. Catequil and Amana were both out, and Coromina I was nearly full, so the landscape was flooded with dim, burnished red light, enough to see by. I passed one of the soldiers when I came to the road, and he lifted his hand at me in a wave before walking on.

The party was a relief after weeks spent cooped up at Star's End. Laila drank too much and threw up in the sand dunes. Paco showed up, driving a beat-up old car, its engine rigged to run on the light from Coromina I. He and I stripped down to our underwear and went swimming in the sea. He kissed me as the waves crashed around us. The bonfire threw long wavering lines of light down the length of the beach. Music thumped against the sand.

Everything was perfect.

I was back in my bed by three in the morning, and I slept for four hours and woke up with my alarm, which I'd forgotten to turn off the night before. Yellow sunlight streamed around the curtains. A bird chittered outside my window. I'd only had a couple of beers, so I wasn't hung over—I thought of Laila and figured she was buried in her bedsheets right now, screaming at her brothers when they came in to wake her up. Still, I lay on my back for fifteen minutes after I silenced my alarm, watching the dust float through the sunlight.

My tutoring session didn't start until after lunch that day, but I couldn't fall back asleep. I thought about the soldier who'd waved at me on the road, and Private Snow promising he wouldn't rat me out to Dad or anyone else. Dad might ignore me most of the time, but slumming it down in the village would be an event worthy of his attention. Given the lack of angry messages on my lightbox, it seemed Private Snow had kept his word.

I wanted to see him again. I'd always known that the Coromina Group manufactured soldiers—providing arms to the militaries was how Dad made his fortune. But I'd never seen an engineered soldier up close before. And yet they were going to become my responsibility some day, just like all the other citizens of Coromina I. Maybe I would be even more beholden to them—after all, these were true Corominans. They had been created here.

I ought to thank Private Snow, I decided. If I thanked him I had an excuse to see him again.

The house was quiet when I left my room, but I slipped out the front door, just in case. No one ever used the front door unless we had guests. Outside, everything was brilliant and shining from yesterday's rain. My feet sank into the soaked earth as I threaded through the garden. The plumeria maze was blooming, scent wafting sweet and heavy on the air. The gardeners were out, clearing away broken branches and fallen leaves from the storms, but they ignored me.

I arrived at the guesthouse. The boots on the porch were gone, but the main door was hanging open, just as it had yesterday. I knocked and called out a hello.

I expected Private Snow to answer, but instead a woman came to the door. She wasn't much older than me, but her body was corded with muscle and her face was hardened in other ways. She leaned sideways in the doorframe, watching me like I might attack.

"Can I help you?" she said.

"Is Private Snow here?"

"Nope. Out on patrol." She jerked her thumb in the direction of the house. "You the Coromina girl?"

"Yeah. Esme."

"Private Abad. Nice to meet you."

"Oh. Do you think you could give Private Snow a message for me?"

"Sure. You want to leave it on the lightbox? He's more likely to get it that way. We're in and out of here. Don't know when I'll see him next." She grinned. "I'll even encode it if you want. CG military-style—no one'll be able to translate it but us."

I shrugged. "You don't have to do that." All the militaries had their own secret codes for sending message between soldiers without threat of interference, but a thank-you wasn't that important.

Besides, I figured she was just indulging me like I was some little kid.

Private Abad let me in. The house was unchanged from yesterday. The two chairs Private Snow had dragged in front of the fireplace remained where we had left them, like they were waiting for visitors. We walked through the living room and into the den, which had been converted into a center of operations; I'd immersed in enough war dramas to recognize one. Private Abad sat down in front of the lightbox and hit a switch. White light filled the room, and that white light was all I could see on the projection screen. The lightbox was encrypted.

She looked up at me expectantly.

"I just wanted to thank him," I said, feeling stupid for making her turn on the lightbox for something so simple. "I mean, for keeping everything a secret—"

Private Abad grinned. "Just say it into the holorecorder, honey."

I laughed, flustered—of course I knew how the stupid messaging system worked, but something about being in the guesthouse made me nervous. She pointed at the recorder, its little pinpoint of gray. I took a deep breath and said, "Hey, Private Snow, just wanted to thank you for not shooting me and everything. And for not telling my dad."

Private Abad watched me for a moment, then switched off the lightbox.

"He'll think that's funny," she said.

My curiosity piqued at that—he thought things were funny! But I didn't say anything. Private Abad stood up and stretched, crossing one arm over her chest. And that's when I saw it. Her tattoo. A black circle dotted with stars, a red silhouette of a dropship hanging in the background. The Andromeda Corps insignia.

"The Andromeda Corps!"

"What?" Private Abad blinked, then looked down at her arm. "Wow, I'm impressed. Not many civvies can tell the insignias apart."

"I can't, usually. I just know that one." My heartbeat had picked up, my palms were sweating. "My mom—she serves in the AC."

"Your mom?" Private Abad laughed. "I gotta admit, I was

wondering about that. Coromina's wife doesn't look old enough to have a teenager." She paused. "Sorry, probably shouldn't have said that."

"It's okay. You're right. She's only ten years older than me."

Private Abad was looking down at her hands like she was uncomfortable, and it occurred to me she thought my mother had died. Soldiers always get weird about death. Mr. Garcia had told me that. They're supposed to think it's an honor, but most of them don't, not really.

"You might know her," I said, "My mom. If you worked for the AC. She's still around."

Private Abad looked up. "I wasn't with them long," she said. "Joined up right out of school. Hence the tattoo." She tapped it. "I got traded though, part of a parley, and wound up switching allegiances. Money's money."

I must have looked crestfallen, because she added, "What's her name, honey?"

"Harriet Oxbow."

I had never said her name out loud, and it felt funny in my mouth, sharp and heavy. But Private Abad's eyes lit up and she said, "Sergeant Oxbow? Hairy Harriet?"

This moment, that flash of recognition, was a gift I'd been waiting for my entire life. I had no idea what to say, so I just blurted, "Hairy? What?"

Private Abad laughed. "That was her nickname, assuming it's the same lady. And that's 'hairy' as in a hairy situation, by the way. A Corps thing. Your mom's Harriet Oxbow?" Private Abad leaned back, arms crossed over her chest. "Wow. *Wow.*"

I looked down at the floor, embarrassed. I must not have looked like my mother's daughter.

"I can't believe she hooked up with fucking Phillip Coromina," Private Abad said, laughing. "My God."

I lifted my head. "What?"

Private Abad seemed to remember that I was in the room with her. She smothered her laughter and ran one hand over her hair, like she was trying to calm herself. "Sorry. Look, Hairy Harriet is kind of—I don't want to say famous, exactly, but she's *renowned*, at least among the AC."

"Really!" A warm, familiar feeling billowed up in my bloodstream, and I tingled with anticipation and a bit of nervousness. It was the same feeling I got whenever I looked my mother up on the newsfeeds, trying to learn about her. "I look her up sometimes but I can never find anything."

Private Abad grinned. "It's not the kind of thing you'd find on the newsfeeds, honey. War stories. We keep 'em to ourselves, usually." She shook her head. "I just can't believe Harriet Oxbow would have even *met* Phillip Coromina. Much less fucked him." Another laugh.

I squirmed, knowing full well that fucking would have had to occur for me to exist, but not wanting to think about it, either.

"Can you tell me some of the stories about her?" I asked. "Even though I'm not a soldier."

"A marine." Private Abad wagged her finger in admonishment. "Learn the difference. Soldiers are in the Army. They don't do shit."

"Oh. Sorry."

"Well, I'd hate to think you've been thinking of your mom as a soldier all these years." Private Abad leaned up against the wall, hips jutting out. "I've never met her, now. Just heard talk, back when I joined up with the AC. She'd served out in the Perre system, during that fucking bar fight they called a war. Waste of everybody's time. But Sergeant Oxbow was out there with a squad, headed toward Perre Red for some reason or another. And they got attacked. Not the Spiro Xu Alliance, but pirates. Fucking pirates!"

Private Abad roared with laughter. I smiled to be polite, because I didn't see what was so funny about a pirate attack.

"Two-bit operation, from what I heard. Oxbow's unit wasn't on an official AC vessel, though; it was this moon-hopper they got off the Perre rebels, and the pirates didn't know better. So, they boarded, took the ship, and Sergeant Oxbow—your mother—she took stock of that situation faster than anybody else in the unit. That's why the call her Hairy—she knows how to worm her way out of a shitshow. Anyway, the Perre rebels had been dragging the AC down for weeks at that point, because they wanted to fight themselves. Didn't understand the point of contracting out to a stand-in military. So, that's why Harriet and the rest were on that crapheap in the first place. The pirates had more weaponry than the rebels did, so Harriet demanded to see their captain, and she managed to talk the assholes into fighting for the rebels for *free*." Private Abad laughed and shook her head. "Although from what I hear, she didn't do a whole lot of talking. Mostly shooting. But whatever gets the job done, right?"

I had no idea about getting the job done. I'd never so much as thrown a punch in my life.

"Wow," I finally said, because I didn't know what to make of any of it. The story made my mother seem less like a mother and more like a character in an Amanan action immersion, one of those trashy ones where you can request extra blood and dismemberment. "That's—thank you for telling me."

"I got some others. You want to hear them?"

Of course I wanted to hear them. The picture I had of my mother was so fragmentary, like a falling-apart quilt. I saw snatches of her from the hologram and from the letters and from the fact that she was a soldier—a marine—and that was it. Private Abad's story was strange and I wasn't sure I believed it, but it was another thing to add to the mosaic.

I nodded.

For the next hour, I sat in the den-or-command-center while Private Abad told me story after story about Hairy Harriet. The stories were more like tall tales, Sergeant Oxbow taking down a Solmored armored combat unit with just a light rifle, or blasting an atmosphere ship right out of the sky. I thought of the woman I'd seen in the hologram, short-haired and heavily muscled. I could picture her doing all those things, easily. But when I tried to picture that same woman holding me as a baby, or kissing Dad, my mind went blank. A malfunctioning computer.

Still, I listened carefully, trying to remember every detail.

Private Abad eventually ran out of stories. "Like I said," she told me, "this is all hearsay. You hear it on the mercenary circuits. Fun as hell to tell, though. You like 'em?"

"Sure." I stood up. My mind was burning with the stories about my mother, like I had the fever that was supposed to preempt the worse symptoms of the flu, the bleeding and the sweating and the dehydration so severe your body mummified when you were still alive. "I really appreciate hearing it. Dad never talks about her, so—"

"That's tough." Private Abad nodded. She glanced over her shoulder, as if she were waiting for someone. "Look, honey, my shift's about to start, but I'll put the word out, see if I hear anything else." Her expression softened. "Something more useful, more like what you were hoping I could tell you."

"What you told me was fine." I gave her a bright smile.

She smiled back at me, looking pleased with herself. I liked her. She was exactly what I would expect from a soldier, but also nothing like what I would expect.

I thanked her again, and she promised to give my message to Private Snow, and I walked back up to the manor, through the warm, lemony sunlight. The house gleamed in the distance, looking like a palace. I went straight up to my bedroom and sat down at my light-box and scrawled out all the stories that Private Abad had told me with my stylus. I didn't want to dictate them. I wanted to feel the words flowing out of my hands. It took a long time, and I worked straight through lunch, finishing just in time for the start of my tutoring lessons. I saved the stories in a sheet of memory glass and stuck the memory glass in my lockbox with the holocube and all of my mother's letters.

When I finished, I felt empty. But happy, too.

That evening, I felt good enough from my talk with Private Abad that I almost looked forward to going down to dinner with my family. I thought I might finally get Dad to tell me stories about my mother.

But Dad wasn't at dinner.

Isabel was upset about it. After the staff brought in the first course, she called Mr. Whittaker into the dining room where we were all sitting around the table with bowls of cold fish soup.

"Will Philip be joining us this evening?" she said in a flat voice.

"I'm afraid not, Mrs. May Coromina. Something came up at the office."

Her face tightened, as if her emotions were trying to escape. "I see," she said. "Thank you."

He scurried out of the room in his little weaselly way, and we ate the rest of our dinner in silence, the only sounds the clink of spoons against porcelain and the twins slopping their food. I didn't tell Isabel that before they'd gotten married, he'd never eaten dinner with me, that the dining room had gone unused. No family meals, no evening dinner parties. It was her presence that had drawn him to the table. Her presence wasn't enough anymore.

My good mood slowly evaporated. Something heavy hung on the air.

"It's the flu," Isabel murmured to herself, stirring her soup around without taking a bite. She wasn't talking to me; I didn't think she was talking to anyone. The twins whispered together and looked over at her, their eyes wide. Isabel dropped her spoon with a clatter and leaned back in her chair. Her belly arced in front of her. She had to be due soon. Another girl. I didn't even know if she and Dad had thought of a name.

That night, I lay awake and didn't think about my mother at all. I thought about Isabel stirring her soup, muttering about the flu. I knew the symptoms. We all did, even if we didn't talk about them. A high fever. And then, an hour later: sweat. Sweat pouring out of your skin, an ocean of your own liquid. And then blood seeped from your orifices, and then you died. It happened fast. Two or three days. If you were sick, though, I imagined that wasn't fast enough.

The official newsfeed had stopped talking about the flu a couple of weeks before. It had moved onto a war in the Uskroba system, some corporate showdown of the sort that happened every few decades, the kind of thing Mr. Garcia said was necessary for a healthy corporate ecosystem. Like forest fires, or predators eating their way through an overpopulated wilderness. Like a virus.

The underground newsfeeds hadn't gone silent on it, although they didn't have much information, only the bits and pieces they could steal from the Coromina Group: there were reports of an outbreak on Catequil, a riot on Quilla. But no one knew for sure, and I had let myself think it was dying out, which was naive of me. I should have known that the flu wasn't gone. It had only been covered up. Contained. Locked away even from the Connectivity Underground, the Galactic Media Standard.

We had talked about the importance of information containment in tutoring.

I fell into an uneasy sleep. Maybe I dreamed about my mother, but I didn't remember it. I woke up feeling scratchy and disoriented. The sunlight in the window was too bright. I rubbed at my eyes. Maybe I'd see Dad today; maybe I'd ask him about my mother. But probably not.

I dressed and went down for breakfast, like I always did. But this morning was different. The dining room was empty, the lights switched off. The table hadn't even been set.

Standing alone in that dark room, still blurry with sleep, I thought backward through my trip from my bedroom to the dining room. Hardly any staff in the hallways, even though morning was when they did most of the cleaning. In fact, the only staff I had seen were Jean and Astrid. They had been huddled together in the corner, speaking in hushed whispers. They glanced at me over their shoulders and went quiet.

I hadn't thought anything of it at the time. But now the pieces were fitting into place. The scarce staff. The empty dining room.

Isabel.

She was always down here at breakfast, sitting with the twins and Rena, projecting the newsfeeds over her meal.

Something was wrong with Isabel.

Miscarriage. I left the dining room and rushed up to her suite on the second floor. I expected to see Dr. Tristany, the obstetrician Dad had hired, or at the very least Mr. Hankiao, the nurse. But the hallway was empty.

I knocked gently on her door and called out her name.

Silence.

I knocked again, harder, and this time, the door opened. Isabel stood in the doorway, her eyes red and puffy.

"Esme?" She blinked at me like she couldn't remember where she knew me from.

I stared at the curve of her belly beneath her dress. My heart pounded. It wasn't her pregnancy.

"Oh, Esme," she said. She rushed forward and wrapped me in a hug, something she hadn't done since we first met.

"What's going on?" I asked into the sweet-smelling silk of her hair. Even though I knew. Dad working late, the empty hallways, the empty dining room, the empty newsfeeds.

"No one told you?" She pulled away, her hands on my shoulders. "My God, I asked Rena to wake you this morning." She pulled away, one hand to her forehead. In the next room, one of the twins started to cry. "They can sense it. Everyone's afraid."

"Afraid of what?" My voice tremored.

"The flu," Isabel said flatly.

For a moment, the room went white. I could hear the blood pounding in my head.

"The flu?" I whispered.

"In Undirra City." Isabel disappeared into the next room, leaving me standing in her sitting room, shockwaves of horror rippling through my bloodstream. Undirra City. Forty-five minutes by car. Twenty by air shuttle.

Isabel reappeared, a weeping Daphne clutching her hand. Adrienne followed behind, her eyes wide and solemn and fearful.

"When?" I said.

"Last night." Isabel knelt beside Daphne and enveloped her and Adrienne in a desperate hug. "My baby girls," she said softly, brushing Adrienne's hair away from her face.

"What's going on, Mommy?" asked Adrienne.

"I told you, sweetheart; it's a grownup emergency." Isabel kissed Adrienne on the forehead. Then she squeezed Daphne again and murmured something into her ear that I couldn't hear. I trembled in place, my thoughts brimming with panic. I wondered how long until the flu came to the village.

"Run back into the bedroom," Isabel said to the twins. "I need to speak with your sister. You don't need to worry, my dears."

They looked at each other. Adrienne seemed doubtful, but she took Daphne's hand. "C'mon," she said, and led her into the next room. Isabel watched them go for a moment, and then stood up and turned toward me. My heart pounded.

"Word came while I was sleeping," she said in a flat voice. "Star's End has been put on quarantine. No one enters, no one leaves."

"Dad—" I choked out.

"He's here. He's the one who brought word. I think this is why he hired those soldiers. He knew it would happen eventually. He denies it, but—" Her expression turned hard, like diamonds.

Hot sunlight poured through her windows, but I was cold. Isabel turned away from me, toward the sound of the twin's voices spilling out of the next room. Bits of dust floated in the sunbeams and swirled around her like stars.

I stumbled out into the hallway. I felt heavy, and breathing was too hard. The staff were nowhere to be seen. No one was mopping the floors or brushing out the curtains. Star's End was abandoned.

Part of me wanted to go up to Dad's office and demand to know everything, demand to know how he could look at us in the eye and claim the soldiers weren't there because of the flu, demand to know how he would act now that the flu was creeping in on our home. Instead, I went to my suite.

As I rushed down the hallways, everything about the estate was quiet and slow and empty, a sharp contrast to the rhythm of panic playing inside my chest.

I burst into my room and stood in the doorway, hands braced against the frame. Rena was perched on the sofa in the sitting room, staring out the window. Her eyes were red, too.

I stopped in the doorway. "Rena?"

She turned to me. "I was supposed to wake you up, but you were already gone." She took a deep breath. "Did you hear about the quarantine?"

I nodded and sat down beside her. I was glad she was here, even if I kept telling myself I was too old for a nanny. She was, after all, the closest I had to a mother. I pressed closer to her, grateful I didn't have to be alone.

My window looked out over the pineapple garden. Right now, it was empty too. In the distance, one of the soldiers cut across the lawn. He held his light rifle in both hands. It wasn't strapped to his back the way the rifles had been before.

"All this time and we never heard anything," Rena said in a hollow voice. "And then suddenly—" She snapped her fingers. "It's at our back door."

I stared at her. I didn't know what to say. Then I slid off the sofa and grabbed my lightbox from the next room. Brought up the official newsfeeds. They were talking about yet another skirmish in the Uskroba system, forty-five thousand light-years and five jumps away.

"They aren't saying anything." Rena knocked the tablet out of my hands and it hit the sofa cushions, the speaker still going on about the skirmish. I switched it off, too stunned by Rena's outburst to do anything more.

"We thought it was over, because the newsfeeds weren't talking about it," Rena said. "But it wasn't." She looked at me and her expression was angry and afraid and I remembered with a sharp jolt that her sister Ella lived in Undirra City, that they spoke once a week or so over Connectivity.

"Your sister," I said. "Oh God, Rena—" I picked up my lightbox. "Let me check the underground feeds. Paco showed me—"

"They don't know shit, either," snapped Rena. I jumped; I wasn't used to her lashing out at me. But then she shook her head, pinched the bridge of her nose. "I'm sorry," she said. "It's just—those underground feeds—the Coromina Group knows how to keep them out of the loop when they need to."

Her words stunned me, but I understood then that I should have made the connection a long time ago. I'd been learning the Coromina Group strategies, but I thought the Underground was omnipotent in a way the company wasn't.

Rena turned toward the window. Beyond the glass, the pineapple garden looked like a painting.

"Ten people are dead in Undirra City already," she went on. "Ella knew. But she didn't say anything. And you know why?"

I shook my head. My heart pounded.

"The Coromina Group has that much control on this planet. They silence not only an entire city but an entire continent. They couldn't contain the flu, so they just forced everyone to stop talking about it." Her mouth twisted. "Thank your father for that. My sister's probably going to die."

"Rena—" I put my hand on her arm. She looked at me and I expected to see rage in her expression but she only looked sad.

"He wants you to be like him," she said.

I knew this wasn't meant to be a good thing.

"Don't look so worried," she went on. "He'll make sure you'll survive. Isabel's carrying a girl, so you're still the heir. The rest of us, though—" She shrugged.

"I'm sure that's not true. I'm sure your sister will be fine."

Rena laughed. "Guess he hasn't quite gotten to you. But you're young yet. This sort of thing is inevitable."

I didn't really know what she was talking about. Inevitable that I'd someday be like Dad? It frightened me that she was going on about my future when the flu was creeping over the southern part of the continent, heading toward the village, heading toward the estate.

Rena stood up. Her eyes were flat. Dead, I thought, like the flu had already gotten her.

"Remember this conversation," she said, and then she left.

For a long time after my conversation with Rena, I sat in silence. A quarantine. Star's End locked away. *Star's End*. It hadn't registered in my mind until now. Only Star's End was under quarantine. The village wasn't.

And then I thought: *Laila*.

I darted over to my couch and picked up my lightbox and switched on the projector. Dusty blue light bolted into the sunlight scattering through the windows. My heart pounded. I watched my lightbox trying to connect with hers. *Please be okay*, I thought.

And then her face appeared, blurred and transparent on the holo.

"Laila!" I cried. "Thank God. Are you okay? I was afraid—"

"Esme! You've heard, haven't you?" Her eyes were sunk deep into her skull and her hair hung lank around her face. "They cancelled school this morning. Last night, these CG guys were coming around taking everyone's temperature." She slumped back and the holo blurred for a moment. "I've been up since three."

"You're okay, though, right?"

She nodded. "Just sleepy. None of us had a fever."

I thought about her family, all her rambunctious brothers and her lovely brown-skinned mother and their house that always smelled of jasmine. They were safe.

"And Paco?" I said. "Have you talked to him yet?"

"He's fine. He's already met up with some of the others, to see about getting in food and medicine in case we go into quarantine—"

Her voice wavered and her eyes flicked away from the holo and that was when I knew, that she knew about Star's End's own quarantine. That I was locked away and she was still out in the open.

"I've been listening to the newsfeeds," she said. "All night. I couldn't sleep. But even Connectivity Underground has been talking about Uskroba." She sighed, a sound like static. I thought of what Rena had told me, about how even the underground feeds were under the company's control. I didn't say that to Laila, though. I couldn't.

"There's a rumor," Laila said, and her voice sounded dry and strained. I frowned at her. "That Undirra City is in quarantine. They're saying—" She hesitated. "They're saying that Alvatech soldiers are shooting anyone who breaks quarantine."

The air slammed out of me.

"It's just talk," Laila said quickly, moving close to the holo. "I'm sure it's just talk."

I nodded. "Just talk," I whispered, but part of me knew better. Dad controlled the planet. He gave orders to any militaries brought in to maintain order.

"I mean, I heard that from Pepe," Laila went on. "You know how he is. It's probably not even true. He doesn't exactly have a direct line to the Coromina Group offices."

"Right," I said, and I tried to smile. Laila gave me a ghost of a grin. I knew neither of us felt like smiling.

"Is anybody sick in the village?" I asked, to change the subject.

She shook her head. "I don't think so. The soldiers are still here, but they're letting people leave. I figure that means no one's been sick."

I nodded.

A shout erupted from Laila's holo—her brother Leo, the youngest one. He climbed into her lap, his long dark hair hanging in his eyes. He squinted at the recorder. Squinting, I knew, at me.

"Mama needs you," he said, still talking into the recorder.

I jolted, thinking, *I don't have a mother.*

"Yeah, I know." Laila slid him off her lap. "Listen, I got to go help with the laundry, okay? Mom's been washing all the sheets in the house."

"That's fine." I felt jittery. "Do you think I'll be able to get ahold of Paco?"

"Maybe." Laila fussed with Leo, who had disappeared into the blurry edges of the holo. "He definitely won't be diving today, and I'm sure he'll want to hear from you."

She looked up at me, dark smudges around her eyes. I wished we weren't talking on a holo, wished I could reach out and pull into her a hug and tell her it was going to be okay, that the Coromina Group cared for its citizens, that none of us had to die.

"Be careful," she said. Then she switched off her recorder, and I was alone.

For lunch, Mrs. Davesa didn't bother with a proper meal and instead laid out cold cuts and slices of bread in the kitchen. I fixed a plate to try to distract myself. I hadn't been able to get ahold of Paco, but if he was working with the underground, that made sense. At least, that was what I told myself.

I ate in my room, sitting beside the window and picking at my food. The day was still as bright and clear as it had been that morning. The idea of the flu almost seemed nonsensical.

Someone knocked on the door of my room, jarring me out of

my skin. "Come in," I said, and the door swung open. It was Isabel. She looked pale and worried, dark circles ringing around her eyes.

"I wanted to see if you'd like to go outside," she said.

"What?"

"It'll be good for the baby." She smiled a little. "It's such a lovely day, and she ought to soak in the sunlight through my skin."

"But the flu," I said.

"The flu doesn't spread on the air." She didn't look at me. "And it does us no good to be cooped up inside."

I stared at her for a moment. The sunlight pouring in through my window was hot against my back. And then I nodded. "Sure."

It felt strange going outside. Dangerous. The staff had set out chairs for us on the lawn, and we faced the plumeria maze, a wind blowing in off the sea.

"It's lovely, isn't it?" Isabel's voice was taut, crackling with electricity. She rested her hand protectively on her stomach. "Such a wonderful day."

"Sure." The maze was blooming, clusters of pink and white flowers letting off scent. I didn't say what I was thinking, that the air seemed poison to me, choked with viruses that would kill us all.

"Phillip says this should all be cleared up in the next month."

Even I could tell Isabel didn't believe this. She sighed and dropped her head against the back of her chair. Adrienne and Daphne sat at her feet, playing with their lightboxes. They projected up into the air butterflies as big as platters that turned transparent in the sunlight. I looked away from the butterflies and up at the blinding blue sky. Coromina I was out, the storm clouds churning across the surface. Amana too, although it was as transparent as the holographic butterflies. An entire other planet, as populated as this one.

Beside me, Isabel sat up. She shielded her eyes with one hand.

"Rena," she said. "Take Daphne and Adrienne inside, please."

Rena emerged from the shadow of the jacaranda tree, where she'd been watching in silence. "Of course, ma'am. Come along, girls."

The twins looked at Isabel with their luminous dark eyes. "Aww!" said Daphne. "Why do we have to go in?"

"Go," Isabel said to them, and her voice was sharp enough that they looked at each other and then gathered their lightboxes and ran over to Rena, who guided them through the door.

"What's wrong?" I felt dizzy and dry-mouthed. Isabel just stared straight ahead, and I looked where she was looking. One of the soldiers marched toward us. Isabel stared at her with a hard, fierce expression. The soldier had her gun out.

"Can I help you?" Isabel said.

"I just need to see Esme." It was Private Abad. She stopped a few paces away from us. "Nothing to worry about, ma'am. But I have something for Esme."

Isabel frowned at me. I didn't know what this was about, but that slamming fear of the flu trickled away, replaced with a tight sense of anxiety. Private Abad knelt down in the grass beside my chair and handed me a slim, disposable lightbox, the cheap kind you can buy in starports. I stared at it in my palm.

"What is it?" Isabel asked, leaning over her chair's armrests.

"It's a message from your mother," Private Abad said to me, and then straightened up, smoothing the lines of her uniform. Isabel slumped back in her chair and pressed her hand into her forehead, looking exhausted.

"My mother?"

"The transmissions into the estate have been blocked."

Beside me, Isabel muttered something angry and unintelligible.

"We've been monitoring them at Mr. Coromina's request," Private Abad said. "I picked up this one. It's your mother. Thought you might like it."

"Are you supposed to do that?" I stared down at the lightbox and my heart warmed a little.

"Nah. But I won't tell if you won't." Private Abad winked at me. Then her face went serious and she said, "Mrs. May Coromina."

I turned to Isabel, who was staring up at Coromina I, her eyes glazed over. "You're not going to tell, are you?"

"Of course not, dear." Isabel dropped her head to me. "But if that transmission has anything dangerous—"

"It's just my mom," I said. "She sends me transmissions all the time." Not exactly true, but close enough.

Isabel didn't seem to hear me.

Private Abad leaned in close to me and said in a low voice, "Don't worry about me getting in trouble. I thought it was worth the reprimand. The enemy won't be coming through transmissions, anyway." She slapped me on the shoulder. Isabel glanced at us, her face cloudy, but I knew what she was thinking: *The enemy?*

Private Abad stood up again and nodded at both of us, and then walked back through the garden, her gun shining in the sunlight.

"The fucking soldiers know more than we do," Isabel said.

I'd never heard her cuss before. She sighed and dropped one hand to the grass, toying with the ends.

"Go on and listen to it," she said. "I'm glad one of us can get a bit of hope in all this."

I wrapped my fingers around the lightbox, measuring the flimsy solidity of it against my palm. Isabel seemed strange to me, lethargic and disconsolate, as if the quarantine were draining her energy. I could understand, though: the quarantine had been draining my energy too, until now.

I slid out of my chair and bounded into the house and into my room. I locked the door. Shoved the lightbox into my holoprojector. My mother's voice filled the room like sunlight. No holo. No image. Just a voice and that staticky thumping interference some of her deep-space messages had.

"Hey, kiddo. I'm on Roxani and had some free time. Thought I'd send you a note. Can't tell you much about Roxani; all top-secret stuff and they'll just static it anyway. But I can tell you I'm doing well, and I hope you're doing well too. You'll be sixteen this year, yeah? Last message said you were still in school. Still the case? I imagine your dad won't let you join up, but I figure you've got some top-notch plans for the future. Hear Ekkeko's nice this time of year. Not too much rain."

Silence. The recording buzzed but it wasn't over yet. I listened to the patterns in the static like they could tell me something. I used to think they could. Now I knew that was just wishful thinking.

Then: "Hell, looks like we're shipping out early. Sorry, kiddo, I was hoping to make this a long one. Maybe I'll have time once we land on Cyter."

The recording fizzed out and then restarted. I listened to it once more before switching it off. I stared at the empty light above the holoprojector. My mother had sent me twenty-seven messages over the years. I sent her responses, too, because I wanted to keep my promise even though I wasn't military. Still, I didn't send as many now that I was older. Any messages I sent had to be sent via the Andromeda Corps; mercenaries couldn't give away their exact location. By the time my mother heard from me, weeks would have gone by. When I was a kid, I'd ask questions she could actually answer, like her favorite color or her favorite immersion. But then I started asking about her missions, like where she went, and whether or not she'd ever seen aliens, and that was when she had to tell me about the censors. Now all my questions would get pinged by the censors. But I kept my promise anyway, tell her about the mundanities of my life. And my mother still kept her promise, too.

I yanked out the disposable lightbox and placed it in the lockbox with all the others. My mother hadn't mentioned anything about the flu. They must not know about it on Roxani, which made sense, as I knew nothing about what was happening on Roxani other than vague rumors about a war, some group of insurgents trying to take over that planet's government. Didn't Roxani have an antiquated government, elected and everything? Not like the Coromina system, which was run by the Coromina Group. The business of civilization.

And I hardly knew about the flu, and it was happening in Undirra City. It made sense that my mother wouldn't know anything. It made sense, but it also made me sad.

I walked over to my window and slid it open, letting in the warm sea breeze. The plumeria maze rippled in the distance. I sat down on the window seat and thought about the waves crashing over the beach and wondered when I would see the ocean again.

That night, I jarred awake in the dark, my heart pounding hard in my chest. A bad dream? I couldn't remember any dreams at all, only an ocean of darkness.

I rolled over onto my back and stared up at the ceiling, everything cast in the murky red light of Coromina I. My bedroom didn't feel real in that light. I took a deep breath. My heart was still pounding. I couldn't imagine going back to sleep. I wasn't sure how I'd fallen asleep in the first place. The day had been so wrought with tension, even though nothing had actually *happened*. It was just this empty waiting. Dad spent the whole time locked in his home office. I didn't see him once. Normally, it would annoy me, but today, it scared me.

I stared up at the ceiling for a few moments before I became aware of a light blinking off to the side, not red like Coromina's light but a bright, artificial white. My lightbox. There was a message waiting for me.

It was only a message. Except we were in quarantine. Nothing was ever only a message.

It could be from Laila.

Or Paco, finally getting back to me.

I was paralyzed with a cold sick fear, terrified of what it would say. The light blinked and blinked, looming larger with each second, until it was as huge as Coromina I itself.

I pushed my blanket away. Kicked my legs over the bed. *Just check it.*

Gunfire exploded outside my window.

I slammed hard against the floor, shaking. The guns kept firing, that bright, mechanical buzzing of light rifles that I'd only ever heard in immersions.

The gunfire stopped. Voices shouted, farther away. There was a panicked urgency to them that made my stomach quake.

More gunfire.

Then: screaming. High-pitched. Sharp. Desperate.

I felt like I was going to throw up. The screaming and the shouting and the gunfire were threading together and I couldn't tell one from the other. Lights flashed outside my window and I let out a gasp of fear and started crawling toward the door. I kept hearing the screaming. I wasn't sure if it was really happening or if it was echoing inside my head.

I made it to the door and pushed myself up and shoved it open.

The hallway was empty but the windows were closed, the curtains hanging limp and still. We never closed the windows this time of year. Not even now that we were in quarantine, apparently.

"Esme!"

I jumped. The voice was male and unfamiliar. I twisted my torso, looked over my shoulder—

It was Mr. Whittaker. He never called me Esme; that was why I hadn't recognized him. He came rushing down the hallway, clutching a little gray box. A butler's jacket was tossed on over his sleeping clothes.

"Get off the floor," he said. "We have to get you to the landing pad."

"The what?" I blinked at him. Gunshots fired off in the distance.

"You're evacuating," he said. "Now get up. We don't have much time before they break through the barricade." He stooped down and grabbed my arm and yanked me to my feet. My head spun.

"Who?" I said. "The barricade?"

"The villagers," he snapped. "Hurry *up*, Miss Coromina; your life is in danger."

My ears buzzed. No. The villagers. The voices beyond the gunshots. The screams—

My lightbox blinking in the dark.

"Oh God," I whispered.

"We have to get the family off the planet before the quarantine comes down." He grabbed my arm and yanked me down the hallway. My head spun. We stumbled into the staff stairwell, narrow and lit with eerie emergency lights.

"But that's not fair," I said, dazed.

Mr. Whittaker didn't respond. We clambered out of the staff stairs and into the kitchen. It was neat, untouched, everything put away for the night.

"There's an armored car waiting for us," Mr. Whittaker said. "Hurry! Don't drag your feet."

"You're coming too," I said.

"Of course I'm bloody coming too. Your father can't live without me. *Now hurry up.*"

I'd never heard Mr. Whittaker speak this way before. Never heard this sort of strained bitterness in his voice. He led me outside, into the delivery courtyard. The night wind was sweet and hot, and I could still hear the screams carrying over through the woods. The car was a big blocky thing, polished black like stone. The door was hanging open. Rena's head emerged, her hair whipping into her eyes.

"Did you get everyone?" Mr. Whittaker asked.

"Yes." Rena's voice was cold and hard. "We're ready."

Mr. Whittaker shoved me in first. Isabel was there, clutching Daphne and Adrienne in each arm, and so was the obstetrician Dad had hired to help with her pregnancy. She looked stiff and worried. Daphne was crying, and although Isabel was silent, I could see that her face was pale and shining with tears.

Dad sat beside her, hooked into a portable lightbox, murmuring in some unintelligible code.

"You're safe," Isabel said when she saw me. She smiled weakly. Dad didn't say anything.

"Clear," Mr. Whittaker said, slamming the door shut. The car shot off. There were no windows. Sound was muffled in there, too. I couldn't hear the gunshots anymore. Or the screams.

"Where are we going?" I said.

"Space," Isabel said. She squeezed Daphne closer to her. "The thermosphere." Her voice sounded far away. The screaming was spinning around inside my head like a song.

"It's not fair," I said softly, and I looked over at Rena. She was looking down at her hands. "It's not fair. Not fair to leave—"

"Of course it's fucking fair." Dad ripped his lightbox away from his face. His eyes flashed in the gloom. "If I die, this system's leadership will default over to the board. Even if you survive, they'll be scrabbling for power and you'll never inherit your birthright. There will almost certainly be a war. So, shut your mouth and do as you're told and don't talk to me about what's fair."

The silence in the car was heavy and thick. I wanted to throw up. The car was jostling around—we couldn't be on one of the roads, then. We must be driving straight through the fields, the fastest path to the launching pad.

I twisted my nightgown up in one fist. The message on my light-box. I still didn't know who it was from. I imagined the villagers breaking through the barricade of the soldiers and spilling into the estate. I wondered if Laila was with them. If she would find her way to my room and see it for the first time. If she would even recognize it as mine. Or if she would even care.

The car slammed to a stop. Isabel let out a little gasp of fear and clutched Daphne tighter.

Mr. Whittaker tilted his head, as if listening to a voice only he could hear. He probably was. Then he nodded once, entered a code into the car door, and pushed it open. White light and hot air swept in. It wasn't the sultry air of the beach but a kind of incineration. A bonfire but bigger. The rocket engines.

"Everyone out!" shouted a voice from outside. "Hurry, hurry!"

Mr. Whittaker went out first and I followed, blinking against the engine-dried air. The glow from the rocket was as bright as day, and for a moment, I couldn't see anything but shadows. Someone shoved me from behind.

"Move!" said the voice. It was gruff and male and I didn't recognize it, although as my eyes adjusted, I saw the dark gray of a Coromina Group security uniform.

I was herded aboard the rocket, up the ramp, into the airlock, everything wide open because we were still planetside. My thoughts were in a blur. Star's End, burning like the rocket engine. The pineapple garden trampled underfoot. My lockbox with all my mother's messages—

I paused on the steps, my heart pounding. My mother's messages, the only piece I had of her, would burn away while I orbited the planet.

"Go, Esme," said Rena, her voice sharp in my ear. I jerked forward, my legs shaking, thinking of the lockbox tucked away inside my closet, wishing I could have said goodbye.

Tears streaked down my cheeks. The doors were sliding shut, blotting out the brightness of the engine's light.

"Prepare for launch!" the security guard shouted, and I'd been on this rocket enough times that my body moved independent of my desires. I stumbled into the seating area and collapsed in the closest chair. The windows were all closed. The lights were still off. People were dying in the village, and we were running away.

The engines roared, the end of a countdown I hadn't heard. The floor rumbled beneath my feet. I felt dry and empty and I closed my eyes as we launched into space.

All my life, the space station had been a jewel twinkling in the left-hand corner of the sky. I used to look for it as a little girl, lying out in the yard, trying to distinguish the stars from the spacecraft.

Now I was aboard it for the first time. I'd been given a cabin to myself, a little room with a bed and a closet and a minuscule bathroom off to the side. It was smaller than the main room of my suite back on Star's End. There was a round window above the bed, but it faced away from Ekkeko, and right now, all I could see was the endless emptiness of space. No lightbox, no media screen. Just the empty walls, the white-noise roaring of the gravity generator tucked deep inside the station.

The station was set to Star's End time, and so it was early in the morning here too, but I was too jangled from the trip to fall asleep. That was what Rena had told me to do, in the exhausted aftermath of our arrival—we were no longer in danger but the adrenaline had worn down, and we milled around the station lobby, Coromina Group stationeers keeping their distance. It occurred to me now, finally, that they thought we were going to bring the disease on board.

Maybe we had.

The thought gave me a shiver. I swallowed twice, not certain if I felt roughness in the back of my throat or not. Surely, there was a way to take my temperature somewhere on the station—but I was afraid of what I'd find. I touched my cheek and my forehead. The skin felt a little warmer than usual, but then, I'd just finished fleeing my home in terror.

I slumped against the wall. It rumbled a little against my back, a reminder that I was in a piece of machinery, that only a few layers of plastic and metal and energy were protecting me from the vacuum.

I heard voices out in the hallway.

Voices speaking in sharp, fervent whispers. Footsteps thumped against the floor, louder and louder, until they faded.

We were in the guest arm, and the stationeers didn't sleep there.

Somewhere, a door slammed.

I crawled forward on my bed. My heart pounded. Something was wrong. We'd only been here a few hours and something was wrong. *We brought the flu with us.*

There were more voices out in the corridor. The same harried, panicked tone. I couldn't stand it anymore. I pushed off my bed and flung my door open, and stuck my head out into the hallway.

It was a pair of stationeers, their uniforms dull gray in the garish overhead lights.

"Who the hell are you?" one of them, the woman, said to me.

Before I could answer, the other said, "It's one of the Corominas." He looked over at me. He had a towel draped over the crook of his arm. Above the towel was a red band. Dread solidified inside my chest. I'd learned this in tutoring: out in the vacuum, the ones who wore red tended to the dead. "Go back into your cabin, sweetheart."

I stepped out into the hallway. "Did someone die?" My voice was shrill. "What's happening?"

The two stationeers exchanged glances.

"Stop it!" I screeched. "Tell me what's going on."

"No one's died," the man with the red armband said. "But you need to go back to your—"

I darted out of the doorway and ran down the corridor, the opposite direction from the two stationeers. I had no rational thoughts—only that I didn't want to be in this arm of the station. I wanted to be far away. Back on Ekkeko. Back in Star's End.

"Hey!" shouted the woman. "What do you think you're doing?"

I ran faster, blood pumping on adrenaline and not much else. Up ahead, the hallway ended at a sliding metal door. The two stationeers were racing after me, feet pounding hard on the carpeted corridor, and I tucked my head down and didn't stop.

The door slid open with a whisper, and Rena bustled out, carrying a first aid kit.

A red scarf was wrapped around her nose and mouth.

I was so stunned I skittered to a stop, veering off to the left and slamming up against the wall. Rena jerked up her head and stumbled backward. The kit banged against her thigh.

"Esme?" She leaned forward, eyes squinting at me over the mask. The two stationeers came to a stop a few paces away.

"She left her room," the man said. He looked flustered and embarrassed, like he'd been caught in a lie. "Just took off running."

"What's going on?" I whispered. I couldn't take my eyes off that red scarf.

"Get back to your cabin now." Rena's voice was hard. "Lock yourself in. I fucking mean it."

"Who's sick?" I realized I was crying. I hadn't noticed until then, but suddenly I knew I'd been weeping all this time, tears falling over my numb cheeks as I tried to run off a space station. I whirled around to face the two stationeers. "Why aren't your faces covered?" I slapped my hand over my mouth and breathed in the scent of my skin.

"We're on a space station," the woman said. "The monitors haven't picked anything up. It's not spread on the air."

"It makes her feel better," said Rena. "If we're covering our faces."

My hand fell to my side. I turned back to her and I felt like I was moving in slow motion. The corridor was too narrow, the lights too bright, the air in the station too stale.

"Is it one of the twins?" My voice cracked.

Rena shook her head. I breathed a sigh of relief. "The doctor, then, Dr. Tristany—"

Rena stared at me and I knew I was wrong. I thought of Isabel clutching Daphne in the car as we drove across the countryside to the rocket, and I went cold all over.

Then Rena shoved the kit into the male stationeer's hands and wrapped me in a hug. I pressed myself close to her. I didn't care that the flu probably traveled by touch.

"Isabel was complaining of chills shortly after we arrived. A fever." Rena's voice was as steady as a metronome and without inflection, as if she were reciting from memory. I was distantly aware of the two stationeers slinking away, the man setting the kit on the floor near the wall. Rena stared at me over the blankness of her mask. "She was tired this evening at dinner, but I didn't think—"

All this way. We came all this way to escape the flu and it just followed us into space.

"Dr. Tristany is hoping she can save the baby. The station is equipped with one of those portable incubators—"

"We were all crammed into that car together!" I couldn't breathe. I couldn't think. "And the rocket. All of us. The twins. And you—"

The mask hid any possible reaction. "There's no evidence that the flu is airborne. The station would have picked up on it." A pause. "It'll also alert us if your temperature goes above thirty-seven degrees. The twins aren't showing symptoms. But you need to go to your cabin. Stay there."

"Does it spread by touch?" I said. "Contact? It has to spread somehow. I don't understand how going to my room—"

"It's the only thing I can do to keep you safe." She sounded so desperate my breath caught.

"What about the vaccine?" I said. "Is that what's in the kit? Dad can stop this, right?" I was crying again, desperate for Rena to say yes. This was the role of a CEO in a corpocratic system. To use the company's boundless wealth to protect its citizens. To provide vaccines when they were dying.

Rena stared at me in that harsh bright light. Then she said, "There is no vaccine, Esme."

"There has to be," I babbled. "That's what the company does. He can't just let us all die."

"If there was a vaccine, your father would have inoculated the family. He wouldn't hide a vaccine from you. Please. Go to your cabin."

I took a deep breath. Wiped at my eyes. Rena stared at me, her eyes glittering. I nodded.

"Good girl." Rena stooped down to pick up the kit. "I'll come check on you as soon as I have the chance. Remember what I said—straight to your cabin, lock the door."

I nodded. Rena scrambled down the hallway and I stared after her. She didn't duck into one of the rooms like I expected but instead disappeared through the sliding doors at the opposite end. Heading toward another wing.

I had her instructions but I couldn't move. Isabel was sick. She would be dead within a few days. The quarantine around Undirra City hadn't protected us. Fleeing hadn't protected us. Dad was wrong. We were the same as the villagers.

I forced myself to move, to walk back to my cabin. The walls buzzed but otherwise the station was silent. I didn't see anyone else. There were no signs of that capricious invader.

I made it to my cabin and locked the door. For a moment, I could only lean up against the wall and stare at the crumpled sheets on the unfamiliar bed. Blood pounded in my ears. My stomach lurched.

I leaned over and threw up on the floor.

When it was over, I felt momentarily cleansed, as if someone had come and stripped away all my fear and panic. I crawled over to my bed and knelt on the floor beside it, dry-heaving. The room spun around.

Isabel was dying. She was, it seemed to me, already dead.

The next morning, someone knocked on my cabin door. I woke up with an aching neck, my body twisted at a strange angle.

The knocking started again.

I sat up, rubbing my neck, and stumbled across the room and pulled the door open.

Rena stood in the hallway, her hair hanging bedraggled around her shoulders, her eyes bloodshot and tired. Last night's mask was gone.

"Your father asked me to tell you," she began, and then she stopped, took a deep breath.

A heaviness formed in my stomach, cold like metal. "What?" I said, panicking. "What is it?"

She closed her eyes as she spoke. "Mrs. May Coromina died last night."

Her words seemed to echo around the room. I didn't know

what to say. Of course she was dead. If you caught the flu, you died.

Isabel was dead. She was dead. We hadn't been friends, but I didn't want her to die.

"The baby, though—" Rena started.

I jerked my gaze up to hers. She blinked, gave me a halfhearted smile.

"The baby," I whispered. The baby that wasn't born yet, that was still a part of Isabel. She would be gone, too.

"We saved the baby," Rena said.

The words didn't make sense at first. I understood them individually, but all strung together, in that particular order, they sounded like a foreign language. But then I worked them out, and a lightness spread through me, disbelief wound together with hysterical giddiness.

She stepped into my cabin and closed the door behind her. "A little girl, of course. She's in the incubator and Dr. Tristany is keeping close watch on her. She doesn't seem to have any symptoms—" Her voice jerked and she pressed one hand to her mouth. "She's breathing filtered air, just in case. The station monitors still haven't identified the virus. If it is a virus. We don't know." Rena leaned up against the wall and took a long, shuddering breath. She was crying, tears shining in the corner of her eyes.

"I'm exhausted," she said. "I've been up all night, tending to her—at least the twins are asleep now. No one's told them yet. I don't—I hope your father—" She stopped herself, and I suspected she was afraid Dad would make her tell them.

I pressed myself to the wall beside her and stared at the doorway leading out into the empty corridor. While I'd lain gasping in my bathroom last night, Isabel had been dying, breathing in her last breaths, feverish and afraid. I wondered if she knew they saved the baby before she died. I hoped she did.

That thought, that Isabel might have died without ever knowing her baby was tucked into the incubator, was the one that drew out my tears. One moment, I was numb and empty, and the next, tears streamed over my face, silent and painful. I could hardly breathe. After a moment, Rena snaked her hand around my shoulder and drew me into her breast, and we stayed like that for a long time, weeping in the space station's false light.

We did not stay long aboard the space station. I suspect the stationeers didn't want us there—and who could blame them when we'd brought a planetside disease into their pristine filtered air? Of course, no one else got sick. No one in the family, and none of the stationeers, either.

And so we went slinking back to Star's End. All of us except for Dad and Dr. Tristany and the new baby. And Isabel. They would fly down on a specialized shuttle in a few days' time. Let the rest of us go first. I didn't know what we'd find when we returned, and during the shuttle ride back to the surface—no one speaking, the twins knocked out with a sleeping pill—I imagined a million nightmares. The gardens trampled and burned, the house gutted. People dead. Of flu, of violence. Whenever I started to drift off to sleep, I heard the gunshots in the distance and the screams of the villagers and I was jarred back awake.

But the estate was fine. We rode in a normal car, along normal roads, back home, and there were no signs of destruction along the way. The palm trees still lined the drive, the gardens still flourished in the bright sunlight.

It was as if we had just been away on vacation.

The next day, I learned that three more people in the household had gotten sick, staff who had had to stay behind while we fled. Beata, one of the cleaning girls, had died immediately, as Isabel had, but the other two had lain in their beds for a long time, dying slowly and painfully. I didn't want to think about it.

The message on my lightbox the night we fled had been from Laila, panicked and crying because her brother was showing symptoms. I contacted her right away. The projection shivered in the empty air as I waited for it to connect. "Please answer," I whispered, my heart pounding hard in my chest. "Please. Please—"

And then her face appeared. Her skin was wan and pale, her hair greasy and tangled. She blinked at me.

"Esme?" she said, and lines appeared in her brow.

"You're alive," I gasped. "You're okay."

"I'm not okay." She stared at me through the holo.

My whole body went numb. Blood rushed in my ears.

"Orlando is dead."

The air whooshed out of me. Orlando. Her little brother. I'd only ever seen him as a blur in the background of her holo, only ever heard him shrieking and laughing as she tried to bat him away.

"Oh, Laila," I said. "Oh God, I'm so sorry—"

"I thought you were dead, too." She trembled. There was a hardness in her expression I'd never seen before. "You never pinged me back. And then I heard rumors about an evacuation."

My cheeks burned. "Dad made me go," I mumbled. I could barely look at her. "Not that it mattered. Isabel died too."

That hardness vanished then. Her shoulders slumped. She looked away from the recorder.

"I'm sorry," I said again.

She nodded and wiped at her eyes. "Yeah. Me too." She looked back at me again, and then she began to talk. In a dull, flat voice, she told me everything she knew. There had been twenty-five deaths before the flu burned itself out. Paco was okay, last she heard, still working with the underground to get information to the people. I should contact him, tell him what I knew. Nothing, I wanted to tell her. I knew nothing. She didn't say anything more about Orlando. I didn't even know if he got a funeral.

We stared at each other through our transparent screens, and I felt a wall go between us that had nothing to do with technology.

They burned Isabel's body and the body of Beata during two separate ceremonies. I was not invited to Beata's funeral, but I went anyway. The flu had wreaked havoc on the village and then disappeared like a bandit, but Dad didn't lift the quarantine until the day of Beata's funeral, the morning after he arrived home, my new baby sister still cloistered away inside a portable incubator. Early that morning, I slipped past the soldiers and down to the village ceremony. It was my first breath of freedom in a long time. The air tasted clean, no poison at all.

The village cemetery was located on the edge of town away from the ocean, heading inland. It was surrounded by banyan trees with long, draping roots, and I climbed up into one of the trees and perched among the branches to watch the ceremony. It was strange to see the staff in white, the women with their faces covered by rectangles of white lace. Beata's ashes were in a simple wooden urn, and they buried that as the priest uttered prayers and incantations no one really believed in anymore. I was afraid of being caught, so I slipped out of the tree as people began making speeches.

I wanted to find Orlando's grave, to see which flowers his family had planted for him, but instead, I just went home.

Isabel's funeral was the next day. I woke up early and put on the only white dress I owned, and then I covered my face with a white scarf the way the women had at Beata's funeral. When I went downstairs, Rena was waiting on the patio with Adrienne and Daphne, who wore matching gauzy funeral dresses and looked as if they didn't understand that the world had almost ended. The priest was there too, a different one from the other funeral. She stood at a respectful distance, gazing out at the trees, and held the urn containing Isabel's ashes to her chest. The bodies of the dead were always entrusted to the priests.

Rena took me in, my dress and my lower-class veil, and didn't say anything.

Dad arrived fifteen minutes later. It was the first time I'd seen him up close since he came back from the space station. I almost didn't recognize him: He was pale and his face so drawn that he looked like a skeleton. His white linen suit hung awkwardly on his frame, and his hair was lank and greasy.

"Is this everyone?" the priest asked gently.

"Yes." Dad scowled at her. "I didn't want to throw a fucking party for my wife's death."

The priest nodded like she was used to these outbursts. I thought that the real reason Dad hadn't arranged for a proper ceremony was because he didn't want any of his colleagues to see him looking so broken-down—looking so *defeated*. Isabel had loved parties and she'd always had lots of friends. Before the flu, she was always inviting them to stay at Star's End. It didn't seem right that Dad was keeping them from mourning her.

The five of us trudged down to the family cemetery on the northern end of the property. It was set on the edge of the woods that stretched out for miles, far beyond the perimeters of the estate. A gateway to the forest.

No one was buried there. Isabel was to be the first. After all, Dad had built Star's End when he made his fortune; it was hardly an ancestral home for any of us. And I imagined that when he set aside the land for the cemetery, he thought he would be the first to inhabit it. The life-extension treatments were new then; he couldn't have imagined he'd live as long as he had now.

A hole had already been dug in the ground when we arrived, the flowers sitting beside it. Dad stared at it like it was an enemy. The priest intoned the prayers, the same as the ones from Beata's funeral, and Rena stood in a patch of sunlight with one hand on each of the twins' shoulders. Leaves and flower blossoms fluttered down from the trees and spilled across the soft, fluttering grass. It was a beautiful day, and that hardly seemed appropriate.

"Would anyone like to speak of the dead?" the priest asked, a cue I recognized from dramas and Beata's funeral yesterday, the only other funeral I'd ever attended. Silence settled over all of us. If Dad had given Isabel a proper funeral, with all her friends, we'd have been there until sunset, listening to stories about her life. But as it was we all just looked at each other, waiting. Then Daphne darted away from Rena, chasing a butterfly, and Rena bounded after her and grabbed her by the arm. Daphne glared at her, and Dad glared at Daphne, and the priest shifted her weight and looked down at her feet.

Part of me wanted to say something, and part of me was afraid I'd say something wrong. I'd known Isabel for almost four years. Half of that time, I'd resented her for taking my mother's place, and the other half, I ignored her. Dad looked afraid to speak, like if he did, we'd see how vulnerable he was.

Then Rena straightened up, clutching Daphne's hand tight. She looked washed out in her white dress. Faded. She said, "Isabel was a good woman and a good mother." She punctuated this statement with a curt nod. Daphne pulled away and ran into a shower of falling leaves. This time, Rena didn't try to stop her. Adrienne followed behind her, the leaves catching in her hair.

They didn't know. They didn't *understand*.

Tears pricked at my eyes. I wiped them away. Dad glanced at me, stone-faced, then turned to the priest and said, "Thank you. We can take it from here."

The priest wasn't intimidated by him. "I'll wait for you at the house. If any of you need to talk." She looked at Dad while she spoke. He looked away, and her shoulder hitched a little. Then she left the cemetery. No one moved, no one spoke. Her footsteps crackled over the grass and then faded away.

"Rena, you take care of the damn flowers." He wouldn't look anyone in the eye. "I have some business to attend to."

Rena nodded. Dad glanced over at me, although I didn't know why. His gaze seemed to weigh a thousand pounds.

"I'll help," I said. I don't think that's what he wanted.

He grunted, turned away, and left. Just like that. The funeral for beautiful and popular Isabel had taken all of fifteen minutes.

"He's grieving," Rena said. "He's just doing it in his own way."

I wondered if she really believed that.

We stood side by side, looking down at the urn tucked away in the grave. Adrienne and Daphne chased each other around the trees, their laughter bright and jarring.

"I guess we should get started," Rena said, watching them. "If we're out here much longer, they'll ruin their dresses."

I nodded in agreement.

One of the gardeners had laid out a flat packing crate of potted flowers before the start of the funeral: mostly heliconia plants, with a tiny twist of glory bower and a sprig of bougainvillea. Rena regarded them for a moment, then picked up the shovel lying beside the crate and began tossing the dirt back into Isabel's grave.

Planting flowers on a grave was supposed to be done by loved ones. Family. Dad should have been there. He should be shoveling the dirt into place; he should be pulling the heliconias out of their canisters one at a time. But instead, he'd left it to us, a servant and a stepdaughter.

And he didn't even let her friends, those women who flitted around the gardens, say goodbye.

I watched Rena fill the grave and promised myself that I'd never become like Dad. No matter which Coromina Group career path I took, I wouldn't carve my heart out the way he did. If someone I loved died, I would plant flowers on their grave. I wouldn't delegate the job to someone else.

Rena finished filling the grave and looked at me. I handed her the first of the heliconias, but she shook her head. "The bougainvillea first. It was always her favorite."

"Oh." I hadn't known that. I brought the bougainvillea over to the grave. Rena dug a space for it, and together we tugged it out of its canister. She let me set it into place. The soil was rich and dark and cool beneath my hands, damp from the moisture in the air.

Adrienne and Daphne wandered over to us from the place beneath the trees. Their faces were serious. Maybe they did understand what had happened. They sat in the grass, holding hands and smearing their white dresses with bright grass stains. Rena called them over and showed them how to place the flowers in the dirt. They planted two before they started throwing clumps of dirt at each other. Rena shouted at them that they were being disrespectful. Daphne just laughed at that and threw more dirt. But Adrienne looked away, her hair hanging in her face. My heart twisted.

Rena and I planted the rest of the flowers. I tried to think of Isabel as I worked, the way you were supposed to. I wanted to think on her in happier times, but I kept seeing her face as we rode in the armored car to the shuttle. She had already been sick, and none of us had known.

When we finished, Rena crouched down behind the twins, her muddy hands resting on their shoulders.

"There," she said. "Whenever you want to visit Mommy, you can come here."

So, Rena had explained something to them. They didn't say anything, though, just stared down at the flowers. Maybe they were in shock. Could kids go into shock? Of course, I was sixteen, and I hardly understood everything that was happening. I couldn't understand why the universe thought this flu was fair, or why Dad wouldn't give her a real funeral.

Adrienne buried her head in Rena's arm and Rena stroked her hair. Daphne just kept staring at the grave. Her face was streaked with dirt and her hair was tangled up with leaves. She looked like part of the forest.

I turned back to the flowers, sparse against the dark dirt. Supposedly, Isabel's spirit would live on in those flowers, because her remains would help them grow. But that was a story for children, and I wasn't a child anymore.

After the funeral, there were no more outbreaks, and we tried to settle back into our old routines, as if the flu had been nothing more than a shared nightmare. But there was an empty space where Isabel had been. The gardens were empty. The guest wing was shut up tight. The house had a black hole at its center, and we couldn't do anything to fill it.

I spent those next few days thinking about the baby. I still didn't know her name, and I imagined her looking the way the twins had when they were born, scrunchy-faced with a thatch of black hair. A tiny life trapped in an incubator. Motherless. Raised by a machine.

I asked Rena one afternoon if I could see the baby—at least peek through a window at her. *Something.* Isabel was gone and I thought I could fill that gap if I at least knew what the baby looked like, if I could at least hold her image inside my head.

"I'm afraid not, sweetie," Rena said. We were sitting outside in the sun, watching the twins play some complicated game of freeze tag out among the pineapples. "Dr. Tristany still isn't sure how the flu affected her. If she's even going to pull through." Rena squinted in the direction of the twins. Daphne shrieked and dove behind one of the larger pineapple plants while Adrienne's back was turned.

I pulled my knees up to my chest, feeling numb. "Does she even have a name?"

Rena kept staring at the twins. "Not yet," she said softly. "Mr. Coromina has—" She took a deep breath. "He's still grieving."

I hadn't seen Dad since the funeral. He spent almost all his time at the office, working. It seemed a funny way of grieving to me.

"She needs a name," I said.

"I don't disagree," said Rena.

The rest of the day stretched out, languid and empty. My tutoring sessions hadn't started up again, and without Isabel, we didn't eat meals in the dining room the way we used to. My life had been ordered before the outbreak, parceled out into blocks of time. Not anymore. There were just hours and hours of hot sunlight that burned away my balance of mind. I couldn't stop thinking about the baby, couldn't stop wondering if she was going to die. It drove me mad.

That evening, I'd had enough of it. I put on a sundress and makeup and pulled my hair back into a sleek, fashionable ponytail. I blinked at myself in the mirror. There I was. Alive.

I didn't worry about the soldiers shooting me as I made my way to the edge of the estate. Death had brushed past me so closely, I had felt the breeze of it on my skin; I couldn't believe I'd ever been frightened of the soldiers' guns.

The sun was starting to set. Lines of color oozed across the sky. I wondered if Laila had opened her food stand again. I wanted to see her, but I didn't think I could stand the thought of going to her house, another place kissed by death. I wanted to see *her*, to hug her and eat some of her fried shrimp and maybe, for just a second, feel like everything was normal. Maybe it wasn't possible. But maybe it was.

I walked along the main road toward the food stands, weaving through the tall sea grass. Cars whipped by. Insects chirped in the trees. The air was balmy on my skin. Soon, I was able to make out the lights from the food stands, already switched on even though we were just edging over into twilight. Laila's seashell was lit up. My heart thumped. I darted across the road without waiting for the signal. A car could have slammed into me at three hundred miles an hour, but I didn't care. Not tonight.

The stands were busier than I expected, families carrying their cartons of food over to the tables set up to look out at the stretch of ocean in the distance. Laila's didn't have a line, though, and I walked right up to the window and rapped once on the glass, the way I always did. Laila pulled the window aside and blinked at me. She looked as if she hadn't slept for days.

"Esme?" She gave me a halfhearted smile. "What are you doing out here?"

"Wanted to see you. I'm so glad you're all right."

Her half-smile vanished. I wished I could vacuum up my words. Of course she wasn't all right. Her brother had just died. I wasn't all right, either.

"I mean, I'm glad you're safe," I said.

She nodded. "I'm glad you're safe, too. You want to come in?"

I moved toward the door, but she held up her hand and said, "No, you know what? I need a break. I'll meet you outside." Then she vanished back inside the recesses of her shell. The lights dimmed. A sign flicked on in the window: BACK IN TEN MINUTES.

Then Laila stepped out of the side door. She activated the lock. I wandered over to her. She pushed her hair out of her face and looked down at her feet.

"You want something to drink?" she said. "I can get usually get a few ales out of the liquor stand." She tilted her head sideways, toward the rainbow of lights erupting out of Sandu's Refreshing Beverages.

"No," I said. "I'm not thirsty."

Laila shrugged and walked away from her seashell toward the little pavilion on the back where stand workers could hide out from their customers. I followed her and tried to think of things to say.

"Have you talked to Paco?" she asked, stopping abruptly.

"For a few minutes the other day." I crossed my arms over my chest. Laila was staring out at the ocean. The waves shimmered in the dying light. "He just wanted to tell me he was all right, that he was doing stuff for the Underground."

Laila choked out a laugh. "The Underground," she said. "Like that helped us one goddamn bit when you get down to it. They act like they're all different, but they're under the company's thumb too. Same as the rest of us."

She darted a glance at me. My cheeks burned. I thought of the screams of the villagers, the rattle of light-rifle fire.

"How was the space station?" she said, her voice as sharp as a wasp's sting.

I looked away, over to the stands, to the people milling around in the lights. Coromina citizen-employees. They almost looked happy. But they couldn't be, not after the outbreak.

I wondered how many of them had seen death too.

"It was terrible," I said.

I could feel an electric prickle on my skin, and when I glanced over, I saw that Laila was watching me with hooded, dark eyes.

"Not as terrible as it was here," she said.

"No," I said. "Probably not."

We stared at each other. I didn't know what Laila wanted from me. If I could have brought back her brother, I would have done it in an instant. The same with Isabel, too. But the Coromina Group hadn't figured out the secret to resurrection. It couldn't even keep us safe from a virus outbreak.

Then Laila sighed and turned away from me. Her lank hair swung through the shadows. "I'm sorry," she said. "It's just been so hard. I can't believe—" Her voice cracked. I could hear the tears trying to get out. I rushed over to her and threw my arms around her shoulders. A backward hug. She wiped at her eyes.

"I can't believe he's gone," she said.

I didn't let go.

"It came on so fast. There were these CG people coming around, scanning people's temperatures from a truck, and they knocked on our door in the middle of the night and said Orlando had a fever and we weren't allowed to leave the house." Her words fell out in a rush. I pressed myself against her. She smelled like the sea, like salt and shrimp. "They put this big black X on our door. And then Orlando started coughing and choking and there was blood every-where—"

She pulled away from me, her hands balled into fists.

"I'm so, so sorry," I whispered.

"I stayed with him," she said softly. "We all did. What else was there to do? I thought I was already dead. And you were up in the sky." She flicked her hand dismissively. "And Paco had run off with the fucking Underground like it would actually do anything, and I was the only one *here*, watching it all happen."

She whirled around. Her cheeks were shiny with tears. I was crying too, little gasping sobs.

"I'm sorry," I said. "I wouldn't have gone, but Dad made me— and it didn't matter anyway; Isabel *died* and it was all so stupid and pointless." I thought about the gunshots again. Who had the soldiers killed? Whose death had been covered up by the company, passed off as a victim of the flu?

"It's not fair," Laila said. She kept squeezing her fists tighter and tighter. "I know it's not your fault, but it's just not *fair*."

I felt hopeless. I had come out here because I wanted things to be normal again. Now I realized they couldn't be. The flu had done more damage than I realized. Killing people wasn't enough.

"I'm sorry," I said.

Laila shook her head. "It's not your fault."

But she stood several paces away from me, and she didn't come any closer.

I ran all the way home. When I made it to the woods on the edge of the estate, I leaned against one of the trees and sobbed. I was to inherit the Coromina Group: in thirty or fifty or a hundred years, I would hold all the power in the system. And yet not even the Coromina Group could save a little boy dying in his family's arms.

I screamed and slammed my fist into the tree trunk. The stinging in my knuckles shocked me, and I gazed down at my hand dotted with blood. I wondered how many other people had died from the flu. The official numbers hadn't been released, of course—it was bad business. Not even the Underground had been able to get ahold of them. But it was probably a lot. More than I could have imagined.

I slumped down in the dirt, leaning my back up against the tree. A hot wind blew in from the direction of the ocean. I could smell the salt on it and it made me think of Laila, my arms thrown around her shoulders while she stood as stiff as a corpse, like she didn't even want me to touch her.

All this death. All this sorrow. My internship was starting next year. Planet Maintenance. It was definitely going to be with Planet Maintenance. No other division in the company worked so closely with the system's people. When I owned the Coromina Group, it would become whatever I wanted. It didn't have to be Dad's vision anymore. We didn't have to manufacture weapons or engineer soldiers—the idea made me queasy, anyway. When the company was under my control, we would manufacture vaccines for diseases like the flu. We would find ways to end hunger. We would do *good* in this system. In other systems, too.

I wiped at my eyes. My hands were still stinging but I didn't care. I stood up, shaking. I was already starting to understand that I had lost Laila, that I might have lost Paco, too—that the older I got, the further I would be pulled away from the village. Company headquarters was going to swallow me whole. It just didn't have to be a bad thing.

I trudged forward, weaving through the trees, back toward the house. The lights in the windows glimmered up ahead. We were going to return to normal eventually. We would shove the memory of the flu aside. But we wouldn't lose our memories of the dead.

Isabel. Orlando. Two souls gone, with only one to take their places. The baby. A little sister. I hadn't been much of a sister to the twins—I'd always just thought that they had each other, that they didn't need me. But I realized I was wrong. The twins and the baby, they would be the first people I kept safe.

This was what I told myself over and over as I picked my way through the cool grass toward the lights of the house. I entered through the garden door, and the cool dry air of the climate control was a relief against my skin. I stood in the atrium, my heart pounding. Somewhere in this house were the three lives I was determined to protect.

I marched up to the twins' suite. It was still early enough in the evening that the twins hadn't gone to bed yet. The door hung open, lemony light spilling into the hallway. I slipped into their play-room without knocking. They were in an immersion, the ghosts of brightly colored cartoon characters swirling around their heads. Rena was reading something on her lightbox. She glanced up at me and frowned.

"My God, Esme, what happened to you?"

My face flushed. I ran a hand over my hair—it must have been wild from the humidity and the wind and my running away. "I'm fine," I said. "I—I just wanted to see the twins."

Rena tilted her head. I thought I might have seen a smile. "They're playing right now. You can keep me company, if you'd like."

I slunk over and sank down into the sofa beside her. Rena switched off her lightbox and cradled it in her lap. "You look like you've been traipsing through the woods," she said. "Is that what brought on this change of heart?"

"It's not a change of heart." I looked over at the twins. Daphne kicked her feet in time to some song I couldn't hear. "I just—I don't want to lose them, too."

Tears brimmed in my eyes. I kept seeing Laila, standing away from me like I could taint her. All my life, I'd pretended there was nothing separating us. But there was, an entire system designed to keep us apart.

"Oh, sweetie," Rena said, throwing her arm over my shoulder. I wiped my eyes, embarrassed that she'd seen me. "I understand." She stroked my hair, the way she had when I was a little girl, and I leaned against her shoulder, still watching the twins laugh at their holos. We sat like that for a moment, and I started to calm.

"If you want," Rena began, "you can help me. With the twins. With the baby, too, when she comes out of her incubator."

My heart fluttered. "Really?" I twisted my neck to peer up at her.

She smiled. "Your father won't like it, you doing servant's work, but he won't have to know about it, will he?"

"I'd like that." I didn't think that taking care of my sisters was servant's work. But I didn't always think like my father.

We sat in silence for a few moments. Then Rena said, "You don't know how glad it makes me, you caring about your sisters." She pulled away and looked down at me. "My sister survived the out-break. I don't think I told you."

I shook my head. My face was hot with embarrassment. I should have asked Rena about her sister. But I'd been so wrapped up in losing Isabel, and then Orlando, that it never even occurred to me.

"Good," I murmured.

"She's safe. For now." Rena gazed across the room, at some unfathomable point on the far wall. "The baby, she's doing better too. I can take you to see her once Dr. Tristany gives us word that it's all right."

I settled into the sofa. The twins were still wrapped up in their immersion. I studied them, looking for those little differences in how they moved, how they smiled, how they laughed. Adrienne moved less than Daphne did, her eyes following the holos around. She seemed to regard them in quiet contemplation. But Daphne chased them as if they were real, laughing in delight.

Rena patted my knee, a motherly gesture that made my chest constrict. I had lost my friends. At least I wouldn't lose my family, too.

Two days later, someone knocked on my bedroom door. I was sup-posed to be studying, but instead, I was sitting by the window with my lightbox balanced on my knees, watching the rain fall over the garden. I hadn't spoken to Laila since the evening at her shrimp stand, but I had gone to the cemetery in the village and sprinkled water over the jasmine growing on Orlando's grave.

"Come in!" I called out.

Rena pushed the door open. The twins were with her, their hair combed back into sleek ponytails.

"I just received word from Dr. Tristany," she said. "It's safe to visit the baby."

My breath caught. "Really?"

Rena nodded. "I knew you'd want to know. And even Daphne and Adrienne have been asking about it, haven't you, girls?"

The twins nodded, their dark hair bobbing against their backs.

Rena smiled at me. I switched off my lightbox and joined them out in the hallway. Together the four of us walked over to the western wing, to the medical suite. Mr. Hankiao, the medical assistant, was there, tapping against an invisiholo fluttering in his line of vision. He glanced up when we came in.

"Hi, Rena," he said. "Came to see the baby, huh?"

"Of course. The girls wanted to."

"Did they, now?" He grinned indulgently at them. I felt like an outsider, like I didn't belong. I wanted to shout that I'd wanted to see her too. "Well, you can go on in. The incubator's air is completely filtered, so no need to suit up." He nodded toward the closed door that led into the resting room.

Rena thanked him and grabbed the twins' hands, and they all disappeared into the dim light of the room. I hung back, a nervous fluttering in my chest. The responsibility of my future weighed on me. Even if it was a responsibility I wanted.

Mr. Hankiao didn't say anything to me, didn't seem to notice I was there at all, so I leaned up against the window. The rain had started a few days after the flu disappeared, like the atmosphere was weeping for the dead.

Rena came out with the twins. We looked at each other. The room was full of the soft susurration of the rain.

"It's okay," she said quietly. "I know you want to see her."

I nodded. Adrienne tugged on Rena's sleeve and said something about needing to go to the restroom, her voice a low, childish whine. Rena sighed and nodded. Mr. Hankiao glanced up at us, the light from his holo shining across the side of his face.

"Go on," Rena said. "You'll be a great sister. I know it."

"There's really nothing to worry about," Mr. Hankiao said, turning back to his holo. "You're not going to make the baby sick."

The baby, the baby. We had to give her a name.

I took a deep breath and stepped into the resting room before Mr. Hankiao could say anything else to me. The curtains were drawn, blocking out all but a trickle of thin gray light. The incubator sat in the center of the room, at the foot of the bed, the glass glowing slightly golden. It made a noise like the wind was breathing, a *whoosh* in and a *whoosh* out. I stared at it and I saw only forms at first, the oblong curve of the glass, the bulky square of the machinery beneath.

Something moved.

An arm, a too-small tiny arm. My breath caught. I stepped forward, hardly daring to breathe. The baby squirmed in the golden light. She was naked except for a cloth diaper, and she was hooked into a tube and wires. I went to the edge of the incubator and peered in. She blinked, her gaze focused on empty space. She didn't look the way the twins had looked as newborns; she hardly looked human at all but rather like some first attempt at a human, scrunched and ill-formed. She'd been born too soon.

The door swung shut behind me.

I jumped and whirled around, my heart pounding. In the darkness, it took a moment for me to realize that Dad was standing in the room.

"Esme?" His voice was rubbed raw. He stepped forward, into the light of the incubator. It cast harsh, geometric shadows over his face. "What are you doing here?"

"Rena told me I could come see the baby."

"The baby." Dad stood beside me and looked down at the incubator. He was close enough that I could see his eyes were rimmed in red. I couldn't imagine my father crying. There had to be some other explanation.

Dad put the tips of his fingers on the incubator's glass, then jerked them away, like the glass was hot. My lungs tightened. I took a step backward, trying to leave, but then Dad said, "She still doesn't have a name, does she?"

"What?" I stopped.

"You called her *the baby*. Still no name."

I hesitated. "I guess not. I guess—"

"We hadn't decided on one yet." Dad tilted his head, still staring down at the baby in the incubator. "Me and—" I swore I heard his voice crack. "I guess I'll have to come up with something."

I didn't say anything. I wanted to leave. The air in the room was all wrong.

Dad wiped at the corner of his eye. "A name," he said, and he turned his head to the side. His cheeks glimmered in the light.

He was crying.

All I wanted was to get out of that room. My sisters were one thing, but I couldn't handle Dad like this. He was supposed to be at his office. He was supposed to have abandoned his family for work. And yet here he was.

Dad turned back to the incubator and wiped at his eye again. I moved backward. The door seemed a million miles away.

"Isabel," he said. His voice trembled, just a little. "Isabel. Isabel."

He murmured her name like it was a prayer. I was sixteen years old and I had never seen true grief until this moment. It terrified me. That it came from my father, a man who treated emotion like a weakness, only frightened me further.

"Isabel," he said again, louder this time. He looked at me. I froze into place, my hand on the doorknob. I was sure he'd forgotten I was here. "What do you think?"

"Um . . ."

"For the name, Esme. Good lord." The sharpness in his voice soothed me. At least it was familiar. "Name the baby Isabel. After her mother."

I didn't understand why he was asking my opinion on this. But I realized I was glad that he had.

"I like it," I said stupidly.

He didn't answer. He just stared down at the incubator, the light flooding around him like a halo.

I fled.

NOW

Will came to Esme's office because hers was more secure. They sat in the two chairs beside the window that looked down into one of the company courtyards. All Esme could see were the tops of trees.

"That's what he wants," Esme said, after she had explained her father's wishes. Talking about them made her exhausted. She leaned back in her chair and looked up at the sculptural light fixtures hanging from the ceiling. "It's insane."

"I don't think it's so insane," Will said, after a moment's pause. Esme looked at him. He sat still in his chair, his back very straight. He was letting his hair grow longer than the R-Troops were allowed to wear it. It curled a little around his jawbone. "People look for redemption before they die."

Will would know about death. He'd certainly seen enough of it. Esme sighed and reached over to pour herself a glass of whiskey. She didn't bother offering any to Will; she knew he wouldn't drink it.

"He's never given one goddamn about redemption." She swirled the whiskey around in her glass before drinking. "I just—" She stopped, staring down at the whiskey. Her office was secure against outside threats, not against the company itself. Not that it mattered so much. She was highly ranked enough that she could be insubordinate if she wanted.

"I know," Will said gently. They had talked about her father before.

Esme drained the whiskey and stood up. She felt agitated. Manic. She paced in front of the window, her feet sinking into the thick carpet. She had taken off her shoes and didn't bother to put them on for Will; they were still sitting in a pile over by her desk. "I want you to be honest with me," she said.

"Always."

She stopped, looked him right in the eye. "Do you think this is a good idea?"

He hesitated.

"I mean, trying to find my sisters?" She threw up her hands and turned to look out the window. "Stirring everything up again?" She watched her lips move in the glass. "They ran away for a reason. Isabel especially."

She wanted to see them. Wanted to see who they'd become. But she was terrified that they didn't want to see her.

Tears pricked at her eyes. She wiped them away before they could fall. It was too late, though: Will had seen, and he walked over to her and put a hand, friendly and comfortable, on her shoulder.

"It's been thirteen years," he said softly. "People change."

Esme said nothing. She knew people changed. She certainly had.

"I think it's worth trying," he said.

Esme smiled a little, tilting her head toward him. "*Trying* being the operative word. I'm not sure I'll even be able to find Isabel and Adrienne." She sighed and ambled back over to her chair. Will followed, sitting down when she did. A gentlemanly move, one he'd learned when he'd first been born. She rubbed her forehead. "We can start with Daphne," she said. "She'll at least talk to me."

Will smiled. "I think that's a good plan. Perhaps she knows where the others are."

"Oh, she definitely knows where the others are." Esme remembered the day Daphne had left. She had been the last of them to go. Isabel was nothing but a memory at that point, and Adrienne had cut off all contact. Star's End had been declared a forbidden zone, to keep citizen-employees from investigating the lies the company had spread about the attack. And Daphne had actually come to Esme's apartment. She had stood in Esme's parlor. She had said goodbye. "But she's sure as hell not going to tell me."

Her eyes prickled again. She poured herself another glass of whiskey, and the alcohol burned her tears away.

"We have other ways of finding them," Will said.

Of course they did. That was why Esme had asked Will to help her in the first place. He had connections to Isabel, however tenuous. She had refused to exploit them before. But this was her father's dying wish. His one chance at redemption, like Will said. She wanted to be hopeful enough to believe in redemption. And she wanted to see her sisters again.

"We'll worry about that later." Esme took a deep breath. She stood up again; the mania hadn't subsided. Will lifted his face to watch her. "I have business on Catequil, anyway," she said. "It gives me an excuse to see her in person."

"I think seeing her in person is good," Will said. "But perhaps this shouldn't be a business trip as well."

Esme's face felt hot. "It's the second breach investigation," she said. "I have to handle it myself." She looked at him, daring him to contradict her. "Dasini's workers have been expressing some concerns. It's probably nothing, like the lab. And Daphne's farm is out near Dasini, so—" She shrugged. She had checked Daphne's files earlier: she lived aboveboard, a full Coromina Group citizen-employee. Not like the other two sisters, who had vanished even from CG records. But her address was the same as it had been four years ago.

"If you think it's the right thing to do." Will lowered his gaze, that subservient gesture that was built into the DNA of all the R-Troops. Esme felt a pang deep inside her chest. She looked away. He didn't agree. But of course he wasn't going to fight her. He hadn't been designed to question authority.

Esme stepped off the shuttle onto the surface of Catequil. The wind buffeted her, warmer than she expected, as warm as the southern seas. It lifted the topsoil in great blustering clouds that swirled and sparkled in the sunlight. Esme had dressed in the layers of loose, sheer, form-covering garments favored by the inhabitants of this part of the world, and she could feel the individual grains of sand pelt against her. A layer of soil was forming over her goggles. She couldn't stay out there much longer.

She should have gone to Dasini first. Should have taken care of her investigation, ensured there was nothing to worry about, not come straight to Daphne's farm. But she was here now. She took a deep breath, gathering up her courage.

Daphne's farmhouse was hidden behind a tall, dark wall in the distance. The wind turbine rose up behind it, a whole forest of them, taller than giants.

Esme strode forward.

The shuttle pilot was one of the new models who could derive sustenance from the energy of the plane itself, and so she left him waiting for her without worry. Not that she would be there long. She would present her case to Daphne, as she and Will had planned, and then she would fly out to Dasini. Easy.

That was all assuming Daphne would speak to her. She'd thought about messaging Daphne while she was flying between worlds, giving her a warning that she was coming, but she decided not to. Perhaps it was cowardice. Or perhaps with the element of surprise, Daphne would be less likely to send Esme away.

The wind battered her as she moved across the dry, empty land. She kept her head down, trying to stop the soil buildup on her goggles from worsening. The house hovered distantly on the horizon like a mirage. Esme took deep breaths through the fabric she wore wound around her face. It helped, but it didn't keep all the sand out of her mouth, and her tongue was dry and thick, like sandpaper. Her muscles quivered; her lungs burned.

And then, unexpectedly, she was at the gate. The wall was reinforced steel, locked into place by Coromina-produced stabilizers. It won the war against the wind, unlike everything else out there. Esme undid the gate latch.

She stepped through.

The other side of the wall was much calmer, although Esme's hair still fluttered into her face. She pulled her mask away. There were plants here: a big sprawling vegetable garden, each row divided by narrow irrigation channels. The farmhouse was a big gray-stone cube with strips of windows running around it in bands. Esme walked up to the front door and rang the bell.

And waited.

The wind howled around the wall, shrieking like a lost woman. Esme rang the doorbell again. This time someone answered: a man, tall and burly, with a guarded, gentle expression. He blinked at Esme. His eyes were as big and damp as a doe's.

"I'm here to see Daphne Coromina," Esme said.

The man frowned. "She didn't say she was expecting anyone."

"She isn't." Esme took a deep breath. "I'm her sister Esme. We talk over the holo sometimes."

The man's face flickered. "Oh," he said. "You."

Yes, Esme wanted to scream. *Yes, me, the one who makes sure the Coromina Group doesn't fuck you and all the windfarmers over.* But she forced a smile out of herself and said, "Yes. I'm sure she's reticent to see me, but I assure you I wouldn't have flown all the way out here if it wasn't important."

The man regarded her for a moment. "Is there anyone with you?"

"Just my pilot, but he's waiting with the shuttle."

The man nodded, considering her words. Then he pulled the door open wider and stepped aside. Esme walked into the house. The interior was bright, compared to the gray overcast outside. The lights all glowed with white intensity.

"She's up in her room," the man said. "You can wait in the parlor while I get her." He nodded at a closed door a few paces away. "Afraid we don't have anything fancy to offer you to drink."

"Water would be fine," Esme said.

He nodded. Water was all she wanted anyway, after walking through that cloud of dirt. The man disappeared down the hallway and she eased open the parlor door. It was a small room, with a tattered sofa and loveseat, an old-fashioned media screen unfurled permanently against the far wall, the corners tacked into place with sealant. Esme collapsed on the sofa with a sigh. She could hardly hear the wind in there.

She wasn't sure how long she'd have to wait, so she pulled out her lightbox and sifted through her messages. Things from work she didn't want to deal with right now. A message of encouragement from Will; a confirmation of her appointment with the city leaders in Dasini. Notifications of the alert warnings that had been sent out to all of the departments, asking them to keep close watch on any R-Troops in their employ, to listen for strange, hissing conversations, mention of unusual dreams. And, at the bottom of the list, sent over eight hours before, while she was still traveling, one from her father:

Good luck.

"Working hard?"

Esme jolted at the sound of her sister's voice. When she looked up, Daphne was leaning in the doorway, dressed in a blue jumpsuit turned brown from the dust. The last time Esme had seen her, it was through the filter of a holo. Here in real life, Daphne was larger and more solid, the only softness a slight roundness in her face that was offset by her close-cropped hair. It was still startling to see her as an adult.

"I was just checking some things." Esme switched off the lightbox and slid it into her bag. Daphne stayed in the doorway.

"Why didn't you message me?" she asked.

"This was too important. I needed to see you face to face."

"The holos are face to face."

"You know what I mean. I needed to see you for real."

Daphne's shoulders hitched. She tapped her fingers against the doorframe, one after another in a steady drumming. Then she sighed and walked into the parlor and shut the door.

"You know you managed to show up at the worst possible time," she said.

"I'm sorry."

Daphne shook her head. "We've got three towers down, and this is the best part of the day to fix them, before the winds pick up again."

Esme didn't say anything, but she couldn't imagine the winds being stronger than they were when she walked across the dirt.

"So, what is it?" Daphne said. "And it better be worth it, because—"

"Dad's dying."

Daphne's mouth hung open, and in that expression of shock Esme saw the little girl Daphne had been before.

"How?" she finally whispered.

"Galazamia."

Silence. The house creaked. Then Daphne said, "He couldn't fucking tell me himself?"

"Would you have let him?"

Daphne fell silent. She looked away, toward an electric painting on the wall. To Esme it looked like nothing but smears of light, shifting in subtle strokes on their plastic canvas.

"You haven't talked to him in years. If he called you up, would you have answered?"

Silence, louder than any wind.

Finally, Daphne said, in a small voice: "No."

"Exactly." Esme straightened. She felt like she was in a business meeting and not a meeting with her sister, and that made her almost sad. "He sent me because he wants me to convince you to come home and see him before he dies."

Daphne looked sharply at her. "What?"

"He wants to see all of us. Adrienne and"—Esme's voice wavered—"Isabel."

A pause. Then Daphne laughed, sharp and cold and bitter. "That's not going to happen."

Esme didn't say that she thought the same thing. "Don't worry about whether it will happen or not. Will you come home?"

"If I say no, then it's definitely not going to happen, right?"

"You can't say no."

Daphne blinked. The electric painting shifted into a hurricane swirl. All the lights in the room dimmed, like the sun going behind the clouds.

"You see?" Daphne said. "No light, slow wind. Best time to fix the turbines."

Esme knew she had overstepped her bounds. Daphne was pulling away. "Look, you don't have to answer right now. I have some business in Dasini—"

"Dasini? What's going on Dasini that they would send you?"

"Nothing," Esme said quickly. "Please, Daphne, could you just think about seeing him one last time? I'll be here for a few days, and we can talk about it more—"

"There's nothing to talk about. I don't mind seeing you, but I don't want to see him."

They looked at each other from across the room. Esme knew Daphne was slipping away. This was pointless. She wondered what her father would do if she failed him at this. He wasn't one to tolerate failure.

"I really need to get out there," Daphne said, and she stood up, crossed her arms over her chest like she was warding off Esme. Or warding off their father. "Where are you staying in Dasini? At the hotel there?"

"I think so, yes."

"Well." Daphne gave a little half shrug. "Maybe I'll call you. We have parties on the weekend. You can come, if you're not too good for us." She peered down at Esme. "And as long as you promise not to talk about him."

"I'd like that," Esme said, promising nothing.

Daphne nodded. Then she left the room, leaving Esme sitting on the sofa.

At least it hadn't gone as badly as she feared.

Esme flung herself on her bed at the hotel in Dasini. Her body felt wrung out from being battered by the winds out on Daphne's farm. At least here in the city, the walls kept things calm.

She had a meeting with the city officials in a little under an hour, a dinner in the restaurant on the top floor of the hotel. She needed to shower and change and look over her notes, but instead she stayed on her bed, listening to the wind whistling outside her window. She felt unmoored. Talking with Daphne had not gone as badly as she had worried. But it had still been a failure.

She rolled off the bed and grabbed her lightbox and sent an update to Will, letting him know what had happened with Daphne. If she couldn't even convince her, she had no hope of convincing the others.

She told herself it wasn't worth thinking about now—that she needed to focus on her meeting, on the work to be done there in Dasini. On the surface, it looked like PM work—a pay dispute, workers at the weapon factory complaining that their job was too dangerous. They worked closely with Radiance DNA; there had been some disruptions. Dreams, from what Esme understood. Miguel thought there was a chance that, if the Radiance did have human help, it was there in Dasini. That was one thing the Coromina Group had learned during the last breach: that the Radiance had ties to all four worlds.

Still, Esme doubted the workers were responsible for the breaches. That was why she wanted to come speak to the Dasini officials herself. Confirm it was just some workers' overactive imagination. Maybe bump up their pay rate. Turn a security check into a Planet Maintenance job.

PM had been her first internship, all those years ago. She had loved it, loved the responsibility of keeping the system running, of making sure all of the Coromina Group's citizen-employees were content. And the truth was, she missed it. The Genetics work, the subsequent weapons design and manufacture—sometimes, she could feel it eating away at her insides, like a parasite.

She went into the shower and rinsed the Catequilian dirt out of her hair. Then she sat in the soft, silky robe provided by the hotel and scanned through the file on the Dasini factory, the information projected by holo over the crisp hotel bed. The factory and the town were both new; they had developed in the aftermath of the war as the Coromina Group began mass-producing the R-Troops for the private militaries. The R-Troops had won the war. Both of the wars, really—the war against OCI, and the war against the Radiance.

Esme switched off her lightbox and changed into the dark, fashionably cut CG Vice President's uniform. She pulled her hair back into a chignon, slipped on a pair of high heels. Then she gathered up her lightbox and went up to the restaurant. She felt calm now, calmer than she had after seeing Daphne. This sort of thing, she knew how to do.

The restaurant was nearly empty, and the lights were turned down to make it easier to see the view outside. The walls were nothing but windows. From this high up, Esme could see the city in miniature and, beyond it, the sweeping, empty plains made desolate by the constant winds.

A host approached her, his cheeks flushed pink. "Ms. Coromina?"

"Yes." Esme couldn't take her eyes off the window. She wondered if she would be able to see all the way to Daphne's farm.

"It is *such* an honor to have you visit us here in Dasini," the host said. "I hope your stay has been enjoyable?"

Esme turned to him, gave him her best smile. "Dasini is marvelous," she said. "All of us at CG are impressed with what you've been able to build in the last ten years."

The host beamed, as if he had himself had built the city. "I can take you to your table," he said. "Mayor Singh Ryvka is waiting for you with the others."

Esme dipped her head in agreement and then followed the host as he led her through the restaurant. They must have closed it for the meeting, she realized. A chance for city officials and her to talk in private.

The city officials were sitting at a table in the back of the restaurant, in front of a view of the weapon factory. It was made of the same dark stone as Daphne's farm, a sprawling structure that ran up to the city's wall.

"Ms. Coromina!" Mayor Singh Ryvka stood up as Esme approached. "It's such an honor to have you here with us. Please, sit. We've already ordered a bottle of wine. I hope you like red?"

"Red is fine." Esme sank down into her chair. She recognized all the officials from their files. The mayor, Olivia Singh Ryvka, wore her black hair draped over one shoulder, a jeweled clip glittering above her left ear. The city commissioner, Eleanora Dixon, sat to her left. She was older but had taken the same rejuvenation treatments Esme's father had, so she looked so much younger, in her early twenties. A child, bright-eyed and rosy-cheeked. And on the right was Terence Stone, the CG factory manager, dark-skinned and handsome. Both Terence and Eleanora had a glossiness to their features, a kind of unnerving perfection. One of the marks of rejuvenation.

"When I was assigned to Dasini," Olivia said, "I never expected that I'd be sitting down to dinner with Esme Coromina! I can't thank you enough for choosing to come all the way out here and help us with our concerns."

"Agreed," said Eleanora, who promptly lifted her wine glass. "To Ms. Coromina."

"To Ms. Coromina," the others said, glasses clinking. Esme just smiled politely. They were laying this on too thick, she thought. Which meant they were scared. They probably thought she was here to shut them down, the factory or the entire town, rather than dealing with the unrest of factory workers. They weren't highly ranked enough to have received the security breach alerts. They didn't even know about the Radiance.

"I appreciate the welcome," Esme said. "But really, it's my pleasure to be here. I want to ensure the safety of everyone in the Four Sisters."

A line of tension smoothed itself out from Olivia's forehead. The others were stolid, too rejuvenated for her to read.

"The chef is preparing a special menu for your visit tonight," Terence said. "They should be bringing the meal out shortly. But please, if you have any questions about our little problem"—he spread his hands out over the table—"feel free to ask."

"Well, I've read through the files." Esme folded her hands on top of the table. "But I'd like to hear what you have to say on the matter. Company reports can be so impersonal."

"So can company interrogations," said Eleanora. Terence shot her an angry look, but Esme just smiled broadly at her.

"This isn't an interrogation," Esme said. "I'm sorry if I gave that impression. Think of it as"—she looked at each of them in the eye in turn—"a conversation."

"A conversation," Olivia said, smiling a little. "I like that."

"This isn't exactly company protocol," said Terence.

"I think we can go off-book just for the evening." Esme lifted her wine glass and took a drink. "I won't tell if you won't."

The three of them all laughed, thinly, and took drinks themselves.

"Now," Esme said. "Let's have this conversation."

She settled back into her seat as Terence began to explain the situation. It was the same information she already knew: Dasini the town had grown up around the weapons factory and existed only to support it; without the factory, all thirty-five thousand of Dasini's citizen-employees would have to be relocated. Things had been going very well in the years after the war, as they had for all of the Four Sisters—it was here that Esme took a longer drink of wine than she should, thinking first about the months of the war itself, and the last time she had seen Isabel, the air thick with smoke from the fires burning Star's End. But the factory workers were unhappy about their latest assignment. Bioengineering. Genetic weapons.

"It's the DNA," Olivia said, leaning forward over the table. "The Radiance DNA."

Esme nodded.

"They think it's dangerous," Terence said. "They've developed— superstitions around it."

Here it was. The possibility of a breach. "Superstitions?"

A bell rang from somewhere deep in the restaurant. It was the chef, announcing that the first course of his special menu was ready for serving. The table fell silent as a line of waiters paraded out with the bowls of steaming soup. Esme *ooh*ed and *ahh*ed over the course, as was expected of her. It was a Catequilian fish soup, a specialty of this world. She'd had it before. But all the while, her thoughts were on that one word. *Superstition*. The report had only mentioned unusual dreams. Superstition implied that they had made a connection between those dreams. That they were attempting to puzzle out the truth.

When enough time had passed, Esme balanced her spoon on the edge of her half-finished bowl of soup. "I would very much like to hear more about these superstitions," she said.

"It's nonsense," Terence said, stirring his soup around. "The sort of thing that tends to crop up among the lower classes."

"I wouldn't be quite that dismissive." Eleanora looked straight at Esme. "They say the DNA speaks to them."

Esme went cold all over. She did not move. She hoped she gave nothing away in her expression.

"And you don't call that nonsense?" Terence asked. His voice sounded a thousand miles away.

"They don't understand what they're dealing with," Eleanora said. "And we can't explain it to them." Her eyes bore into Esme's. "The company keeps too many secrets."

Of course they did. The exact nature of the Radiance DNA was Level Ninety-Nine. To the rest of the people of the Four Sisters, to these three city officials sitting across the table, the R-Troops were powered by a synthetic DNA strand, a blend of cloning and genetic manipulation. If they knew what had won them the war against OCI, what had vaulted the Coromina Group into the top echelon of corpocratic systems in the galaxy—there would be panic and outrage and, worst of all, *disorder*. Esme had seen that happen at Star's End. She had seen it happen within her own family.

"Have there been any incidents," Esme asked, "that might lead the workers to develop these ideas?"

The three city officials exchanged glances with each other. Esme leaned back in her chair and waited.

"No," Olivia finally said.

Inwardly, Esme flushed with relief. Outwardly, she did not move.

"It's just a ploy to get more money," Terence said. "They came up with this bullshit about the DNA being dangerous so they'd get paid more."

"Yes," Esme said. "I saw that in the files."

The bell rang, the next course was announced, the waiters marched in. Esme had a moment to consider her options then. The easiest solution would be to give the workers the money they wanted—the company certainly had the income for it. But if she gave in too easily, it would suggest that the workers had a reason to worry about the DNA. Perhaps they did.

But Esme could not reveal that to anyone ranked below Ninety-Nine, could she? The exact nature of the Radiance must remain a secret, hidden away in the multilayered fabrics of reality.

"You can see our conundrum," Olivia said, when it was polite to speak of business again. "We insist and insist that the DNA is safe, but the workers don't believe us."

"We've heard rumors of a defection," Terence said. "Nothing substantial, but the threat is there."

"That serious?" Esme said.

"I told you it wasn't just nonsense," Eleanora said. Olivia hushed her.

"It's a high-ranking factory," Olivia said. "The threat of defection is always there. We've never had trouble before."

"Yes," Esme said. "I suppose that's true." She wondered what the workers had heard. What they had *seen*, what images had materialized inside their thoughts. She had found nothing at Hawley Lab, but it seemed she and Will had been looking in the wrong place. They were going to have to investigate Dasini further. She and Will would have to speak with some of the workers, at the very least. Find out if Miguel was right, if the Radiance had found human aid inside a weapons factory.

But first she would have to soothe the worries of the Dasini officials.

"I glanced over the financial reports for the last quarter," she said breezily, poking at the pile of sautéed root vegetables draped across her plate. She couldn't eat any more; all her food tasted like ash. "The factory has done tremendously well for the company."

"Yes." Terence beamed at her. "We're routinely ranked among the top five factories of our type in the system."

"Well, there you go." Esme lifted her wine glass in a halfhearted toast. "I imagine the company will have no trouble unearthing the funds to give the workers the raise they want. We find that's the most effective method for quieting rumors of defection."

"Of course," Olivia said, and Esme wondered if the defection rumors were true, or if they had just been a ploy to get the raises. Not that she cared; it was a useful fiction. The company could afford it; it would make the workers happier as the company launched its more in-depth investigation. And higher wages meant easier investigations.

"So, it's settled," Terence said. "We give them the raise." He clapped his hands together. "Excellent."

But Eleanora didn't celebrate with the others. She stirred her vegetables around, her eyes downcast. Esme's chest tightened. Eleanora believed the workers, then. Perhaps she'd seen the whispers from the Radiance herself.

As soon as dinner was finished, Esme would have to go back to her room in the hotel and send an encrypted message back to the Coromina Group main campus. It would identify Dasini as a place of interest, and it would list Eleanora's name, too. If there was even the smallest chance that the Radiance's influence had crept up that high in the company's infrastructure, Esme was required to act, and quickly. Workers and new recruits were one thing; officials, even minor city officials, were another.

Esme studied Eleanora as the meal continued on, Terence and Olivia's chatter fading into the background. With that one message, Eleanora would be removed from her position and placed in prison, under surveillance. Just in case.

This was the universe they lived in now.

Daphne's farmhouse at night looked like a light painting. The windows glowed from within, mutable colors that streamed one from the next at the same rhythm as the howling of the wind. As Esme approached, she caught the sound of faint strains of music, a low, soft melody that seemed at odds with the wild, screaming wind. She ducked in through the gate and peeled off her goggles and shook the sand from her veil. A couple stood kissing in the corn. They didn't notice her. She was glad for that.

She shouldn't be there. Not just because she was no longer the sort of person who could come to parties like this, but because there was a chance that the breach was very real. But in this moment, standing in the farmhouse, the Radiance felt unimaginable.

She draped the veil around her neck like a scarf and walked up to the front door. It hung open, party sounds spilling out into the nighttime. Music, conversation, laughter. Esme stood on the outside, listening in. Two hours earlier, she had sent a report to the Coromina Group central campus, requesting that the Dasini factory workers be given a raise before launching a more thorough investigation, and that Eleanora Dixon be detained immediately as a possible Radiance contact. One kindness, one cruelty.

She pushed the door open and went inside.

Those color-changing lights flooded the hallway, blue washing over her and then fading to a sickly, thin green. She followed the melancholic beat of the music into the living room, where people who were nothing like her gathered together with drinks in their hands. The room was soaked in red light, then orange, then yellow. A rainbow washing over all of them.

"Esme! You made it!" Daphne ambled over. She had fixed her hair so that it fell in waterfall curls over her right shoulder, and for a moment, she looked the way Esme had remembered Adrienne, and Esme felt a sharp, sudden pang in her chest. "Can I get you something to drink?"

Yes, thought Esme, but she shook her head. She needed her thoughts clear tonight. If she could convince Daphne to come see their father, then she could leave this place, she could go back to Ekkeko and focus on stopping the containment breach.

"Oh, at least have some goddamn punch," Daphne said. "No alcohol. I know you're probably afraid we're gonna get you drunk and pull a bunch of company secrets out of you."

Esme heard the mockery in Daphne's voice. She sighed. "Fine. Punch would be fine."

Daphne breezed off to a table set up across the room. Esme shifted her weight, aware of how much she stood out at this party. She wore civilian clothes, not the Coromina Group uniform, but she knew they were all wrong anyway. The material was too expensive, too precious. You wouldn't wear handspun silk on a windfarm in Catequil. She watched the other party guests, taking in their threadbare clothes, their wind-tangled hair, and thought for the first time in years about the parties she had gone to in the village when she was younger. They had always been on the beach, a bonfire raging to light up the night, but otherwise they were identical to this one. The same kind of music, the same kind of people.

Esme pressed herself against the wall. The air in the room was very still, no fan, no climate system circulating it through the house, even with all these people milling around. Maybe it was because the farmers were in wind all day, and so they wanted stillness when they were inside.

"One punch for the CEO of the company." Daphne shoved a glass of ruby-colored liquid at Esme's chest.

"I'm not a CEO." Esme took a long drink of the punch. "Just a vice president."

"Oh," said Daphne, rolling her eyes, "*just* a vice president."

Esme drank her punch to keep from replying. She didn't know what to say. Everything she thought of was too corporate. A business proposal, as if she were luring a new employee from a rival company, and not trying to convince her sister to come home to her family.

But then Daphne said, "Thanks for coming, by the way."

"What?" Esme looked over at her. Daphne was staring out at the party, the changing colors sliding across her features.

"I didn't think you would." She drank from a bottle of cheap beer, the sort you could buy from Coromina Group grocers. "Figured you were too good for this kind of thing."

"I don't think that," Esme said softly, and she realized she wasn't lying.

Daphne shrugged, sipped at her beer. The changing colors made Esme's head hurt.

"You want to talk about Dad, don't you?" Daphne said.

Esme didn't answer.

"I can tell. You were never as subtle as you thought you were."

Esme smiled. "I never thought I was subtle at anything."

Daphne laughed, tossed back her beer. "Guess not." She paused for a moment, and Esme waited. It was more like a business meeting than she wanted to admit. Never talk first, as her father always said.

"So, let me guess," Daphne said, watching the party. "He was an asshole when we were kids, but he's different now, right? He's relented? He's a changed man? Maybe found some religion or another?"

For a moment, Esme considered lying. She considered telling Daphne what she wanted to hear, what she thought would bring her back to Ekkeko. But she couldn't bring herself to do it. "No," she said.

Daphne blinked in surprise.

"He hasn't changed at all. He's still an asshole. He doesn't—" She took a deep breath and steadied herself. "He doesn't regret what he did. Especially the—you know."

Daphne did not look away from her. She knew. It was the reason they left, the reason all of them left, one by one over the course of two years. All of them except for Esme, who was a coward.

"So, why should I go see him?" Daphne said. She leaned toward Esme, beer bottle dangling from one hand. "Convince me, Ms. Vice President."

"He's dying," Esme said.

Daphne frowned, slumped up against the wall. The lights turned a murky blue-green and it was as if they were underwater, it was as if they were drowning.

"That's all you've got?" she asked. "He's dying?"

"It's the truth."

Daphne looked at her. "You never tell the truth."

Esme looked away, her cheeks stinging.

"I mean, none of you in the company. That's how you get things done, isn't it? We've got a representative we have to deal with once a month, whenever we go into town to sell the energy loads. He's a real dick. Smarmy. I never believe a word he says."

She paused. In the slowly shifting light, she looked older than she should. The party went on around them, people laughing, the music shimmering. Esme tried not to think about the meeting with the Dasini officials, the report she'd sent afterward.

"I believe this, though. Dad just wants to see me because he's dying. I guess even someone like him starts feeling nostalgic once in a while." Daphne laughed bitterly. "You know what I expected you to do?"

Esme shook her head. With all the business negotiations she'd done for the last twenty years, she'd learned to recognize early on whether one would end in her favor or not. But right now, with this negotiation, she had no idea.

"I expected you to spin some long sob story about how Dad wanted to beg our forgiveness or that he regretted what happened. The usual sort of nonsense. But you didn't." Daphne nodded. "I appreciate that."

Esme's heartbeat surged. "Thank you."

Daphne shrugged. "It's nothing. You could have bullshitted me and you didn't." She leaned up against the wall, her arms crossed over her chest. Laughed sharply. "I can't believe you came all the way out here to tell me he's still an asshole."

"I figured you wouldn't believe me even if I did lie," Esme said.

"Probably." Daphne took a drink of her beer. "After you left yesterday, I was thinking about what you said. About going to see him one last time."

Esme listened.

"I figured if I invited you tonight, you'd ask again, and I'd need to answer. A definite answer. And I thought about it the whole time I was out there with the turbines. Just me and the wind and this worst decision I've probably ever made." She looked at Esme. Her eyes were dark and serious. "I decided if you showed up, and you didn't bullshit me—I'd do it. I'd go see him."

Esme exhaled a long breath. It had been a long time since the truth had been the best approach.

"For you," Daphne added. "I'm going to see him for you. Are we clear on that?"

Esme blinked, taken aback. She couldn't imagine any of her sisters doing something for her, not even Daphne. But she managed a nod.

"Thank you," she whispered.

Daphne looked grim. "We talk sometimes. Me and Adrienne. I try to tell her you're not as full of shit as he is. She doesn't buy it, though."

Another surprise, although Esme thought Daphne was probably wrong. Eleanora Dixon's face flashed in her memory.

"I'm just telling you this so you know I'm the only one you're going to convince." Daphne looked hard at Esme. "The only one you're even going to find."

Esme knew better than to say anything.

"And I'm not telling you where they went."

"I didn't expect you to."

"Good." Daphne drained the last of her beer and tossed the empty bottle across the room. It landed on the sofa. For a moment, the two of them stood in silence. To Esme, the party felt like an entirely different universe. She wondered if this was what it was like for the Radiance when they peered between the boundaries of the two dimensions.

"I can arrange your travel," Esme said.

Daphne shook her head. "Not necessary. I can do it. I'm not a complete failure."

"I didn't mean that."

Daphne sighed. "I know you didn't."

They stood in silence.

EIGHTEEN YEARS EARLIER

It was the first day of the rainy season and the first day of my new position in Genetics. I arranged for the car to pick me up early, hoping I could make it to my office before anyone else did. I'd been working at the Coromina Group for the last five years, ever since I was seventeen, and even though I didn't want this transfer, I knew by now how to play the game. Get there early and leave late. I never learned that in tutoring, but I learned it well enough from Dad and from experience.

Rain pummeled against the roof of the car. I stared out the window at the banana trees lining the road. The sun hadn't risen yet and everything shone yellow from the floating lamps, and although I was familiar with this road and those trees, in the light and rain and early morning haze it all looked brand-new.

We left the village and sped past the corporate enclave, an enormous swath of land set aside for high-ranking employee-citizens. I could see some of the houses from the road. A few of them had lights on in their windows. Most were dark.

I turned away, switched on my lightbox, set the holo into privacy mode. I'd skipped breakfast—it was too early to eat—but my stomach roiled anyway. Nerves made my skin jangle like I'd been struck with electricity.

I reread through the debriefing files I'd been sent over the weekend. Genetics' big focus was on the soldiers manufactured on Quilla and Catequil, and my taking over the department at such a young age was a major coup for my career. Most of the Coromina Group's profits came from Genetics and the soldiers. It'd been that way since Dad first shifted the focus away from terraforming and into weapons manufacture, long before I was born.

The car pulled onto the Coromina Group campus. I hadn't looked out the window since the road, but I could tell because we slowed down and the light coming through the window changed from the yellow of the highway lamps to the soft white glow of the Coroshine lights that the company manufactured as a subsidiary of Planet Maintenance, where I'd spent the last five years.

I locked down my lightbox and slid it into my bag. The car pulled up to the main building and I waited as the driver came around the side with his umbrella. It was raining harder now, sheets of water falling across the dry soil.

"Gonna be a bad one this year," the driver said, his voice muffled by the roaring of the rain. He was young and recently hired. I was pretty sure his name was John.

"Is that what they're saying?" We walked side by side to the building's main door. Light bounced off the curving orgo walls—the building hadn't actually been built but grown, back when Ekkeko was being terraformed, and its shape was organic enough to give its origins away.

"Yeah. Lots of flooding this year." We made it to the door. John pushed it open for me and grinned. Raindrops sparkled down the left side of his body.

"Have a good day, Ms. Coromina," he said, and I nodded at him and went inside.

The lobby was empty and clamorous from the rain beating against the glass skylights. I went to the elevator and almost pressed the button for five before remembering that no, I was going all the way to twenty-seven now.

My stomach twisted. Up I went.

The elevator doors slid open a few seconds later, revealing the

Genetics lobby: the administrator's desk tucked away in the corner, the big crystal light fixture that had been designed to suggest strings of genetic code. I'd only been up there a handful of times, for my interviews.

All the lights were off.

"Coromina 825," I said, to switch them on. They came to life immediately. Then I strode past the empty administrator's desk, past the rows of offices where the technicians and the salespeople spent their days. There was something about an empty office that always made me feel lonely, and that loneliness was amplified today by the rain and by my own anxiety. In Planet Maintenance, I had been Assistant Director, second to Celina Hen, the Vice President of Operations and the person in charge of overseeing the concerns of the citizen-employees of the four planets of the Coromina I system. When I started my first internship, a few months after the flu outbreak, Assistant Director to the Vice President of Operations was the job I wanted. I climbed my way up so quickly because no one else in the Coromina Group cared about Planet Maintenance. It was a nowhere track. Not enough glory in it, they said.

I didn't care. Planet Maintenance was where I'd always wanted to be. The reality didn't exactly line up to my teenage daydreams—because of the company's focus on weapons manufacture, it was much more frustrating and difficult to make any real progress. But I still loved it. Loved working there, listening to the concerns of the people of the Coromina I system. I flew all over Ekkeko, from city to village to town, meeting with the local franchise representatives and drawing up compromises so that they could get their new road or their school or their medicine and the Coromina Group wouldn't lose any money in the process.

Then Dad started Project X.

I didn't know what Project X was. No one did—or at least, no one in my clearance level, and my level was pretty high. When people did talk about it, they did so in lowered voices, like they were discussing a taboo. Rumors circulated; I pretended to ignore them. There was the usual talk of sentient aliens, that myth that had followed humanity as we delved into the stars. A lot of people still held out hope, although I was of the opinion that if we were going to find aliens, we'd have found them by now, considering how deep into the galaxy humanity had gone. Some people thought it was tied to the flu outbreak six years before, and to me that seemed the more plausible choice—an alien, but not the kind people want. That flu outbreak had haunted my family for years, and the only way Dad had of dealing with a ghost was monetizing it.

In the end, though, it didn't really matter *what* Project X was, only that it existed. When Dad started it up, he called me into his office on the top floor. I stood in front of his desk and looked out the huge picture window that rose behind it, revealing the glittering expanse of the ocean.

"I'm transferring you," he said.

"What?" I looked away from the ocean, startled. "Transferring me? Why? I told you I wanted Planet Maintenance when I started, and you—"

Dad scowled. "Planet Maintenance is a bullshit department. You deserve better."

"It's responsible for the well-being of the *entire system*."

"It's a legal requirement. You're supposed to be CEO, Esme. If you while away your time in PM, it doesn't matter what my fucking will states; Adrienne is going show up with a squadron from Spiro Xu and dispose of you before my body's even started to cool."

I sighed, tapping my fingers against the arm's chair. Adrienne had some interest in the company, it was true, but hiring out a military wasn't her style. Wasn't mine, either. Besides, my father's death seemed a million years away; I wasn't, in fact, certain he *could* die.

"You're not taking this seriously."

"I want to stay in Planet Maintenance."

"Too bad." Dad leaned forward. He looked older in the sunlight, his hair shining gray and the thin lines in his skin deepening. "I'm starting up something new. Clearance Level Ninety-Nine, so don't bother asking questions. But I need someone I can trust in Genetics—"

"You want to put me in *Genetics*?"

"Yes." Dad nodded. The ocean scintillated behind him, out of place next to the quiet rage currently simmering inside me.

"I don't know anything about Genetics."

"You didn't know anything Planet Maintenance, either. Your job is management. It doesn't matter where I put you."

I glared at him. It did matter. I actually cared about PM. I cared about keeping the system inhabitants happy. I didn't want to manufacture soldiers.

"Anyway, the project has a bit of overlap with Genetics, so I'll have men dipping in and out of the department as I see fit. That's why I need you. You're one of the only people in this company I can trust."

My cheeks burned. In that, he was right. He could trust me. He was my father.

"I don't want to do this," I said.

"You've made that abundantly clear, but I'm afraid you don't have much say in the matter."

"I could just quit."

Dad looked at me. "You're not going to quit."

I glowered. Of course I wasn't going to quit. I didn't want to be completely on my own—the likelihood that anyone in the Coromina I system would hire me under the table, even as a pearl diver or a tour guide, after I'd left the Coromina Group was so small, it was basically nonexistent. I'd have to go to another system; I'd have to lie about my background.

"What if I'm terrible at it?" I said.

"You aren't terrible at anything," Dad said. "You're too scared to fail."

I looked away at that, over to the cluster of leather chairs, imported from out of system and deliriously expensive for it. I'd never seen someone sit in any of them.

Too scared to fail. He was right about that, too.

"Are you going to make any more feeble protestations?" Dad asked. "Because I have a meeting with the laboratory director in ten minutes, and I'd really like to get some prep work done."

"This is a mistake," I told him.

"You don't have the whole picture," he said. "This is the only decision I could've made. Now get out."

That conversation had happened a week and a half ago. Now I was sitting in my new office on the twenty-seventh floor, syrupy office light pouring around me. I'd toyed briefly, in that week and a half, with putting in the worst performance of my short career, with taking six-hour lunches and missing meetings and simply *not caring*. But Dad was right. I was too scared to fail.

But I'd had a revelation while I was out on one of my last field visits as PM Assistant Director. I was in a little town on Catequil, one of those windswept places where the people always looked blown back and battered. I'd sat in the city offices and listened to grievances, my lightbox recording the voices of the townspeople as they pleaded with me to help repair the town windfarm. And I said the thing I always said in those situations, except I said it wrong— "I'll try my best." Not *We'll* try our best, royal *we*, company *we*, like I'd been trained.

"I'll try my best," I said, looking down at the farm couple, two old men with faded clothes and dust in their hair. The sentence echoed around inside my head. What could I do in Planet Maintenance? Nothing, not without the say of the company. But in Genetics, I'd have real power. I'd work my way up the clearance level. I could order repairs to a wind village on Catequil without asking permission.

After that, I didn't complain about the transfer. All I needed to do was bide my time. As Dad worked on whatever subterfuge he was playing at with his ridiculously named Project X, I would gain control of the company in tiny increments, and I could go back to helping the people of the Coromina I system the way I wanted.

It was a game. And I knew how to play, so I did.

My first day in Genetics proceeded as I expected. The sales team started trickling in around eight o'clock and let out little startled cries when they saw the lights were all turned on. Most of them stopped by my office to introduce themselves. The man I'd replaced, Mr. Muraski, had been transferred to a higher position in Terraforming. He was an ambitious type and grateful that I'd replaced him, since it gave him a link, however tenuous, to Dad. He called a couple of times during the day, asking if I needed any help. I didn't.

I read through the project lists and checked up with the sales team on the day's progress. I recorded messages of greeting for each of the five militaries we currently had contracts with; one of them was Andromeda Corps. My mother was still stationed with them, last I'd heard, and as I stood in the bright white light of the holorecorder, I wondered, like I was a little girl again, if she'd see my message. But of course she wouldn't. It was encrypted for the Andromeda Corps general and no one else. She might have seen the message I sent her directly, telling her about my promotion. I didn't know. I hadn't received a response yet.

I took lunch with Joan and Allison, a couple of friends from PM, picking at my shrimp salad as they talked about a new initiative to build roads over on the Tiess Atoll, halfway across the world. When I got back to my office, I sat at my desk for a few moments, staring out the little square window that looked over the jogging trail below. It was still raining. It would keep raining for the next six months.

I sighed, wondering how long it'd take me to get to the clearance level necessary to do the work I wanted.

After meeting with the sales team that afternoon, I sat down at my computer and started contacting the laboratories the company ran offworld. As with the generals, I wanted to introduce myself and check up on the state of the projects, but since Quilla and Catequil were both in-system, I didn't have to resort to a holo recording.

We had five labs total across the two moons, and I dialed up the smallest first. A wiry little man answered, although he wasn't looking at the screen, but off to the side, distracted.

"Mr. Targowski?"

He turned to me. "You said my name right."

"I make sure to look those things up."

"Who are you?" He squinted at the bottom of the screen, where the identification information would be displayed. "Oh, you're from headquarters. Genetics? What happened to George Muraski?"

"He was transferred."

Mr. Targowski sat unmoving for a moment, then nodded and said, "Ah! I remember now. He told me a few weeks ago. Are you his replacement?"

I nodded. "My name is Esme Coromina. I just wanted to introduce myself."

Mr. Targowski's brow furrowed. Everyone in the company reacted to my name in some way or another—their eyes narrowed, they recoiled from me as if I were poison, they broke into big, disingenuous smiles. It was a reflex. None of them could help it.

"Well, it's a pleasure to meet you, Ms. Coromina."

I smiled. "Please, call me Esme. And it's a pleasure to meet you as well."

It seemed to put him at ease, the reassurance-through-civility that I wasn't my father.

"I don't have any major questions at the moment, but I did want to check up on production status. Nothing formal, just what you know off the top of your head."

Mr. Targowski grinned. "We've been meeting quotas left and right the last few months. You came onboard at a good time. Mostly we've been filling orders for Zimconia—they've got a list of requests they like, night vision and that sort of thing."

"Their deployment is out in the Zimmer system, isn't it?" I paused, rifling through my memorized corporate history. "They started out as a subsidiary of Zimmer Corp's military branch, right?"

"I believe so, yes. Now they're going rogue. I don't keep up with it myself. Just produce the damn things."

I smiled politely.

Mr. Targowski used that as an excuse to launch into a detailed description of Zimconia's most recent order: a squadron of pilots whose genetic code could interface directly with the military-grade shuttles the Coromina Group had put out a few years before. I knew from all my tutoring sessions that the shuttles had been designed with that specific purpose in mind—any weapons or aircraft we produced could be used only with a Coromina soldier.

I eventually cut Mr. Targowski off, claiming I had a meeting. From there, I called the second-smallest lab and had an identical conversation. Same with the next two. The largest lab was different, though—it inhabited an entire landmass on Ekkeko, called Starspray City, and it really was a city unto itself, with housing and schools and most everything that a typical midsized Coromina city had. It was the first lab the company had built, back when Dad had the idea for the soldiers, after the Coromina Group made its first trillion off the Triad Sector Wars.

An administrative assistant answered my call, rather than the head researcher herself. The assistant had a snappish countenance that smoothed out when he heard my name.

"Ms. *Coromina*," he gushed. "So glad to meet you. Ms. DeCrie will be with in *just* a moment."

The screen flashed to the hold screen. I sat back in my chair and waited. Speaking with the other labs had made me realize how little I knew about what Genetics did. I'd gone over it in my tutoring sessions—I'd gone over everything the company managed—but I'd always been interested in Terraforming and Planet Maintenance, never weapons production. I was going to have to study up on it in my own time, if this plan of mine was to work.

As I sat there waiting, the Coromina Group logo spinning in endless circles, I thought of the first engineered soldier I'd ever seen, that marine who came to the estate before the flu epidemic. Private Snow. It always left me unsettled that he'd been born in a laboratory. It struck me as unfair to *him*, to deny him a mother and a father and a real life.

Of course, I didn't really have any of those things myself.

The holding screen faded away and Ms. DeCrie shimmered into view. "Ms. Coromina, such a pleasure to meet you. When I heard you were taking over the department, I have to admit, I was pleased to hear it wasn't another old man." She laughed. She looked young—maybe a few years older than me—but her skin had that telltale glossiness. Rejuvenation treatments. Hardly anyone in the upper echelons of the company appeared older than thirty, and so age was meaningless unless someone lived for centuries, like Dad. It was different in the village. The young and the old had different places in the world. But not here. We let the company rank us, One through Ninety-Nine. "I was hoping you'd come visit Starspray City if you have the chance. I think it's important to keep in contact with headquarters, and I'd *love* for you to see the facilities."

"I was thinking the same thing," I said, and smiled even though I didn't mean it. Going to visit the largest lab was exactly the sort of thing I should be doing now that I was in charge of the department. It showed an interest in my work, the way showing up early did. But showing up early was easy.

Fortunately, Ms. DeCrie had given me the opportunity. And if she was inviting, she'd schedule the flights and accommodations. Sometimes, there's benefit in waiting.

"Wonderful!" Ms. DeCrie clapped her hands together. "I'll have Cameron get in contact with your people about arranging travel. When would you like to come out?"

"Sometime soon. In the next few days, maybe." I was falling so easily into this role, although it didn't feel right, like a dress a size too small. "I'll be interested in looking at some of your most recent projects. I've spoken with the other labs, but I know Starspray City's been working on the Alvatech contract, and I'm very interested in seeing how that's progressing." An easy lie to tell. Which was good, because it was going to be nothing but lies from here on out. They were worth it, though, if it meant making this company what it should always have been from the beginning.

Adrienne asked the cook to prepare a formal multi-course meal that night, to celebrate the first day of my promotion. Twenty-five years old and I still lived at the estate—I'd mentioned to Dad that I might like to have a townhouse in the corporate enclave, but he'd snapped at me and told me it was dangerous. "You're protected here," he'd said, gesturing out at the yard. I knew he was talking about the soldiers patrolling the perimeter. The soldiers were new; he swapped them out every year, never explaining why. They were all genetically modified these days.

I still didn't know what the soldiers were protecting us from. I'd gone looking when I started at the company, but that information was too highly classified for me to access. All I found were locked files and encrypted holos that, for me, only played static. The security protocols at the enclave were some of the highest in the system, but they didn't involve constant coverage from a squad of engineered soldiers. Now that I was in Genetics, maybe I could find out more. Maybe.

The dining room table was too big for just the five of us—me, Adrienne and Daphne, Rena and little Isabel. I always made sure to eat dinner with them if I could. I knew what it was like to grow up with that unused dining room reminding you of the family you wanted.

We were on the second course now, bowls of watercress soup, a traditional start-of-the-rainy-season dish. I'd never cared for it, but since Adrienne had asked it to be prepared, I ate it out of politeness. She was in her usual spot, sitting with a straight spine, play-acting at being a princess. Daphne didn't seem too interested—I knew she didn't like the soup much either. Isabel slurped at hers, still young enough she didn't realize it was rude.

"So, how was your first day?" Rena asked.

Daphne poked her head up. "Did you get to see any of the soldiers being made?" Her eyes gleamed.

I shook my head. I had already visited the labs by the time I was her age, but Dad didn't expect them to take over the company someday. He ignored them most of the time. I couldn't decide if that was better or worse.

"I will, though," I told her, stirring my soup around. "I'm going to Catequil later this week. To Starspray City, to visit the lab there."

"Starspray City!" Adrienne's eyes went wide. "That's where they filmed the last *Intensity of Days* storyline!"

Daphne rolled her eyes. Eight years old and Adrienne was already the romantic, lapping up those Amanan dramas as much as she could. Daphne didn't have time for them. I just smiled at her, though. I remembered that storyline. It had been part of a campaign put out by the Psychology department, to sell the citizen-employees of the Coromina I system on the importance of manufacturing soldiers. I never told Adrienne about that, though. She just loved the romance of it, the ill-fated affair between the scientist and the soldier she helped create.

"Do you think you'll see Artus Falk on your trip?" Adrienne asked, her eyes wide. One of her favorite actors from the show. Had he played the soldier? I couldn't remember.

"Probably not. I think they're filming on Amana again."

Adrienne sighed dramatically. Daphne made a face at her and I gave her a sharp look, which she ignored. They didn't really obey me. Rena, she was their surrogate mother. Me, their half-sister, my mother still alive even if I hadn't seen her in person since I was a baby—that put me in some other, harder-to-define category.

The staff swept in and cleared our bowls away, then brought in plates of lemon-butter trout. I know Adrienne was enjoying the formality of the dinner more than the rest of us.

When Isabel saw the trout, she threw her fork on the table and pouted.

"What's the matter, dear?" Rena asked mildly.

Isabel didn't answer. I took a bite of fish—flaky and almost sweet. Isabel's pout turned into a scowl.

"What did we talk about?" Rena said.

Isabel paused for a moment before letting loose a long stream of babbling, hissing syllables. It startled me; I knew about this made-up language of theirs but had never heard it myself. It didn't sound like noises a human being could make.

Adrienne answered Isabel in the same language. Her eyes were narrowed in annoyance. Daphne watched them both, her head cocked to the side, listening. I felt a stirring of pain in the part of me that was still a lonely little girl—*Why didn't they teach it to me, too?*

Rena set down her fork, crossed her arms over her chest, and turned a steely gaze to Isabel. The babble fell away and she gazed back up at Rena, her dark eyes wide.

"What," Rena said, "did we talk about?"

Isabel looked down at her plate. "Only speak Corominan at the dinner table."

"Very good. Now will you share what you were saying to Adrienne to the rest of us?"

Isabel hesitated. Then she said, "I don't eat fish anymore."

"And why's that?"

"I dunno; I just don't *like* it."

Rena frowned. "Well, fish is what we were served, and so fish is what we'll eat."

Isabel sighed. "I knew you were going to say that," she muttered. Then she picked up her fork and shredded her trout into pieces without eating any. Rena didn't push the matter.

I'd first heard about the language from Grace, the girl who brought me breakfast in the mornings. She had chattered about it when it first started up, how all three of them had just suddenly started talking nonsense to each other, but nonsense that they apparently understood. No one could figure out where they picked it up. I told her one of them must have made it up, but she just shrugged and said, "You think they made up an entire language?"

I didn't think it mattered so much. They were better adjusted than I had been at that age—we were all motherless and growing up at Star's End, but at least they had each other. I liked to watch them from my window when I was working. They'd drag their kid-sized table and chairs out into the garden to have tea parties. Sometimes, they disappeared into the plumeria maze, three by three, their arms all linked. They were kids. They had some whole world created out there in the garden, and no adult was ever going to see it. Not even me, as much I wished I could.

The staff cleared the fish away. Brought in dessert. It was another rainy-season dish, little bowls of sweet rice pudding with a square of dark bitter chocolate tucked away at the bottom. I was touched that Adrienne had thought to ask for it. One bowl would always have a coin instead of chocolate, and whoever had the coin was supposed to have good luck during the following rainy season—well, good crops, specifically, but we weren't rice farmers.

"Do you know which one has the coin?" Daphne asked Evonne, the server.

"I most certainly do not. Where would be the fun in that?" She set a bowl down in front of each of us and stepped back against the wall, gazing beatifically down at the kids.

"Don't eat yet!" Adrienne cried as Daphne picked up her spoon. "We have to dip in at the same time so we don't ruin the surprise."

Daphne groaned.

"Everyone's served," Rena said. "You can eat now."

And even though I was an adult and in charge of Genetics at the Coromina Group, I still shivered a little with excitement when I dipped my spoon all the way to the bottom of my bowl. When I pulled it out, melted chocolate swirled together with my pudding. No good luck for me this year.

Daphne and Adrienne both sighed with frustration, but Isabel held her spoon over her bowl, a flash of gold glinting in the chandelier light.

"I found the coin." She squinted down at the spoon. "Do I eat it?"

"No!" Rena laughed. "Here, set it on your napkin. I'll wipe it off for you. You can keep it in your jewelry box for luck."

"Luck," whispered Isabel carefully.

"It means something good will happen to you before the dry season starts," Adrienne said.

Daphne scowled, although her scowl disappeared as she began eating the rice pudding. Isabel dropped the coin on her napkin and stirred her own pudding around. I remembered the first time I'd found a rice coin—I'd been around her age, six or seven. Rena told me the same thing about keeping the coin in my jewelry box.

The rest of us finished our desserts, but I noticed that Isabel hardly touched hers. She only swirled it around and around, smiling to herself.

My shuttle touched down on Starspray City's landing pad, out in the churning black ocean. Even though I knew it made me look like an idiot, I peered out the window to catch my first glimpse of the city. I'd been to Catequil before, of course, but only to a handful of the civilian cities, and I'd never come this far south.

Everything about Starspray City looked haunted. The buildings rose up in a series of twisting metal tubes, and amber lights shimmered through the white fog lifting off the ocean.

"Ms. Coromina?" The attendant smiled down at me. "We're ready to disembark."

"Yes, I'm ready." I jerked my gaze away from the window,

slightly flustered that she'd caught me gawking like a tourist, and fumbled for my bag. I was the only person on the plane save for the pilot, who I never saw, and the two attendants. I'd assumed that Ms. DeCrie would book one of the Coromina shuttles for me. And maybe she had. But when I received the confirmation for my flight to Catequil, my lightbox chimed ten minutes later. It was Dad, telling me that I should take his plane and also that he was uploading a file to my personal directory that I'd be able to open once I was in Starspray City. The file would give me instructions before fizzling away on my lightbox's hard drive.

"I need you to check up on some things for me," he said. "Clearance Level Sixty-Four."

Then he vanished from my screen.

The attendant waited for me as I gathered my bags and wrapped my hair in a scarf. The wind whipped off the ocean, throwing stinging dots of saltwater across my face. *The Winds of Catequil*—that had been the name of a drama I used to watch. The first I time I visited there, I saw the name wasn't just poetry.

The walkway took us to a covered ferry that sat bobbing in the sea. I left the attendant standing on the walkway, her uncovered hair flying up around her face like a lion's mane, and took a seat in the ferry's inner room. The room was empty, and almost as soon as I sat down, the ferry pulled away from the walkway. I pulled out my lightbox and tried to open Dad's file. A message box materialized instead:

Sorry, Esme, not in Starspray City yet.

I scowled and shoved the lightbox back in my bag. This was supposed to be a routine visit, the sort of thing any new manager in Genetics would have done. But already Dad was turning it into something else. Something I didn't even have clearance for.

Starspray City loomed ahead, the lights and pipelines looking like a star map. No trees, no landscaping. Just rocky soil and the twist of metal buildings. Ten minutes later, we arrived.

A young man waited for me on the dock, standing beside the windbreak with a portable holoprojector at his feet, beaming up my name in my big, glinting letters.

"Ms. Coromina!" he said when I walked up to him. "So wonderful to meet you in person."

I recognized him, then, by the gush in his voice, as Ms. DeCrie's administrative assistant.

"Cameron," I said. "Yes, it's nice to meet you as well."

"Are you ready to tour the facilities?" He bent down to switch off the holoprojector. My name evaporated. "I know Ms. DeCrie has everything set up."

I nodded. The wind blowing off the ocean was cold and damp and seemed to cut straight to my bones, slicing through my clothes and my skin and my musculature. It howled through the buildings like the voices of the dead.

"It'll be nice to be inside," I said.

Cameron laughed. "You get used to it." He led me down the docks to a covered electric cart that ran on tracks into the tangle of buildings. The wind buffeted us as we rode along, but Cameron didn't seem concerned, and he just kept chatting about the Alvatech account and how pleased I'd be with the products. I looked past him as he talked, out the window, to the gleam of buildings zipping by, and wondered about the file on my lightbox.

The cart rattled to a stop. Cameron hopped out and opened the door for me and I exited, turning my face against the wind. We stood in front of a tall, glittering building wrapped in pipes, like a tree covered in parasitic vines. White steam poured out of a smokestack. The air smelled unnaturally sweet, like rotting mangos.

"Here we are," Cameron said. "The main lab. Ms. DeCrie's waiting inside."

He led me up the steps, and I was aware of the building towering above me, this oppressive steely height, another sign of Dad's power, and his power over me.

Cameron scanned his eyes at the identification lock and we went in. The front door opened into a cavernous lobby with clean white walls and tile floors and a few tasteful chairs tucked away in the corner. I heard Ms. DeCrie before I saw her, the *click click click* of her shoes against the tile. She strode across the lobby, one hand raised in greeting. No one else was there. Not even a receptionist. They didn't need one, not when they had an identification lock.

"Ms. Coromina," Ms. DeCrie said. We shook.

"You can call me Esme," I said automatically.

She grinned with delight. "And I'm Flor. I've never been fond of that old Earth formality; don't you agree?"

I nodded. Flor gestured with one hand at the echoing lobby. "You're standing in Catequil's pride and joy. This was one of the first buildings established once the planet was terraformed."

"Interesting," I said, although I'd already known. The history of the Coromina I system, and all of the Coromina Group's involvement with it, had been the focus of my tutoring as a child. My entire future was built from the past.

Flor walked toward the elevators at the end other end of the lobby. "I'm sure Cameron told you, but we'll be looking at the Alvatech project today. Given some of the tensions the company's been having with OCI, Mr. Coromina asked me personally to look into developing soldiers that might serve us if we ever came to blows." She winked like she was talking about some ballgame, but I felt a tightness in my chest. I didn't want the Coromina Group to go to war with OCI. The Coromina Group going to war meant all of the Coromina I system could serve as collateral. Sure, we hired out soldiers these days, but battles didn't always stay in space.

I stepped onto the elevator with Flor—Cameron had vanished out of the building—and the doors whisked shut. Flor scanned her eyes, then stepped back and gestured for me to do the same. It was the first time I'd been anywhere remotely high-level, and there was a brief flutter of anxiety that the scan wouldn't take, that my promotion had all been some prank on Dad's part.

But the lock beeped in satisfaction and the elevator shot upward.

"The products are still in the development stage," Flor said. "Vat level. But they're the current standard design—increased strength, stronger bones, less need for sleep—"

"The Kalevala models." I watched the numbers on the elevator blink higher and higher.

"Yes! Of course, you *would* know. I'm just used to giving the pitch to the generals."

I didn't say anything. I was familiar with the Kalevala models not because I'd read up on them in my transfer (although I had) but because the soldiers currently stationed at Star's End were all Kalevala. Dad had switched over to a group of entirely engineered soldiers a few years before, for reasons he hadn't bothered to divulge to me. And on my own, I hadn't been able to learn anything but their model name.

The elevator stopped. We stepped out into a narrow, brightly lit foyer. "This way," Flor said, and led me to the right, through a corridor lined with windowless doors, the locks at their sides all blinking red—activated. The floor was silent save for the hum of a generator in the background.

Flor stopped at a door like all the others. Scanned her eyes. I did the same.

The door snapped open. Inside the room was a gurgling like a river. Flor held the door for me and I went in. I took a deep breath to steady myself.

The room was lined with vats filled with human beings.

The door clicked shut and the lock reactivated. Flor stood at my side.

"We keep all the Kalevala models in this room," she said. "These guys are in the later stages, just about to be extracted." She smiled at me. "Go on, have a look around. The farther back you go, the younger the products become. Let me know if you have any questions."

My ears buzzed. I thought about my trip to the bioengineering lab when I was a little girl. It had looked like this, only smaller, scaled down. A child-sized version. That visit had been a taste of my future. Now I was at the banquet.

The vats bubbled and hissed, as if the people inside were sighing. The room smelled like chemicals, strong enough to burn at the inside of my nostrils. I forced myself to walk over to the closest vat. It was a woman, almost fully grown, like Flor had said. She floated in the clear preservation fluid like a mermaid, bobbing slightly, her eyes closed. A few inches of dark hair drifted around her head. I touched the info pad at the base of the vat and her vitals and designations popped up in glowing blue holoprojection. NO. 39083-F. EST. EXTRACTION: 39-8-2813. Heart rate, blood pressure, respirations: all beeped steadily on.

I touched the pad again and the information disappeared. This was the Alvatech order; she might face my mother in battle someday. The thought made my stomach twist around.

"She's close," I said, because I had to say something. "To extraction, I mean."

"Yes." Flor nodded. "If you wanted to stay a week or two longer, you might be able to watch. Not that there's anything to see. We pull them out of the vats and let them wake up in one of the suites on the seventy-third floor."

"Are they ever confused?" I moved away from the woman, down the aisle of floating future soldiers.

"What do you mean?"

"When they wake up." I stopped in front of another vat, this one containing a person not as developed as the woman. The designation information noted that he was a male, but I couldn't tell from looking at him—the body was smooth and featureless, not yet fully formed. It wasn't a child's body, more like a doll that hadn't been painted on. "How confused are they, about who they are, where they are—I was never clear on that." I looked at Flor, mostly so I wouldn't have to look at the soldier.

"Oh!" She laughed. "Oh, yes, I know what you mean." We moved away from the vat and continued to walk down the aisle. "No, they aren't confused. We program all that information at the genetic level. It's a neat trick, and it's pretty much common practice now. Not just with the Coromina Group."

"So, they know everything?" I wondered what that was like, waking up as an adult, your childhood a dream from before you were born.

"Not *everything* everything. Not how to brush their teeth and dress themselves and that sort of thing. But they're all so easily adaptable, and they learn extremely quickly. Takes about a week or so to teach a new extraction how to function in the world. But they do wake up knowing speech—Coromina Standard, of course; we don't get that fancy—as well as who and what they are, and what they'll be expected to do." She shrugged. "It's been this way for decades. Back when bioengineering was the new thing, they'd have some problems—"

"Yes, I know." My voice was sharper than I expected, cutting her off. The Coromina Group had been the major pioneer of this sort of technology, solely because Dad had been looking to profit off the Triad Sector Wars. Terraforming was not a high-enough earner. But the early soldiers had been unpredictable. They didn't follow orders; they questioned authority. Technological advances solved the problem, although we'd only ever touched on them in tutoring.

We arrived at the far end of the room. The vats were smaller, the air warmer.

"The babies," Flor said brightly.

They didn't look babies—more like baby-sized adults, only even more smoothed over and featureless. They didn't have eyes, and their mouths and noses were tiny slits in their smooth oval faces. I drew up the designation on one, and the sex hadn't even been marked yet.

"We're doing some of the more fiddly engineering work with them right now," Flor said. "Appearance, mostly. Personality, too—we like to mix up the personalities a bit, within the range, so that woman-born soldiers will be more comfortable interacting with them."

I nodded, staring at the tiny blank slate of a human floating before me. I remembered seeing the twins and Isabel when they were born and not knowing what to make of them. But I knew what to make of this. Everyone did. Its fate had been decided before it ever existed.

At least Adrienne and Daphne and Isabel had had a choice. They could take their lives where they wanted.

Or maybe they couldn't. I hadn't been grown in a vat, but in half an hour, I'd be running some secret errand for my father because he told me to and I didn't say no. I couldn't say no.

I did not want my sisters to have that future.

* * *

Cameron drove me to the hotel on the edge of Starspray City. It was a reinforced brick building situated behind a windblock, and when I stepped out of the electric cart, I could smell the salt of the sea. I thanked him and checked into my room, which was on the top floor of the hotel with a view of the ocean. There wasn't much to see, just glassy black water and curls of white mist. Still, I left the curtains open.

I was tired from travel, from seeing those soldiers in their softly bubbling vats, but when I sprawled out on the bed, I pulled out my lightbox anyway. I brought up the file Dad had asked me to open. Tapped on the icon. This time, the lightbox chimed and the file blossomed open into a holo recording, tiny and hazy in the light of the hotel room. It was Dad.

"Esme," he said, his voice tinny. "You'll only get to listen to this message once, so be sure to pay attention. If you take notes, they must be destroyed before you leave Starspray City. Do you understand?"

A message box popped up on the touchscreen, YES OR NO. I rolled my eyes. Dad must have been watching too many espionage dramas lately.

I tapped YES.

"Good. I'm holding you to that. If I ever find out that any part of this exchange was not kept secret, there will be repercussions. Do you understand?"

Another message box. Another YES OR NO. I considered tapping NO just to see what happened, but I tapped YES.

"Excellent." Dad almost smiled. "There is a man working in the records building who has a file for me. The material on it is far too sensitive to transmit over Connectivity, so I'll need you to go to his office and collect it physically from him. He will complete a retinal scan to confirm your identity. I would suggest doing it sooner rather than later—I'll feel safer knowing the file is with you."

A little warmth of happiness worked through me, even though I knew the trust was just Dad's nepotism.

"Do not lose the file! It is imperative that it gets back to me as soon as possible. I suggest keeping it on you at all times. Whatever you do, do not leave it in your hotel room—it's not secure enough. Do you understand?"

Another message box. I pressed YES.

"Good. Your contact's name is Walter Indisch. As I said earlier, he works in the records building. The hotel concierge will be able to arrange transport for you. Don't ask Ms. DeCrie's assistant—the boy couldn't keep a secret to save his life. Do you understand?"

Another message box. I sighed, hit YES. "I'll go *right now*, Dad," I said, as if he could hear me.

"Remember: Walter Indisch, records building. Identify yourself and he'll know what to do from there. This file will corrupt in five seconds."

I lay back on the bed and counted to five in my head. When I checked the lightbox again, the holo had frozen into a fan of empty light. I blinked at it, listening to the distant whistle of the wind outside. So, this was why Dad needed me in Genetics. Running files like a character in a story. Like we were just playing some father-daughter immersive, like none of this was real.

I rolled over onto my back. The ceiling hung low and oppressive. Maybe I wouldn't get the file after all. Maybe I would just stay in my room, pull down the media screen, watch an old episode of some drama.

But I knew that wasn't really an option. Not if I wanted to do my undercover PM work. I needed the high ranking, so I'd do what I could to get it. Then I could start tending to those villages that the company liked to forget about. Make sure they got the money to rebuild roads, to run schools.

So, I pulled on my coat and walked down to the lobby. The concierge smiled at me like she hadn't just checked me in five minutes earlier.

"I need transport to the records building," I said.

"Of course." Her fingers moved through the glow of her lightbox. "It's ready for you outside."

I thanked her and stepped out into the damp, chilly air. The wind howled behind the windbreak. An electric cart waited for me on the rails, empty. When I climbed in, the doors clicked shut and the cart flew away, its path to the records building marked on the map glowing on the screen set into the dash. I watched my progress. I didn't feel nervous, really. Only annoyed. Put out. Put *upon*.

The records building was squat and unassuming and nestled between a pair of high-rises belching steam. I walked through the door and into a fluorescent-lit lobby. No receptionist, no guard. Just another glass screen like the one in the cart. TAP HERE FOR ASSISTANCE glowed in white letters. I tapped.

A few moments later, a short, round man walked through a swinging dark door. He blinked at me, waiting.

"Mr. Indisch?" I said.

"Yes."

"I'm Esme Coromina."

"Oh! Esme! Of course, yes, I've been expecting you. Come on back." He didn't look at me as he spoke, as if he were straining to be polite. He held the door for me and I stepped into a big room filled with row after row of industrial lightboxes. I'd never seen so many in one place, all of them glowing faintly at their core. They were powerful enough that they let off a soft, mellifluous humming. It almost sounded like a song.

Mr. Indisch didn't even look at them as he led me to an office in the back corner. The office had a big, clear window, but when he closed the door, the sound of the lightboxes cut out, and there was only silence and a faint glow through the glass.

He sat behind his desk and pulled out a portable retinal scanner.

"Per Mr. Coromina's instructions," he said.

I nodded and leaned forward. The laser ran over each of my eyes and chirped that I was the right person.

"Now let me find it." Mr. Indisch dropped the scanner back in his desk drawer. I crossed my arms over my chest and peered around the office as he dug through a metal chest of drawers in the corner. It was cramped but also very sparse. No pictures on the wall or on his desk. No plants growing in the corner. He had one window that looked outside, but its only view was of the skyscraper next door.

"It's in here somewhere," Mr. Indisch said. "I've got drawers and drawers of physical files—that's why Mr. Coromina asked me to hold this one for him, I think." He didn't sound happy about this. Nervous, maybe. Scared. My heartbeat fluttered. "I really ought to work out some sort of system—ah! Here it is!" He stepped away from the cabinet. The file was a glass square. Mr. Indisch handed it to me, leaning over his desk. I gripped it by its edges, the same way he had, and held it up to the light. But of course I couldn't see anything. It was completely transparent. I hadn't seen a file like this in ages.

"I've got a case for it. Hold on." He rummaged around his drawer and pulled out a thin plastic sheath. I slid the file into place and then dropped it into my purse.

"Thank you, Mr. Indisch." I stood up and tossed my purse over my shoulder and moved toward the door.

"Wait."

I looked over at him. He was pale, his skin gleaming in the residue of the lightboxes.

"You're his daughter, aren't you? You've got the same last name."

I hesitated. "I thought everyone in the company knew that."

"It's a big company, Ms. Coromina. I wanted to make sure."

"Yes, I'm his daughter."

Mr. Indisch shifted in his seat. The chair creaked. The wind howled between this building and the next.

"You be careful with that," he said. "Just 'cause you're blood relatives—" He shrugged. "It's scary stuff, isn't it? What he's planning."

"I don't know what he's planning," I said flatly.

"Neither do I," Mr. Indisch said. He grinned. "I was asking you. I'd just heard some rumors. About—" His voice lowered. "Aliens."

At headquarters in Ekkeko, this sort of thing—sniffing around for information above his clearance level, spreading rumors—could get him fired. But he didn't seem concerned, and I didn't care enough to report him. I'd heard the alien rumors too. Wishful thinking, the way alien rumors always were.

"Have a good day, Mr. Indisch," I said, and I walked out the door, back into the hum of information.

* * *

I arrived back at Ekkeko in the middle of the afternoon, two days later. I was exhausted. After my initial tour, Flor showed me the genetics lab as well as one of the learning barracks, which had been half-full with young men and women who straightened their spines when I walked in. They watched me, eyes distant, expression blank. Dad's stupid file was a weight in my purse the entire time.

The shuttle brought me to the Coromina Group landing pad, walking distance from the main building. I went straight to Dad's office. He was available—a break, it seemed, between meetings. His assistant smiled at me and said, "Good timing, Ms. Coromina," before returning to her lightbox.

Dad was jogging on his treadmill when I walked in, looking out his picture window at the glittering ocean. He didn't acknowledge me. Not a surprise. I slouched down in one of the guest chairs and waited for him to finish.

"Esme," he said a few minutes later. He was still running, still looking at the ocean. "Did you do what I ask?"

"Yep. Never let it out of my sight."

He stopped the treadmill and rode it backward until he could jump off. He turned to me. "Well, let's see it."

I pulled the file out of my purse and handed it to him. He slid it out of the case and held it up to the sunlight. It sparked like a match going off.

"This will be our victory," he said.

"Our victory?"

He glanced at me like he'd forgotten I was there, and swallowed the file up in his hand. "Nothing you need to worry about, dear. At least not yet. All in good time."

I hated the way he said *dear*, as if it were a joke. He walked over to his desk and set the file down. I waited for him to tell me I could leave.

"Have you been home yet?" he asked.

"What? No. I just arrived on-planet."

He nodded. "You need to go home. There's an emergency. I told them not to contact you—I didn't want you distracted."

"An emergency?" I stared at him. "What kind of an emergency?"
He didn't look at me. "A family one. Rena can explain it better."
"A *family* emergency? Then why aren't you home?"
He went still and I knew I'd said something I wasn't supposed to.
"Because I have duties here." He turned to me again, and his eyes
were cold. "You can sort it out in my place."

I stood up, pushing the chair away from me. "Fine," I said, and
stalked out of the office. Part of me was angry with him, but a
bigger part of me was worried. The last time we'd had a family
emergency, the flu had come to Star's End.

I asked his assistant to call for a car and went down to the lobby
to wait for it. I'd had my luggage sent home, but I had my lightbox,
of course, and I tried to connect with the staff line. But no one was
on the other end to pick up.

I set the lightbox in my lap, my throat dry.

The car pulled up to the doors and I climbed in, my heart pounding. The trip seemed to take a hundred years. When the manor
finally loomed up on the horizon, I had a sudden sinking feeling
of foreboding. I tried to push it aside—if this were a serious emergency, a life-and-death emergency, Dad would come home. He'd
done that much for the first Isabel, all those years ago.

We pulled into the drive and I thanked the driver and climbed
out. The rain had stopped for the time being, and the air was warm
and unsettlingly still compared to the air of Catequil. It felt like
everything was dying. But at least it smelled of jasmine instead of
brine and dead fish. I went in through the front door.

"Hello!" I called out. "Anyone here?" One of the staff should
be nearby. I made my way toward the kitchen. The house seemed
empty. "Hello?"

Nothing.

It was suddenly hard to breathe. This wasn't some small thing.
The house's emptiness crackled with dread. The molecules themselves were disordered and out of place.

I picked up into a run. "Hello!" I shouted. "Rena! What's going
on?"

By the time I slammed into the kitchen, I had whipped myself into a panic. There was only Alicia, the cook's assistant, sitting at the table in the corner. She jumped up when she saw me and smoothed down her gray uniform.

"Ms. Coromina!" she cried. "You're home."

"What's going on?" I demanded. "I heard there was an emergency. Where is everyone?"

"They're out looking," she said, cowering a little. I took a deep breath, reining myself in.

"Looking for what?"

She hesitated. Her hand curled around the edge of her skirt.

"For little Isabel," she said. "She went missing this morning."

The kitchen froze over. I stared at Alicia, convinced I'd heard wrong.

"She went *missing*?"

"Yes, ma'am." Alicia's voice trembled. "Gerard saw her last." Gerard was one of the gardeners. "She was walking to the cemetery. She does that sometimes, you know?"

I nodded.

"He didn't think anything of it, because it's not the first time she's walked out there. But he didn't see her walk back, and an hour or so had gone by, and when he went to check—" She took a deep breath. "She wasn't there."

I slumped down in the chair. Drops of rain pinged against the windows in a slow, drizzly shower. Isabel had gone missing and Dad was still in the office. And he *knew*. He had fucking *told me about it.*

I thought I might throw up. Instead, I took a deep breath and looked up at Alicia. "And everyone's out looking for her?" I asked.

She nodded.

"What about Rena? Daphne and Adrienne? Are they okay?"

"Rena's with the others, yes. Grace is watching over the twins. They're safe."

I stood up. Alicia blinked at me. I left the kitchen and walked out to the back patio, not caring about the drizzle dampening my suit. The pineapple gardens were empty, the colors of the plants bright against the gray light. But distantly I heard voices calling out Isabel's name.

I slid off my heels and stockings and tossed them inside the house. Then I ran into the garden, dizzy with anxiety. I ran barefoot across the grass, through the lawn and past the plumeria maze, winding around the property until I came to the cemetery. Some of the staff were there, huddled beneath an umbrella. And one of the soldiers too. It startled me, seeing him so soon after the visit to Catequil. I imagined him floating in the murky liquid of a vat, nothing but a designation number. They didn't get names until after they were born, and even then, those names were based on whichever lab had produced them.

"Private Sun," I said, and he looked up at me. Sun meant he came from the small lab on the hot part of Quilla, the one I'd visited as a child. These names were really designations too, assigned to them when they left the labs. "Have you found anything? What's going on?"

"You heard what happened," Mrs. Davesa said, rushing out from under the umbrella to pull me into an embrace. "It's terrible, terrible." She wiped at her eyes, although I didn't know if she wiped away tears or rain.

Private Sun watched us with a calm expression. "We didn't see anything, Ms. Coromina. I reviewed the security feeds myself. The girl goes into the cemetery and never comes out."

My thoughts pounded with my heartbeat. I'd sworn to myself that I would keep my sisters safe, that I wouldn't lose them the way I had my village friends or the first Isabel or my mother.

And now Isabel was gone.

I curled my hands into fists. "I want to see," I said. "There may be something you missed."

I knew how stupid that sounded. Private Sun was engineered so that he never missed anything. But he didn't question me, only nodded and said, "Yes, ma'am."

We left the cemetery. The drizzle had soaked me through completely, but I didn't care. Dad would have cared, and I didn't want to be like him. Not right now.

The soldiers' house was locked up tight. No one was there. "All out looking," Private Sun said, and I nodded, not expecting anything less. He led me into the security room, where the monitoring equipment was set up on a piece of plywood that had been laid across the bed. He flipped one switch and suddenly the room flooded with a three-dimensional holomap of the estate. It took up the entire room. I stood in the middle of the house—the woods were over in the corner, crawling with tiny figures.

"Private Wind-3 has a feed of the woods going into his eyepiece," Private Sun said. "Scanning for her that way. He was originally monitoring from the room, but after an hour of not finding anything, he thought the old-fashioned way might be a better choice."

I nodded, numb. Where the hell could she be, if they couldn't see her on the map?

Fear turned my whole body to stone.

"Can I watch the video of her entering the cemetery?" I asked, trying to keep my voice calm.

"Of course." Private Sun tapped out a pattern on the control panel and the map spun around the room. The cemetery grew larger and larger and the rest of the estate shrank down to insignificance. Another pattern, and the cemetery jumped and transformed: Mrs. Davesa and the rest of the staff disappeared, and the light changed from the gray drizzle of the present to an eerie golden glow.

Everything began to move.

At first it was just the leaves in the trees, rustling back and forth. Then Isabel appeared, wearing a party dress, the one with the frilly petticoat and the big blue bow in the back. I frowned. She carried a bouquet of flowers from the garden, which she set on her mother's grave. For a moment she stood in place, staring down at the soil, and I thought about how she was only six years old, and when I was six, I didn't understand death at all. I thought death was my mother living two galaxies away, sending holos whenever she could.

The wind picked up, and Isabel lifted her head, looking into the woods.

Her lips moved.

"There!" I said, pointing. "She said something."

Private Sun nodded. "Yes, but it's just gibberish, as far as we could tell. The recording quality is not very good that far out from the house—"

"Gibberish." I shook my head. "No, no, you don't understand—let me listen." My heartbeat quickened.

Private Sun didn't make any indication of what he thought about my request. He followed orders without question and traced a pattern on the control panel. The recording reset.

The room filled with a crackling and the low whine of electronic feedback. Isabel turned toward the woods. Opened her mouth. The sound didn't quite line up with her mouth's movement, and it was almost drowned out by the feedback, but I could still hear it, that hissing, garbled speech she and the twins shared.

"It's not gibberish," I said. Private Sun stopped the recording and looked at me.

"It's not? We ran it through our language analyzers and didn't come up with anything—"

"Because she made it up. Or the twins did. They all speak it together sometimes."

"Oh." Private Sun looked crestfallen. "We didn't know. I'm glad you watched the recording."

I waved my hand, dismissing his concerns. It was good to scour the woods anyway. "Let me see the rest of it."

The recording started back up. She seemed to be speaking with someone—she would speak, and then there would be silence, and then she'd nod and speak again.

And then she skipped off into the trees.

"That's all there is," Private Sun said. He froze the image. "Would you like to watch it again?"

I shook my head, staring at that empty, hazy cemetery. She vanished into the woods. The recording should have followed her into the trees.

"Is there any way to strip out just the sound?" I asked. "I want to play it to the twins."

"Of course." Private Sun went back to the control panel. I dug my nails into my palms. She had to be on the estate somewhere—maybe the girls were playing some game.

I watched Private Sun and thought again about Dad running on his treadmill like it was an ordinary day. Like this was an ordinary emergency. And for a moment, I was paralyzed with rage.

But then the holo flickered, and there was Isabel again, looking down at her mother's grave. I stopped thinking about Dad. He didn't matter now. Only Isabel did.

I'd find her. I had to. It was just like my mother said on the first holo she ever sent me: Oxbow women didn't break promises. So, I didn't. Not even the ones I made to myself.

Music drifted through the door of the twins' suite, the lilting hypnotic jingle of one of the shows they liked to watch. I knocked. Grace answered, her face lined with worry. She gave me a hopeful smile.

"Did they find her?"

I shook my head. Her smile vanished. Behind her, the twins were stretched out on the floor, staring at their media screen, where a cat rolled around in a grassy field. Daphne laughed in delight.

"I need to talk to them," I said in a low voice. "I don't want to upset them, but—it may be important."

Grace twisted her mouth. "I don't think you'll upset them," she said carefully.

Daphne laughed again. Adrienne stared at the screen with a bright, curious intensity. I shivered. They didn't seem to care that their sister was missing.

Grace stepped aside, holding the door for me. The twins' room was bright, painted with pictures of Earth animals long extinct, tigers and eagles and zebras. Neither one of them turned toward me. They were too engrossed in their show.

"Adrienne. Daphne." The show drowned out my voice, and they ignored me.

"Girls," Grace said sharply. "Esme needs to ask you some questions."

Adrienne sighed and twisted around to face me, although she didn't look happy about it. Daphne kept staring at the screen, and Grace reached over and turned it off.

"It's about Isabel," I said quietly.

"Oh," said Daphne. "You don't need to worry about her."

I frowned. The chill from earlier rippled down my spine. I looked over at Grace for an explanation, but she looked as baffled as I felt.

"And why's that?" I sat down cross-legged on the floor. The twins leaned against each other, looking bored.

"Because she's fine," Adrienne answered. "Everyone's upset over nothing."

"Do you know where she is?"

"Nah." Daphne shook her head, her long dark hair splaying around her shoulders. "We weren't invited."

Adrienne nodded in agreement.

The chill turned to a sick weight of dread in my stomach. "Someone invited Isabel away?"

They both nodded.

"Who?"

Adrienne rolled her eyes. "Why don't you go talk to Rena? We told her all this already."

"Rena's out looking for Isabel," I said, more sharply than I intended. "Something very bad could happen to her. Who invited her?"

The twins looked at each other, and then Daphne started to murmur in their hissing language.

"No!" I said. "You'll only speak Corominan in front me; do you understand?"

They gave me dark glares. I'd been sharper than I should have; I hated how that language put up a wall between us.

"Who invited her away?" I asked.

"Her friends," Adrienne said.

"We've never met them," Daphne added. "Isabel says they're scared of us."

I looked back and forth between their calm, implacable faces. Dread threatened to swallow me whole. I had seen Isabel talking to someone in the woods—Private Sun had as well. But who? If it was someone on the estate, the soldiers would have seen them. Even if the kidnappers had cloaked themselves in camouflage technology, the soldiers could see on all levels of the light spectrum. And since the soldiers were engineered, none of them would have been bought off. That's why you paid premium for engineered soldiers. Their loyalty was built in from the beginning.

I was shaking.

"You don't know anything else about these friends?" I asked.

They shook their heads. "She doesn't talk about them much," Adrienne said.

I took a deep breath. I was aware of Grace standing off to the side, watching us, studying us, passing judgment on me, her employer who couldn't find her sister.

"Can we go back to our show now?" Adrienne said.

"Not yet." I pulled out the recording of Isabel's voice from the security feed. "I'm going to play something for you. It's Isabel, and she's speaking in that language of yours. I want you to translate for me, okay? I know you think Isabel's fine, but you've never met these friends, so they may very well be capable of hurting her. Do you understand? It's important that you translate this."

They looked at each other again. Daphne leaned over and whispered something to Adrienne, and Adrienne whispered something back. Normally, I though this kind of thing was cute, the twins conferring among themselves. But not today.

They turned to me. "We promise."

"It's really important that you tell me the truth," I said. "I don't want anything to happen to Isabel. Or to you two."

"Yeah, just play it." Adrienne sighed dramatically and flopped back against Daphne's shoulder. I didn't understand how they could be so calm, why they didn't see the danger in Isabel's disappearance. Perhaps I didn't understand them as well as I'd hoped.

I activated the recording. Isabel's voice filled the room, crackling and dim and strange. The twins listened intently. When it ended, I asked them if they needed to hear it again.

"No, it was easy. There wasn't much." Daphne shrugged. Adrienne nodded in agreement.

"What did she say?"

A pause. The rain beat against the windows. The air was thick with humidity and I wanted to shake the answer out of them but I knew I couldn't do that.

Finally, Adrienne answered. She stared straight me as she spoke, and her words paralyzed me with fear.

"She said, 'Hello, my friend. I'm excited to go play with you today.'" Adrienne blinked. "'What are we going to do?'"

I kept the household feed on all night. It was quiet, just a few updates on the search as staff slowly trickled back in for the night. If they found Isabel, I wanted to know. But I also wanted to know when Dad came home.

I couldn't sleep. I hadn't expected to, but I tried anyway, tossing and turning and twisting the sheets around my legs. The rain picked up around midnight, pummeling hard against my windows, turning the evening light murkier than usual. Finally, I gave up. I climbed out of bed and sat down with my lightbox and drew up files from work. It was routine stuff, brainless: mostly approving work orders from the various militaries. The bulk of the approval work had been done already by the head of sales, so any anomalies had already been sorted, but I read over their requests myself anyway, checking them against the labs' different abilities before pressing my thumb against the screen to finalize the deal.

As I worked, my mind wandered—to Isabel, to the twins' insistence that she was with friends. I'd taken the information to Private Sun as soon as I'd found out. He had listened closely, head tilted, frown deepening as I spoke. I knew he had reached the same conclusion I had, about the reality of a "friend" who dragged six-year-old girls out of the woods. Later, I wondered how he'd learned about the darker parts of the universe. If it was part of the genetic programming to come into this world fully cognizant of the atrocities of human beings.

When I finished, he put a hand on my shoulder and said, "We'll find her."

I wanted to believe him. I stared at him and told myself he was better equipped for this than I was—stronger senses, more stamina, a clearer mind. Surely, the attributes necessary for survival in a war were enough to rescue a little girl from whatever monster had stolen her away.

"I promise," he added, and smiled at me, a crooked, imperfect smile that didn't seem engineered.

But that was earlier in the evening, when the sun had been able to peek through the clouds and turn the drizzle into diamonds. Now it was storming, and Dad still wasn't home, and I couldn't stand the thought of working any longer.

I shoved away from my lightbox and paced around the room. The feed was silent save for an occasional burst of static, interference from the soldiers' equipment. I paced over to my window. Stopped. Opened it, something I hadn't done during a storm since I was a girl. There was enough of an overhang that the rain fell like a sheet half a foot away, and the only water that got in was a sweet-scented mist that dusted across my face like sea spray. I breathed in the rain. I told myself I wasn't going to cry.

And then the feed rippled with voices. I turned away from the window, away from the roar of the rain, and listened.

"I'll go tend to him." It sounded like Mr. Whittaker. "I was expecting him a little later, actually. Tell Alicia to prepare his bedroom."

"Shameful." It was a woman's voice; I didn't recognize it, but I agreed with what she said. "Staying late on a day like this. Absolutely horrific."

Mr. Whittaker just said, "He's a busy man."

Bullshit. I fumed at Mr. Whittaker for taking his side, although that wasn't surprising, given the way Dad always fudged the rules for him—technically, Mr. Whittaker was a Sixty-Five, but I suspected Dad told him information above his rank. He always seemed to know more than he should.

I switched off the feed and threw my robe around my shoulders. It was psychopathic for Dad to stay late today. Psychopathic for him to keep Isabel's disappearance from me until I arrived home—forcing me to put work first, just like he did.

I stalked through the empty halls of the house to Dad's suite. The door hung open; Alicia was in there, dressed in a robe, setting out a stack of towels on the coffee table in front of his sofa. She didn't notice me until I slipped through the doorway.

"Ms. Coromina! You startled me." She pressed one hand to her chest. "Do you need anything? It's awfully late—"

"No, I don't need anything." I sat down on the sofa. "Just waiting for my father."

She nodded once, as though she understood why I was there. She finished putting out the towels and gave me a quick smile before disappearing into the hallway. I tapped my fingers against the armrest. Normally, I'd be terrified at the thought of confronting Dad, but in the wake of the day's panic, an inexplicable calmness had washed over me, and I stared at the empty doorway, ready for whatever happened next.

Voices drifted in from the hall. Dad and Mr. Whittaker. Dad barreled into the room, Mr. Whittaker trailing behind him.

"—not be disturbed tomorrow. I've got a big call-in, and I'm taking it at the house for security reasons. You'll need to tell the marines to activate the shielding—"

He froze when he saw me.

"Esme." His voice had a hard, brittle edge to it, even as he smiled. "You really ought to be asleep. Between-world travel can be *exhausting*."

"I couldn't sleep." I stood up. My heart was pounding. Mr. Whittaker kept looking back and forth between Dad and me. "Because of the emergency you told me about? Isabel? Your daughter? She's missing."

Mr. Whittaker looked personally affronted. Dad waved a hand at him, dismissing him from the room. He slid away, shooting angry looks in my direction, closing the door as he left.

"I was very busy," Dad said.

"She's *missing*, Dad. She fucking *disappeared*. No record of her on the security feeds, a squad of *genetically engineered* soldiers haven't been able to turn her up, either with technology or themselves. What does that say about our company's product? That they can't even find a little girl in a manicured forest?"

I was crying. Dad stared at me, his face expressionless. "This outburst is unbecoming, Esme."

"She's probably dead." Speaking it aloud was the only way I'd allow myself to think it. "And you don't even care."

"Of course I care. I'm deeply upset." He didn't sound upset. His voice was flat. "But Project X has taken up a large chunk of my time, and—"

"Project X? *Project X?* You care about some obfuscatory bullshit business plan while your own daughter is probably being murdered—"

"It's not bullshit!" he snapped. "And I doubt she's being murdered. The estate is big. No one saw her leave." He must have seen the surprise on my face, because he added, "I may have been in the office, but I kept in contact with the soldiers. Don't be so quick to judge."

I glared at him. "So, she'll be murdered on your own property."

"She isn't being murdered!" His voice roared out of him and I jolted back.

"How could you possibly know that?"

"I have my reasons, and they are none of your business. Now get out. I have a call-in tomorrow and I need to be rested for it."

"You're an asshole."

"Out!"

I glowered at him one last time, my face hot with rage. He didn't care.

I went downstairs the next morning in a haze. The staff were scarce, just Alicia and Grace cleaning up Dad's breakfast. He'd had *breakfast*, as if it were a normal day, as if his daughter hadn't been missing all night. I couldn't breathe.

"Would you like anything?" Alicia asked gently.

"No, I'm fine." I shook my head. "Some water, that's all I need."

She filled me a glass, and when she turned to hand it to me, her face was lined with concern. "You really ought to eat something," she said. "It'll make you feel better."

My stomach was walled off. I couldn't stand the thought of food. But she and Grace were watching me, the remains of Dad's breakfast—a pan dirty with scrambled eggs, a mangled grapefruit husk—spread out on the counter. I sighed and said, "I'll take some oats. In the sunroom."

Alicia nodded and I left the kitchen. Everything was in a blur. Rain pattered against the roof, the steady silver drizzle that was the default this time of year. The sunroom was cooler than I expected. I'd gotten used to the heat of the dry season. The plants were all wilted, like Isabel's disappearance had affected them, too.

I had chosen the sunroom because it faced the direction of the cemetery, and if I couldn't do anything else, I would sit and watch the empty yard, the rain and grass and trees. A dark-hooded figured trudged past, and my heart leapt—but then I saw the gleam from the light pistol. One of the soldiers. Still searching.

Alicia brought my oats and set them on the table without saying anything. They floated, unappetizing, in their milk. I didn't touch them. Dad spent tens of thousands from his personal account hiring engineered soldiers to keep us safe from an unnamed threat, and then when Isabelle went missing, he didn't even care. It made no sense. It didn't make *financial* sense.

The rain kept falling. I picked up my oats and stirred them around, taking a bite and tasting nothing. The rain beat a rhythm against the sunroom's glass wall, tracing snaky paths down to the soil. And through those paths, I watched the woods, and I saw nothing.

I saw nothing, until I didn't.

It was a small movement, flickering from the trees. I shoved my oats aside and stood up. It wasn't a person—more like a shadow, a trick of sunlight. But there was no sunlight right now.

The rain. The rain was making me see things.

It happened again, a flicker of darkness, like something moving on the periphery of my vision, even though I was looking right at it. And I thought about how the soldiers' security feeds had seen only Isabel, talking to ghosts.

My head buzzed. Some cloaking technology? A new sort that our espionage agents hadn't uncovered? OCI was rumored to be working on something—God, I'd been stupid, to assume the soldiers could see through any cloaking technology a kidnapper could bring planetside. Someone was out there.

I opened the sunroom's door and burst out into the rain. It roared around me like a monster. I knew I should call the soldiers, but I was afraid this flicker in my vision would disappear and I'd lose her.

"Isabel!" I screamed.

The rain answered with its dull gray static. I ran across the lawn. The trees loomed ahead, the branches sagging. Water ran into my eyes and into my mouth and it tasted steely and cold. The world was a blur.

"Isabel!" I shouted again. I was almost to the tree line. I stopped, whirled around in place. I was alone out there. Fear prickled at my chest. I could feel eyes on me, but everywhere I looked, I saw only emptiness.

The rain pummeled my bare skin, and the grass poked at my bare feet. My fear built and built. I should go back. She wasn't there. She was probably dead.

"Esme?"

I thought her voice was a hallucination at first, some willful lie my brain told me. But when I turned my face toward the woods, I saw her, wearing the same dress she'd been wearing in the security feed.

"What are you doing out in the rain?" she asked.

"Isabel!" I bolted toward her and scooped her into my arms. All thoughts of an unseen voyeur vanished, replaced by a flood of relief that I'd found Isabel—I'd done what Dad could not and *I'd found Isabel.*

"Esme?" Isabel squirmed away from me, slippery from the rain. "What's the matter with you?"

"Where were you!" I cried. "The entire household's been looking for you! We thought you were—" I stopped myself. *We thought you were dead* maybe wasn't the best thing to tell a six-year-old.

Isabel squinted at me. She didn't look like she'd been harmed. She didn't even look hungry or tired. "Did I miss dinner? Is that why you're upset?"

"Did you—" I shook my head, not understanding. Dinner? She thought she'd missed *dinner?*

The rain was cold. The rustle of it through the trees pounded at my head. "Let's go inside." I took her by the hand and led her across the lawn. She didn't protest, just half-skipped alongside me like the way she did when she was happy. I led her into the sunroom and we stood dripping on the tile. Isabel looked around, blinking and wiping the rain from her eyes. When she saw my bowl of oats, she stopped and stared at it.

"Isabel?" I knelt down beside her and put my hand on her back. "Are you okay?"

"Why are you eating breakfast?" she asked.

Dread threaded itself through my stomach. "Because it's breakfast time," I said.

She looked at me. For the first time, I saw something like fear in her expression. "Breakfast? But I was only gone for an hour."

Everything turned to ice. Everything froze. Even my heart stopped.

"Isabel," I said, trying to find the words, "you've been gone since yesterday afternoon. Overnight."

"Overnight?"

I nodded.

She looked down, her face scrunched up like she was thinking. I felt sick. Something terrible had happened. She was fine, yes, but something terrible had happened.

She looked up at me again. In the filtered light of the sunroom, with her pale skin and tangled black hair, she looked like a woodland imp from a story. Not human at all.

Rena stepped out of Isabel's bedroom, easing the door shut so it wouldn't make any noise. "She's asleep," she whispered.

I nodded and we walked together down the hall toward the library, where we could talk in private. It was a cavernous room with big windows and skylights designed to flood it with light. That didn't happen during the rainy season, however. Instead, it was as if we were underwater.

Rena collapsed in one of the big leather chairs and rubbed her forehead. The lines of her face were deeper than they had before I left for my trip.

"Mr. Hankiao looked over her," Rena said. "But he didn't find anything wrong with her. No injuries, nothing." She paused, gazing up at the ceiling. "I tried speaking to her again. But I couldn't get anything out of her either."

"Really?" I frowned, frustrated. "She didn't say anything new?"

"Only what she told you. She thought she was gone an hour. When I asked her where she'd gone, she said the cemetery, and when I told her we went to the cemetery and she wasn't there, she clammed up."

I shook my head. "If someone did hurt her," I said, "do you think they—they *threatened* her, or—"

"I don't know." Rena's voice was calm, soothing, the voice she used on me when I was upset as a child. "But we know she wasn't hurt. At least physically. And she doesn't seem to be in any emotional pain, either."

"But she had to have been on the estate!"

"I know, sweetness."

I stood up and paced around the library, passing shelves lined with the glass squares containing all of Dad's dull histories of business and war. It wasn't much to look at, and so Dad had filled the empty spaces with polished stones and vials of sand and dried flora from all the Coromina I planets. The library wasn't so much a library as it was a monument to Dad's corpocratic acumen.

"Esme," Rena said gently. "Maybe you should rest for a bit. The office can wait another day, and Isabel's back safely—I know you didn't sleep last night."

"This is going to bother me." I stopped next to the window and looked out at the rain-soaked garden. "I just—God, I just want to find out what happened."

Rena stared at me. I'd never told her that I'd promised myself I'd keep my sisters safe. But maybe she knew anyway. She didn't ask me to explain.

"I'm going to see the soldiers," I said. "Have another look at the security feeds." I hadn't told her about the flicker of movement I saw before Isabel appeared. It was a clue, but I kept it to myself. I guess I wanted to be the one to figure out what happened.

"I really wish you'd rest," she said.

"I've gotten by on less sleep. Let me know if you find anything else."

I swept out of the library without waiting for an answer. I'd already called in to the office to explain I had a family emergency and wouldn't be in until tomorrow at the latest, but when I took a meandering route so that I could walk past the garage, I saw that Dad's car, a prototype of some new technology, with mind-links for the drivers, wasn't there. Dad had gone in. He knew we'd found Isabel—Mr. Whittaker had assured me he'd given Dad the message. But I'd been with Isabel all morning and hadn't seen Dad once.

Had he even bothered to check up on her? Did he even *care*?

I told myself it didn't matter, that I cared, and Rena cared, and that was enough. But I didn't believe it.

The sun had come out from behind the wispy gray clouds, although showers of rain still sprinkled over the garden, dampening my hair and clothes and catching in the light so that they sparkled. *Diamond-rain*, we used to call it when we were kids. Children always have lots of name for rain, but by the time you're an adult, you forget them all.

The soldiers' door was open except for the screen. I banged on the frame. "Hello?" I called out. "It's Esme Coromina! I'd like to watch the security feeds again."

Private Snow answered, a different Private Snow from when I was a teenager. This one was a woman, tall and broad-shouldered, with pale hair she wore in a soldier's buzz cut. She was my age, but she reminded me of my mother. I didn't like talking to her.

"Oh," I said. "Is Private Sun here?"

"No, they're all out scouting the perimeter. Your father has them looking for evidence. Seems to think we're cops now." She paused. "Sorry, that was inapp—"

"Evidence?" I frowned. He didn't care enough to visit Isabel before he left, but he sent the soldiers out sifting through the grounds. He only cared about us in the abstract.

"Yeah, told us to look for whatever we could find. But Private Sun thought you'd be stopping by to look at the holos again, and it was my turn to stay in, anyway. Glad to hear the little girl turned up all right." She shifted her weight like she was uncomfortable.

"Yeah, me too."

She unlatched the screen and let me in.

"Did he give you any idea at all what you're looking for?" I blurted the question out. I felt like Dad was keeping something from me. But then, I always felt like that.

"Not really. Just said if we found anything *unusual*." She shrugged. "You'd get more information out of him, I imagine."

"No, I wouldn't," I said.

She didn't respond.

We went into the security room. I waited while Private Snow got the recordings to the right place.

"Take it back a few moments before she walked out of the woods this morning," I said. "And zoom out. I want to see as much as possible." Private Snow didn't question. The lawn filled up the room, watery gray light casting shadows over our faces. The position wasn't the same angle I'd been watching from the sunroom, but it was close enough. I stared hard at the place where I'd seen the flickers, but there was nothing on the recording. Then Isabel stepped out of the trees, small and bedraggled.

I still didn't think I'd imagined those flickers.

"Go back," I said. "I want to watch again."

She did. This time, I zoomed in on the place where Isabel emerged. It was only a meter or so from where I'd been watching the flickers. Weird that I hadn't noticed her right away, but I'd been distracted.

The trees rustled. Shadows shifted over the grass. And Isabel stepped out of the darkness like she was walking through a doorway.

"Does that look weird to you?" I asked Private Snow.

"Does what?"

"The way Isabel walks out of the woods—could you go back? Thanks." The recording reset itself. "Now watch. It looks *weird*, how she walks out of the woods."

Everything moved again. Silvery rain, rustling trees. The shadows lengthened over the grass and Isabel stepped out of them. That was the only way to describe it. She stepped out of a fucking shadow.

Private Snow paused the recording. "That does seem strange."

She frowned, fiddled with the controls, and paused the recording right at the moment Isabel appeared. All I could see on the holo was a black, mud-caked shoe and a skinny calf.

"That can't be right," I said.

"It's probably the recording." Private Snow lurched the holo forward moment by moment. Isabel materialized from the feet up. "I mean, damn. I've never seen anything like that."

"Really?" I turned to her. "There isn't any kind of, I don't know, stealth equipment that can do that? I know we've been working on something, but nothing we've got is anywhere remotely on that level." I hesitated. "I was worried it might be OCI tech, but—" My voice trailed off.

Private Snow looked at me. Her eyes were big and dark brown, like a deer's. They didn't seem like the eyes of a soldier. "With all due respect, Ms. Coromina, you'd know more about it than me. All non-Coromina weapons on the Four Sisters are banned, so if—"

"Oh, please," I snapped. "Just because something's banned doesn't mean people won't have it. Especially the sort of people who kidnap little girls."

Private Snow shook her head. "You'd be surprised, especially with the scanners they have up in the atmosphere. But there's nothing like that in *use* that I'm aware of, certainly not on that level. I imagine this whole thing is a just a holo-trick. The light was bad— the recording's pretty dark, all told." She shrugged.

I turned back to the holo, frozen in place on a shot of Isabel staring off to the left. Staring at me, I knew, although the zoom had cut off all but my right hand, a tiny white blur on the edge of the projection.

"Maybe," I said.

"Look." Private Snow hesitated. "I can ask around, but you got to promise me some kind of immunity, right? If people hear me asking about non-Coromina weapons—"

"It's fine," I said. "I'll talk to my father and make sure he gives you and your contacts immunity. Just for this." I held up one finger, and she nodded. I wasn't sure this was a promise I could keep, but I needed to know for sure. And even if Dad didn't care about Isabel, he'd want to know about non-Coromina weapons making their way into the system.

I turned back to the holographic version of Isabel, staring off into space. I didn't believe it was a holo-trick. Dad had been *so sure* she was fine that he hadn't even come home when she went missing.

He knew what was lurking in those shadows. And I wanted to know what it was too.

After Isabel's return, I had her run through a full gauntlet of tests, both physical and psychological, and the end conclusion was that exactly nothing had happened to her.

"She just ran away into the woods," Dr. Clavé told me. She was the psychologist I had hired to talk to Isabel. "It's a huge estate. I'm surprised this didn't happen with Daphne and Adrienne." She smiled. "Or with you."

"She was gone overnight!"

"Plenty of children run away from home for a day or so. It would be a matter of concern if she came back injured or distraught, but she didn't."

There was nothing more for me to say to that. Dr. Clavé was right: Isabel was thoroughly unharmed by the experience. I watched her for the first week after she came back, and she seemed herself, eating her usual foods without complaint, playing hologames with Adrienne and Daphne in their suite, growing restless from the rain. I asked Rena and the other staff if they noticed anything unusual about her behavior, but they hadn't either.

I also heard back from Private Snow—but she wasn't able to learn anything about true invisibility technology even existing, much less being brought onto Ekkeko as contraband. Another lead thwarted.

There was still their strange, hissing language, though. The girls would speak it to each other when they thought no one was listening, and one afternoon, I happened to overhear them. I came home early, tired of the bright off-white lighting in the Coromina Group building, and I passed the playroom on the way to my home office. The hissing stopped me dead in my tracks.

I didn't know why. I'd heard it before. But after hearing it on the security holo, where it was tied inexorably to her disappearance, I associated it with danger.

The playroom door was cracked open, and I hovered outside it, listening. It still sounded like gibberish, all those low, growly sibilants. I closed my eyes, trying to parse the words. I couldn't.

The girls dissolved into giggles. My eyes flew open and I had a brief moment of panic, like I'd been caught breaking some minor corporate rule. I peered into the room. Isabel and the twins were sitting in a circle on the floor, the set of wind-up metal dolls I'd brought them back from Amana arranged in the center of the circle. Adrienne lifted one of the dolls and said something in their language, and then Isabel did the same.

I pulled away and took a deep breath. There was nothing sinister. Just little girls playing a game.

Except I didn't believe that, not really. Not because of Isabel, who was clearly all right—and I was grateful for that, I was— but because of Dad. I was certain that he knew something about her disappearance, and I hated that he was keeping it from me. He'd shoved me into Genetics because he could trust me, and yet he wouldn't reveal whatever dangerous secrets were lurking in the woods of the estate.

Things were busier at work, too. We were in the process of adding new improvements to the standard soldier model—fiddly stuff, mostly, that had to do with the body's immune system and means of recovery. It was my first big project in Genetics and I wanted to get it right. Gaining a higher security clearance seemed even more important now that Isabel had disappeared, because the higher the clearance, the more likely it was I could find out what the hell was going on.

And then messages from Dad started to materialize. Questions and tasks, mostly, out of the blue. *Did Flor DeCrie suggest anything in your meeting today, and if so, what was it? Dr. Vanya is working on an update to the white blood cells—could you prepare a report of his progress?*

I answered them dutifully, knowing those kinds of inanities

were the way to a high security clearance. But I also paid attention to them. They'd started up after Isabel's disappearance, and even though Dad tried to make them as ordinary and as bland as possible, I knew that couldn't be a coincidence. I searched for the pattern, just like I had with my mother's messages all those years before. This time, though, I knew the pattern was actually there, even if I couldn't quite see it.

Some of the questions dealt with the immune-system work we were doing, but most of them didn't. Most of them were just Dad angling for reports of my day-to-day activities, and I might have thought it was Dad checking up on me if I hadn't known there was an entire network of corporate watchdogs set in place to do that for him. I was *sure* the questions tied to Isabel's disappearance somehow. I suspected as well that they were linked in some way to Project X, since only something like Project X would require this level of obfuscation. Which was a disturbing thought, that one of Dad's corporate projects involved my little sister. But I was old enough to expect that sort of thing from Dad.

I knew that if I could figure out what the connection was, then I'd be better equipped to protect Isabel and Daphne and Adrienne from the machinations of my father.

But I couldn't find a pattern. The questions came through, about immune systems, about meetings with the lab-wranglers, about my lunch with the liaison to the CG marketing division, who was one of Dad's little favorites, which just complicated things even more. I knew Dad was probably sending me false questions as well. Still, I'd filter out my messages so all I could see was a list of questions, and I read through them, over and over, trying to make sense of them. But they may as well have been a code.

Then one afternoon, Dad called a meeting.

There weren't many people there—just Dad and me and Alexander Fforde, the lab-wrangler, who managed the scientists and reported directly to me. We met in a room up on the eighty-ninth floor, with a huge picture window that, as with Dad's office, looked out at the ocean. I couldn't see anything, though, because it was storming that day, rain buffeting against the glass. Every now and then, lightning burned up all the light in the room. Fitting weather.

"Genetics will be starting something new," Dad announced from his place at the front of the table. "Something internal."

Alexander and I glanced at each other.

"Do we have the budget for that?" I asked, trying to play my role to the fullest.

Dad glared at me. "We always have the budget for self-defense."

The room went quiet except for the rain.

"Self-defense?" Alexander squeaked.

"Yes. OCI has been making some movements I'm not happy about. Trying to recruit my own people out from under me, making inquiries into the two smaller labs. I don't like it." He grinned. "I suspect they're after the latest Ninety-Nine project, but so far, they haven't even come close."

"That's good," Alexander said.

"Are you hoping to go to war?" I asked.

Dad looked me straight in the eye. "No one ever hopes to go to war."

I glared at him for lying. We all knew a war could be very profitable for the Coromina Group.

"But to answer your real question," Dad went on, "I'm not *expecting* to go to war. I just want to make a few preparations, to speed up the work on the project. We were planning to start production at the end of the rainy season, but I want to move it forward. Which is why I need your help." He pointed at Alexander and me in turn. "What I'm about to tell you is classified Level Eighty-Seven."

My heart fluttered. A jump that big, so soon?

But then Dad went on: "I'm not increasing your security clearance. This is the only piece of information you're getting. I assume you both know what it means if this information leaves this room?"

My excitement faded. Of course I did. Termination, blacklisting. I suspect it could also mean something far harsher and just as permanent, but no one ever expressed those concerns aloud.

Dad nodded, satisfied. We were trustworthy; that's why we were there.

"This new project will be based out of a lab here on Ekkeko," Dad said. "Close to home." He grinned. I sat still, feeling cautious and uncertain. "Unfortunately, the lab's not currently equipped to manufacture soldiers from scratch—we're still working on that part of the building, because, remember, we weren't expecting to have to use it until the end of the season. No matter. I just need the two of you to arrange for some in-house blanks. Twelve to start with; we'll be doing one squad."

Alexander slumped in his chair. Internal work, without a security increase, meant our jobs would be broken down into minor projects so we couldn't see the full picture. I thought about all of Dad's strange questions and assignments. Looked like he'd had me doing work on these new soldiers already.

Isabel disappeared, Dad got the security patrolling the perimeter of the estate, he announced a new lab related to Project X. The pieces were all there. But I just couldn't see the connections.

I studied Dad's face, hoping for a tell, a hint of an explanation. But there wasn't anything.

"I have some specifications." Dad pulled out his lightbox. On cue, so did Alexander and I.

We all set our lightboxes on the table, and in unison, their screens flowered to life. Dad's specifications appeared instantaneously on my holoscreen.

"It's encrypted," Dad said. "If you want to access it alone, it will need to scan your fingerprints and eye retinas."

Alexander made a coughing, choking noise, which Dad ignored. I looked up at Alexander, and when he caught me looking, he shrugged, a bewildered expression on his face. I understood. This was a lot of subterfuge for a spec list.

"Read them over now," Dad said. "Let me know if you have any questions."

I did as he asked, scanning it quickly. Even with my short time in Genetics, I suspected that his requests were unusual, and the increasingly bewildered expression on Alexander's face confirmed it for me. Dad wanted the soldiers developed to stage four, at which point they would be shipped to Ekkeko. He wanted us to remove the first wave of personality imprinting as well as the general behavioral modifications.

"So," Dad said, breaking the silence. "Do you have any questions?"

He was daring us to question him. Trying to prove I wasn't the daughter he could trust. Part of me wanted to hurl my lightbox at his head, to ask him why this stupid project and these stupid soldiers meant more to him than his family. Than Isabel. Than me.

But I only shook my head and asked, "When do you want them delivered?"

I went home after the meeting. I told my assistant that I had a headache and wanted to lie down. It wasn't exactly the truth.

My lightbox chimed on the way home, and the Connectivity in the car whispered to me that Alexander had put in Dad's order, placing it with Starspray City. That was quick for him—Dad knew how to frighten his employee-citizens into action. I pulled out my lightbox and approved the order. I watched as the order went through, and then I closed my eyes, trying to decide what to do next. I refused to believe there wasn't a connection between this new assignment and Isabel's disappearance. Had some rival corporation kidnapped her? But no, she'd been fine when she came back. It wasn't like she had information they'd be looking for, anyway.

I knew there was a connection. I just had no idea what it was.

By the time I arrived at the estate, the rain had slacked off, transforming from a wall of water to a thin gray mist. I asked John to drop me off at the back of the estate so I could slip in through the side service door. My curiosity was burning me up from the inside, and I didn't want the staff to know I was home. I had some investigating to do.

It had been a long time since I'd listened to the underground newsfeeds. A long time, really, since I'd thought about the Underground at all. It used to make me sad, thinking on it, because those crackly, distorted voices reminded me of Paco and Laila, of a whole life I'd never be able to touch again.

Today, though, I needed the rumors, and I shoved aside my

blue-tinged nostalgia to get to them. I locked myself in my suite and switched on my personal lightbox, the same one I'd had since I was a teenager. For a moment, I sat there staring at the holoscreen. It felt absurd to hook into the Connectivity Underground while I was still wearing my Coromina Group uniform, but I knew if I wanted to learn something, I was going to have to go there. Asking around in the company itself would only lead to problems. It would only reveal me as untrustworthy, and I couldn't have that. Not now.

I tapped in the code for the Connectivity Underground—an old one that Paco had given me years before. It still worked, the holoscreen swirling with colors and data until I was in.

Nothing had changed. There were still the same scrolling headlines, the same distorted voice chattering in the background. Right now it was reciting an anti-corpocracy manifesto, calling for the dissolution of corporate control, a return to the democracies of humanity's past, when we all had a say in our future. I tuned it out because there was no way to turn it off without being shut out of the Underground completely. A long time ago, that rhetoric might have spoken to me. But now I knew better.

I scanned the scrolling headlines, but it was all the same sort of thing that you always found in the Connectivity Underground, detailed accounts of corporate atrocities, old information about Dad's start as a war profiteer, profiles of CG's upper staff. I wondered if I would see my name. Wondered what they would say about me—if they would include the fact that I had slept with one of their own, that at one point I had truly believed in their message.

But my name never appeared.

I kept scanning; the voice kept chattering. The manifesto had become more specific; now the voice was listing Coromina Group injustices in a rhythmic, singsongy way, as if it wanted to turn the company's darkness into a poem: "Gassed anti-corpocracy protesters on Amana and placed them on a hyperdrive ship for banishment in the OCI system. An entire village has been wiped out—they say it was a natural evolution of the market, but we say they murdered those villagers for spreading anti-corpocracy ideas."

I didn't believe any of this, of course—I knew for a fact that the village had been drying up for years because I had visited it when I worked for PM, to meet with the mayor and discuss ways to bring business back into town. No one was killed. They just moved away.

But then I heard the phrase *Project X* in the voice's distorted cadence, and I froze.

"What is this Project X?" the voice said. "According to the Company, it does not exist. And yet we have internal memos which refer to it directly." A pause. My heart pounded in my throat. "From Flor DeCrie, head of the Catequil death lab Starspray City, to Sterling Segal, one of the head honcho's main men himself. 'I agree that the DNA shows a great deal of promise, but I am uncertain of Philip's claims that it can bind to human DNA. With all due respect, he is not a scientist, and he is perhaps too close to the subject to see things for what they are.'"

I shrieked and stared at my holoscreen in horror. *Too close to the subject.* The voice was asking the wrong questions, about what this DNA could be, and why it was separate from human DNA, but all I heard was *too close to the subject* and I thought of the first time I'd seen Isabel as a baby, and how Dad had stared through the glass at her, his face haggard, and I'd almost thought he loved her.

Too close to the subject.

I shut off the lightbox and shoved it aside. I could still hear the voice echoing around inside my head. My heart pounded. I stood up, shaking, and pushed my hands through my hair. My thoughts were wild. I didn't know what it meant. The memo sounded real. If the Connectivity Underground was going to fake a memo, they would have made it sound more horrific. They weren't good with subtlety.

I made my way downstairs. I needed time to mull this over, to decide what exactly I thought it meant. It was late enough in the afternoon that the staff were scarce, resting up before it was time to prepare dinner. The house was dim from the rain. I went out through the garden door and stood on the porch. Rain pattered across the yard. I could have grabbed my raincoat, but the truth was the rain helped me think.

The dampness misted over my clothes and hair as I strolled across the lawn. The pineapple plants rose in spiky clumps up ahead; the trees trembled from the rain. I thought back to the day Isabel had come back. Dad had demanded that the soldiers case the yard. Perhaps theirs was the DNA in the memo. Was he training Isabel to be a soldier? No, that didn't make sense.

Something flashed in the periphery of my vision.

I stopped, a cold prickle climbing up the back of my neck. It was like someone was watching me. But when I turned, scanning over the lawn, I didn't see anyone.

Except—

I froze. There it was again, that flicker of shadows, the same thing I'd seen before Isabel came back. This time, it blinked by the hibiscus bushes, a smear of darkness amidst the vivid color of the blossoms.

"Isabel?" My voice trembled. No answer. I felt like an idiot.

Another flicker, more pronounced. It was almost in the shape of a man, and it was rimmed with a sickly yellow light. Just for a flash, and then it vanished.

I gasped, jerking back. I was certain I'd seen it, certain this wasn't a trick of the shadows or some momentary flaw in my vision— something, *something* was moving over by the hibiscus.

I took a deep breath and walked across the lawn with slow, careful steps. I did not look away from the hibiscus. The misting rain made everything hazy, and every now and then, I had to wipe at my eyes to keep drops from forming on my eyelashes.

When I came to the hibiscus bushes, I stopped. Rain pattered gently against the leaves. The blossoms bobbed up and down. I thought I smelled something faintly chemical, but then I only smelled the rain.

"Hello?" I called out, tentative. I immediately felt like I'd made a grave mistake. No one answered. I didn't see any more flickers, any more shapes of yellow light.

But that creepy cold feeling still lingered. No one was there. But someone was watching me.

What are you doing, Dad? I thought.

I twisted my head around, trying to examine the lawn from all sides.

No one there.

My clothes were soaked through. I didn't want to be out there anymore. The rain was no longer a comfort, and I couldn't get rid of that unshakable sense of eeriness. I turned in place one last time, looking for anything unusual, and I saw only the lawn.

I walked back inside.

As soon as I passed through the doorway, the cold inkling of paranoia dissipated. I leaned up against the wall and I tried to make sense of what I had seen. Maybe it wasn't a rival company that had developed invisibility armor. Maybe it was the Coromina Group. Maybe Dad was testing it—on me, on Isabel, on all of us. Maybe Private Sky had lied to me.

I rubbed my forehead. I felt suddenly very tired, and I knew snooping around the Connectivity Underground wasn't going to get me the answers I needed. It was just going to make me paranoid. Had I even seen a shape moving through the rain? In the dry safety of the house, it seemed impossible.

I wondered what Dad would do if I cornered him and demanded answers. That sort of thing had never worked before. But maybe I was finally old enough to do it right.

In my dream, the world rattled.

"Ms. Coromina! Ms. Coromina!"

The voice was far away and desperate. I couldn't quite latch onto it.

"Ms. Coromina! *Esme!*"

One last shudder and the dream was gone, forgotten, and I was stretched out at a crooked angle on my bed. Alicia hunched over me, her eyes red and scared, her face pale.

"You've got to come quick." Her voice brimmed with tears. "Quick, quick—down to the lawn—Mr. Coromina, he's on his way—"

I sat up, trying to rub the fuzziness out of my eyes and head both. Pale sunlight slipped through the windows. I'd stayed up late last night, waiting for Dad to come home so I could confront him. Except he never had, and I'd fallen asleep with my head full of questions.

"Please! You have to come right now! Something horrible has happened!"

Her words slammed into me, and for the first time, everything about this scene started to make sense. "Something horrible?" I stood up. "Isabel?"

Alicia stared at me, her lower lip trembling. Horror rose up in my throat. But she shook her head. "No. Rena. Ms. Coromina, Rena's—Rena's dead."

Everything froze. All I could hear was the roaring of blood in my ears. It reminded me of the village beach. I hadn't been there for months. Rena—

"Dead?" I whispered.

Alicia nodded. "They found her out on the lawn, near the hibiscus bushes, and—" Her voice turned into an atonal whine. *The hibiscus bushes.*

The flickers of movement.

The cold prickle on the back of my neck.

The sensation of being watched.

I fled the room. Alicia jumped away from me with a shout, then called out my name. I ignored her. I pounded through the hallways, my chest squeezing itself shut, adrenaline the only thing keeping me alive. The back entrance was crowded with the staff, all of them huddled together, some of them weeping: Mrs. Davesa, Grace, the gardener Claude, the faces all shiny with tears. When I burst into the room, every single one of them looked up at me like they'd never seen me before.

"Ms. Coromina!" cried out Mrs. Davesa. "We sent Alicia. It's terrible, terrible—"

"What happened? Where is she?" I pushed through the crowd, my whole body shaking. Through the distorted glass of the door's window I could make out the blurred shapes of the soldiers. "Are my sisters safe? Where is system security?"

"Your sisters are up in their rooms with one of the soldiers. I'm not sure they understand what happened, but they're being protected." Mrs. Davesa stepped close to me. She wore a mask of bravery. "System security is flying in from Undirra City. Mr.

Coromina has been contacted. Poor Claude found her a few minutes ago—he went to the soldiers first, and they asked us all to stay inside."

Of course they did. I plowed up to the door and flung it open. The early-morning light blinded me but slowly shapes came into focus—the hibiscus plants, the soldiers standing in a clump with their guns. One of them, I couldn't recognize his face in the shadow of his helmet, moved toward me, calling out my name.

"You need to go inside, Ms. Coromina. We don't know the extent of the situation—"

"What happened? Where is she?" I shoved forward. The soldiers shuffled closer together, trying to block my view, but in their movement, I saw a flash of pale skin.

Rena.

Rena's body.

My stomach lurched. I turned away, focusing on the hibiscus, looking for a flicker of movement, a shiver in the shadows.

But everything was still.

"Ms. Coromina, I have to insist you go back inside." The soldier's hand was on my arm. It was Private Sky-3—I recognized her voice. "We don't know what happened, and for your safety—"

My safety. Whoever had been there earlier was gone. There was no cold sensation on the back of my neck, no insistence in my head that I was being watched. *Dad, did Dad do this*—

"Let me see the body," I said in a soft voice, steeling myself.

"Ms. Coromina, I have to insist—"

"This is a direct order. Let me see the body."

Private Sky-3 fell silent. I watched her, waiting. Then she looked over at the other soldiers. Nodded once. They parted like the sea.

I told myself I wouldn't react, and I didn't. But there in the grass lay Rena, the woman who had raised me, her sternum split in two, a jagged bloody hole where her heart should have been. Everything else about her was pristine: her face, her bare limbs. I wondered if the rain had cleaned everything away.

Suddenly, all I could smell was blood. It reminded me of the scent of Undirra City, especially in the crowded quarters close to the docks. The world spun around, faster and faster, until the lawn and the garden and the soldiers and the planets in the sky flashed by me in an unintelligible blur.

Only Rena was still.

NOW

Esme met with her father in his office. He seemed to have shrunk inside his suit, his shoulders jutting out like folded wings. But when he peered up at her, he was the same man she'd always known, his eyes as hard and glittering as diamonds.

"Well?" he said. "What have you got for me?"

"I met with Daphne. She's agreed to come see you, although it will be in a few weeks' time, since she has to arrange her schedule around the schedule of the farm."

Her father nodded. "Excellent. Where are you with the others?"

Esme sighed. The windows looking out over the ocean were darkened, and the overhead lights were dimmed. The murkiness made her head spin. "I'm going to start looking into the records we have about Adrienne. I've got an appointment at Hawley Lab this afternoon about the breaches. I'm sure you read my report on Dasini."

"I did. It's troubling. But I thought Hawley had been cleared?" Her father frowned.

"Among the new recruits, yes." Esme shifted her weight. Eleanora Dixon had already been detained; Esme had received the notification that morning. She didn't want to think about it. "But one of the original R-Troop soldiers is stationed there. Sergeant Woods. Now that we know a breach is likely, Will wants to—to talk with him." They wouldn't really be talking, of course. Sharing thoughts. What Isabel had called Seeing, all those years ago.

Her father nodded. "Get that locked down," he said. "I want you focused on finding your sisters. So, you're going to look for Adrienne. What about Isabel?"

Esme tugged at her skirt. There were no records on Isabel at all— she had vanished the night Star's End had burned. "I'm going to ask Will to help with that. Because of his—connections."

She looked up at her father, wanted to see if there was any guilt in his expression. Any hint that he knew he'd done wrong.

He was unreadable.

"Good. Will's a good resource for finding Isabel." He leaned back in his chair, the springs creaking. He looked so pale in the dim light. Pale and old. Because of the rejuvenation treatments, all her life he'd appeared middle-aged, some graying in his black hair, some thin lines crossing out from his eyes. He preferred to look a little older, some throwback to when he was young, when the signs of experience could still earn respect. But right now, in the shadows, he almost looked his true age. Three centuries of life. He almost looked like a corpse.

"How are you doing?" she asked him. "Are the treatments working?"

"I don't want to talk about the galazamia," he said. "Get to your meeting. I want you working on finding the other two as soon as you can."

Esme's eyes narrowed. He had six months, he'd told her. She wondered if he'd been lying.

"Go, get out of here." He waved one hand dismissively. "I have some business to attend to."

Esme left. It wasn't worth questioning him further; she doubted he would be willing to talk about it in the building, anyway. You never knew who might have an ear in the wall. Homes were always safer for gossip.

She rode out to Hawley Labs even though it meant she would be early—she didn't want to go back up to her office, didn't want to respond to holos or check up on the progress for the latest upgrades to the R-Troops. She didn't really want to go to the labs, either, but at least there she would have Will at her side. He always made her feel calm.

The meeting on Dasini had unsettled her. The breach five years earlier had been difficult, a constant reminder of the last days of Star's End, of all those memories she had tried so hard, for a while, to forget. Now she let herself remember them. But who knew what another breach would bring.

Thirteen years earlier, she had watched Star's End burn as she and the rest of her family made their escape in a helicopter. This was what the last breach had forced her to remember. The fire had been so big and so bright that it had stained the ocean red. It was the last time she had seen Isabel, too, in the strange echoing space that belonged to the Radiance. Her father had put out a massive search for her, not, Esme knew, because she was his daughter but because of the secrets locked away inside her body. She was a security threat.

And she was gone.

This was what the Radiance did, Esme thought as she walked into the cool, climate-controlled corridor of the laboratory. They complicated everything.

She only had to wait a few moments for Will; he breezed in and smiled when he saw her. "Here we are again, huh? How was Catequil?"

She knew he was asking about Daphne, not Dasini. "It was fine." She stood up from where she'd been sitting. He already knew Daphne had agreed to come home; she had told him over holo when she had made the arrangements to go for a second meeting at the lab. But that had been a quick conversation, businesslike, and she hadn't wanted to talk about Daphne over Connectivity, anyway. "If you want to get lunch after this, I can tell you more."

"Sounds good to me." They walked down to the conference room. This time, it wasn't a lab assistant who was waiting for them but Dr. Goetze himself. He straightened up as they approached, smoothing one hand over the bald spot on the top of his head. "Ms. Coromina," he said. "Mr. Woods."

Esme smiled to put him at ease—this wasn't about a problem with his labs. It was a problem with the Radiance. "Well, this is an unexpected pleasure, Doctor."

Dr. Goetze's features flickered, as if he couldn't decide if he should smile or not. "Your message concerned me, Ms. Coromina. After the first interview, you said there was no sign of a containment breach."

Will stepped forward, gave his easy golden-boy grin. "And there wasn't. We're just here so I can link up with Sergeant Woods. A company matter."

"We explained this on the request," Esme said sweetly. Both of them, she and Will, acted as if this were routine, as if they had Dr. Goetze's best interests in mind. Lying was what business was all about.

Dr. Goetze frowned. "I read the request, yes. I'm just here to protect my own neck."

Esme did not let her smile falter. "I completely understand."

The three of them walked into the conference room. Dr. Goetze was ranked highly enough that he was allowed to listen in, even though Esme wished he wouldn't. The fewer people who knew, the easier it was to keep information within the right circles. But as a Level Ninety-Three, he had the right.

One soldier waited for them this time; one was all they needed for this. He was not a new recruit—he was, in fact, part of the original batch of R-Troops. He and Will had been brothers-in-arms, along with ten other soldiers. Half of those soldiers had been lost at Star's End. Esme could see his history reflected in the way his face, with all its standard features, seemed worn down. He watched them with a steely glint in his eye, his mouth a thin line. Unlike the recruits from the other day, he was not afraid.

"Sergeant Woods," Will said, giving him a nod. "It's been a long time."

Will and Esme sat down at the head of the table; Dr. Goetze stayed standing, hovering just behind Esme's shoulders. Sergeant Woods glanced up at him, scowling, looked back at Esme and Will.

"There's no breach," he said. "I monitor all the soldiers under my watch, and I know the other sergeants do too. If we see anything—any dreams, any voices, any of that shit—we cut off the infected soldier and close up their mind. The Radiance are not getting through here."

"We know that," Esme said. "We spoke to some of your soldiers the other day. This is about a potential breach on Catequil."

"Catequil?" Sergeant Woods frowned. "Why aren't you harassing the labs out there, then?"

Esme sighed. Will shifted in his seat—he might be uncomfortable; he might find this amusing. Sometimes it was hard to tell, with him and the R-Troops. Especially the last of the original squadron.

"The breach is tied to a weapons manufacturing factory," Esme said. "The workers there are not enhanced, but they are producing enhanced weaponry—specifically, the guns your fellow R-Troops can link up to in battle."

Sergeant Woods smirked a little, rolled his eyes. It caught Esme off guard, but she knew how to recover. "I asked Will to come and link minds with you to see if you can find anything. The worry is that the Radiance may be creeping in through the production process."

Sergeant Woods sat very still, watching her as if she were prey. He leaned back in his chair. "So, this is one of those espionage jobs?"

"Is that what they're calling them now?" Will asked.

Sergeant Woods gave a hard bark of a laugh. "You need to get out of the goddamn corporate system. You were always one of the best. You're too good a soldier to waste on this shit." He gestured at Esme, and she felt her cheeks warm. "But yeah, that's what we're calling it now. Ain't that what it is? Peeping in on them where they live? Sniffing around to see what they're up to?"

Will's shoulders hitched a little. "I suppose you could look at it that way."

Sergeant Woods looked at Esme. "You ought to go in and talk to them yourself sometime. Bet you'd be surprised by what you found."

"Sergeant," Dr. Goetze said sharply. "You're being insolent."

"It's fine," Esme said, looking at Sergeant Woods and not Dr.

Goetze. She didn't want the sergeant to know that his words had gotten to her. First Dasini, now Sergeant Woods—she thought she was used to these sorts of things. To the idea that some people had to be unhappy in order for a corpocratic system to function. But she realized now that she had only managed it because Isabel was gone. Because she had allowed herself to forget the extent of what the company had done to her sister. Of what they had done to the Radiance, too.

Esme sat unmoving as Will walked over to Sergeant Wood's side of the table. He sat down and they looked at each other. The R-Troop's mind-link didn't look like anything to an outsider. If Isabel were here, she'd know what they saw as they delved into each other's minds.

These soldiers, genetically engineered, infused with Radiance DNA, only existed because of Isabel. Because of what had happened to her. Esme thought she had come to terms with her own part to play in all of that a long time ago. She had come to terms with the fact that she had chosen to be like her father and not like her sisters.

But sitting in this stuffy conference, watching Will and Sergeant Woods speak with their eyes closed and their mouths shut, she knew she had been lying to herself.

Adrienne's records were waiting on Esme's lightbox when she came home after the meeting at the laboratory. She felt drained, indistinct. Will and Sergeant Woods hadn't found anything unusual when they dipped into the space where the Radiance lived. No sign of a breach. Dasini was going to have to go on lockdown until they got this sorted out.

When Will had left the lab, he seemed shaken. His skin was like ash. She didn't ask him what he'd seen, other than to confirm that there was no breach. She knew it could be difficult for him, connecting with his old squadron. Hardly any of them were left. Of the ones who had survived Star's End, a few had gone on to be killed in other wars, and the rest of the survivors were scattered throughout the galaxy.

Esme didn't open the file right away. The sight of it made her chest hurt, and so she left it, the lightscreen still up, beaming images into the clean air of her apartment. She ate a CG nutritional packet and her hunger slowly faded, along with the faint anxious churning in her stomach. The packets always did that; they were designed to calm in cases of emergency.

Esme sat down in front of her lightscreen and tapped on the file. It shimmered into existence on the air above her bed.

Adrienne Adele Coromina, the report said, *current whereabouts unknown*.

No surprise there.

The report listed Adrienne's past in chronological increments: *Year 2902 to 2920: Star's End in the village of Undirra, the continent of Izal, Ekkeko. Year 2920 to 2923: Marzal College in the city of Etzin, the continent of Starr, Quilla. Year 2923 to 2927: Jaconet College of Design in the city of Cordova, the continent of Starr, Quilla.*

Esme already knew all of this, and she knew about it in more depth: Adrienne had always wanted to work for the Coromina Group. She had studied for it under Mr. Garcia's tutelage for years, and she had trained for it with her internships as a teenager. But not long after Isabel left, so did she. Off to study art and then terraform design on Quilla. She messaged home sometimes. It was before Daphne had left. She had rarely spoken to Esme.

Esme deactivated her lightscreen. The report blinked out, and it took Esme's eyes a moment to adjust to the darkness.

Adrienne had stopped messaging when she graduated from Jaconet. She didn't come back to Ekkeko for holidays. Slowly, without Esme even realizing it, she vanished completely. Then Daphne left and there was no one. Star's End had been gone for nearly two years by then.

When Esme went to bed that night, she thought about the war as she waited to fall asleep. She thought about the R-Troops, the miracle that won the war. The weapons that were now the pride of the Coromina Group. Products, not employees. Certainly not citizens.

Slaves, Esme thought, staring blankly at the empty wall of her bedroom. Adrienne had said that, right before she left for college.

"They want freedom too. People shouldn't be weapons." And then she was gone.

The next morning, Esme asked her driver to take her by the tourist shacks along the Undirra expressway before work. She wanted a cup of coffee from Seaside Coffee, which grew their own beans on a farm down on the other side of the village and which had, in Esme's opinion, the best coffee in the village. She felt better this morning, after a night of deep and dreamless sleep.

"Wait here," she told the driver when he pulled up to Seaside Coffee. She didn't know why she said it; he would have waited anyway. But it was a politeness she wanted back. When they had unenhanced drivers, when she was younger, she had always thanked them.

The driver, for his part, just nodded and looked back at her, his eyes glowing blue from the Connection.

She climbed out of the car and crossed the lot and bought her coffee. The Seaside Coffee building stood in the same place that Laila's shrimp hut had, all those years ago. But the old seashell facade had fallen into disrepair and Laila had disappeared from Esme's life long before that. Esme ought to put in a request to find her. Probably have better luck than finding Adrienne.

She carried her coffee down to the overlook. The driver was still plugged into the car. She could see the blue of his eyes from there.

The overlook was always empty that early in the morning, and that time of year, there weren't many tourists, anyway. It faced the ocean glittering off in the distance. The water was red from the light of Coromina I, which was full and heavy-looking today. It hung low in the sky, and Esme sat down on top of a picnic table and watched the storms creep across its surface. Isabel used to read her fortune in those storms, although she never saw what eventually happened to her. Esme wished it were that easy, to look up at the clouds of Coromina I and find the answer to your questions.

The wind stirred the sea grass, bringing in the scent of fried plantains from the cluster of tourist shacks. If you ignored the whine of cars on the road, it was almost peaceful out there.

Her lightbox chimed.

"Wonderful," Esme muttered. She dug it out of her purse and activated it. The holo appeared, pale in the early morning sunlight.

It was her father.

"Just checking up on your progress on Adrienne," he said.

"There wasn't anything in her records I didn't already know." She balanced the lightbox on her knees, and her father's skeletal face hovered next to hers. He looked worse than she'd ever seen him, like a ghost. She resisted the urge to swipe her hand through the holo. "The last entry talks about her attending college on Jaconet."

"What?" Her father closed his eyes, defeated. "Are you sure there's nothing after that?"

Esme nodded.

"That's impossible. We keep pristine records; you know that. Even if she left the system, we'd still have a record of it."

Esme sipped her coffee and shrugged. "I guess the records have been blocked. Ever since she left college, there's no record of her at all."

Her father's holo stared at her. Seeing him this way, built out of light, just made him look all the more transparent, all the more weak.

"That's not possible." He frowned. "You put it through the official channels? You did—"

"I know how the system works," Esme said. "There must be some kind of block. Or the information got erased."

"That's not possible," he said. "You've got Ninety-Ninth clearance; there shouldn't be any blocks. And you know damn well no information is ever really erased. Not for a Ninety-Nine."

Esme didn't say anything. The wind stirred at her hair. There was a vein of coolness to it.

"Have you looked up—" He stopped. "Anyone else?"

A curious pain throbbed in her chest. He couldn't even say Isabel's name. "Not yet." She paused, trying to read his expression through the holo. She couldn't. "I'll keep looking into Adrienne, though. All I have to do is go down to the Records Office and scan in. Once they've got my clearance level established in person, it should be fine." She looked past her father's holo, out to the hazy crimson ocean in the distance. "I'll go there now."

"Let me know what you find out." And he switched off abruptly, the way he did when they were discussing business.

Esme sighed. She drained the last of her coffee and slipped her lightbox back in her purse. She wondered if she was right about the block, or if Adrienne had managed to vanish out of the system entirely. Maybe she'd learned the trick from Isabel. Esme knew there was no trace of her in the Coromina Group records, either.

The Records Office building was one of the newer Coromina Group buildings, more industrial than organic—lots of flat panes of reflective glass and white stucco walls. The car dropped Esme off in front of the entranceway and then zipped away, back to the enclave to pick up some other Coromina Group employee. Esme stared at her reflection in the glass door. People moved on the other side, as transparent as ghosts.

She took a deep breath and went in.

The lobby was crowded, but Esme rarely noticed crowds anymore, because they didn't affect her, not at the Ninety-Ninth level. She strode through the milling clumps of people, passing up the public elevators in favor of the high-ranking elevator tucked away behind a locked door. She pressed her thumb against the sensor and stepped into the hallway. The elevator was sleek and silver. "Citizen-Employee Records," she said. The elevator dinged to acknowledge her request.

"Fifteen seconds," the elevator said in its charming woman's voice. Esme crossed her arms. It was quiet there in the foyer, especially after the din of the lobby.

The elevator arrived and slid open. It was empty. Esme was the future CEO. She had a Ninety-Ninth-level security clearance. She never rode in an elevator with another person unless she wanted to.

The elevator took her to the twelfth floor. Citizen-Employee Records hummed like a beehive. Coromina Group employees scurried between the open office doors. The receptionist at the front desk was speaking to someone over the computer, but he waved at

Esme as she walked past. She'd never seen him before, but he had certainly recognized her.

She threaded over to Gerald Conto's office and knocked.

"Come in!"

Esme plastered on a smile and pushed the door open. Gerald had his holo up, his fingers dancing through the illuminated air. "Esme!" he called out. "Did you get the records you requested? Was there anything missing?"

"Yes, most of them." Esme sat down in his guest chair. Gerald looked at her through the hazy glow of the holo.

"Most of them?" He frowned. With a swipe of his hand, the holo disappeared. He leaned forward on his deck. "I'm afraid I don't understand."

Esme sighed. "My God, did you even look at that file?"

Gerald laughed and held up his hands. "You caught me. It's been crazy around here, so I just signed off on it, sent it on its way." He paused, watching her closely. Gerald never acted less than amiable, but if you looked him straight in the eye, you could see a streak of corporate savagery. He sized you up; he looked for weakness. And he always made you laugh as he did it.

"I understand. It's not anyone's fault." Esme laid her lightbox on the desk and activated the holo. Adrienne's whereabouts, ten years out of date, materialized on the air. "I suspect she's blocked her records."

"Strange." Gerald squinted at the holo and squeezed the bridge of his nose. "She must have connections, if she was able to pull that off. Legal or—*illegal*. I hear the anti-corpocracy hackers have been advertising for ways—"

"I'm sure it was legal," Esme said, even though she wasn't. She didn't know what to think, not about Adrienne, not anymore. "At any rate, I need the block removed."

"Well, then you better hope it's legal." Gerald chuckled. "Hard to remove a block that's not meant to be there."

Esme nodded, keeping her expression chilly if civil. She wished he wouldn't chatter on so much and instead would just find out what was wrong. She wanted to know where Adrienne was, she realized, and not because her father asked for it—but because *she* wanted to know. Maybe finding Adrienne would be a chance for her to apologize. She doubted very much their father cared about redemption. But Esme was starting to realize that she did.

"Good thing you came in." Gerald drew up his monitor again. "A lot of the Nineties end up thinking they can put in a digital request and we'll get it taken care of, and I've got to tell them every time: *Nope, need your DNA.*"

Esme gave him a polite smile. "How quickly will it take to lift the block?"

"Depends on who called for it. If it was your daddy, just a few seconds. Otherwise—" Gerald shrugged. "We'll have to take it from there, won't we?"

Her father hadn't put the block on the records; Esme knew that much. She sighed as Gerald reached into his desk and pulled out a portable sensor and set it down in front of Esme. She laid her forefinger on it, where she was greeted with tiny *zip* and a sharp, minute burst of pain. Gerald nodded in satisfaction at something only he could see on the sensor's screen.

"Looks like you are who you say you are." He grinned. "Seriously, though, it won't even work without your blood."

"I know," Esme said.

Gerald brought up his holo again. He was well trained enough to keep his face dispassionate. He had to know Adrienne was a relative, if not her sister—the name, the old address at Star's End. Gerald was old enough to remember Star's End.

"Ah, well, this is a bit of bad news."

Esme frowned. "What? What is it?"

"She married a Tarcza diplomat."

Esme was relieved to find that Adrienne hadn't turned to illegal means to erase her family. A diplomat—that sounded like her. Esme remembered the dinners where Adrienne wore the latest dresses and styled her hair the way girls did in the fashion feeds. She knew better than any of the sisters that fashion was a perfect shield. Fashion and courtesy. Esme was surprised that Adrienne hadn't become a diplomat herself.

But a diplomatic block was still a hindrance.

"I'm sorry, Ms. Coromina," Gerald said. "I can't lift the block without permission from the Tarcza government. You know they don't trust corpocratic systems."

"Yes," Esme said quietly, and disappointment settled around her.

"I can request the permission, if you wish."

Esme shook her head; there was no point. Adrienne would refuse it. Adrienne understood the importance of propriety. But she also knew how to hold a grudge.

"Thank you," she said, and she stood up, her emotions a bewildering churn in her belly. Pride at who Adrienne had become; disappointment that she was locked out completely.

Esme swept out of the office. *Will.* The R-Troops were spread out across all the militaries, including in Tarcza's house military—that was why there was a Tarczan embassy in the Coromina system in the first place. Will would be able to connect with those soldiers, maybe find her the information she wanted to know. If Will went after information about the diplomat and his wife, it would not tip off Adrienne as much if it were Esme asking questions.

Perhaps this was a sly way to approach the problem, but, Esme was sure, it would be worth it in the end.

That afternoon, after Esme contacted Will and told him her plan—he agreed, cheerfully, said he hoped he'd be able to find the information she needed—a driver showed up at Esme's office. Her admin assistant showed her in, and she blinked at Esme with the blank eyes all drivers have when they are not connected to a car.

"Your father," the driver said in a flat voice, "has requested you come to his home immediately."

Esme froze, her fingers lifted to her lightscreen. She stared at the driver.

"His home?" she said. "You mean he's not in the office?"

The driver shook her head. "I'm afraid I don't know anything more, only that it's urgent."

He's dead. The thought slammed into her like a punch. He'd looked terrible on the holo. But no—if he'd died, she wouldn't have found out this way. He wouldn't have been able to send a driver, for one. But he could be close. It could still be too late to bring home her sisters.

She gathered her things and followed the driver out of the office. On the ride to her father's home in the company enclave, she sent an encrypted message to Will: *We may have to hurry on finding my sisters, something's happened. More later.* Then she slumped down in the seat while the scenery whisked by. Her lightbox chimed; it was from Will. *Good luck.* She closed her eyes. Took deep breaths. The car slowed, and when she looked out the window, she saw they were passing by the big sprawling houses that belonged to the members of Coromina Group upper management. One of them could be hers if she'd wanted it. But she'd never bothered to upgrade.

Her father's house was tucked away in a cul-de-sac, surrounded by camphor trees and plumeria shrubs. The sight of them always made her chest hurt; but these plants were not sculpted like the plumeria at Star's End had been. They were not genetically engineered. They were just ordinary flowers.

A soldier stood outside the door, light rifle slung over his shoulder. He was linked into a scanner, and when he looked at Esme, she felt his eyes go straight through her. But he gestured for her to go in, and she did. Her father's house felt more like a tomb than it usually did. Everything was cold and sterile and there was a shivering reverberation as her heels clicked against the stone tiles. "Hello!" she called out into the foyer. "Dad? What's happened?"

"Esme." Miguel stepped out of one of the side rooms. "You made it. Thank God. He's been asking about you."

Esme felt a twinge of anger—why the hell did Miguel find out everything before she did? "What's going on?"

"I don't know. I just got here. He won't tell me anything without you."

Esme blinked in surprise. That was new.

"He looks bad, though. You may want to—to brace yourself."

Esme nodded. Her mind raced with worry. She and Miguel walked side by side, unspeaking, up the stairs. Esme realized she had no idea where her father's bedroom was in this house.

It didn't matter, though; a doctor was waiting at the end of the hallway, her back pressed against the wall, her hand pressed against her forehead. She lifted her gaze as Miguel and Esme approached and gave them a thin smile. "Good," she said. "You're here."

"Is he dying?" Esme spat out, even though it was a stupid question. Of course he was dying. But the doctor seemed to understand what she meant.

"He still has time. But he's getting worse, and he needs to . . ." The doctor took a deep breath. "He *has* to transfer power before the board finds out. I advised him to do it now."

Every cell in Esme's body went still. *Transfer power.* It was finally happening. Everything she had been groomed for since the moment she was born. At the same time, though, it felt too soon. Her plans with the immortality treatments—they weren't quite ready. And she had so much else to worry about.

And why was Miguel there? Was this one last trick of her father's, one twist of the knife?

"Go in," the doctor said. "He's waiting." She pushed the door open. Miguel stood back, let Esme go in first.

The room smelled of medicine, sharp and chemical. Her father sat in a tremendous bed in the center of the room, blankets folded around his waist. Seeing him was a shock. He looked even more like a corpse, like a skeleton, than he had on the holo. The final stages of zamia came on fast. He lifted his head, blinked his sunken eyes.

"Esme," he said roughly. "I'm sorry you have to see me like this."

Esme stumbled forward. Her eyes were heavy, like she might start crying. She didn't know what exactly she would be crying over— was she really going to grieve for him the way she had grieved for her mother? It seemed impossible. But maybe that wasn't it at all. Maybe it was just that seeing him reminded her that death eventually came for everyone.

"Philip," Miguel said. His voice startled Esme. He rushed to the side of the bed. "You look—"

"I look like a three-hundred-year-old man dying of galazamia." Esme's father croaked out a laugh. "I'm sure both of you know why you are here."

Did they? Esme glanced over at Miguel again, but he was just staring at her father in horror.

"I'm not dead yet," her father said. "And the doctor says I have a few months left in me." He turned his gaze on Esme when he said this, and she knew that it was his way of warning her—*You have two months to get your sisters back to me*. "But I can't go into the office looking like this. The board's already started asking questions."

Esme's chest was getting tighter and tighter. She squeezed at the cuffs of her jacket, her palms damp with sweat.

"We need to change over the power," her father said. "Esme, you will take my place as CEO."

All her life, she had known this would happen. And yet hearing it now felt like a cold wind.

"Miguel, you will take on Esme's old job, of Vice President of Genetics. You two will run the company in my stead." Her father looked between them. His neck was so thin, it seemed incapable of balancing his head. His mouth seemed too red. "The board may try to wrest power from you. Don't let them. Work together to protect yourselves."

A cough rose up in her father's chest, like tectonic plates shifting beneath the surface of a planet. He doubled over, spots of blood splattering across the bedsheets. Esme's stomach twisted. The doctor rushed in—Esme hadn't even realized she was in the room—and pressed a med needle against the side of his neck. The coughing subsided and he rolled to his back, swatted the doctor away. She stepped back, her face grim.

"I'm fine," he said. "We need to make everything official. I have the files set up on my lightbox. You two just need to get scanned."

Miguel nodded, his eyes wide with barely concealed excitement. Esme felt dizzy. All this power being handed over to her. It was early, yes, but she could still finally run the company the way she wanted, the way she'd promised herself all those years earlier. And it wasn't as if she were completely unprepared. She would just have to contact the scientists working on the immortality treatments, let them know it was time to switch over, that their research needed to focus on eradicating diseases, not living forever.

Her father pressed a button laid into the frame of his bed, and a holoscreen appeared, flooding the room with light. There were the files, just as he promised. Esme stared at hers, at her official image staring back at her. It had been taken last year, and even then there was a tiredness around her eyes.

"It needs your DNA signature," her father said. "I have it set with a scanner. Just walk right through. Miguel, you go first."

Miguel glanced over at Esme. He was beaming. She gave him a thin smile in return and wondered if he would try to undermine her somehow, try to find a way to steal her power. He was ambitious enough, but his ambition had always felt benign.

He took a deep breath and stepped through the holo. The image shimmered around him like stars. When he was on the other side, the official title on his file had changed: VICE PRESIDENT, GENETICS.

"Esme." Her father's voice was rough in her ear. Power, she thought. All the power in the Coromina Group. She could do whatever she wanted.

Maybe she could finally become someone other than her father.

Esme could feel her father watching her. She wondered if he'd ever thought it would be this easy. Just watch her walk through a curtain of light and have everything taken away from him.

She stepped up to the holo. She could feel the energy radiating off it. And when she crossed the boundary, she held her breath. The scanner pricked at her skin like tiny needles, and when she came through to the other side, she felt as if a layer of herself had been stripped clean away.

"It's imperative you find your sisters," her father said suddenly, his voice startling her. "I need them in person, too."

Esme turned to look at him. The prickling dizziness of the holo faded away. Of course. She had always known it wasn't just about redemption.

"The board," her father said, coughing a little. "The board could use them. They have to abdicate their portions of the company—I'm just trying to protect you, Esme. Protect you both."

"Of course," Miguel said.

Esme nodded. She glanced over at the holo, the light filling up the room. It wasn't the abdication itself that bothered her—the truth was, it would protect them, too. They could no longer be used for bargaining pieces if the board found them first. But some part of Esme had hoped her father had changed, even if she hadn't let herself believe it. Some part of her had hoped he really had just wanted to apologize.

She should have known better.

Esme invited Will to have dinner at her condominium, and to talk about what to do next. It felt like the safest option. She certainly wasn't willing to discuss things at the office, where the board might have found a way to listen. Out in public wasn't always safe either. But in her own home, where she controlled the surveillance, she felt secure.

She laid out the food she had ordered on the table—herb-crusted fish, a rice pilaf, vegetables that were grown in the Coromina Group gardens—and then poured herself a glass of sweet white wine. She knew not to offer Will any; the R-Troops never drank alcohol. It interfered with their system of unspoken communication.

"I have some good news," Will said, cutting into his fish. "I think I found Adrienne."

Esme looked up at him. She had been so preoccupied with her promotion that she hadn't given much thought to Will's own search. "And you didn't tell me when I contacted you earlier?"

Will grinned. "I wanted to tell you in person. See your expression."

Esme smiled, shook her head. She hadn't told him she was CEO of the company yet. She wondered if that would change the way he treated her.

Or if he'd already been treating her the way he would a CEO. Technically, she owned him. Technically, she could control him if she wanted.

"She's in the system," Will went on. "On Amana."

"Really?" That was a stroke of luck, that Esme wouldn't have to make the jump to the Tarcza system. It would be easier to get to Adrienne, at least.

"Yeah. I'll give you the address and such when we're done

with dinner. I didn't want to transmit it over Connectivity, even encrypted." He looked up at her, his fork hovering in midair. His eyes gleamed. "Given the way I, ah, acquired the information. I don't imagine either CG or Tarcza would be happy to know that I linked up with a Tarczan R-Trooper."

The food on Esme's plate suddenly looked lumpish and unappetizing. "I shouldn't have asked you to do that," she murmured, before taking a long pull of her wine. When she set it aside, Will was staring at her, frowning.

"I didn't mind," he said.

Did he mean it? Esme studied him. She couldn't tell. Sometimes, he kept his emotions tucked away inside of him. She couldn't always read his expressions.

"Well, I appreciate it," she said. She hesitated. Her mouth felt too dry. "I have some news of my own, by the way."

"Oh?"

Esme nodded. She lifted her gaze to meet Will's. He blinked at her, expectant.

"Dad made the transfer," she said. *Just spit it out, get it over with.* "I'm CEO of the Coromina Group now."

It felt wrong, saying it out loud, as if the rules of the universe were coming undone. For a moment, the room drowned in silence. Then Will broke into a bright smile, and he became more human than Radiance. "Congratulations!" he said. "Shouldn't you be drinking something nicer than that?" He nodded at the wine. "Or, for that matter, having dinner out at the Veiled Garden or something?"

Esme's cheeks warmed. "I'm perfectly fine having dinner at home." *With you,* she thought, although she didn't say it.

Will laughed. "Staying humble, then. That's good."

They ate for a few moments longer—well, Will ate, and Esme picked at her food, her stomach still roiling around, so she didn't have much of an appetite. Then she said, "I think I'll go see Adrienne in person."

Will paused. "Yes," he said. "I think that would be a good idea."

"I should do it as soon as possible." Esme pushed her food around. "Dad's probably going to die soon." A knot formed in the base of her throat as she thought back to the sight of her father in his bed, as if his atoms were collapsing in on themselves. She could never imagine him dying. Even when she had received word that her mother had died, in battle, the way she would have wanted—even when faced with that reality, Esme couldn't imagine her father dying. Her mother, she had expected to die someday. Her father had expected to find immortality, to cheat the universe of his death.

And he lost. One of the few failures in his life. But she could use his failure to shape the future of the company.

Esme pushed away from the table and grabbed her lightbox. She felt a weight on her shoulder—Will's hand, she realized with a start. She looked over her shoulder at him.

"She's living in Santos," he said softly. "Her house has a name instead of an address. Let me get the information for you."

Esme nodded. Santos. It made sense. It was one of the more fashionable cities in the Four Sisters. A place artists lived, trying to keep away from the scrutiny of the company.

"Here," Will said, taking her lightbox. He pressed his own lightbox against it, like a kiss, and then activated her lightscreen. The information flowered into place. Adrienne Lanka, wife to the Tarczan diplomat Oliver Lanka. So, she really had stripped all remnants of her family. Hadn't even kept her name, as was custom here and on Tarcza too. No Adrienne Coromina Lanka, like tradition dictated. No attempt at honoring her father's name.

"There," Will said. "Winslow Place. Should be easy to locate."

"Yes." Winslow Place. The name wasn't familiar to Esme, but that probably just meant that it was some embassy house belonging to Tarcza.

The alert light began blinking on Esme's lightbox. Bright white and urgent. She sighed, tapped it. A holo of Asenka Wymer, one of the board members, materialized in the air of Esme's apartment. She jerked back, startled.

"I see it's already starting," Will murmured.

"This encrypted message is for Esme Coromina only," Asenka's holo said in a prim, stiff voice. "Room scan will begin in ten, nine, eight . . ."

Esme looked at Will apologetically. "Guess you better wait out-side."

"I wonder what would happen if I stayed?" he asked, although he was already on his way to the door.

"Nothing good."

He slipped out into the hallway just as Asenka said, "One." A bright blue light flashed out of Esme's lightbox, blinding her for half a second. Then it faded, leaving ghostly impressions glimmering in its wake.

"Room clear," Asenka said, and the holo flickered; Asenka's image jerked to the left, leaving her in a different position from where she started. "Esme," she said, her voice still prim. "Let me be the first to congratulate on your promotion to CEO."

Esme smiled, because really, it was Will who held that honor.

"I look forward to working with you. Because of the sudden nature of this changing of the guard, so to speak, the rest of the board and I have agreed it best to call a meeting tomorrow morn-ing, to discuss what these changes mean for the company and how we wish to proceed. Your presence, of course, is strongly requested."

That meant *required*. Esme sighed. She would have to attend the meeting, then fly out to Amana to face her sister. A meeting like this should have been inevitable. She knew damn well it wasn't out of concern for the company but out of the board's concern for itself. They wanted to know what new power structures she would bring to the company. What new games she would play. If she was weak, or if she was strong, without the presence of her father always lurk-ing overhead.

"Please confirm here if you'll be able to attend," Asenka said, just as a message screen appeared, floating near her head. *Yes, I'll be there* versus *No, not this time*. Esme stared at it for a moment. She knew it was only the illusion of a choice. Say no, and the board would descend on her. She'd be out of power before her father's death.

She was going to have to prepare something, too. Some show of strength. She already knew what it would be, because she'd been preparing for it for the last five years. Perhaps it was a bit prema-ture. She didn't care. She could work around the problems.

She looked at the door leading out to the hall, the door Will was waiting on the other side of. She thought of the last time she'd seen Isabel. The entire night had been red with flames.

Esme confirmed her attendance.

Esme made sure she arrived at the board meeting fifteen minutes early, a guarantee that the board would not attempt to pass any decisions without her presence. Doing so was technically forbidden, of course, as she was now CEO, but that had never stopped anyone in the Coromina Group from playing their games when it was prudent.

She was not the first to arrive; Miguel was there already, but she wasn't worried about him. He gave her a quick smile of solidarity, which she returned. Then she slid into the chair at the head of the table. Her father's chair.

Not anymore, she reminded herself.

Esme took a deep breath. She set up her lightbox. Then she reached under the table and found the button that would turn the windows transparent, so they would have a view of the landscape during the meeting. A small thing, but it would let in the reddish light of Coromina I, which was waning in the west. A reminder to the rest of them of who she was, where she came from.

She had her plan. It was not going to make the board happy. It wasn't going to make her father happy, either. But she'd been preparing for this moment for a long time.

"How's it feel?" Miguel asked as the dark tint in the windows slowly faded away. He leaned forward over the table, his eyes bright. "Being CEO?"

Esme paused, considering. "I've been expecting this since I was a little girl," she finally said. "But I still didn't expect it to happen so soon."

Miguel nodded sagely. What Esme did not tell him was that the knowledge that an entire planetary system was now her responsibility was like an ocean pressing down on top of her. She did not tell him that nearly thirty years earlier, she had promised herself that she would keep her sisters safe, and she had failed at that.

What business, then, did she have protecting the people of the Four Sisters?

The door swung open; it was Kara Bewick Skillings, the oldest member of the board. A potential ally, too, as she had no real interest in a true leadership position within the company. She had been a friend of Esme's father early in his career; she had taken the same rejuvenation treatments as him, so although she was two hundred and fifty, she looked as if she were in her forties, a sleek curtain of silver hair the only real acknowledgment of her advanced age. She nodded at Esme and Miguel, gave her congratulations.

Esme's heart thudded. She took deep, paced breaths, hoping she wasn't being too obvious. The other board members trickled in, sometimes alone, sometimes in pairs. Esme took notice of the order, of the partnerships—Martin Lieb and Tyrel Shew could be a problem, as could Ollie Mata. When Flor DeCrie breezed in, her hair curled and teased so that it draped around the line of her neck like she was some Amanan immersion star, Esme felt herself go stiff. She had not seen Flor in years. She had always delegated any necessary interactions with her. But she was not going to let Flor's presence unravel her.

Flor slid into the seat near Esme and flashed her a bright smile. She didn't look any older than she had thirteen years before. Esme knew that she did; she had only started her rejuvenation treatments two years earlier, when she turned forty. Flor had always been meticulous with hers.

"I was so happy to hear the news," Flor said through bared teeth.

"So was I," Esme said. She was not going to think about what she had done to Isabel.

What her father had done to Isabel.

What she had done to Isabel.

When the last board member slid into the room, Esme did not waste any time. She looked coolly out at the board, meeting the gaze of all eight of them, including Flor. Flor's eyes glinted like diamonds. Had some part of her thought she might make CEO someday if she did everything Esme's father asked of her, even the unthinkable?

"Let me begin," Esme said, "by thanking Asenka Wymer for

suggesting we have this meeting. I agree that it's prudent to discuss our positions going forward, now that my father has stepped down from his position."

Some of the board members nodded; Esme made note of which ones.

"With that in mind," Esme said, "I'll hand the reins over to Asenka so that she can state any questions or concerns she might have."

Always good to start with a show of generosity. To not let them know she understood what this meeting was really about: a way of undermining her power.

Asenka coughed into her fist. "Yes, thank you, Ms. Coromina. I don't have concerns, per se."

Esme kept her expression blank.

"But I did want to get a sense of your plan for the company," she continued. "Do you plan on continuing your father's work?"

Esme's heart pounded harder. Her face felt hot; sweat dripped along her spine. So, Asenka was going straight into it. She was not going to dance around the subject. She was going to lay everything in the open.

Everyone, including her father, expected the answer to that question to be *yes*. Her father had not died yet; he would still want to exert control over the company. And she would let him, in certain ways. But not in this one way. She couldn't do it anymore. She had decided this nearly five years earlier, when she started up the immortality research, hiring scientists who were loyal to her and who understood that the immortality work was a temporary cover for her real plans.

"For the most part," Esme said.

The board members shifted in their seats. Exchanged glances. Murmured to one another.

"Oh?" Asenka tilted her head, eyes curious. "And what does that mean, exactly?"

Esme took a deep breath. She gazed down the table. She had never seen this room from this position before. The window opposite her looked out in the direction of where Star's End had been. It was already overgrown, a green tangle hiding the charred remains of her childhood home. She could see the village, though, the little houses like toys among the greenery.

When Esme spoke, her throat was dry and scratchy. Her head spun. She kept her gaze fixed on the ghost of Star's End.

"I'm shutting down weapons manufacture," Esme said.

FOURTEEN YEARS EARLIER

Dad wanted to see me, which couldn't mean anything good. Anytime he called me into his suite at Star's End, it meant bad news. A potential security breach somewhere in the lower tiers of the company. OCI uncovering classified company secrets. He was transferring me out of Planet Maintenance and into Genetics.

I sat on his sofa, waiting for him. The windows were propped open, an electronic insect screen buzzing in the background. Occasionally, a bug would fly into it and it would let out a *snap* like a piece of plastic breaking in half. It was the dry season, and the heat pressed down over Star's End. I didn't know why he had the window open. I was already sweating in my simple cotton clothes.

Dad strode in from the back of his suite. He glanced at me but didn't say anything, just poured himself some water from the chilled pitcher sitting on the coffee table. "Want some?" he asked.

"Yes," I said. "Why is it so hot in here? Why do you have the windows open?"

"I like the heat." He poured me a glass. These days, he treated me like one of his trusted employees. "When you get as old as me, you need it, like a lizard. The rejuvenation treatments only go so deep. You should start thinking about starting those, by the way. Twenty-eight is pushing it."

He handed me the water and I took it and drank greedily. "Maybe I'll start a new trend of looking older." I wanted out of this room. Sweat beaded around my forehead. Dad didn't laugh, only frowned, then dropped the subject.

"So, I wanted to talk with you about something." Dad sat on the couch beside me, crossing his ankle over his knee. *No shit*, I thought, but I knew better than to say anything.

"About Isabel, specifically," he said. "I think it's time we get her an internship."

I frowned. Isabel was only fourteen. "Isn't she too young?"

"She's about the age I was when I had my first job," Dad said. "Working on the Martian docks. I guarantee a cushy internship in the Psych department will be a hell of a lot safer."

"The Psych department?" A strange choice for a fourteen-year-old. Psychology was a euphemism, really, for what they did—it was the propaganda department, a subset of the company focused on deciding the best ways to make changes and reveal information to the citizen-employees of the Four Sisters with minimal outcry.

"They need an admin," Dad said, shrugging. "Someone to help with filing and the like. It'll be easy work, and it'll give her something to do besides watching Amanan dramas all day."

I looked over at the window, at the insect screen letting off its thick, wavy lines of energy. An admin in the Psych department. I looked at this decision from all angles, trying to see what Dad really wanted there. But I found nothing. Psych was actually responsible for the dramas Isabel loved so much, so it made sense, in a weird sort of way, to place her there. Admin work was pretty typical for a first internship. Both Adrienne and Daphne had just started theirs, too, Adrienne at Terraforming and Daphne in Planetary Resources. It felt too altruistic for Dad, to have all three of them start around the same time, but perhaps he had some self-serving reason for doing so. I studied him, trying to read his face the way I could clients. But he was always unreadable.

"You don't approve?" he said, raising an eyebrow. "I know you've taken it on yourself to be mother to those girls."

"You mean your daughters?" I snapped back.

Dad didn't even flinch.

"I just don't understand why you want to start her so young," I finally said, leaning back against the sofa. "I mean, fourteen?"

"She's old enough," Dad said. "I want their positions in the company squared away. If it makes you feel any better, you can oversee her internship. Make sure Flor DeCrie isn't mistreating her."

"Flor?" I frowned. "Why the hell is Flor her supervisor?"

Dad sipped from his glass. "She transferred there last year," he said. "Wanted a change of scenery."

I sighed. Psych was a strange department for someone who had once worked out at Catequil. At least Dad had been up front about it. "That does make me feel better," I told him, glad it was someone I'd worked with. Flor was generally willing to listen, to reach agreements. "Thank you."

Dad nodded, stood up. "Then it's settled. I'll speak to Isabel, let her know the plan. I hope to get her started in the next few days."

I didn't say anything, even though I thought he was moving too quickly. There had to be a reason for it—I just wished I could see what it was. At least he was going to let me keep an eye on her. That was something.

Dad moved across the room, toward the hallway. My cue to leave. I drank the last of my water and slipped out, back into the cool climate-controlled hallway. It was like stepping onto another world.

Two days later, I rode to work with Isabel. I felt uneasy with her scrunched up in the seat beside me, gazing out the window as the scenery bled by. She was as awkward as I had been at that age, but it was a different sort—she was gangly rather than hulking, a tangle of arms and legs that meant she'd probably grow up to look like her mother, just as I had grown up to look like mine.

"Are you nervous?" I asked her.

She shook her head, still staring out the window. I wondered if she was telling the truth.

"Good."

"Daphne said it shouldn't be that bad," Isabel went on. She curled a piece of her glossy black hair around one finger. "And she said Psych puts out *The Intensity of Days*."

"It does," I said. "Maybe you'll get to meet one of the actors."

Isabel shrugged. "They all live on Amana, don't they?"

"Yeah, but they come to headquarters sometimes." This was a bit of a stretch, but I could tell she was nervous, even if she insisted she wasn't. "So, you could get lucky."

Isabel finally turned away from the window and looked at me. She studied me very closely, the way she always did with people, as if she were trying to memorize their features.

"Can I ask you something?" Isabel said.

"Of course." I hoped it would be a question I could answer—the truth was, I didn't know much about Psych. I'd been so wrapped in Genetics these last few years, as well as my personal PM projects, that I hadn't paid it much mind.

"You know how I like to go into the woods? To visit the grave-yard?"

I blinked, startled. What did this have to do with her internship?

"Well, I was out there the other day and I saw this man with some kind of machine, a lightbox, maybe, and he was scanning the trees and it was—weird." She looked down at her lap, her hair fall-ing around her shoulders. "He didn't see me. I mean, I tried to stay hidden. But I just—do you think that's why Dad is making me do this internship?"

I stared at her, bewildered. A man with a lightbox in the woods? What could that possibly have to do with an early internship? I had been part of the company long enough to know that you shouldn't dismiss possible conspiracies as coincidence, but I couldn't see the connection there at all. Even my own concern about Dad's motiva-tions didn't fit.

"What did the man look like?" I finally asked.

"Just a guy," Isabel said—quickly, I thought. "He was wearing a CG uniform."

"It wasn't one of the soldiers, was it?"

She shook her head, looked at me with dark, imploring eyes. "Why would he be scanning the trees?" she said. "It was so strange. Do you think the flu is back?"

I stiffened. No, it wasn't the flu. I was high-ranked enough to know about that. But this, a man scanning the trees? I hadn't heard anything. I wondered if it was related to Project X. Dad still hadn't let me in on that one yet.

"Dad's got something going on," I said. "Very high-clearance. I imagine it's related to that. But I can't tell you anything more."

"Because I don't have the clearance?" Isabel asked.

"Because I don't. I don't know why that man was in the woods. If I hear anything, I'll tell you, but until then—it's not something you need to worry about, okay?" I wanted to tell her more, wanted to find out all the details I could, wanted to warn her to stay away from CG men in the forest. But we were almost to the office, and I didn't want to scare her. I'd look into it on my own. She didn't need to harbor company conspiracies. That was my job.

I had instructed John to bring us around to the Psych department rather than dropping me at the usual place. I hadn't spent much time in the Psych building, not even during my PM days—PM was about making things easier for our citizen-employees, whereas Psych was really about making things easier for the company. It was a newer building, a shining glass-and-stone structure that jutted out sharply against the backdrop of the orgobuildings that made up the rest of the campus. I glanced over at Isabel; she was staring out the window, her eyes wide, her mouth hanging open.

"This is where Dad wants me to work?" she breathed.

"Apparently." The car pulled to a stop and I stepped out. A hot, dry breeze ruffled my hair. Isabel scurried over to my side, tilting her head back, peering up through the trees. Coromina I rose over the horizon, an angry red bruise in the sky.

"The Luca configuration is close," Isabel said without looking at me. "That means chaos, you know."

I smiled, didn't say anything. I never had the heart to tell her astrology was nonsense. But Isabel had it all worked out, how Adrienne and Daphne had been born when Catequil was approaching Coromina I, and so they were strong-willed and skeptical. Or how I had been born when Coromina I was ascending, which made me a natural leader.

"I'm not sure this was the best day to start my internship," Isabel said.

"It'll be fine." I put my hand on the space between her shoulder blades and guided her toward the doors. They slid open with a sigh and we walked together into the Psych lobby, a big room filled with red-tinted sunlight, like all the lobbies in the Coromina Group. Flor was waiting for us. She looked the same as she had the last time I'd seen her, a few years before on Catequil, her skin glossy with the rejuvenation treatments.

"Esme!" she cried, strolling toward us. I put my hand on Isabel's shoulder, wanting suddenly to protect her. How much did I know about Flor, really? We worked well together, but she'd always struck me as the ambitious type, and moving from Genetics to Psych was not an ambitious move. Maybe I could find some internship for Isabel in Genetics. She could file for me, not for Flor and whatever she was scheming about in Psych.

But Isabel stepped away from me, sliding out from under my touch. She blinked up at Flor. Sizing her up, the way she always did with new people. Even with us, sometimes.

Flor gave her a big, shining smile. "And you must be Isabel," she gushed. "I've heard so much about you."

I wondered from where. Dad? It seemed doubtful. But it was the right thing to say to Isabel, because her shoulders loosened a little.

"Yes," Isabel said softly.

"Only good things." Flor looked up at me. Her eyes were sharp and intelligent. She looked at me like I was a rival—most people didn't, since most everyone in the company knew I would be CEO someday. "We'll take good care of her over here at Psych; don't worry."

"Glad to hear it." I returned her gaze. I didn't want to leave Isabel there. I felt like I was setting her up as a pawn in some kind of convoluted Coromina Group power struggle. But then Isabel turned toward me and said, "Don't worry, Esme. I'll be fine."

I started; she did that sometimes, say something like she knew what I was thinking. I nodded. "You know you can contact me through the campus Connectivity if you need anything."

Isabel nodded, just as Flor said, "Oh, we'll be just *fine*. You'll have lots of fun interning with us, I promise." She circled her arm around Isabel's shoulders and guided her toward the elevators. "You know we work with Amana to produce the dramas, right?" she said to Isabel. Isabel nodded silently. "Do you watch them? I've only been able to keep up with *The Intensity of Days* myself—"

I stood in the lobby until they had stepped into the elevator. Flor kept chattering away, and Isabel gave me a little reassuring wave. I told myself I didn't need to worry. That both of the twins had internships, and they were fine. No one played games with them. It was just because Isabel was the youngest. I'd always been over-protective of her, ever since she vanished for a day back when she was younger.

I left Psych and followed the walking paths back to Genetics. The storms churned across Coromina I's surface. No one was out; it was too hot to be outside, really. But I needed the time to calm myself.

That first day of Isabel's internship, I waited for her to contact me over Connectivity. My eyes kept flicking over to the signal light on my lightbox, and if it was blinking, my heart leapt high in my chest—but it was never Isabel.

I went home early that evening. Isabel was already there, sitting out in the pineapple garden watching *The Intensity of Days* on Adrienne's lightbox. The actors' faces danced in ghostly patterns above the lawn, all the colors leached out from the bright sunlight. Coromina I had set; the light was ordinary again, lemony and clear.

"How was it?" I said, kneeling down in the grass beside Isabel.

"Boring," she said. "They made me sign a bunch of waivers, and then I had to organize some files."

Adrienne reached over and paused the display. "So, you didn't get to hang out with any actors?"

Isabel rolled her eyes. "It was exactly what you said it was."

That made me feel better. Boring was good. I stood up, dusting the grass from my skirt. The girls turned back to the projector. They were more involved in whatever the love affair of the week was than anything I had to say.

A week or so went by. Isabel went back to the company one more time—more filing, she reported over dinner that evening. My worry finally started to subside. It didn't help that a huge order came in from the Spiro Xu military, and I spent all day in a holo-meeting, having long, encrypted conversations with the Spiro Xu representative as she argued with my scientists about the specific features the military wanted in their new soldiers.

Things carried on. We fell back into our usual patterns. I spent longer and longer days at the office, something I hated doing, but the military requests kept pouring in, one after another, and it felt like every single one got diverted to me personally. I barely had time to catch up with my sisters. Mostly I'd just see them at breakfast, when they were bleary-eyed and sleepy, and I had an entire day to deal with at the office.

But then one afternoon, I came into my office after a particularly exhausting lunch with some reps from the science division, and a message was waiting for me on my lightbox. I figured it was yet another military with some complaint or another about production taking too long, but when I played it, Adrienne's face materialized above my desk, her eyes wide and her face pale.

"Esme," she said. "I hope you get this soon. You need to come home, okay?"

My whole body went very still. I gripped the edge of my desk to keep myself from toppling over.

"Daphne and I—" Her voice wavered and it was like a stab through my heart. "We're really worried, okay? Please come home. I know you're busy but you need to come home."

The message flicked off, and for a moment, I just stared at the empty light radiating above my desk. Then everything became a blur. I locked down my lightbox and grabbed my things and rushed out of the office, shouting at my admin to take any messages for me. My thoughts were a riot. Isabel. I knew it was Isabel. She had disappeared again.

I cursed at myself as I rode the elevator to the first floor, as I waited for my car to come around and pick me up. All those projects—had they been piled up on top of each other on purpose to distract me? But no, Flor didn't have that kind of power.

Did she?

"Hurry," I told John, sliding into the backseat of the car. He glanced back at me, brow knitted in concern.

"Everything okay?" he asked.

"I don't know. Just—just hurry." My heart was pounding so hard, I couldn't catch my breath. John jerked the car out of the drive and sped down the freeway. I pulled up my portable lightbox and put in a call for Adrienne. She didn't answer. Neither did Daphne. I took a deep breath and whispered Isabel's code. The holo shimmered above my wrist. Isabel never appeared.

"Fuck," I said, and shut the whole thing off. I couldn't tell where we were on the freeway; everything was a blur, green forest and blue sky. I sighed and slumped back against my seat.

"Almost there, Ms. Coromina," John said. "I told the car it was an emergency. Should have shaved off about ten minutes of our drive."

"Thank you." Staring out the window left me queasy, so I stared up at the ceiling of the car. A thought came creeping in, cold and unsettling: I had been so tied up with work that I had ignored my sisters. And that was something our father would do.

The car slowed; John pulled up to the front of Star's End. It looked closed off, all the doors and windows shut tight against the dry-season heat. I flung myself out of the car and raced up the walkway and slammed in through the front door. "Adrienne!" I shouted. "Daphne! Isabel!" My voice rebounded off the walls. I kept flashing back to that day Isabel vanished as a child. It had been the rainy season, I remembered. Everything damp and cool.

"Ms. Coromina!" Alicia bustled around the corner. "Oh, I'm glad you're here. I keep trying to get ahold of Mr. Coromina, but he's not answering, and Daphne is so upset—"

"What's happening?" I said, stopping her. "I got a message from Adrienne but she wouldn't tell me what was wrong."

Alicia sighed, her shoulders hitching. "Isabel," she said. "She's disappeared again."

I had expected her to say this, but hearing it just made me feel dizzy and light-headed. At least she wasn't six years old this time. "Have you sent anyone to look for her in the village?" I said. "I used to sneak down there when I was her age."

"Not yet. We've been sweeping the woods. But I can send one of the maids to go down there. Maybe Lily? They've always gotten along."

I nodded, then told her I was going to talk to Adrienne. I remembered when this happened before, I'd been swept up in a panic. But this time, I just felt numb.

The door to Adrienne's room was hanging open, and I could hear her and Daphne murmuring softly to each other inside. I knocked and went in. They were both draped on the couch, and Daphne's eyes were red from crying.

"Esme, you're here!" Adrienne jumped up from the sofa and threw her arms around me.

"Alicia told me what happened," I murmured into the soft flower-scented sweetness of her hair. "Why didn't you answer your holo?"

"We wanted to talk to you about it in person," Daphne said.

I looked over at her. She rubbed furiously at her eyes.

"Daphne—we—we think this has to do with Isabel's internship," Adrienne said.

The room seemed to lurch, throwing us all sideways. So, I wasn't the only one with paranoid suspicions. But I didn't want the girls to know that. I needed to soothe them over, calm them down. Then I could find out what was happening.

"Why do you think that?" I asked carefully, walking Adrienne back over to the sofa. Daphne watched us with hard eyes. "Did Isabel say anything to you?"

"No," Adrienne said.

"The whole thing just feels suspicious," Daphne said as I sank into the sofa beside her. "She wasn't supposed to have an internship this young! And now she's gone."

"Wait," I said. "Start at the beginning. We need to be methodical."

I didn't feel methodical. I wanted to jump up and storm up to my father's suite and rip his expensive light paintings from the walls until he gave me answers. But I was the eldest. I was the adult. I couldn't act like a child to get what I wanted. "When did you notice she was missing?"

"This afternoon," Daphne said. "That's when we decided to send you the holo, and we told Alicia so she and the soldiers could start looking in the woods."

"Like last time," Adrienne said.

"Yes." I hesitated. "I remember then, she had said something to you about meeting friends?" A wild shot in the dark, but Daphne just rolled her eyes.

"She doesn't have imaginary friends anymore," Daphne said furiously. My face burned; of course not. Isabel had outgrown that a long time ago. She'd outgrown that made-up language, too. "She didn't come to breakfast, which she usually does."

"She sometimes does," Adrienne said gently.

Breakfast. I hadn't seen them at breakfast that morning. I hadn't seen them at breakfast for the past week, because I'd been so busy, leaving the house early enough in the morning that the sun hadn't even risen, and it was just the soft glow of the half-illuminated worlds watching me wind through the streets to the office.

My stomach knotted in on itself.

"When did you see her last, then?" I asked.

"Same as you," Daphne said. "When we were all sitting in the parlor last night, after dinner."

I hadn't been sitting in the parlor. I'd rushed through, on my way up to my room to finish some last-minute work. But all three of them had been there. Isabel had been sitting next to the window, a holo balanced on one knee. She'd been playing music, colors swirling in time to the beat.

She hadn't seen scared or upset. She had seemed like herself.

"And this morning, she was gone," Daphne said.

"Why do you think this is related to her internship?" I asked. Panic was building up inside me but I managed to keep my voice calm.

"Daphne says she said something about it last night," Adrienne said. "But I was there and I don't remember anything—"

"She said something about Flor," Daphne said. "Her supervisor?"

My chest constricted. "What exactly did she say?"

"Just something about Flor picking her up tomorrow. And I was like, why would she pick you up? But then she got real quiet and turned her music up and wouldn't answer me." Daphne's voice was wobbly with tears. "She's not in the woods, okay? She tells us when she's going out into the woods, and she's never gone that long—"

"It could be OCI," Adrienne said quietly. "Which is about a million times worse, so I think that's where we need to focus our attention."

"It's not OCI," I said, because Adrienne sounded like she was on the verge of tears, and because I didn't want to think about the possibility of a rival company snatching my sister out from under my nose. But Flor DeCrie, that was another matter.

"Alicia told me the soldiers are looking for her," I said, standing up, taking charge. "I want you two to go down to their house and keep track of what they find. Can you do that for me?"

A pause. They looked at each other. Then Adrienne nodded, solemnly.

"Good." I took a deep breath. "I'm going to try and get ahold of Flor. See if we can settle this."

Adrienne and Daphne both looked stunned, but they stood up, moving by rote toward the door. I looked out the window at the plumeria maze, the blossoms glossy in the heat. One of the soldiers strolled past, a lightbox held out in front of him, scanning. And I thought suddenly of those odd questions Isabel'd had, about the CG man scanning the forest. They had slipped my mind in the rush of work. But I felt a clenching in my chest—what if someone *had* come into our forest to snatch away Isabel? Not OCI necessarily, but anti-corpocracy rebels maybe, someone who'd gotten hold of a CG uniform.

Or the company itself, working above my security level.

I left Adrienne's room, my heart thudding, and went to my own suite. I pinged Flor first thing, but she didn't answer and so I left a message with her admin. But I also didn't want to wait around for her to contact me back. Alicia had said they weren't able to get ahold of my father, but I had a private channel on Connectivity that I could use to contact him during emergencies. I activated the holo, white light fanning out above my desk. Keyed in my father's private code. No answer, but I didn't expect one: this system didn't work in real time.

"Dad," I said, speaking to the camera. "Isabel's missing. I've got the soldiers looking for her but I want to know—" I hesitated. The holo light burned my eyes. "I want to know if you know anything about this. If it's related to her internship. We need to rule that out before investigating other options."

Blood pounded in my ears. I switched off the holo and slumped back in my chair. My room felt too quiet. I hoped Lily would find Isabel in the village and this whole thing was some stupid misunderstanding.

I paced around my room, my palms slick with sweat, and thought about the day Isabel returned the first time, how she had seemed to step out of the shadows. I'd always dismissed it as a trick of my eye, or of an exhausted mind. I peered out the window at the shadows and hoped I'd see her this time.

I didn't.

My holo chimed. I whirled around and there was my father, his image faded by the holo light. "Esme?" he said. "You there?"

He was contacting me on the ordinary Connectivity, and so it was a live feed. He peered around, looking for me. I stepped into the camera.

"Where's Isabel?" I said.

"That private Connectivity channel is for emergencies only," my father said.

Anger flared inside of me; I smothered it down. "And your daughter vanishing isn't an emergency?"

"She hasn't vanished," Dad said. It was hard to make out his features on the holo. I wondered where he was—not on Ekkeko, surely; his Connectivity was too weak. One of the other Sisters, then. "She's perfectly fine. She's with me."

This did not calm me at all. "And where the hell is that?"

"Above your ranking."

My anger swelled into a tide of fury, but on the outside I stayed very still so he wouldn't see.

"So, what," I said, "you couldn't tell me? Or Adrienne and Daphne? They were freaking out—they contacted me at work—" And they were right, too. It was related to Isabel's internship. But I kept that knowledge to myself.

Dad flipped one hand dismissively. "DeCrie and Banski are working on a high-level project—"

"Banski!" I shouted. "What the hell does he have to do with Psych?" Dr. Banski was one of the scientists at Starspray City.

"It's a cross-departmental project. They needed an intern with them to do some filing."

"Since when do we use interns for high-level cross-departmental projects?"

"When the interns are my daughter," Dad snapped. "You think you had the typical intern experience? That work you did in PM was Level Thirty at the very least."

I trembled with anger. "This is higher than Level Thirty."

"Isabel is fine. You don't need to worry about her."

Dad switched off his holo before I could say anything more. I stood in front of the empty holo light, curling my hands into fists. I had known something was wrong with this internship since the beginning, and I had done nothing to stop it. I had ignored my instincts.

Now Isabel was gone.

The next morning, I went to Psych first thing. I was still fuming from the conversation with my father, and it had worsened when I came down to breakfast and Adrienne was slouched in her seat, poking at the rice cakes Mrs. Davesa had made for her special. Daphne was still in bed. Last night, I had told both of them what Dad had told me, but I was sure I had just made them worry even more.

The Psych building glittered in the sun. All that glass, all those sharp edges—it hurt my eyes to look at. I slipped in, walking briskly, heels clicking against the tiles. I tried not to think about dropping

Isabel off on her first day. I should never have let her intern there. I should have fought it, brought her over to Genetics. Followed my instincts.

The secretary glanced up from behind the desk, her eyes widening when she saw me. "Ms. Coromina!" she cried. "What can I do for you?"

A secretary like this wouldn't have a clearance level above twenty-five or so, but I didn't need her to answer all my questions. Just one. "I need to speak with Flor DeCrie." I met the secretary's eye and spoke clearly, cleanly. "In person."

"Oh!" The secretary's hand fluttered near her chest. "Oh, oh dear, I'm afraid she's offworld right now."

My stomach twisted, and my mind went back to the Connectivity connection last night. Dad was offworld, too.

"Well, that is a conundrum," I said, managing to keep my voice calm. "Do you know when she'll be back?"

The secretary shook her head. Her eyes kept getting wider and wider. She was scared of me. I was Philip Coromina's daughter, after all. Funny how I didn't feel that power, not right now.

"She's offworld," I said, "not offsystem, right?" The *right* came out short and tense. I was afraid the answer would be no.

The secretary gave me a happy smile. A question she could answer, I thought. "Oh, no," she said. "She just went to Catequil. To Starspray City. I just don't know when she'll be back."

Starspray City? Of course, Dad had mentioned Dr. Banski's involvement last night. For one brilliant second, I thought maybe this was all in my head, that Dad hadn't lied, that Isabel really was out there to do admin. But then—why wouldn't he have told me? Starspray City was part of my purview, as Assistant Vice President of Genetics.

Maybe that was why he'd kept it from me, I thought with a jolt.

"Have you tried her holo?" the secretary asked. It took me a moment to realize what she was talking about. "I know she was going to have limited availability on her trip, but if you were to contact her and leave a message, I'm sure she'd get back to you."

I nodded. My thoughts were all in a haze. "I'll do that, thanks." I turned and stumbled out of the building, back into the pervasive heat. I wasn't going to try Flor's holo again. It was too easy to lie on a holo.

I went back to my office and sank down behind my desk. The climate control dried the sweat on my skin. For a long time, I just sat there, trying to put the pieces together. A man scanning the woods. An early internship. The interference on Dad's holo.

He was there too. Catequil. I was certain of it, with that weak connection: the winds always interfered with the holos there.

Dad and Flor had taken Isabel to Starspray City.

I activated my lightbox and booked the first shuttle I could.

"Take us with you," Daphne said.

I shoved another uniform into my suitcase. I'd already packed three; I had no idea how long I would be in Starspray City. As long as it took for me to find Isabel and bring her home. Or at the very least make sure she was okay.

"I don't think that's a good idea," I said.

"But she's our sister, too!"

I stopped, straightening up. I didn't want to tell Daphne the truth—that it could be dangerous. That I didn't know what I was going to find out there.

"I know she is," I finally said. "But you're too young."

Daphne scowled at me. It was a cop-out answer and I knew it. I zipped up my suitcase and pulled it off my bed.

"What if you need help?" Daphne pleaded. "What if we have to bust her out?"

"The company's not keeping her imprisoned," Adrienne said suddenly. She'd been in my room while I packed too, but she had kept quiet, sitting in the little alcove next to the window, her knees pulled up to her chest. Now she looked over at us. Her eyes were sunken into her face, and she looked like she hadn't slept. "I mean, they wouldn't do that, would they?"

I didn't want to lie to her. But she and Daphne were both staring at me with big dark eyes, and I had to say something.

"Isabel hasn't done anything wrong," I said. "And Starspray City isn't a prison."

Neither were lies, at least.

Adrienne sighed and turned her gaze out the window. The sun was just starting to come up, and the pink light spilled around her. "I don't understand why she didn't tell us where she was going. Even with the high clearance. I mean"—her shoulders hitched—"we're her *sisters*."

I glanced at the clock on my wall; I still had time before I needed to be at the starport. I hadn't requested a company shuttle, not for this. Too much of a chance that Dad would find out I was coming ahead of time. I hadn't told my sisters that, though. I didn't want my subterfuge to give them ideas.

I went over to the alcove and knelt beside Adrienne and wrapped my arms around her waist. She stretched out her legs and pressed her head on top of mine. "You don't know what Flor told her," I said. "We don't know what her assignment is. She probably had to sign a waiver."

I didn't believe anything I was saying. I didn't know what I believed.

"I mean, she didn't even tell me," I added.

Adrienne glanced at me. "But it's different," she said. "Our mom *died*, Esme. We have to watch out for each other."

Her words were like a slap. For a moment, my whole body went numb. Daphne smacked Adrienne on the arm.

"You think I'm not worried about her?" I gasped. "That I don't really think she's my sister?"

Adrienne sighed. "That's not—that's not what I meant. It's just hard, okay? Because we"—she tilted her head at Daphne, who looked down at her hands—"we remember her. Our mom. And Isabel doesn't. And we just . . ." Her voice trailed away. My face was still burning. Part of me understood where she was coming from. It was like the language from when they were children. Something that bound them together and excluded me.

"It doesn't matter," Daphne said, breaking the silence. "She should have told one of us. It's not like we're going to run off to OCI or something." Daphne looked over at me. "I mean, don't you think this whole thing is shady?"

I stood up. I put aside thoughts of mothers, missing and dead. "I don't know what I think. I just want to make sure Isabel's okay."

"So, you think there's a chance that she's not?" Adrienne said. "But she's under company protection!"

I closed my eyes. Adrienne had a child's view of the company: that it was a benevolent protector. I didn't understand how she had gone so long without realizing otherwise. But then, she had been too young to remember the flu outbreak. And she never went into the village. Adrienne was too much of a good girl to cross those unspoken class lines. I doubted she'd ever logged into the Connectivity Underground, either. I wondered if Isabel had. If that might explain why this was happening.

But no, I'd never been punished for it.

"I'm going to find out what's going on," I said. "I'll send you updates over the holo."

Adrienne nodded. Daphne scowled. "I still wish you'd take us with you."

In response, I just scooped her into a hug, which she begrudgingly returned. Then I grabbed my suitcase and told them it was time to go. Daphne nodded. Adrienne kept staring out the window.

"I promise I'll find out what's going on," I told them.

The citizen shuttle did not fly directly into Starspray City, so I had to land in Rasok, on the edge of the continent closest to the lab, and then ride the boat across the choppy, windblown waters. The boatman confirmed my DNA with a quick blood sample, and he actually gasped when he saw my name splash across the lightscreen.

"Why'd you fly in here, Ms. Coromina?" he asked. "You know the CG shuttle has a landing pad out at sea—"

I reached across the counter and set a money chip in front of him. I had loaded it with enough credit to cover his salary for half a year; to me, that sort of money was nothing. "I'm trying to be discreet," I told him. "I'd very much appreciate your help here."

The boatman stared down at the money chip for a second, like he thought it was some kind of trick.

"It's fine," I said. "I'm not asking you to do anything illegal. But the company shuttle isn't very discreet."

He picked up the money chip and scanned it and made a little choking noise in the back of his throat when he saw how much money it contained. "I understand, Ms. Coromina. We can leave right away."

He opened up the hatchway and I walked through the corridor to board the boat. The wind battered hard against the corridor walls, and it swayed back and forth. I pressed one hand against the wall to steady myself. The flimsy material bulged disturbingly from the wind.

The trip across the water was unpleasant, as I expected it to be—the Coromina Group discouraged travel to Starspray City for all but the upper tiers of the company, and it did so in all the ways it could. This boat from Rasok only existed so that the janitors and admins who worked in Starspray City would have a way to access the mainland. Or in case there was some sort of emergency. It was not designed for comfort. The boat tilted with the waves, jerking me sideways in my seat. Nausea swelled up in my stomach and I eventually stretched out on the floor, my suitcase as a pillow, because it was the only way to feel comfortable. I stared at the ceiling, hoping a focal point would calm my seasickness. It didn't do much.

An hour later, we arrived at the Starspray City docks. I thanked the boatman for his trouble—"No, thank *you*," he said, bowing a little, patting the pocket where he'd slipped the money chip. "Have a nice trip, Ms. Coromina."

I stepped off the boat into the swirling, rushing wind. Usually when I visited this place, I was greeted by a city admin. Not this time. There were no covered carts to take me to the hotel. I could call for one, of course, but the carts were automated, and there was no way to pay for a computer's discretion.

So, I walked.

The hotel wasn't far, only a couple of blocks, but the wind made it feel longer. By the time I saw those spinning mechanical doors, my body ached as if I had been beaten. But when I stepped inside, the stillness was disconcerting. The lobby of the hotel felt dead.

The clerk glanced up at me, frowning. She checked her lightbox. I hadn't contacted them ahead of time, and the hotel in Starspray City was not a place where travelers just happened to find themselves.

"I won't be in the system," I called out, strolling across the lobby. It was empty, for which I was grateful; it was risky, coming there, because this was where Dad and Flor would be staying. But there was only one hotel in Starspray City.

"Oh?" the clerk raised an eyebrow. I pulled out another money chip and curled it up in my palm. This was a much more expensive trip than I had led Daphne and Adrienne to believe.

"I'm Esme Coromina," I said. "I've stayed here before." I set the money chip on the counter and the clerk stared at it. "I should be in your files. I'd like a room, although I don't know exactly how long I'll be staying. I'd also appreciate your"—I nodded at the chip—"discretion."

The clerk's hands were already flying over her lightbox display. "Ms. Coromina," she said, glancing between the lightscreen and my face. "Yes, I see you here. I hope you won't mind terribly if we confirm your identity?"

I held out my hand by way of an answer. After she had checked my DNA, the second pinprick sting of the day, she slid the money chip off the counter.

"Welcome to Starspray City, Ms. Coromina."

She had given me one of the lower-tier rooms, a detail I appreciated and one I hadn't thought to ask for. It occurred to me, as I dragged my suitcase in the small, cramped room, nothing more than a bed and tiny closet of a bathroom, that the hotel staff knew how to handle under-the-table visits. I suspected I wasn't the first Coromina Group employee to come to Starspray City outside the proper channels. The thought made me queasy. I wasn't there to betray the company. I wasn't some OCI spy. I just wanted to find my sister.

I changed into a fresh suit—the one I'd been wearing was damp and coated with a fine layer of salt from the wind and the sea spray. I brushed the wind-tangles out of my hair, yanking hard on my scalp, and then finally pulled the whole mess back into a slick bun. I stared at myself for a moment in the mirror. I had come all this way, crossing the inky black of space, and I still didn't know what I was going to say to Flor or my father when I found them. In business, I always prepared my statements ahead of time. I did not like to be caught unawares. But this wasn't business.

I left my room and went back down to the lobby. It was still empty, the chandeliers throwing off hollow fragments of light, the seats at the bar waiting for revelers to fill them. The clerk nodded at me as I made my way to the underground path that connected the hotel to the laboratory's guest building. I knew damn well I wouldn't find Flor there; the guest building was a formality that rarely went used, as anyone visiting Starspray City should already know where they are going. But it was a place to start.

The tunnel was well lit, and carpeted, so my footsteps didn't echo off the walls. It was decorated with light photos of the soldiers produced in Starspray City, their portraits hovering in the air. I recognized all their faces, even if I didn't know these particular soldiers. The Coromina Group had baseline models, with features chosen to represent the Corominan ideal. Thick black hair and golden-brown skin. Strong jawlines, sharp cheekbones. It wasn't that the models all looked the same but more that they were imprints of each other, copies of copies that followed me all the way to the guest building.

The lobby of the guest building was Starspray City's cathedral, a huge, cavernous room with skylights that revealed the gray, stormy skies. It was empty save for a single white desk, behind which sat a man with black hair and golden skin—a soldier. Except he wasn't a soldier. He was just one of our models, grown not to fight in foreign wars but to sit behind this desk and greet anyone who came snooping around the laboratory. He lifted his dark eyes when the door slammed behind me, the sound echoing up through the empty space.

"May I help you?" he said.

"My name is Esme Coromina," I said.

He didn't react. I began walking the massive space that separated us. His eyes followed me the entire way. When I reached his desk, I said, "I'm Assistant Vice President of Genetics. I need to speak with Flor DeCrie. I was told she was in Starspray City."

"I'll need to scan you."

I held out my hand. Whenever I came there on official business, I didn't have to deal with this kind of security. And I knew with each prick of blood it became more and more likely that my father would learn I was planetside.

"I see," the guard said, his lightscreen flowering into life. "Welcome, Ms. Coromina. But it says here you don't have any scheduled business here in Starspray City."

"That's right," I said. "I'm here to see Flor DeCrie."

"She's not expecting you." He watched me with careful eyes. A created person, designed and built by the Coromina Group. I hadn't thought of the engineered soldiers like that in years. But for some reason, in that moment, it was all I could think about.

"No," I said. "I couldn't get ahold of her holo. But the matter couldn't wait."

The guard watched me, said nothing.

"It's a security concern," I said, drawing up my spine, gazing at him coolly from under my lashes. "A potential OCI propaganda breach involving our manufactured soldiers."

Did his face flicker when I said *manufactured soldiers*? We designed them specifically so that they wouldn't see their existence as anything unnatural—a few genetic tweaks here and there, some light training when they were first decanted. But sometimes things slipped through.

"OCI propaganda?" He frowned.

"Yes. I can't say anything more than that." I tapped my foot against the tile, lifted my chain. "It's a high clearance level. Please let me speak with Ms. DeCrie."

The guard sighed. "Give me a moment, Ms. Coromina." He turned to his lightbox. All I could see was a pattern that reminded me of the wind blowing outside, abstract swirls spiraling in on themselves. He was typing his message, whatever it was. Typical practice in all the labs. The messages would be encrypted and then dissolved once they reached their target. No chance for eavesdroppers.

It felt as if years had passed. Eventually, the guard turned to me again. "She'll be here in just a moment, Ms. Coromina. You may go into the waiting room if you wish." He pressed a button under his desk and a door slid open in the wall, revealing a room with plush seats, a table filled with food.

"Thank you." I breezed in. He didn't close the door behind me, and I could look out at the big empty lobby. I wondered if she was really coming to see me, or if this was some kind of power play, if she would leave me waiting for as long as I could stand it. I checked the time on my portable lightbox. If she wasn't there in ten minutes, I would start making demands again.

I sat down. Scrolled through my messages—nothing urgent, just some specifications that needed approval, some production notes from the lead scientist at one of the smaller labs. Nine minutes passed. Flor still wasn't there. I went back out into the lobby.

The guard looked up at me like he expected to see me.

"Did you tell her this was urgent?" I asked.

"I'm sorry, Ms. Coromina," the guard said. "But she was on the other side of the city. It will take her time to arrive here—"

"Nothing is more than seven minutes, if she's taking a cart," I snapped. "Contact her immediately and tell her that my time won't be wasted."

My words were sour on my tongue. I preferred a more slippery approach to business, a kind of meandering around the matter until I could convince my partner to reach the same decision as me. But, I kept telling myself, this wasn't business.

The guard typed out his message on his lightscreen. His expression didn't change. "She assures me she's on her way, Ms. Coromina."

I checked the time. "Seven minutes," I told him, and then I went back into the waiting room. I was too restless to sit. I poked around at the food, all of it prepackaged and unappealing. I didn't have an appetite anyway. I looked at my lightbox—five minutes. I scowled. I didn't want to harass that poor guard again.

And then I heard the *click click click* of heels on tile.

I stalked out of the waiting room to find Flor striding across the empty lobby. She was trying to keep her expression cool and dispassionate, but she was failing—there were tells in the way her brow was creased in irritation, the way her eyes flashed when she saw me.

"Where's my sister?" I said, walking up to meet her.

"I'd prefer not to discuss this in the guest lobby." She didn't smile at me, didn't pretend to play nice or try to soothe me down. In a way, I appreciated it.

Flor brushed past me, heading toward the waiting room. I followed. The guard watched us. He was better at keeping his emotions under wraps than Flor was.

"Close the door," she told him as we walked into the waiting room. The door whisked shut, as if it were automatic.

Flor stopped in the middle of the room. She didn't turn around to look at me.

"All right," I said. "We're alone. Where the hell is my sister?"

"Isabel is fine," Flor said, her back still turned. I scowled at it, then walked over to her side to force her to look at me.

"Where is she?"

"*We* are working in one of the production labs." Flor stared at the pile of packaged food spread out on the table. "She's sorting files for me. It's a huge project, and I don't want to interrupt her."

I glared at Flor. I didn't care about keeping my emotions under wraps either. This wasn't some delicate business meeting with a foreign dignitary. This was a colleague, a woman in my own company. Of course, secrets were necessary in a corpocracy like the Coromina Group. But my sister did not need to be a part of them.

"I don't know why you're so upset," Flor said. "Her father knows she's here. We didn't kidnap her, for God's sake." Flor gave me a small, cruel smile.

"I'm aware my father knows she's here," I snapped. "It still feels like a kidnapping. She didn't tell me or her sisters. She just vanished. You can't blame me for getting upset when things are so unstable with OCI right now."

"She didn't tell anyone because she was instructed not to. This is a high-clearance project."

"I want to see her," I said. "Now. I have the clearance level to go into the production labs."

Flor finally turned to face me. She was smiling again, her mouth cutting her face in half. I faltered. I did not like the look of that smile.

"You don't have the clearance for this," she said.

I blinked, stunned. Flor had a higher clearance than me? *Isabel* did?

"No Psych project has that high a clearance," I said, "and if this really is an interdepartmental project with Genetics, I have a right to know—"

"You don't have the clearance." Flor moved toward the door.

I stepped in front of her. "I have permission from Mr. Coromina to oversee Isabel's internship. You'll let me see her immediately."

Flor blinked at me. "I'm afraid I can't do that." Then she stepped around me. I watched her, not knowing what to do. I hadn't expected this, to be shut out because of clearance levels. I thought it was my father and one of his byzantine plans of action. He always scattered them into pieces. But I still thought I could get access if I demanded hard enough. Especially since Dad had promised me he'd let me check up on Isabel's internship. But it also didn't surprise me he had lied. I was used to him breaking his promises by now.

"When Isabel is finished," Flor said, "I'll send her over to you. I assume you're staying at the hotel?"

I nodded—too late now to pretend otherwise.

"She should be done in about an hour or so. Just go back to your room and wait." Flor smiled again, but this time it was sweeter, a placating smile. "I promise you she's quite all right. We're just very busy."

"What are you working on?" My voice was edged with malice. I didn't care.

Flor kept smiling. "You know damn well I can't tell you that. Not until you're a Ninety-Nine."

Her statement pounded around inside my head. I stared at her. A Ninety-Nine. The highest clearance in the company. For all my connections, I was only at Level Eighty-Six.

"How is Isabel working on a Level Ninety-Nine project?" I whispered.

Flor shrugged. "Ask her when she stops by."

She walked over to the door, pressed her palm against the lightscreen. The door hissed open. She glanced over her shoulder at me, one last time. I felt deflated. And confused. Bewildered, really. A Ninety-Nine project? And Isabel?

Flor's eyes glittered. She knew she had won. All I could do was watch her walk away.

This first thing I did when I got back to my room was try to contact my father's holo. I tried the ordinary connection as well as the encrypted one. The second thing I did was contact Daphne and Adrienne. Adrienne answered, her eyes wide. Daphne crowded in behind her.

"Did you find her?" she asked.

"Isabel's here," I said. "I haven't spoken to her yet, but I will. Flor promised to send her over to my room when she finished her work for the day." I didn't tell them about the project being at Level Ninety-Nine, and I didn't tell them about Flor's mocking smiles. I didn't want them to worry. "We'll both holo you when she's here, okay? I promise."

They nodded. Daphne wanted to stay on the holo, but Adrienne reminded her they had tutoring, and I sent them on their way. Tutoring should be enough of a distraction. And honestly, I wanted some time alone.

My room had one little square window—no balcony, the way my rooms usually did. I pulled the curtains aside and looked out at my view of a city street. A single tree grew out of the cement sidewalk, its trunk twisted to the right so that it was almost parallel to the ground. Hardly anything grew out here except for those trees, which grew deformed, brutalized by the wind.

Nothing about this trip made any sense. An intern working on a Level Ninety-Nine project was unheard of. Level Ninety-Nine projects were, in general, unheard of. Only a handful of people had that clearance level, and it still left me rattled that Flor was one of them. I wondered if this was all related to the tensions with OCI—it would have to be, right? Some kind of propaganda project, maybe involving an engineered soldier or two? But why would such a thing be Level Ninety-Nine? And why would they bring in Isabel for filing?

My thoughts spun around as I waited for Isabel to come to my room. The glass rattled in the window frame. I stared out at the twisted tree. My chest felt empty.

Eventually, I pulled out my lightbox. Work would distract me, just like I wanted it to distract the twins. I plunged myself into my messages, fingers flying over the lightscreen, responding to and confirming and approving one project or request after another. It worked, but it worked too well. When I had finished, I glanced at the time and saw that two hours had passed.

Two hours and Isabel hadn't shown up.

For a moment, I was numb. Then I switched off the lightbox and stood up, my legs shaking. Flor had lied. That shouldn't have surprised me, but it did, a little. I had honestly believed that if I came to my room, if I waited, I would get to see Isabel.

My sisters made me naive.

Anger surged inside of me; I spun around the room, looking for something to throw, to break, to destroy. I wound up slamming my fist into the soft pile of the pillows on my bed. Hot tears sprouted at the edge of my eyes. Then I took a deep breath. Anger solved nothing. I smoothed one hand over my hair. I was Esme Coromina. I was going to be CEO of this company someday. And I was not going to let them keep secrets from me.

The guard in the guest building had told me Flor was on the opposite side of the city. It could have been a bit of obfuscation, but I doubted it—it would put her in the main laboratory, which was exactly the sort of place I would imagine there to be Level Ninety-Nine projects going on.

Level Ninety-Nine. God, none of this made sense. It left a strange feeling in the pit of my belly, like whatever I was going to find was going to be worse than not knowing.

I called the lobby and asked for a cart to take me over to the main laboratory. There were no quibbles over my identity, at least; I'd been to the lab before. I went down to the lobby. It was still empty. Starspray City was an isolated place even at the best of times, but ordinarily there would be a few mid-ranking Coromina Group officials drinking at the bar, laughing with some of the scientists or technicians from the labs. Especially this late in the day. The lobby was eerie as an empty place, those lovely chandeliers glittering for no one but the bored clerk behind the desk.

The cart was waiting for me when I stepped through the revolving doors, preprogrammed for the main lab. It wound through the city streets, rocking to the rhythm of the wind, and I focused my thoughts on Isabel: finding her, tearing her away from whatever project they had her working on, bringing her home. I didn't care if she was just sitting in some back room, swiping through files. I didn't care if she had no access to Level Ninety-Nine information. I didn't like this, and I wanted her back at Star's End.

The cart rattled to a stop in front of the main lab. Staring up at that curving organic building, I felt momentarily paralyzed, fear gluing me in place. Because it was one thing to decide that I would do whatever I needed to in order to keep Isabel safe. It was another to actually do it. To actually defy my father. Because that was what I was doing there, right? Defying my father. If he wanted, he could spin this, turn me into an OCI spy. Exile me, or worse. We did worse sometimes. Capital punishment was supposed to be a cruelty from a barbaric past, but there were times it was necessary.

Not this time, I told myself, stepping out into the wind. Dad wasn't going to kill me for snooping around for my sister. He wasn't insane.

I walked up to the door, wind battering all around me. I expected it to slide open on my approach, but it stayed put. Locked. But the doors were never locked.

Panic gripped at my chest. I tried tugging on the door, to pull it open, but it didn't work.

The main laboratory of Starspray City was locked down.

A lightscreen was set into the wall, inset deeply enough to protect it from the wind. I activated it. A cheery message illuminated the lengthening dusk: AUTHORIZED PERSONNEL ONLY. PLEASE CONTACT FLOR DECRIE FOR ENTRANCE PRIVILEGES.

"Fuck!" I slammed the side of my fist against the wall. This really was Level Ninety-Nine work. The main lab of Starspray City had never been locked in all the times that I had visited. And it certainly shouldn't be locked to me, Level Eighty-Six, the Assistant Vice President of Genetics.

I stomped back to my cart, slammed back inside, activated my lightbox. My fury made me tremble, but I knew too there was a faint undercurrent of fear there as well—because I did not understand why Isabel was involved with any of this.

I connected to my father's holo channel. The holo light flooded through the cart, hurting my eyes. But I was not going to leave this place until he answered live.

The holo light flickered. My father's face materialized above the dashboard of the cart.

"What the fuck are you doing in Starspray City?" he asked.

At the sight of him, some of my resolve shimmered away. I slumped back against my seat. But I forced myself to look him in the eye, even if it was just the eye of a holo.

"I'm worried about Isabel," I said. "Flor told me I could see her, but she never showed up at my hotel." I swallowed. Dad's face was unreadable in the blinding holo light. "This isn't typical intern work, and you know it."

My father studied me. "You came all this way just to make sure your sister was safe. You didn't believe me? You thought I would lie to you?"

Yes. "No. I just wanted to see for myself. Adrienne and Daphne were in a panic."

Dad moved out of the line of the holo, leaving a transmission of his background—some kind of office. Not his office at the main campus. I didn't recognize this one.

"You're just going to walk off?" I said, anger surging because of the fear beneath it. "You're not going to answer my questions?"

Dad reappeared, suddenly, streaks of holo light radiating off him. The winds of Catequil, interfering with the Connectivity.

"I was resetting the permissions for the laboratory doors," Dad said. "You can get in now."

My mouth dropped open in surprise. "You're letting me in?"

"Don't make me regret it," Dad said. "I'll meet you in the lobby."

"With Isabel?"

Dad's eyes glinted. The holo twitched. My breath was in my throat.

"No," he said. "With an explanation."

And then he switched off.

Dad was waiting for me in the lobby when I barreled in, my hair windblown, my clothes rumpled. He looked as unflappable as he always did, in his neat gray Coromina Group suit. I stopped halfway across the lobby and stared at him, my arms hanging limply at my side. I didn't know what to say.

"Let's talk in the courtyard," Dad said.

I shook my head, curled my hands into fists. "I want to see Isabel," I said. "Now."

"Isabel's sleeping."

I was ready to protest, to fight for more information, but this was so straightforward and so simple that the words just evaporated in my mouth.

"What?" I whispered.

"She's had a difficult last few days," Dad said. "But let's talk about it in the courtyard." He held out one arm, as if inviting me. I drifted toward him, feeling dazed. All those unanswered messages, all of Flor's lies—and yet here was Dad, telling me what I wanted to know. He was almost being honest.

Dad put one arm around my shoulder, gave me a squeeze that was not quite a hug. I wanted to put my guard up, but instead, I just melted against him. We probably made an awkward pair. Father and daughter. CEO and employee. I was so used to being the employee that I didn't know what it was to be the daughter.

"Have you ever been out to the courtyard?" Dad's arm slipped away from me as we walked toward a darkened glass doorway on the other side of the lobby.

"Probably," I said. "I don't remember. I don't exactly come out here to sightsee." I shook my head. "I'm not here to sightsee tonight, either. Where's Isabel? At the hotel? Why didn't she come see me?"

"She's not at the hotel." Dad pushed open the door and stepped out into the courtyard. I had been there, once before, for some lunch meeting. A glass ceiling shielded us from the wind, and the night-time plants glowed. They were the product of genetic engineering, experiments that would go out into the galactic market in a year's time. But pomegranates that cast an incandescent shimmer of red, beautiful though they were, would never be the primary income of the Coromina Group.

"Where is she, then?"

"Here. At the lab." Dad sat down on a metalwork bench. An awning of softly glowing moonflowers stretched overhead. He patted the seat beside him, but I stayed standing, arms crossed over my chest.

"Will you please just give me a straight answer?"

"You won't like it."

"Dad."

He peered up at me. His eyes seemed suddenly very old, a reflection of his true age. Maybe it was the light.

"One of the ID scanners pinged her as being infected with Lasely fever."

It felt as if something had slammed into my stomach. I gaped at him. "You can't possibly be serious. She's fourteen."

Dad shrugged. "You were fucking that village boy by the time you were fourteen, if I recall correctly."

Paco. He was talking about Paco. My cheeks burned, and I looked away from him, at the manicured growth of the courtyard. Lasely fever was sexually transmitted; there was no other way to catch it. If the ID scanners had spotted the virus in her blood, she might not have been showing symptoms yet.

"I really didn't want to have to tell you this," Dad said. "I know you treat her like she's your own child."

I floated over to him and sank down beside him on the bench. The plants swayed around us; the building let in just enough wind to create a breeze.

"I don't believe it," I said. "I don't under—" I stopped myself, glanced sideways at him. "And I wasn't fucking anyone when I was fourteen, by the way."

Dad shrugged. "Congratulations. Isabel was. I brought her here for the surgery—we caught it early enough that we could go in and burn it out of her system. It's a new method of disease eradication we're trying out. That's why Flor was being so damned squirrelly."

I turned to him in horror. "You tried an experimental surgery on her!"

"It wasn't experimental," Dad shot back. "It passed the experimental stage ages ago. You probably signed off on the damn test subjects and forgot about it."

I scowled. He could be right, since the medical division used engineered soldiers when they needed human subjects. I didn't like thinking about it, signing away the permissions. "Then why the hell did Flor go on about it being Level Ninety-Nine?"

Dad snorted. "Power-play bullshit. Flor is Level Ninety-Nine. This isn't. Look, I'll take you up to see Isabel. She's knocked out right now, but you can see that she's okay. The surgery is tough, but she's young and she pulled through just fine. Now she gets to go home, be good as new, and no one has to know she got a damn STD."

He looked at me expectantly. I sighed, tried to work everything through in my head. It made sense, mostly. I thought about how Isabel always snuck out to the woods. She'd be gone for hours, sometimes, but she always came back, smelling of the soil and tree sap. It never once occurred to me that she could be meeting someone out there, some villager who told her sweet things and suggested a whole wider world than the one she knew. But I didn't have to think on it long to understand that it made sense, too. That it made more sense than her spending hours in the woods alone.

"She could have told me," I mumbled. Something in my heart stung. It was like when my sisters were younger, when they had that strange hissing language that I couldn't understand. "She didn't need to keep it a secret from her family."

"She was embarrassed," Dad said. "And she should have been. Lasely is a prostitute's disease."

I glared at him.

"I'm not saying she's a prostitute," Dad said, "only that this is why I never liked you girls going down to the village."

I stood up. My face was hot. "I want to see her. I want to talk to her."

"You can see her," Dad said. "But she's gonna be too knocked out for you to talk to her." He shrugged. "Price to pay for a virus that wouldn't otherwise have a cure."

I left Dad at the bench and walked back inside. The air in the lobby smelled sanitized. Too clean. For a moment, I just stood there alone. I hadn't thought about my childhood friends from the village in a long time. This was the last place I'd expected to be reminded of them.

A *whoosh* as the door swung open; Dad's footsteps clicked across the lobby floor. "This way," he told me, and we walked over to the elevator. Dad pressed his palm to the lightscreen, and when the elevator confirmed his identity, the doors slid open and we both stepped inside. The elevator hummed around us.

Then Dad said, "I'm sorry."

"What?" I jerked my head over at him. He stared straight ahead.

"I'm sorry," he said. "For not telling you. I just wanted to give Isabel her privacy."

I trembled. Dad was not the type to apologize. And part of me wanted to know why he was doing this, what angle there could be in it for him. But the rest of me was exhausted with worry and lack of sleep, and that part of me knew that when I saw Isabel lying safe and convalescent in a laboratory bed, I'd actually forgive him.

The elevator dinged. Dad stepped out and I followed. We were in a part of the lab I'd never been before; it looked more like a hospital than a laboratory. A man sat at a desk surrounded by lightscreens. He nodded as we passed.

"One of the nurses," Dad told me. "There are two, to ensure there's always someone to watch over her. But so far, her condition has been stable."

He stopped in front of a closed door, one of a whole line of closed doors. My chest tightened. He pushed it open. Nodded for me to go inside.

I did.

Isabel was there, as Dad had promised. She was asleep, curled up on her side beneath the blankets, a vitals monitor blinking at her temple. I could feel Dad hovering in the doorway, watching us. I walked over to the side of the bed and knelt down and brushed her hair out of her face. Her breathing was deep, steady. But her skin was pale and dark lines traced along the veins of her arms. I ran my finger down one arm, then looked over at Dad.

"Side effect of the surgery," he said softly. "It'll fade in a few days."

I studied Isabel. I wanted to find something wrong with her. Some implant, some sign of illness. Something to show that Dad was lying to me. But there was nothing. She seemed frail, yes, but that would make sense, after recovering from a surgery.

I stood up. My legs trembled as I stumbled out of the room. The lights in the hallway were too bright.

"See?" Dad said. "Safe and sound."

I leaned against the wall, took a deep breath. Safe and sound. For once, I believed him.

I wanted to stay in Starspray City until Isabel woke up, but one of the lab doctors told me that it could be as much as a day before she did—"She's fine, she's stable, but she needs to sleep off the after-effects of the surgery," she told me, sitting in a little office with a view of the storm-swept seas. Isabel's files floated on the air above the desk, a confusing jumble of medical terminology I only half-understood. "You're welcome to stay, but I'm sure your work is piling up. I'll be happy to have Isabel contact you as soon as she wakes."

I shifted in my seat, thinking back on Flor's lies. But this doctor wasn't Flor. I outranked her.

"Your sister's going to be fine," the doctor told me.

In the end, I checked on Isabel one more time. I watched her sleep for about half an hour, the climate control in the lab buzzing in the background. And then I went home. Guilt tugged at my chest, but the doctor had been right: my work *was* piling up, and I knew I could always come back to Catequil if I didn't get a holo from Isabel within the next day or so.

Star's End was a contrast to Starspray City, the air hot and bright and still. I felt as if the gravity of the world had changed, like it was easier for me to walk through the garden, my movements as graceful as a dancer's. I needed to catch up on work, but I wanted to tell Adrienne and Daphne what I'd learned, too. I wondered if Isabel really was as embarrassed by catching Lasely fever as Dad had implied, or if he was the one who was embarrassed, his daughter coming down with a low-class venereal disease. Either way, I wanted to tell the twins. I couldn't imagine that Isabel would mind.

Alicia told me they were in the plumeria maze, sunning themselves by the center fountain. I hadn't gone into the plumeria maze since I was a child, but the path came back to me as I followed the twists and turns, spiraling toward the center. It was bright enough that the glow from the genetically engineered flowers was barely visible—a fact I was grateful for, since the maze reminded me of the courtyard at the lab, and reminded me of the conversation with my father.

I found Daphne and Adrienne stretched out side by side in lounging chairs. Adrienne was studying on her lightbox, but Daphne just lay there with her hands folded on her belly. I thought she was asleep, except she was the first one to notice me.

"Esme!" she cried, jumping to her feet. "Did you find Isabel? We didn't hear anything from you—"

"Isabel's fine." I wrapped my arms around Daphne, squeezing her close. Adrienne shut off her lightbox and scooted up on the lounge chair so she was sitting cross-legged. She draped her wrists over her bare knees.

"Is she with you?" Adrienne asked.

I shook my head and then sat down on the edge of the fountain. Droplets of water splattered across my spine, a few sweet spots of coolness. Daphne frowned, put her hands on her hips. They were both in bathing suits, their skin already turning pink from the sun.

"Isabel—Isabel was sick," I said. "Dad flew her out to Catequil to perform a surgery to get rid of the virus. It's a new method—*not* experimental, just something they'll be rolling out in the next few months or so." On the shuttle ride back to Ekkeko, I had gone back through my old correspondences. I'd found the requests to use engineered soldiers to test a new method of disease eradication. Dad's story had been true.

"What virus?" Adrienne frowned. "Isabel didn't seem sick."

I took a deep breath. "Lasely fever."

Adrienne and Daphne both stared at me.

"You're shitting me," Daphne said.

Adrienne shot her a dirty look; Adrienne, always so proper, hated profanity. But then Adrienne shook her head. "No," she said. "No way. Isabel wasn't having sex."

I sighed. "That you know of."

Adrienne glared at me. "That *you* know of, you mean. I don't work twenty hours a day. I know Isabel."

I looked away, my cheeks burning. That was a low blow, and Adrienne knew it. "She got it somehow," I mumbled. "I saw the test results myself. In her files."

The only sound was the gurgle of the fountain. I looked back at Adrienne. Her head was tilted down, her hair falling around her shoulders. "I know she's not having sex," she said, insistently.

"I dunno," Daphne says. "She goes to the woods an awful lot. Won't let us come with her."

"She would have told me!" Adrienne's voice rang out, too loud in the enclosed space of the maze center. "Maybe not you, but she would have told me."

"We all have secrets," I told her, trying to be a comfort. But she didn't listen, just slid off her lounging chair and stalked toward the maze exit.

I covered my face with my hands. I wanted to be the rock, the big sister who told them not to worry. I wasn't about to tell them about my doubts, that I had thought the same thing—Isabel couldn't be having sex! But I had seen the test results when I met with the doctor. She had explained everything to me, showed me how the surgery had worked.

Daphne sat down beside me and put her arm around my shoulder. I lifted my gaze up to the plumeria blooming in effulgence.

"She has that friend," Daphne said quietly. "That girl, the one who lives in the company enclave. Maybe her?"

I knew the friend Daphne was talking about, but she was a manager's daughter, and managers' daughters shouldn't get Lasely.

But then, Isabel, the CEO's daughter, had.

"It's not that big a deal," Daphne said. "Especially since they were apparently able to get rid of it?"

"Yeah," I said. "Although it was a major surgery. She was asleep the whole time I was there. The doctor promised she'd have her send a holo. If she doesn't, I'm going back."

Daphne nodded. She laid her head on my shoulder. "Good. I think that sounds good."

The holo came through that evening, when I was up in my office at Star's End, working methodically through the backlog of military requests I'd let pile up during my trip to Catequil. My lightbox chimed and my heart jumped—it was late enough that I knew it wouldn't be a client.

When I activated the holo, Isabel stared back at me. She was still in her hospital bed, and her hair hung lank to her shoulders.

"Isabel! Oh, thank God. How are you feeling?"

She blinked, gave me a dazed expression. "Groggy," she said. "They told me—I was sick?" I heard the question at the end of the statement, an upward lilt that tore at my heart. Did she not know ahead of time? Dad had made it sound as if it had been her idea, to keep all of this secret.

"Yes," I said gently. "But it's fine. You're fine now. They got rid of the virus."

Isabel nodded. "Lasely, they told me it was Lasely fever . . ." Her voice trailed off and her holo turned and gazed at some point Isabel could see and I could not. Suspicion surged up inside of me.

"Is it—" My voice stuttered because I wasn't sure how to ask this question. "It's possible, right? That you could have Lasely?"

Isabel blinked. She looked down at her hands. "Yes," she said. "It's possible."

My heart twisted. "Nothing—nothing bad ever happened to you, right? It was always your choice?"

She blinked, looked up at me. "Yeah," she said. "I don't want to talk about it, I mean—" Even on the holo I could see the embarrassment in her features, and my own face was burning hot, too. As long as it had been her choice, I didn't care.

"Just be careful next time," I said.

She nodded.

We sat in silence for a moment or two. Isabel's holo never looked up at me, never quite met my eye. I didn't know if it was because she was embarrassed about the Lasely, or if there was something else, something insidious lurking beneath the surface, that I couldn't see. All the pieces had fallen into place, and here was Isabel, speaking to me over the holo, alive and safe. I knew it was her.

"Are you okay?" I finally said. "In the hospital?"

She nodded. "I just want to go home."

"You'll be home before you know it." I had no idea if this was a lie or not. "I promise."

She lifted her gaze then. I smiled at her. She didn't return it.

Isabel came home two weeks later. I was at the office, but Adrienne sent me a holo, a short one, while I was in a meeting. "She's back!" she cried, and behind her Daphne ran by, shouting something, her words blurred. I switched off the holo and leaned back in my chair and looked out my window, at the trees rustling in the yellow sunlight. I was light with relief, but at the same time, there was a weight dragging me down, something I couldn't identify.

I had another meeting that afternoon, with some of the scientists over in R&D, but I postponed it for the next morning and went home myself. I found all three of my sisters in the backyard despite the heat, sipping fizzy lime drinks. They wore their bathing suits, and Daphne and Adrienne's hair was damp. They must have gone down to the beach.

"Isabel," I said, rushing over to her. "I'm so glad you're back."

I gathered her up in a hug, which she returned limply, one arm sticking out, still holding her lime drink.

"Yeah, me too," she said, and then she took a long drink. I stepped away from her and surveyed the three of them lolling in their hammocks, their feet coated with sand. I felt separate from them in my suit, my hair pulled away from my face. They looked carefree, like they had no idea what responsibility was. But I knew that was a mirage.

"Why are you sitting out here?" I said. "In this heat?"

"It's not so bad," Daphne said. "Besides, we were down at the water. Isabel didn't swim, though."

"I didn't feel like it," Isabel said into her drink. I frowned. That didn't sound like her.

"Do you feel okay?" I said. "You're not still hurting or anything? From the . . ." I didn't want to say *surgery*, didn't want to upset this sunny, happy scene with any reminder of what happened.

Isabel shook her head. "I just didn't feel like swimming."

"Go change," Adrienne said, kicking out one of her long legs. "And come hang with us. We're trying to get Isabel to tell us about Catequil."

"I told you," Isabel said sullenly. "I didn't see anything."

"There's not much to tell about Starspray City anyway," I said, but I still couldn't shake that twist of concern. Isabel seemed like she had retreated into herself. She kept sipping at her drink and glancing over at the woods. She twisted one finger around the strap of her bathing suit, twisting twisting twisting and then letting it drop and then doing it again. A distracted, nervous gesture.

That night, Mrs. Davesa whipped up a celebratory dinner for Isabel's return. Chilled soup and pizza with vegetables from the garden. A perfect meal for such a hot day, and two of Isabel's favorites. But she only picked at her food, pulling the pizza apart without eating it, stirring the soup around.

I watched Isabel over the table as she toyed with her food. I wondered if she was embarrassed about catching Lasely fever. None of us had brought it up, as far as I knew. We certainly didn't talk about it at dinner. Adrienne was going on about the episodes of *The Intensity of Days* that Isabel had missed, and Daphne kept rolling her eyes at the more absurd plot points. It should have been a safe conversation. No mention of an embarrassing illness. No mention of the surgery, or even of Catequil. But Isabel just seemed to pull further and further away, until she was alone at the table, the spoon in her soup bowl going around and around.

And then she pushed away from the table, jerking back suddenly. Adrienne looked up at her, frowning.

"Where are you going?" she asked.

"Yeah, we haven't even gotten dessert yet." Daphne tilted her head. "Pineapple ice cream. Your favorite!"

Isabel sighed. She curled her hands around the top of the chair. "I'm just tired," she said. "I'm sure there'll be ice cream for me left over."

Tired. Of course. She had just left the hospital and flown across the black. She was probably exhausted.

"Why don't you get some rest," I said. Isabel turned to me, her eyes half-hidden behind her hair. "We'll be fine without you. Won't we?" I glanced over at Adrienne and Daphne. Daphne shrugged. Adrienne poked at her soup.

Isabel nodded. "I think that's what I want," she said. "To rest."

I stayed up late that night to catch up on some of the work I'd missed because of Isabel's surprise homecoming. Or at least trying to—it was hard to concentrate, and my thoughts kept drifting back to that afternoon and evening. To Isabel. Did I really believe she was just tired and embarrassed? Or had something else happened out there on Catequil?

I couldn't imagine what. All of the parts of Dad's story checked out. They all fit together like a puzzle. But worry still nagged at the back of my head.

A knock came at my door.

I jumped, startled by the loudness of it. Then I sighed, shut down my holoscreen, and walked over to the door. I expected one of the staff. Mr. Whittaker, maybe, serving as my father's envoy. Who else would be up this late?

But it was Isabel.

"Isabel?" I blinked down at her, taking her in. She wore a flimsy nightgown, and her hair was mussed like she'd been trying to sleep and failing. "What are you doing here?"

"Couldn't sleep," she said. "It's too hot."

I nodded, pulled the door open wider. Even with the climate control, the thick dry-season air turned everything heavy. The day's heat seemed to seep into the walls of the house.

Isabel slipped in. She glanced around my room like she hadn't seen it before. Her eyes settled on my lightbox. "You were working?" she asked.

"Yeah, but it's not a big deal. If you want to talk . . ." I shrugged, held out my hands, trying to invite her to tell me what was wrong.

But she didn't. She turned toward me and stared at me for a moment, not saying anything.

"Isabel," I said, stepping toward her. "You can talk about this if you want. I promise I'm not going to judge you."

"I know," she said, and I thought I heard a tremor in her voice. It tore at my heart, and I didn't stop to think about it, I just swept over to her and gathered her up in my arms, pulling in for a real hug. This one she returned, burying her face in my neck.

"I was so worried," I said to her. "We all were." But I wasn't thinking about my worry, even though it was true. I was thinking about Dad trying to tell me everything was fine when I knew it wasn't.

Isabel pulled away and looked at me, her eyes intent.

And then she reached out and pressed her hand to my face.

It was such a strange, intimate, unfamiliar gesture and I had no idea how to react to it. So, I just stood there, staring stupidly down at her. She pressed her palm against my cheek. Then she gasped and yanked her hand away.

"Isabel?" My skin tingled from where she'd touched me. "Isabel, what are you—what's wrong?"

Her eyes were shining with tears.

"You *knew*," she said.

"What?" I shook my head. "Why did you touch me like that? What do you think I knew?"

Her chest rose and fell, tears burned in her lashes.

"About the surgery?" I reached out to her and she pulled away. "I found out about it when I went to Catequil. Isabel, why did you touch me like that? What's—"

"You *knew*," she said again, louder, her voice edging into a shriek. "You knew he was going to do something to me! You knew everything was wrong!"

I felt cold. I had known, hadn't I? Or at least suspected. And I hadn't done anything to stop it.

But how could Isabel know that?

"Isabel." I moved toward her but she turned and raced out of my room, slamming into the hallway. I darted after her and watched as her nightgown fluttered behind her just as she dove into her own bedroom. I heard the lock activate.

Maybe I should have gone after her, pounded on her door and demanded answers. But instead, I slumped against my doorway. The nighttime silence fell around me, and I could hardly breathe.

NOW

Amana at night was like a fever dream of the inside of the human body. It was a circulatory system of light. Esme watched those veins of illumination from the window of the shuttle as it descended over Santos. She hadn't been there in years. There wasn't much Genetics work in Amana. It was almost all propaganda. Psychology. Actual Psych work, not the cover her father had used when he was doing his work on Isabel.

The shuttle touched down at the Coromina landing pad, just outside the city limits. Esme was the only person aboard aside from the flight staff, and they smiled at her as she disembarked, wishing her good business and congratulations on her promotion. They wouldn't know about her shutting down weapons manufacture. That announcement hadn't yet been made public.

A company car waited for her at the end of the landing pad, the driver standing beside it with his hands tucked behind his back. He greeted her with a bland, polite "Good morning, Ms. Coromina." She had to do the calculations to see that he was right: it was three o'clock in the morning, Amanan time.

"Would you like to go straight to the enclave?" he asked, opening the door for her. "Your house has been prepared for you."

Esme hesitated. As much as she wanted to get this whole awful business over with, she doubted it would do much for her cause if she showed up at Adrienne's house so late—no, so early, here.

"Yes, that would be fine."

She climbed into the car and they sped off into the brilliant darkness of Santos. Esme pressed her forehead against the window, the glass cold against her skin. Santos was farther north than the main Coromina Group campus, more temperate than tropical, and the night was cool and breezy.

The car moved so fast through the abandoned streets that all Esme could see of Amana was a blur of light. It made her motion sick. She closed her eyes and imagined tomorrow's scene.

I chime the bell. Adrienne answers. She slams the door in my face.

I chime the bell. Adrienne answers. She reminds me that I betrayed our sister, and then she slams the door in my face.

Esme sighed. She couldn't imagine any situation in which this would work.

The enclave loomed out of the darkness, the streets as twisted and confusing as the enclave on Ekkeko. The car had slowed enough that Esme could make out the houses in the pools of bone-colored streetlights. Squat and nondescript, just like the houses in her enclave at home, although these were built of brick and not teak and sea stone.

Her temporary house was just as squat and nondescript as all the others, low-slung and sunken into the ground. The driver led Esme up to the front door, dragging her suitcase behind him. He produced a key and handed it to her with a quick bow. "So you may come and go as you please, Ms. Coromina. A shuttle runs every fifteen minutes during the day to take you to the campus or into the shopping district, if you need anything. You can also call for a car, if you prefer." He spoke with bright, even clarity and didn't sound tired at all, as if he too was on Ekkekon time.

Esme thanked him and went inside.

The house was eerie, filled with the same pale prefab furniture that came standard in all the enclave houses. That furniture hung like ghosts in the shadows. Esme switched on the lights and everything suddenly was too garish, the prefab furniture trying too hard to be tasteful. But it was better than being haunted. She dragged her suitcase down the hall until she came to the first bedroom, switching on lights all the way. She stood in the doorway and looked at the white sheets on the bed, at the white curtains hanging from the window. One of the windows was cracked open and the curtains fluttered and Esme was reminded, suddenly, of Star's End. She dropped her suitcase to the floor and marched across the room and tried to draw the window shut. It wouldn't move. She sighed, stepped back. A flaw in this perfect enclave house. If there was anything that better summed up her father's entire existence, it was that.

Esme twisted the curtain away from the window so it wouldn't move.

She knew she ought to sleep, but she also knew she'd be space-lagged tomorrow either way. That was what happened when you booked the earliest possible flight: you got stuck with poor landing times.

No matter.

Esme went back into the living room and sat down with her lightbox. The message light blinked; she knew it was her father, that he had heard from someone about her announcement at the board meeting. She didn't want to deal with him yet, though, so she brought up the map to Adrienne's house and readied it to download into the driver tomorrow morning. She toyed with the map out of boredom, calculating distance based on her current location and drawing out potential itineraries past restaurants and coffee shops. Adrienne lived on the opposite side of the city from the enclave. A car driving at full speed could get there in fifteen minutes. But they probably wouldn't be able to drive at full speed.

Esme tossed the lightbox aside and stretched out on the sofa. The ceiling was painted a dull, nondescript white. It felt like it could swallow her whole.

At first, all Esme could see of Adrienne's house were flashes of sunlight flickering through the curtain of pine trees that lined the road. But then the car turned down the drive and the house materialized, a great modern white box lined with windows. It didn't seem like a place where Adrienne would live. But Esme didn't know Adrienne anymore, not really.

"Shall I wait for you?" the driver asked when they came to the end of the drive.

Esme didn't even hesitate. "Yes, I would appreciate that." A pause. "If you don't mind."

He nodded. The drivers never minded—the implants subdued those parts of their brains. The technology for the drivers had grown out of the technology used by the engineered soldiers. The method of linking to a machine, the cultivation of the right kind of personality. For one scintillating moment, Esme wondered what she had done, ending the weapons manufacture program. It had been the entire foundation of the company for the last two hundred years. No wonder her father kept pinging her.

She took a deep breath. She would worry about that later, after speaking with Adrienne. She had an appointment with the director of the weapons program there on Amana—she would start the company changes there, on this planet of propaganda. The immersion department could help. Even though she had been planning for this shift for the last five years, she hadn't expected to become CEO so quickly. Everything was moving so fast.

Esme stepped out of the car. The air was still cool out despite the sun being up, and she hugged her arms in close, wishing she'd brought a warmer coat. The house loomed up ahead. She focused her attention on this matter. On bringing Adrienne home.

I chime the bell. Adrienne answers. She slams the door in my face.

Esme walked up to the porch. Sunlight bounced off the windows and scattered across the yard. There wasn't a doorbell. Adrienne had a sensor installed, the same that their father had at his house. It read the identity of the person touching it and fed the information into the house's Connectivity.

Esme reevaluated the scene in her head:

I activate the sensor, no one answers.

She took a deep breath. The air nipped at her skin. She laid her thumb against the sensor. It didn't make any sound, but warmth singed against the pad of her thumb. She dropped her hand and waited.

Waited.

Waited.

She hadn't realized until this moment that she would stand on this porch until Adrienne spoke to her. It was madness, but it was a madness she had brought upon herself all those years before, when she kept producing the R-Troops even though she knew where the genetic material had come from.

Shutting down weapons manufacture, coming to find Adrienne: they were the same thing, really.

Esme pressed her thumb against the sensor again, then she sat down on the edge of the porch to wait. The car was still parked in the driveway, the driver sitting behind the wheel, his head bent low over a lightbox. He had disconnected from the car. Esme hugged her knees. The Amanan sky was clear and bright blue, a blue you didn't often see on the equatorial line of Ekkeko. The cold wind last night must have swept all the clouds away.

The door opened.

Esme jolted; she hadn't expected an answer so quickly. She jumped to her feet and turned around, holding her breath as if that would force her to speak when faced with Adrienne. But Adrienne didn't stand in the doorway. A stranger did, a woman dressed in slim black trousers and a white shirt.

"May I help you?" She spoke with a Tarczan accent and wore a streak of blue in her hair, a Tarczan custom. Esme couldn't remember what it signified.

"I'm looking for Adrienne Lanka."

"Is she expecting you?"

Esme shook her head.

"May I ask why you need to speak with her?"

Esme's head buzzed. She ought to lie. Maybe the woman hadn't seen the sensor readouts; maybe she hadn't recognized Esme's name. And so, this was Esme's chance to get inside the house, to at least *see* Adrienne face to face, to maybe have a chance to explain—

"I'm her sister," Esme said. "Esme Coromina."

The time for lying was over.

The woman gave no suggestion that this was a surprise or a problem. She only nodded and said, "You can wait in the foyer if you like."

"Thank you."

The woman held the door open and Esme stepped in. After the cool air outside, the house felt too warm.

"I'll be just a moment," the woman said, and then she disappeared down the hallway on whispering, slippered feet. Esme tucked her hands into her coat pockets. The foyer was filled with sunlight from the windows carved into the ceiling. Some unidentifiable plant, tall and wild with growth, lurked in the corner. It was not a species native to any of the worlds of the Four Sisters.

Footsteps. Esme's heart leapt in her throat. But it was only the woman again.

"Mrs. Lanka says that she will give you five minutes," the woman said. Her face was expressionless. "If you violate her hospitality, she'll call the Tarcza consulate."

So, Adrienne didn't even trust the local police. Esme wondered if she trusted anything about the Coromina System anymore.

"I understand," Esme said, in the same voice she used for the boardroom.

The woman seemed immune. She nodded and said, "This way," and walked off in the direction that she had come. Esme followed. Her heart fluttered fast against her sternum. Daphne felt easy in comparison. Daphne still called home. But Adrienne had worn her hurt and betrayal out in the open. She had trusted the most in the company when they were children. Her disillusionment made her bitter.

They walked into a big open room even more flooded with sunlight than the foyer. A glass chandelier hung from the ceiling and threw rainbows against the walls. Esme recognized it immediately: it was the same chandelier that had hung in the foyer of the estate in *The Intensity of Days*, that drama Adrienne and Isabel had loved so much. Seeing it twisted something in her chest, and for a moment she was young again, and Star's End still stood, and her sisters were lying out in the garden, watching a holo with that chandelier glittering in the sun.

But then the moment passed. Esme was back in this unfamiliar room. And at the center of the room was a table and at the head of the table was an elegant woman in a silk dressing gown.

"Adrienne?" Esme said.

The woman lifted her head from her plate of fruit. It was Adrienne, only older, her face sculpted by surgeons in small ways—sharper cheekbones, a narrower jawline. It was a trendy face. Her hair was pinned back. She wore no makeup.

"What are you doing here?" she said, and her voice was more like Adrienne than anything else about her.

"Adrienne, I—" Esme started toward the table, moving to pull out one of the chairs. But Adrienne held up one hand.

"Don't bother sitting. I'm not letting you stay long." She leaned back in her own chair and crossed her arms over her chest. The sleeves of her dressing gown pooled in her lap. She was as imperious as a queen, and Esme felt like nothing in her presence.

"It's about Dad," Esme blurted out. "He's dying."

Adrienne didn't move. The climate control must have turned on because the rainbows began to dance around the room. One of them slid back and forth across Adrienne's face.

"I thought you were here to apologize," she said. "But I see now I was thinking more highly of you than you deserve. Get out."

Esme's cheeks burned as if Adrienne had physically slapped her. "That wasn't my fault," she said softly, her refrain from thirteen years earlier.

It was a mistake to say that. Adrienne plucked her napkin off her lap and hurled it at the table. "We're not having this conversation again, Esme." Adrienne looked up at her. "You forgot the rest of it, what you used to say. That it was Dad's fault."

Esme looked away.

"It was Dad's fault, and now you're coming to tell me that he's dying? I don't care."

"He's your father," Esme said.

"And she was your sister!"

Silence filled up the room. The rainbows kept dancing over the walls.

Adrienne gave a cold, bitter laugh. "I can't believe this. How did you even find me? No—I don't fucking want to hear it."

Esme let herself bear the weight of Adrienne's anger.

"That company is poison," Adrienne said. "And so are you. Now get out of my house before I call the consulate. I'm a Tarczan citizen now, and no one from the Coromina Group has any say over what I do. Not you, not *Philip*, not anyone." Her cheeks were flushed. She gripped the edge of the table and Esme was almost afraid of her. Almost. But she'd dealt with worse threats than this in her time at the company.

"Now get out," Adrienne said.

"You can make me leave your house," Esme said. "But you can't make me leave Amana. And I'll stay here until you let me explain."

She whirled around and stalked toward the exit, even though she knew Adrienne would have the last word.

"There's nothing to explain!" Adrienne shouted, her voice echoing down the hall. "Because you've already explained just how horr—"

Esme slammed out the front door. The silence on the porch was overwhelming.

For a moment, she thought she was going to cry. But she didn't.

Esme woke early the next morning, still groggy with space lag. The sun had not yet come up, and she lay in her bed, staring at the ceiling. The climate control hummed through the house, a hollow sound that reminded her she was alone. Lights rippled across her bedroom: surveillance drones keeping watch over the enclave. Those made her feel alone too.

Her lightbox chimed an hour later. It was around seven in the morning, Amana time. Her alarm. She'd avoided looking at the lightbox as she lay not sleeping, but she had to grab it now in order to turn the alarm off. A new message from her father.

She stared at it for a few seconds, her hands trembling. She kept thinking about Adrienne in her room of light and rainbows, sitting beneath a chandelier from a drama she had loved so much. Adrienne, who had believed so deeply in the company. She had taken her rage out on Esme because she had believed Esme should have been better than their father.

And she was right.

Esme rolled over onto her side and played the message. Her father's holo'd face appeared over her bed, distorted from the transmission across space.

"I need to speak with you about this nonsense at the board meeting," he said. "I know you're meeting with Adrienne, but we need to talk about this immed—" Esme switched off the holo. Later.

The sun was finally starting to come up, and that made it all right for her to get out of bed. She sat up and her eyes were bleary and she was already tired from the day's trials. Her meeting with the Amanan branch of the weapons division was scheduled for that afternoon, and she had already done all the preparations on the shuttle over. But she didn't want to try Adrienne again. Not without devising a plan of action.

Esme realized now that she couldn't treat Adrienne the way she had Daphne; she had to treat Adrienne like an employee from a rival company, someone the headhunters had brought in for her to woo. And what did Esme do when she was trying to bring over talent from OCI or Glowka & Oldster or any of the others? She certainly didn't go banging on their doors unannounced.

"Stupid," Esme murmured to herself. The house answered with silence. She stood up, stretched, dressed in comfortable day clothes. Whenever she spoke to a potential transfer citizen, she researched them. She looked for their weaknesses; she looked for their strengths. She had made the mistake of thinking that the Adrienne in the white house was the same Adrienne who had lived at Star's End. But she wasn't. That Adrienne had disappeared when Isabel did.

The house's kitchen was fully stocked with food and supplies. Esme had never really learned to cook in her time at the penthouse suite, but she could at least scramble some eggs in a frying pan. She sat down with her eggs at the breakfast table. Activated her lightbox. Since she was in the enclave, she had access to the company's Connectivity, which meant she should be able to tap into the civics information the Amanan offices had about Adrienne Lanka.

It was all blocked.

Esme cursed, even though she had expected it. She supposed now she would have to drive down to the records office and throw her weight around, convince the clerk there to break the law for her. She leaned back in her chair and stirred her eggs around. The files swam through the air like fish, all of them struck through with a red line. Blocked. Blocked. Blocked.

Esme sighed and deactivated her lightbox. She hoped the Amanan offices would have something useful. They'd probably have more than what Will was able to find. Individual worlds kept their own records; it was easier that way. Made for less clutter.

She entered the code for a driver to come pick her up, changed into a suit, and went outside to wait. The cool breeze rustled through the trees, all as prefab as the houses. The air smelled different there, on Amana, cool and smoky and faintly metallic. Esme wasn't sure if she missed the scent of the ocean or not.

The car pulled into the driveway. A different driver than yesterday. His eyes glowed from behind the windshield, watching her as she made her way down the drive. She could have waited for the shuttle, but she was a Ninety-Nine and the daughter of Philip Coromina. Thirteen years ago, she would have waited. Not anymore.

"I need the records building," Esme said to the driver. "I'm not sure if it's on the main campus or not." She arranged herself in the backseat, strapping herself in, smoothing down her skirt.

"Of course, Ms. Coromina."

They drove through Santos. The Coromina Group campus was perched on the top of a hill at the city's center, looking out over the landscape like an ancient Earth castle. The car had to slow down in order to reach the top, winding through the narrow, curving roads. Esme felt like they were driving up to the sky itself, still and flat and cloudless. Coromina I hung in the west, half in view. You couldn't see the storm as well from this world.

"Approaching Records Office," the driver said. The campus there was newer than the one on Ekkeko: it had been built after the terra-forming, and like Adrienne's house, it was mostly glass and plaster. Unfamiliar fir trees filled in the gaps between buildings. Esme stared out the window like she was a little girl again, seeing Undirra City for the first time.

"We've arrived," the driver said.

"You're very formal," Esme told him.

He glanced up at her in the mirror. The glow hadn't faded from his eyes. "It's part of my job."

She smiled at him and climbed out of the car. Wind slapped across her face, colder here on the top of the hill than it was down in the valley. She hugged herself and darted forward. She should have brought a heavier coat.

At least it was warm inside. The glass amplified the pink-stained sunlight and turned everything in the lobby rosy. Esme asked the receptionist for records and rode the elevator to the fourth floor. Her new status as CEO gave her priority: she pressed her thumb against the sensor and the other people waiting for the elevator shuffled and sighed and moved back, tilting their heads low so they didn't meet her eye. It seemed the rumors of her decision to shut down weapons manufacture hadn't made it there yet, either. Good.

The records office there was smaller than the one on Ekkeko and much less busy. A man sat behind the receptionist's desk, fiddling with the control to his holo.

"Excuse me," Esme said, and her voice made him jump. "I need to speak with—" She checked the name on her lightbox. "Ms. Rose-mary Silvers."

The man peered up at her. "Do you have an appointment?"

"I don't need one." Esme reached across his desk and grabbed the sensor he had sitting in the corner, next to a stylus. She pressed her thumb against the sensor, and her blood activated the white hazy glow that signified she was not only a Ninety-Nine but CEO.

"Oh," the receptionist said. "Oh, I'm sorry, of course, I should have been paying attention to the elevator—" He fumbled around on his desk. Esme stepped back and watched him with her arms crossed. This was what she did to people now. She made them fumble.

"You can go on in." He tapped a pattern on his holo and the image flickered. He grinned at her. "Ms. Silvers is waiting, Ms. Coromina."

"Thank you very much." Esme stalked away from him, keeping her head high. Voices silenced as she walked past. He must have sent word: a Ninety-Nine is here. Philip Coromina's daughter.

Esme felt hollow.

Ms. Silvers's office door was open. Esme knocked on the frame to be polite, then peered in. Ms. Silvers sat at her desk, although she stood up the moment she spotted Esme. "Ms. Coromina!" she cried. "I heard you were onworld. But I didn't realize you would be making—a—a visit."

"I'm not." Esme knew that when Ms. Silvers said *visit,* she meant *audit.* "I'm here about a citizen of Amana who has placed a diplomatic block on her personnel files." She cleared her throat. "I need access to them."

"Oh, I see." Ms. Silvers's smile flickered. "I'll see what I can do. Can you give me a name?"

"Adrienne Lanka."

Ms. Silvers danced her fingers across the lightscreen, pulling up the files. She stopped.

"Everything's blocked," she said. "I don't know if there's anything I can do—"

Esme pressed her palms against the desk and leaned forward. She looked Ms. Silvers in the eye, and Ms. Silvers leaned back, her skin going pale.

"I understand that I'm asking you to do something untoward," Esme said in a soft, quiet voice. She smiled a little. "But I'm sure you can manage it. Just this one time. We aren't dealing with the main company files, after all."

Ms. Silvers closed her eyes. "No," she said. "I suppose not."

Esme sat back in her chair. She didn't dare do this before. But she was CEO now. She could break laws.

"If I'm found out . . ." Mrs. Silvers began.

"You won't be," Esme said. "I swear that to you. As your new CEO. It hasn't been officially announced yet, but it will be." And she pressed her hand against her heart and smiled. Ms. Silvers gave her a fluttery sort of look, her cheeks pinkening. She turned back to the lightbox.

"Of course, Ms. Coromina," she murmured. Esme sat with her back very straight as Ms. Silvers dove into the files, her fingers flying across the air. Esme felt a vague twinge of guilt—*I'm exploiting her.* But she needed that information. She needed something to find a way to Adrienne.

"Adrienne Lanka," Ms. Silvers said softly. "I've spoken with her husband once or twice. They're great patrons of the opera house here." She gave a strained smile. "I do hope there's no trouble." Her eyes widened, as if she realized she'd overstepped her bounds.

"Oh no," Esme said. "It's nothing like that." She paused. The glow from Ms. Silvers's holo tinted her vision blue. "A personal matter," she said.

"Of course." Ms. Silvers tilted her head demurely. She worked in silence for a few moments more. Then she sighed, brushed an invisible strand of hair away from her forehead.

"All right," she said. "There we are. Shall I add them to your lightbox?"

Esme nodded and pulled it out of her purse. It didn't take long for the files to transfer.

"Thank you, Ms. Silvers." Esme stood up. She attached her lightbox to her wrist; she wanted to keep it in sight. "I'll see to it personally that this doesn't come back to you."

Ms. Silvers just nodded. Her hands were shaking.

Esme left the records office. In her empty elevator, she waited until the door slid shut before she leaned against the wall and gasped for air. She was struck by a dizzying wave of sadness. She thought she might start crying. Was this how it started for her father? Asking for favors, small things to help fix family matters? Was that why he wound up torturing his own daughter, her own sister?

"No," Esme whispered to her reflection in the elevator. "No, no, no."

When the elevator deposited her on the ground floor, Esme rushed through the bustling lobby to get back outside, into the crisp, clear Amanan air. She ran her fingers over her lightbox, as slim and delicate as a bracelet, and took a deep breath. The trees rustled around her. The sun was pleasant on her skin. Her thoughts cleared, and she no longer felt weighed down by her own sorrow.

A line of cars waited at the end of the drive, each of the drivers' eyes glowing. She climbed into the nearest car. "Home," she said, and pressed her hand against the sensor. It read her blood, and whispered the address through the cables of the car, into the driver's ear.

"The Lorna Street Enclave," the driver said. "I'll get you right there, Ms. Coromina."

She slumped back against her seat and fiddled with the lightbox dangling around her wrist. All of Adrienne's secrets wrapped around her like jewelry. And she realized, as the car zipped along the wide streets of Santos, that she wanted to know what the files said, and not just to convince Adrienne to come home. She wanted to know more about Adrienne. When her sisters disappeared, it had hurt like she'd lost part of her own soul.

"Privacy," she said, and the privacy screen buzzed into place. She pulled up the files, spreading them out across the back of the car. OCCUPATION. FAMILY. ARRESTS & CITATIONS. TRAVEL. POLITICAL AFFILIATIONS. She touched ARRESTS & CITATIONS: Adrienne had gotten involved in politics at university. She'd been picked up at an anti-corpocracy rally in Etzin, and then, a few months later, issued a citation for passing out non-CG-approved food handouts. But Esme knew this already; Adrienne had still been talking to her when it happened. She went back to the main file and selected POLITICAL AFFILIATIONS.

Member of the Four Sisters Freedom from Corpocracy Group, 3921 to 3928.

Wife of Tarczan diplomat; dual citizenship.

Allegiances to anti-corpocracy groups on the Tarcza planet Zatan.

Esme read all of this with a curious detachment. She had not realized how deep her sister's radicalism had gone. She'd never been particularly political herself, but she'd always held to the notion that corpocracy was the best way of running a planetary system.

After all, a corporation is better equipped to support its citizen-employees. A corporation is always looking to please their customers. And a citizen, as Mr. Garcia had told her over and over, is a customer born into your trust.

A link floated into view. WATCHLISTS. Heaviness settled in Esme's stomach. She tapped the link and the lists blossomed out, over ten of them: POTENTIAL TERRORIST THREATS. POTENTIAL CORPORATE RIVALS. KNOWN ANTI-CORPORATE SYMPATHIZERS.

With a start, Esme realized that she still thought of Adrienne as a teenager eager to work her first internship at the Coromina Group, a teenager who dressed up for dinner and always knew the right things to say, who studied her lightbox lessons while her sisters were swimming at the beach. But that teenager didn't exist anymore, and Adrienne had rejected the life that raised her.

Esme cleared the files away and deactivated the lightbox. So, Adrienne had gone from a model intern to a radical after it happened. Their father's sins were enough to poison Adrienne against her own family.

The car arrived at the enclave. Esme climbed out, in such a daze that she forgot to thank the driver, and stumbled up to the front door. The house wasn't hers, and it didn't *feel* like hers, either. Living there reminded her of those first few weeks after she moved into the penthouse. It wasn't Star's End, and it wasn't right.

She set her lightbox on the dining room table and activated it. Brought up the files again. They scattered across the room. She switched off the overhead lights so she could see better. This time, she touched OCCUPATION.

A new file system materialized into place. Everything was arranged by dates. Esme skipped over the files from Adrienne's time at college and touched the one labeled 2927 TO PRESENT. An image of a world appeared. Not a full one, not a corporate one—an asteroid, from the looks of it. Small. A private world.

Halcyon, said the the subtitle. *Designed by Adrienne Lanka in 2930 for Tarcza Preeminence Alexis Zurita. Considered an anti-corpocracy haven; see Political Affiliations.*

Adrienne had become a world designer.

All the considerations about Adrienne's politics flew out of Esme's head. She tapped the image of Halcyon and it grew larger, enveloping the text until the planet was all that remained, spinning above the car seats. The planet was shrouded in pale, silvery mist, although bits of green sneaked through. Esme tapped the planet. It stopped spinning. There didn't seem to be a way to look at the surface, and Esme realized how disappointed that made her. This was her sister's biggest accomplishment: not the protests, not rebelling against corpocracy. This lovely designer world.

Here was a reminder of the Adrienne Esme had known all those years ago.

Esme scanned over the rest of the file. Adrienne was employed by the Sweeting firm, a privately owned Tarcza company. She'd worked on several other projects over the years, but Halcyon was the only one where she was head designer, and the only one of any interest to the Coromina Group. Esme slid the files aside and asked her lightbox to run a search for Adrienne Lanka, rather than Adrienne Coromina, on Connectivity, to see if there was any private information among the Four Sisters. It was a long shot, but she was curious.

"It'll help convince her," Esme muttered to herself, but she knew that wasn't it, that wasn't it at all. She just wanted to see her sister's work. But she couldn't find anything.

Esme drew up the Family system. Immediately, all the floating files collapsed into a point in the corner, and a message flashed over the table, filling the entire car with red light:

WARNING: PHILIP COROMINA'S DAUGHTER. ESTRANGED. PROCEED WITH CAUTION. DO NOT KILL.

Esme stared at the warning. Its light burned into her skin.

DO NOT KILL.

DO NOT KILL.

DO NOT KILL.

"Acknowledged," Esme said. Her voice cracked, but the message vanished anyway, leaving a darkness in its wake. Esme felt hollow.

The files resumed their previous positions. Esme tapped on the file concerned with Faust Lanka, Adrienne's husband. A holo appeared: Ambassador Lanka, his lower half hidden by a podium.

"The Tarcza system is working as closely as we can with the Coromina Group," he was saying in his tinny hologram's voice. "These new revelations concerning genetic experimentation are troubling, but I urge the people of Tarcza to resist passing judgment until all facts have been gath—"

Esme paused the holo. Lanka's mouth froze into an *ahh* expression, like he was silently screaming. Genetic experimentation. Adrienne must have told him what their father had done. Why else would this video be included in her file? But Esme didn't want to watch it, not right now.

She read up on Lanka's history. He had attended Cusson (a quick search on Connectivity told her it was the best university in the Tarcza system) and became a diplomat not shortly after, first to Barazani Incorporated and then to the Coromina Group. He did not have a business background, but the file was unclear as to what background he did have. Which meant the Coromina Group didn't know. No matter. It wasn't anything that would be useful. She didn't need information on Lanka; she needed information on Adrienne.

On her sister.

There were so many gaps of information in an official Coromina Group file. Esme could learn where her sister worked and who had she married, but that wasn't enough to fill thirteen years. She didn't know how Adrienne and Faust met; she didn't know who made the first move or which one proposed. She didn't even know if it was a marriage of convenience or of love. And Adrienne's job, designing planets—why did she choose that? Did she like it? Was she trying in some way to best their father, to create worlds completely unlike the worlds of the Four Sisters?

Question after question after question, as all the pieces of Esme's sister swirled around her.

Esme sat down at a table set up next to a vast, shimmering lake. Mina Weston, Amana's Head of Weaponry, was already there, her expression cool. "Welcome to the Cafe du Lac," she said. "I was surprised to hear you'd never eaten here."

"No." Esme sank down in the chair. The wind blowing off the

lake had an icy edge to it, and she shivered, not bothering to take off her coat. Mina had, of course—she must be used to the chill, having not lived her whole life in the tropics. Esme had no doubt that she chosen this restaurant, with its lakeside table, specifically for this purpose. "I haven't spent much time on Amana at all."

"Pity." Mina activated the menu, holographic images of the restaurant's dishes spiraling around the table in a slow, lazy arc. "We should start with drinks. Their cocktails are the best in the system."

"Serena isn't here yet." Esme glanced at the path she had walked on to get there. The table was isolated, and no doubt protected with invisible security shields to ensure their conversation stayed private. Despite being in the center of one of the largest cities in the Four Sisters, Esme felt as if she were in the middle of nowhere, as if she and Mina were the only people in the universe.

"Serena Cowrie is always late," Mina said, still flicking through the holo menu. "It's so typical of those immersion people. Here, let's have the rosemary infusion. It's to die for." She tapped the holo three times and the menu vanished. Then she leaned back in her chair and studied Esme. Esme didn't blink.

"So, I read the message about your—decision," Mina finally said. "That was a bold move, to put it lightly. When do you plan on making the official announcement? To the citizen-employees?"

Esme gave a thin smile. "That's what I wanted to talk with you about. And I'm afraid some of them have probably already heard about it."

"Just rumors." Mina tossed one hand dismissively. "But vicious ones, I've heard. They're afraid they'll be rendered obsolete. That there will be no place for them in the company." She paused, letting her words sink in, as if she didn't think Esme had ever considered that possibility. "I know I'll be safe; I'm highly ranked enough. But the people in my factory—"

"I don't take these concerns lightly," Esme said. "This plan has been building for the last five years."

Mina raised an eyebrow at that, just as a figure appeared on the horizon: it was Serena rushing down the stone path, her hair billowing out behind her. She raised a hand in greeting and called out, her voice rising and dipping with the wind, "Sorry I'm late!"

Mina scowled, briefly, wiping the expression from her face before Serena was close enough to see.

"Hello, hello." She spoke with a harried breathlessness. "Have you ordered yet?"

"Just drinks," Mina said. "Rosemary infusions. They should be here soon."

"Rosemary infusions! A classic." Serena turned to Esme, and a beat later, she straightened her spine, as if just remembering that Esme was CEO. "Hello, Esme. I hope you're doing well. Congratulations, by the way."

Esme smiled. "Thanks for meeting with us."

"I have some ideas," Serena said, settling into her chair. "About the rollout. We'll need to counteract the rumors, of course; people are already talking and there is a fear that the, ah, decision will run the company into the ground."

"As I was telling Mina," Esme said, "I've been developing a plan for a while now."

The waiter crested the horizon, bringing their drinks. Esme watched him approach, a dark shadow against the vivid green backdrop of the surrounding countryside. The wind picked up, but it didn't feel as cold as it had earlier. Maybe she was getting used to it. Maybe talking business just made her warmer.

"Your infusions," the waiter said, setting them down one by one on the table. Esme could smell the liquor and the rosemary, a pungent combination that made her head spin. "Would you like to order your meals in person or via the holo?"

"The holo is fine. Thank you." Esme was expected to answer for everyone now that she was CEO. She picked up her infusion and took a drink, barely tasting it.

When the waiter had gone, Mina said, "You have a plan."

"Yes." Esme set her drink down on the table. The wind ruffled the tablecloth. The air had a dampness to it from the lake. "This is level Ninety-Nine information."

Serena's eyes went wide, but Mina was unfazed.

"My father, before he retired, was working on a cure for death." She paused. "Immortality."

Mina snorted. "You can't be serious."

Esme glared at her, squaring off her shoulders. She was still CEO. "Let me finish," she said icily.

Mina leaned back, pushed aside a few wayward strands of her hair.

"Immortality is nonsense," Esme said. "Even if we could achieve it, there are questions about how it would affect corpocracy, as well as the obvious ethical concerns." That was a statement she doubted her father had ever said. *Ethical concerns.* But she was a new CEO, and this was a new company. "But I volunteered to spearhead the research because it could aid tremendously in curing diseases— diseases like galazamia, which I'm sure both of you know is the reason my father has retired."

Mina blinked in surprise; she wouldn't have expected that, would she, an admittance of weakness. Serena tilted her head, listening. Already thinking of how to spin this, no doubt. The storylines they could use on the dramas. Esme wondered, just for a flash of a second, if Isabel still watched them.

"I hired scientists who understand our real purpose. For the last five years, they've been surreptitiously running tests on new medical treatments, under the guises of chasing after immortality. That means we have a five-year head start on new approaches to medicine." Esme paused. "All weapons manufacture will be converted to the production of these new approaches. It may be shaky to start, and we'll have to work around that. But it isn't necessary for us to sell weapons and exploit people in order to maintain our corpocracy."

"What about the soldiers?" Mina said. "The R-Troops? The entire basis of our economy?"

"They are not the entire basis of our economy." Esme felt a flare of anger. "They will be granted citizenship and given the freedom to choose how they will serve the Coromina Group. I imagine most will stay as soldiers. Others will find other work."

Mina laughed. "This is outlandish, Esme. This will never work."

Esme sat in the cold, trying to formulate a response. But she didn't have to. Serena spoke up first.

"Anything can work," she said. "With the right spin. Remember when the existence of the Radiance was leaked? We thought there would be panic in the streets. But a few choice dramas, a bit of subliminal messaging, and people dismissed the rumors as nonsense." She shrugged. "We can shape the people's perception however we see fit."

Esme studied Mina, trying to see if she was convinced. Her expression wasn't quite as hard as it had been before—a good sign. It wasn't going to be easy, shifting the entire focus of the company. But at least here was a start.

"We should order," Esme said. "And finish our discussion over food."

Serena nodded, but she was on Esme's side in this. Mina sat for a moment, and Esme's irritation coiled up inside of her. The cold wind from the lake was bad enough—were they really going to fight it out over food, too? But then Mina tucked her hair behind her ear. "I think that would be a good idea," she said, and activated the holo.

The meeting continued. It grew easier the further they went into it. Esme laid out her plans and ideas, Serena chimed in, Mina listened. By the time the waiter brought their mugs of steaming coffee and a trio of tiny chocolate cakes, Esme felt assured that she had secured Amanan support. Granted, she would still need to meet with the Amanan officials, particularly the mayors of the affected cities, but that was a courtesy more than anything else. They weren't the ones with the real power. She also would have to deal with the three remaining worlds, and Ekkeko would be the hardest to convince. But she had a start. Her position as CEO was a little less precarious than it had been before lunch.

After the meeting, Esme wandered down to the shore of the lake. She was alone; Serena and Mina had left together, chattering about new alliances between the immersion team and the former department of weapons manufacture. Esme told them she wanted to admire the lake, but really, she wanted to think: not about the new path of the company but about her sisters. About Adrienne.

The lake glittered in the sunlight, a cold sparkle that reminded Esme of diamonds. She slipped off her shoes and walked barefoot across the cold sand, down to the water's edge. It wasn't exactly the village beach, where she had spent so much time growing up. Up close, the water was murky, choked with slimy plants, and the wind whipped sharp and freezing across her face. But it was close.

Esme stared out at the expanse of water. She just needed to get Adrienne to agree to see her one more time. The new decision about weapons manufacture hadn't been officially announced yet, and Adrienne didn't work for the Coromina Group, not anymore. She wouldn't know. Esme should have thought of it when she went to Adrienne's house the first time, should have spat it out as soon as she saw that beautiful, elegant woman who had once been her sister. But she'd been too stunned by the changes and too guilty about Isabel. She was still guilty. That would never go away. But she was going to make it better.

Esme waded into the water. It was so cold she gasped, but she didn't move away, just let the icy lake burn at her ankles.

This time, Esme wasn't nervous. She understood now that her anxiety two days ago had come from not knowing what she was going to say. She'd been space-lagged, her thoughts soft. But now she had her approach.

The door to Winslow Place swung open. It was the Tarczan woman again, this time dressed all in black.

"I'm sorry, Ms. Coromina," she said. "But Mrs. Lanka gave me strict orders—"

"Tell her she was right," Esme said. "She was right about everything. I'm not here to convince her to come home. I only want to apologize. To make amends."

The woman hesitated. Esme's chest tightened. But then the woman said, "Wait here."

She did not invite Esme into the foyer. The door slammed shut. Esme sighed. She could feel the driver staring at her, but she didn't turn around to acknowledge him. It was a different driver from yesterday, younger, handsome, with a sly air about him. She would have had a crush on him when she was a teenager. But she wasn't a teenager anymore.

Time passed. Esme didn't bother to check her lightbox, and so she had no concept of how much time it was. Long enough that the driver pulled out a lightbox of his own and played through what looked like a newsfeed, faces and headlines flashing one after another.

The door opened.

Esme turned around. If the woman said no, she would have to push her way inside, demand to see Adrienne. She was family and she was CEO. She had the right.

But it wasn't the woman at the door. It was Adrienne.

She was dressed this time, properly, in a russet silk dress, the back cut in a V. Esme was vaguely aware of it as a fashionable style, at least on Amana. Adrienne's hair was curled and set in a pile on the left side of her head, another fashionable style. She looked sleek, and modern, and adult.

"I told you I wouldn't let you in my home," she said.

"And you don't have to." Esme smiled. "We can speak out here."

"We won't speak at all." She moved back into the glimmer of the house.

Esme stuck her hand out and grabbed the door. "I came to apologize. You were right. About everything. To run away like you did, and block your records. I—please, just let me talk to you. Ten minutes."

Adrienne's face was dark and guarded, but she didn't close the door, only leaned up against the frame. She seemed tired, and for a moment, Esme caught a glimpse of the Adrienne she used to know, the teenage Adrienne, sleepy at dinner after an evening with her internship.

Esme's heartbeat quickened. If Adrienne said no, she'd have to come up with another way in, spend another several days in that house in the enclave.

"Fine," Adrienne said. "Ten minutes. But we'll talk in the garden." Adrienne pointed to the left. "That way. The path will lead us around." She stepped onto the porch and slid the door shut behind her. When Esme turned around, she saw the driver staring stead-fastly at his holo. She wondered if he was engineered to hear. Some of the drivers were, to help the company better learn the secrets of their employee-citizens. Maybe she would change that, too.

Adrienne breezed past Esme. She was barefoot despite the chill on the air, and it was an odd combination, her bare feet and stylish dress. Esme followed her. She practiced what she would say in her head, the way she did with any potential transfer citizen.

The garden was tucked away behind a metal gate, the trellis overhead filled with drying vines. Adrienne's garden was dying for the winter.

"Did it take long to get used to?" Esme said. "Four seasons instead of two?"

Adrienne glanced over her shoulder. "No," she said.

They sat in chairs on a veranda arranged between a pair of dark, thorny bushes. Those bushes probably became roses in the summer. Adrienne crossed her legs and set her hands on the armrests.

"Ten minutes," she said.

"I kept thinking about what you told me," Esme said, in her clear businesswoman's voice. "That you thought I should have apolo-gized. And you were right, completely right. I shouldn't have let Father use Isabel the way he did. I know I told you this already, and I understand that it really doesn't matter, but I *didn't know*."

Adrienne looked away, out at the garden rustling in the wind.

"I didn't know, and when I found out, I was as disgusted as you. But—"

"But you didn't do anything about it. You went *along* with it." Adrienne turned to back to Esme, her eyes burning. "Of the three of us, you were the one who could have done something. You could have stopped production, you could have quit the company—hell, you could have refused to participate in that goddamned cover-up you two were so proud of! That would have sent more of a message than me running off to Amana. Do you honestly not understand that?"

"I do." Esme took a deep breath. Adrienne's chest rose and fell. Esme would have to tread carefully now, if this plan was to work.

"I was scared. Not like you. And you know what? I admire you for it. I do. And I did, at the time. I remember when Alicia showed me the holo—she showed me and Father at the same time, in his office. I'll never forget what you said." Esme paused. The sunlight caught in Adrienne's hair and gleamed. Adrienne's face was a mask. *"I can't ever look you in the face again. Either of you."* Esme leaned back. "It hurt me, it did. Because I understood why. I could hardly look myself in the face either."

Adrienne was silent for a moment, her face unreadable. Esme was breathless. She hadn't lied. It had hurt, watching that holo of Adrienne staring at her across the chasm of space, condemning her in a recorded voice. It had almost been a physical pain.

"I'm not going to see him," Adrienne said. "I don't care if he's dying. He should have died two hundred years ago, during the Triad Sector Wars. Men like that shouldn't exist."

Esme didn't point out the obvious: that if their father had died during the Triad Sector Wars, none of them would exist. Not Esme, not Adrienne, not Daphne. Not Isabel.

"I understand," Esme said.

"Do you?" Adrienne said sharply.

Esme hesitated. "Not completely," she finally answered. "I'm trying to understand. And I realized I couldn't do that without apologizing." She swept her gaze around the garden. It was unsettling to her, the way the plants here curled up on themselves in the winter, instead of blooming all year round. "I have something else to tell you, too."

Adrienne stared at her. "What, that you're CEO now? I heard."

"Not just that, no."

Adrienne tilted her head to the side—Esme had surprised her. She recognized that look, that quick flash of curiosity, which was just as quickly subsumed by Adrienne's mask of indifference.

"It hasn't been officially announced yet," Esme said. "Rumors are already starting to fly around, of course, but that's always how it is."

"What are you talking about?" Adrienne said. Her voice was low and dangerous.

"I'm shutting down weapons manufacture," Esme said. "I'm changing the focus of the company."

Adrienne's mouth dropped open. But then she shook her head, her eyes closed. "To what?" she said. "What could you possibly—"

"Medicine, to begin with," Esme said. "Dad's been working on immortality treatments—"

Adrienne rolled her eyes.

"I know; it's absurd. But the research can do some good in stopping certain incurable diseases." She looked Adrienne in the eye. "I'm also granting the R-Troops, and all engineered soldiers, full citizenship."

Adrienne didn't say anything for a long moment. The cold wind tousled a loose curl of her hair. Esme studied her, tried to see what she was thinking.

But then Adrienne let out a laugh, sharp and cruel.

"Medicine," she said, shaking her head. "And I'm sure you'll charge good money for these miracle cures of yours, won't you? Make sure only the wealthiest systems can afford it?"

Esme thought back to Adrienne's files, to all the anti-corpocracy radicalism in her history. She would see it that way, wouldn't she? Adrienne, who had trusted in the company so thoroughly when they were younger. She had seen the benefit of this system before.

"I don't want to exploit people," Esme said carefully. "We're in our earliest planning stages. But I will always find a way to work within corpocracy. I'm not a radical like you."

Adrienne smiled. "I'm not a radical. If I were a radical, you think I would be living in this house?"

Esme sighed. "It doesn't matter. I'm going to make this work, okay? I'm not going to be like Dad."

Adrienne regarded her with dark eyes. Esme sat very still, as if she were being scanned.

But then Adrienne uncrossed her legs and stood up. "Thank you for apologizing," she said. "Although you really ought to apologize to Isabel and not me."

Esme stood up too. She had promised she would only stay for ten minutes, and surely those ten minutes had passed by now. She didn't know if she was successful. But perhaps she'd at least planted the idea in Adrienne's mind.

"I don't know where Isabel is," Esme said. "But if I ever find her, you know I will."

Adrienne was an extension of the garden, a statue positioned on the veranda.

"I should go," Esme said. "I said I would only take up ten minutes of your time." She stepped down onto the path. Adrienne stayed standing on the veranda, one hand at the base of her throat, her fingers moving back and forth across her décolleté.

Esme walked back toward the front of the house.

"Goodbye, Esme," Adrienne said.

Esme stopped, glanced over her shoulder at her. Adrienne had lifted one hand in a wave. Esme returned the gesture.

As she walked down to the car, she realized she didn't care if Adrienne came home or not. She was just grateful she'd had the chance to apologize.

The next morning, Esme woke to the sun streaming white and golden through the windows, the alarm chiming her out of a half-sleep. She had decided, after meeting with Adrienne, to stay one more day in Santos. Serena hoped to discuss the official announcement about dropping weapons manufacture as a company focus, and Esme wasn't sure she wanted to face the board in person again. Not yet.

Esme lay in bed for a few moments, readjusting to the daytime. Then she showered and dressed and put on her makeup. Brewed some coffee and stood drinking it by the back window so she could look out at her garden.

No, she corrected herself. Not my garden. But she thought of it that way nonetheless, a mental tic that she couldn't shake. It had embedded itself in her brain and so there it was: her garden. Her house.

The doorbell rang.

Her doorbell rang.

She jumped in surprise and almost dropped her coffee cup. Serena? No, their appointment was this afternoon, at the Immersion offices.

Maybe it was her father, tired of waiting for him to return his messages. Or maybe it was someone here to tell her, in person, that her father had died.

She drained the last of the coffee and set the cup face down in the sink. Then she smoothed down her uniform and strode through the house into the foyer. A shadow moved on the other side of the front door, distorted through the glass.

Esme pulled the door open.

It was Adrienne.

She didn't say anything, just blinked like she was surprised to find Esme on the other side. She was dressed up in faux fur and white gloves, a woman about town. A shiny silver personal car waited in the driveway. No driver. Of course. Adrienne wouldn't have the taste for genetically engineered drivers, would she? Not anymore.

"Adrienne," Esme said, stunned. "What are you doing here?"

"You're not the only one who can show up unannounced at people's houses."

Esme nodded. She deserved that. "Would you like to come in?" Esme asked. She stepped out of the doorway and Adrienne glided in, glancing around the living room with a dispassionate expression. She slipped off her fur and draped it on the sofa.

"Would you like some coffee?" Esme asked.

Adrienne sat down on the sofa and folded her hands in her lap. Her eyes flicked over the images on the walls. "This is more decorated than your suite at Star's End."

"It's more decorated than my condominium back on Ekkeko, too." Esme sat down on the sofa beside Adrienne. "The offer still stands for coffee."

"I don't want any." Adrienne squeezed her hands together. Esme didn't say anything; she would let Adrienne speak when she wanted. A technique she had learned in business, but it worked for sisters, too.

Adrienne glanced at Esme out of the corner of her eye. "Do you understand why I left?"

Esme blinked, taken aback. "I thought I did," she said. "But then, I stayed."

Adrienne shook her head. "I had my life planned out; did you know that? An internship in Terraforming—at the time, I thought it could catapult me up to Psych or PM. Immersion production. I wanted to show the people of the Four Sisters how wonderful it was to live here."

Esme looked down at her hands, remembering her own idealism. It felt as old as starlight.

"I assumed I would marry a company man, and we'd live on the estate until we had a high-enough ranking to get one of the bigger houses in the enclave—" She laughed bitterly. "I used to get John to drive me past them; did you know that? The big ones on the beach. Flirted with him, too. It drove Daphne mad." Adrienne covered her face with her gloved hands. "And then I saw what the company was really about."

Esme said nothing.

Adrienne fixed her with a cold, dark stare. "I wanted to be the bigger person. I wanted to show Dad that I was bigger than him. It wasn't a matter of proving it to myself, because I *knew* that, knew it as well as I'd known that one day I'd live in an enclave just like this one." She turned away. "And I wound up with something better than an enclave."

The house buzzed from the climate control. Adrienne stood up. Esme tried to figure out where this conversation was headed. She couldn't, and that made her feel lost. Unmoored.

Adrienne looked at Esme. For a moment, nothing but silence passed between them.

"I didn't want to accept your apology," she said. "But I remember the way you used to be. Before—" She glanced at one of the windows. It looked out at the empty street outside. "Before Isabel. I think your plan is—corpocratic, at its heart. But *your* heart is in the right place."

Esme stood up and walked over to Adrienne. She wanted to throw her arms around her and hug her, like when they were younger. But she stopped herself. Adrienne walked over to the window and put her hand on the glass. Her expression was far away.

"I'll come back to Ekkeko and watch Dad die," Adrienne said.

"What?" Esme sputtered. This was the last thing she'd expected; she'd accepted her failure in bring Adrienne home. She'd thought it didn't matter anymore. But now, hearing Adrienne say it—she realized it did.

"I was the bigger person all those years ago," Adrienne said. "Now I want to be the smaller one. I want to sit by his bed and make sure that he'll never hurt anyone again."

That was when Esme grasped what Adrienne had really said—she wanted to watch their father die. She didn't want to say good-bye at all.

"Oh," Esme said. "Thank you. I can make the travel arrange-ments for you—"

Adrienne flicked her wrist. "Don't bother. I'll have Faust do it."

Esme expected her to leave, to stride out the front door. But she only turned around, her gazed fixed on a stand of electronic flowers buzzing in the corner.

"I know where Isabel is," she said, in a flat voice.

Esme's throat felt dry. Her head spun. "Is she all right?"

Adrienne sighed. "No."

Esme opened her mouth, trying to find the words for the ques-tions she wanted to ask.

"How do you expect her to be," Adrienne said, "when her own family used her body the way they did?"

Esme looked away.

"I'm not going to tell you how to find her," Adrienne said.

"We have our records," Esme bluffed.

"You don't have hers." Adrienne smiled again. "I have work to do, so I'm afraid I can't stay much longer. But I'll be back on Ekkeko soon. Tell Daddy I'm so looking forward to it."

She turned and walked away. The door slammed behind her, echoing into silence.

Esme wept.

THIRTEEN YEARS EARLIER

I lay in bed, listening to the rain pound against the windows. I'd managed to fall asleep for a few hours earlier, which was more sleep than I'd managed these last few weeks.

The Coromina Group was going to war.

It wasn't official yet, but I was high-ranked enough to know anyway. A man from OCI had been caught with Coromina Group secrets. An act of corporate espionage. The company had waged wars for less.

I rolled over onto my stomach and pressed my head into my pillow. My blood pounded in my ears, my heart thudded in my chest. It was like I'd gone jogging, not like I'd been stretched out unmoving, thinking that if I could fool my body into thinking I was asleep, I'd actually fall asleep for real.

Over in the corner, my lightbox lit up, a square of pale white telling me I had a message waiting—a message that had been sent through Coromina Group Connectivity. My chest tightened and I wondered if this was it, *the* message, the one that would tell us we were going to war.

I kicked my blankets off. Sat up. I wasn't going to let a message like that go, not while I was awake. Not knowing would eat me.

I took a deep breath. "Play message," I said, my voice unnaturally loud in the quiet stillness of the nighttime. I closed my eyes, all my muscles tense. If it was war, the lightbox would want a DNA sample, confirmation that I was who I said I was.

Hey, Esme, it's me, Miguel. Just wanted to let you know that I looked into that project—the roads in Tirem, on Quilla? It shouldn't be too much to shift some funds around to get them fixed, if that's really what you want.

He hadn't bothered with a visual recording. Just his voice, wavery through the Connectivity. He would still be on Quilla—it was morning there. Late morning.

I slumped down on my bed. War delayed for another minute, hour, day, week—I didn't know. At least Tirem, that little village in the desert, would get its new roads before everything went to hell.

It was risky, continuing my secret PM projects without permission from Dad. The closer war got, the higher he pushed my ranking—I was a Ninety now, which was high even for Genetics. High enough that it meant I learned things I didn't want to know. But high enough, also, to order repairs on little villages, to try and make the Four Sisters a better place for its inhabitants. I tried to focus on that. I was doing what I'd set out to do when I first started at the company.

It wasn't enough of a consolation, though. Not with war coming.

I shoved myself out of my bed. My heart was still pounding. It pounded a lot these days. Mr. Hankiao said it was anxiety due to work stress and gave me medicines manufactured by the Coromina Group. They didn't help.

It wasn't work stress.

I shuffled over to my window and gazed out at the rain-drenched garden. Shards of planetlight broke through the storm clouds, turning everything an eerie tarnished color, like the world had gone bad. I pressed my forehead to the glass. I'd only fallen asleep this evening out of pure exhaustion; when I woke, it had been because of a nightmare. I dreamt of Starspray City. It was flooding, the ocean waves rising higher and higher, and Isabel was there. She was locked away in one of the buildings, and there was nothing I could do to save her.

Something had happened on Catequil. I still didn't know what, only that Dad's story, about Lasely fever, about a new medical surgery, didn't sit right with me. Isabel had come home almost six months ago. She was the one part of Dad's story that didn't fit. She acted strange now. Withdrawn. Quiet. I couldn't get anything out of her. Neither could the twins.

Trying to find out what had really happened to her was impossible. I'd tried. I'd made the calls; I'd visited the right offices. I'd done everything but ask Dad, which was the one thing I didn't want to do. After that strange outburst, when she accused me of knowing something—I still didn't know what—Isabel started brushing off my attempts to find out more. Said it was just surgery, it was nothing. But she'd come back a different Isabel. I knew damn well it couldn't just be nothing.

The sun would be up in a couple of hours, and at that point, I'd have to get dressed and go back to the office and pick up where I left off yesterday. The Alvatech general was still waiting to hear from me, to confirm deployment of the soldiers we'd paid for two weeks ago. Our Andromeda Corps troops had already been deployed—it had been weird and scary and a little thrilling to make that call. As Level Ninety, I'd made sure the Andromeda Corps was on our side. Made sure the right squadrons would be engaged.

For the first time in my life, my mom was making her way to the Coromina System. I'd finally been able to draw her there.

The next morning, the house had a pallor to it, the way it usually did those days. I was up early, sick of lying in my bed, waiting for sleep. The hallways were empty and still. Not even the staff was moving around, tending to their chores.

A door swung open, nearly slamming into me. I jumped away, startled. No one else should be up.

Isabel stepped into the hallway, her face pale, her eyes dark. We stared at each other across the empty space.

"Hi," I said, and I gave her a smile. She didn't return it. "You're up early."

She watched me, guarded. "I wanted to go outside before the rain started again."

"Isabel," I said, and her name stung my tongue. "Isabel, I—" I floundered for something to say. Anything. "I want us to be friends—" No. Wrong relationship. "Sisters. I want us to be sisters again."

Her eyes narrowed. She snorted. "You're not my sister."

I jerked back as if she'd slapped me. She had never said anything like that to me before.

She turned away and loped down the hallway and then vanished down the stairs. I listened to her footsteps echo against the wall and her words echo in my head. *You're not my sister.*

I thought about the first time I'd ever seen her lying in that incubator, a miracle wrapped in blankets. I'd sworn to take care of her that day. Some job I'd done of it.

I trudged downstairs. Isabel's outbursts were burning away at me. What the hell had Dad done to her? I'd tried all the avenues I had to find out. Asked all the people I knew. I'd even taken Flor out to dinner in Undirra City, at one of those trendy floating restaurants that drift languorously over the city lights. But she wouldn't say a thing.

I wandered into the kitchen, my thoughts hazy and sad. No one was in there; it was still too early for even Mrs. Davesa. I started up the coffeemaker and then sat down at the staff's table, feeling vaguely like I was a little kid again, tucked away for one of Dad's parties. I pulled out my lightbox. The message light was blinking, a cold white square fading in and out like a patch of sunlight.

My chest clenched up, and for a moment, Isabel flew out of my thoughts and I wondered if this was it, if this was *the* message, the one that would tell me were going to war.

I was alone down there, so I went ahead and pressed my hand against the message alert. There was a pause; the holo illuminated but it didn't show me anything.

"Come on, come on," I murmured. And then a face materialized on the holo. It was the last face I expected to see, but after what Isabel had told me, it was the face I needed to see right now.

It was my mother's.

All the breath went out of me. She was talking but I couldn't make sense of any of the words; her voice sounded like static, like air. She was clearly older than she'd been in the last holo, and she had a new scar, an angry red slash above her right eye. But her hair was still cropped short, and she was still wearing the black and red uniform of the Andromeda Corps.

"Replay," I whispered, but my lightbox didn't do anything. I raised my voice. "Replay, dammit. You stupid thing."

The holo froze. It flickered. And then my mother was talking to me, and this time, I heard her.

"Hey, baby girl." My mother smiled, rubbed distractedly at her ear. "I guess you're not such a baby anymore, huh? Well, I know it's been a while, but Andromeda Corps's been deployed—looks like we're fighting on your side. You probably knew that already." A crooked, sideways grin. "I'll be pulling into Ekkeko tomorrow. Why I was able to send this through CG Connectivity. Anyway, I got special permission from my CO to meet up with you, if you'd be into it." She'd looked away from the holo recorder then, and run her hand over her shorn hair. "I know I ain't been much of a mother, but—I do hope Philip's been treating you right. You want to meet up, just let Andromeda Corps know. Sure do hope I get to see you."

Her image flickered out. I sat there in the kitchen, the coffee-maker gurgling behind me, staring at the empty holo light. She had contacted me. She wanted to see me. Part of me had been afraid she wouldn't. I hadn't heard from her in so long. I still had all her old holos, though, tucked away in my suite. I was overcome with an urge to watch them again, to listen to those strange patterns in the static one more time. I'd been so convinced she was trying to tell me something. Now I knew it was just interference.

I told the holo to play my mother's message again. Her voice washed over me.

The starport was a seething mass of travelers. The lines to get on the jump-ships were longer than I'd ever seen, stuffed with families dragging their weight-restricted trunks behind themselves. The air was smoky with anxiety and the threat of impending war.

Everyone was trying to get offworld, to Coromina ally planets like Esteller or Occamy, before the fighting started and the travel restrictions came down.

I waited at the disembarkation lobby, tapping my fingers against the side of my thigh. I'd almost come down there in my gray uniform, but Grace pulled me aside just as I was about to dash out the door. "You shouldn't," she whispered. "Not right now."

"What?" I glared at her. "I have to! It's one of my only chances to see—"

"No, that's not what I meant." Grace closed her eyes. She looked so much older. Even though she took Rena's place, she'd always been my employee, not my nanny. Now I wondered if she hadn't seen our relationship the way I had. "You shouldn't go dressed like that. Be yourself."

I'd looked down at the suit fabric shining in the house lights, and I knew she was right.

So, there I stood, in the bustle of the starport, wearing dressy civilian clothes for the first time in weeks. I was always in my suit or the old lounging outfits I wore when I worked from home.

Her shuttle had landed. I could see it through the windows, a smear of white light against the sunny backdrop. I replayed her message in my head as the shuttle emptied its passengers into the starport. All of them were military. Entrance into the Four Sisters had gone into martial mode, even though we weren't at war yet. Citizens and soldiers only.

This was a woman-born squadron, none of them engineered. The Coromina Group was trying to rent as many of the militaries as we could out from under OCI—even with our troops of CG-branded engineered soldiers, we still employed the old-fashioned soldiers, the ones who worked their way through the system. I got a kind of weight in my stomach, thinking about it, that my mother was being flown out there to make a statement more than anything else.

Even though they weren't engineered, the soldiers had a tendency to look the same, like they wanted to fool you into thinking they were the top of the line. They all had my mother's short haircut, and they all carried narrow collapsible trunks with the Andromeda Corps logo emblazoned on the side. The kids waiting to get off the planet stared at them with big round eyes. I felt like one of those kids myself.

And then I saw her.

I'd been afraid I wouldn't recognize her, that the holo would have distorted her image so much that when she stepped out onto the starport, I'd just see another soldier. But no. I caught the glint of her platinum hair, the swell of muscle in her arms. It was her. My mother.

I felt something heavy inside my chest, like my lungs were trying to collapse.

She walked to the edge of the embarkation lobby, a few meters away from me. Dropped her trunk. One of the soldiers slapped her on the back as he walked past, said something that sounded like *good luck*. She scanned the starport, looking for someone.

Looking for me.

She stood with one hand on her hip, her fingers tapping against her side. She kept sweeping her gaze back and forth, and I wondered if that was how she looked when she was on duty, when she was casing the perimeter. I couldn't move.

And then her eyes stopped on me. For a moment, she took me in like a soldier, looking for rank and identification tags, friendly or hostile, military or civilian. I'd seen that look a thousand times the last month, from a thousand different soldiers. But then her expression changed, became complicated and unreadable, an expression I'd never seen on anyone, soldier or otherwise.

"Esme?" she whispered.

The starport seemed to spin around. The voices of the crowd turned to radio chatter, distant and indistinct. I nodded, my mouth too dry to speak. I didn't know what to call her anyway. Not *Mom*. Not *Harriet*. Certainly not *Sergeant Oxbow*.

Then my mother laughed, that sharp, masculine laugh I'd heard so many times in holos. "God," she said. "You look so much like your father in person."

I felt like I should apologize for that, but instead I smiled, gave a weak "Hello." We stared at each other. Up close she looked older, her skin leathery and lined, her hair brittle. The Coromina Group had the secret to long life, but eternal youth wasn't something you'd ever find in a soldier. That was what an Alvatech general had told me once. "At least not on the outside," he'd said, winking.

"God, I'm sorry," my mother said. "I don't—I'm not used to this kind of stuff." She gave a sheepish grin and picked up her trunk. "I was hoping we could talk, though. Get to know each other. You can only do so much through holos."

"Yeah," I said, although I wanted to tell her that even those holos had been enough, that when I sent them to her, I would be exhilarated for days. I wanted to tell her that I'd kept all of the holos she'd sent me, still tucked away in the same lockbox I used when I was a little girl. That I'd treasured them so much, I'd been certain she had woven in extra messages just for me. I wanted to tell her that even now I watched them sometimes, in those hours when I couldn't sleep, her holographic ghost casting watery light across my room. The confession built up behind me but I didn't let it break free.

"I hated that I couldn't respond to them quickly." She paused, studying me. "It always bothered me that we had to go through all those loopholes just to talk to each other. But you know. Andromeda Corps policy."

"I understand." I smiled weakly. "It's a policy I approve of too. Wouldn't want our soldiers' locations being broadcast to everyone in the galaxy."

She laughed. "You sound like your father. Did you feel that way when you were a kid?"

I heard a hopefulness in her voice, a sort of childish naiveté. A sharp, sudden pain erupted in my chest and disappeared. Part of me had always believed that she didn't really care about my holos to her, that she sent messages only out of a sense of duty. Soldiers have duty; it was a quality that translated to mothers, too.

"No," I said. "It drove me crazy how long it would take to send things." I was grateful that my voice didn't crack.

She beamed.

"I booked us lunch at the Veiled Garden," I said. "It's on the edge of Undirra City. I know you have to get back to your squadron pretty quickly, but I did get special permission from Commander Sky to drop you off at the base."

"Well, listen to you," she said. "You must be pretty high up on the ladder, to get Commander Sky to break up his squadron like that."

"Everyone knows I'm Philip Coromina's daughter," I said.

I immediately regretted it—I was Philip Coromina's daughter, but not Harriet Oxbow's? But she only shook her head and laughed and said, "Oh, I bet they do."

"The car's waiting." I gestured toward the exit. "I can call the driver in here if you'd like him to carry your things."

"I'm not some visiting dignitary. I got it." She hoisted the chest up on her shoulder, and together we wove through the starport toward the revolving glass doors leading outside. The heat blasted across us we passed the threshold, steamy and humid. My mother let out a low whistle.

"Good God," she said. "I'm going to have to get used to this."

"Was it cold where you were?" I asked politely. "I know you can't say exactly—"

She laughed. "Sure makes it easier, you working with the company and knowing all the rules. But yeah, it was colder. It was autumn, actually. The trees all looked like they were on fire."

We didn't have autumn on this part of Ekkeko. I'd never experienced it properly, only passed through that crisp, chilly air on business.

The car waited for us at the end of the walk, the first in the line of CG taxis. My mother threw her trunk in the back and we climbed in. I'd already told John where to take us, so he pulled away from the starport without a word. Harriet leaned against the window as the starport flashed by. She looked like a little kid.

"Never been in one of these, can you believe it? Andromeda Corps transports us in those fucking open-air hover cars. Abominations. They can't get off the ground half the time. Everybody bitches about them, but what can you do?" She grinned at me. "We bitch about everything."

"I didn't know that." It was a stupid thing to say, but I didn't want the silence to swallow us whole.

We drove along. The starport was situated out in the wild, where it was easier for the shuttles to land and where people wouldn't have to live in the clouds of exhaust particles the shuttles expunged from their engines. John veered off down a fork in the road that led us through the natural forest. I'd asked him to take the scenic route.

"So, tell me about yourself," Harriet said.

I leaned back in my seat. Dappled sunlight flickered across her face and body, illuminating her like a painting.

"Your last holo said you'd been bumped up to Genetics," she said. "You work with the soldiers?"

There was that hopefulness again, but I didn't know how to read it this time. Did she think I was curious about her? Or did she want information about Project X?

"I deal with military orders. I review them and make sure they're filled properly." I was too shy to tell her that I'd put in the request for her squadron to land on Ekkeko.

Harriet nodded. "You like it?"

No one had ever asked me that before. Not my sisters, not any of the staff, certainly not Dad. I realized I didn't know how to respond.

"Yeah," I said, "I like it."

It was the expected answer.

"Well, that's good. No point wasting your two hundred years on something you hate, right?"

"Do you like being a soldier?"

The question spilled out. It seemed a natural follow-up, and I'd always been curious. It was the sort of question that would get censored if I'd tried to ask it in a holo.

She gave me an odd look. "Yeah, I do. Makes some things harder, but—" She shrugged, and I knew she was talking about me, about giving me up.

My chest started to hurt again.

"So, where is this restaurant?" she asked, after a few moments had passed. "You sure this isn't some OCI trap?"

She laughed, but my cheeks burned anyway. "No, of course not. We should be there soon. I didn't want to take you some place too far away from the ba—"

"I was joking." Harriet grinned at me. "Philip raise you not to take a joke?"

He didn't really raise me at all, I thought, but all I did in response was smile.

We rode along in silence. The jungle crowded around us, a green blur outside our windows. Eventually, the car slowed enough that the trees became distinct, great towering ohia trees spangled with feathery red flowers. Harriet gazed out the window like she'd never seen anything like them.

"Just gorgeous," she said. "We don't spend a lot of time on the nicer worlds, as you can imagine. Hell, we're lucky if they're even fully terraformed when we're dropped off."

She didn't seem to be talking to me, really, just talking. The restaurant sign appeared, a holographic display projected against the trees so that it looked like an extension of the forest. THE VEILED GARDEN, it read in ropy, shimmering letters the same green-gold as the sunlight. My heart started to pound. What if Harriet didn't like it? What if she thought it was pretentious? What if they didn't let her in? She was still in her traveling uniform, red on black. I should have worn my suit. It gave me legitimacy.

The car slid to a stop. The restaurant was built behind a holographic facade that mimicked the surrounding jungle. It wasn't just a gimmick, though, but part of what made the Veiled Garden so elite—to eat there you had to know how to look for the restaurant itself, had to learn to tell the difference between reality and falsehoods.

"Well, isn't this tricky," Harriet said, after we'd climbed out of the car. She squinted up at the holos of the jungle. "Guess that's where the name comes from, huh?" John pulled away, the car disappearing into the trees. "Where the hell he's going?"

"There's a parking area down the road. They don't want to ruin the effect."

Harriet laughed. "I guess most folk can't tell the difference, can they? Between the mirage and the forest?"

"Can you?" I blinked at her in surprise, then immediately felt a twinge of disappointment, a twinge of guilt. I wanted to show her how sophisticated I'd become, that I could weave through the maze of holograms and drooping jungle plants into the Veiled Garden dining room. And yet Harriet, this gruff military woman, had seen right through it.

"Oh, hell yeah. Dango's MC pulled this shit all the time back on Beamish. Not a jungle, though. The world wasn't quite done and the only landscaping were those ether trees they grow first for the atmosphere—you ever see them?"

I shook my head and began edging toward the entrance. The false plants shimmered in the sun like they were wet with dew. It was hot out there, and humid, and the air was difficult to breathe.

"They're a sight, I'll tell you that. Towering things. Thirty stories tall, some of 'em. Weird colors, usually, since they react to the soil—these were all yellow and sort of brownish red. 'Cause they're not true plants, right? Can't be, since you grow 'em without oxygen."

"Yes, I remember studying these with my tutor."

"Yeah, I forgot about your tutor." Harriet shook her head. The holographic jungle rustled around us, moved by false wind I couldn't feel. "Lord, you did grow up special."

"Dad wanted us to learn about the company in addition to all the normal stuff."

"I'll bet he did," she muttered.

We came to the entrance of the restaurant, a solid glass door standing in the middle of the trees. No walls, no ceiling, only a door. Through it I could see the maitre d' and the asymmetrical glass chandelier that threw off scatters of dots all through the dining room. Harriet smoothed one hand over her hair.

Maybe she was nervous too.

I pulled the door open and the cool climate-controlled air rushed over us. The maitre d' plastered on a shining smile that matched the chandelier. "Ms. Coromina," he said. Of course. I didn't have to wear my uniform there. The sensors picked up on my identity when I passed through the doorway. I'd forgotten; not many restaurants did that, although it was becoming more common. "Oh, and a soldier, a sergeant of the Andromeda Corps. Welcome. We do appreciate your service in this time of strife."

Harriet gave a solemn bow. "Just doing my duty, sir."

And her job, although that was a truth no one ever acknowledged in polite company. I had been at the meeting the day that Dad signed over the payment to the Andromeda Corps. One and a half times their usual fee. That's the problem with mercenaries: they're trained professionals, and thus better than roping some innocent kid into war, but at the same time, your enemy can always pay a higher rate.

The maitre d' led us to our table, tucked away in an alcove reserved for Coromina Group upper management. One wall of the alcove was an enormous picture window so that we could see the spray of vegetation outside. The humidity had turned to rain since we'd gone into the facade, and drops splattered against the glass, leaving narrow trails that glowed green.

"This is something," Harriet said as we took our seats. The holo activated immediately, a calm woman's voice explaining the prix fixe menu that I'd arranged for us earlier, images of the food flashing one at a time.

"I hope you like everything," I said. "Prix fixe is the best way to get a taste of all that Ekkeko has to offer." As soon as I said it, I realized it was the same thing I told clients. This whole trip had been like a client meeting. The small talk, the walk through the facade-maze, this fucking table.

"You get used to eating anything when you're a serving merc." Harriet stared out the window. I switched off the holo and arranged my hands on the table.

"So, you were telling me about the ether trees."

"Ah, yeah." Harriet turned back to me, grinning. "Well, we were on this half-formed planet; can't tell you who it was for, unfortunately, but I *can* tell you we were up against Dango's Military Corporation. Tricky bastards. They used holos like the one outside to make the ether tree forests thicker, then scrambled our Connectivity once we were good and mired. Pain in the ass while it was happening, but we sure learned a lot." Harriet nodded at me and winked. "Might even throw out our own version when we're up against OCI. Heard they're using a house military, eh?"

"That's what our intel says." I didn't want to talk about the war, but as a precaution, I reached under the table and activated the privacy shield. There was a reason this was the Coromina Group's table. Harriet must have noticed it—the shield emanated a faint ripple of electricity, meant to be as nonintrusive as possible— because she gave me a sly, knowing smile. "We're still not sure we trust it, though, so we've been scooping up private militaries when we can."

She laughed. "Oh, you corporate types are all the same. You just wanted to talk strategy."

My cheeks burned. This wasn't how I wanted this to go. I had a million questions, about her and Dad, and why she left me at Star's End, and about the patterns I'd seen in her message, but I didn't know how to just *ask* because she was my mother but she was also a stranger. "No!" I said. "I just—I didn't want to risk—"

"I was kidding." She leaned back in her chair. "I don't mind if you want to talk shop. All we've been chattering about. Haven't had a proper war in quite some time. Just a few skirmishes, some protection gigs."

"I don't want to do that." And to prove it, I deactivated the privacy shield. "No business talk at all. How does that sound?"

Her eyes glittered. "Sounds good to me."

The waiter approached with our first course, two bowls of mango gazpacho. My face was still hot; I was glad the soup was cold. I stirred it around, poking at the chunks of fruit and cucumber. Harriet slurped at hers.

"This is good," she said. "Better than AC chow, at any rate. So, what should we talk about, if it ain't military?" She peered up at me, and once again, I couldn't read her expression.

"I want to know everything." I took a bite of gazpacho, sweet and spicy all at once. "Everything you couldn't say on your holos. I mean—how did you and Dad even *meet* each other?"

She looked at me for a moment, and I tensed, afraid I'd said something wrong. Then she threw back her head and roared with laughter. A couple of gray-suited CG managers at the next table over glanced at her and then whispered together. I shot them a dark look.

"You mean your father never told you?"

I shook my head.

She laughed again. "Sounds like him. He likes his goddamn secrets, doesn't he?"

I didn't want to agree with her, not here, not out in public. But she didn't seem to expect a response. Instead, she leaned back in her chair and gazed up at the ceiling, like the memories were playing out there. "Well. Let's see."

I leaned forward, my gazpacho forgotten.

"He'd rented out the AC to help with some security issues. For the Four Sisters."

I frowned at that. "What kind of security issues?"

"Oh, typical corporate paranoia about rival companies." She flicked her wrist dismissively, but she wasn't looking me in the eye. A chill ran down my neck. "I remember floating around Ekkeko in the space station, looking through the windows down at the surface." Her face had gone flat. She stirred at her soup. "Your father came to visit the station. Make the rounds. Stop by the bar." She looked up at me then and smiled, and the flatness in her voice vanished. "He was handsome as hell, I'll tell you that much."

"He still is," I muttered.

"Oh, tell me about it. With those rejuvenation treatments, he looks the same as the day I met him." A laugh. I wondered if I'd imagined the weird little blip from earlier. Or maybe it was some soldier thing. A flash of PTSD that slipped through the treatments. The thought made me sad. "He came swaggering in like he owned the place—which I guess he technically did, at least till our contract terminated." She chuckled.

The waiter approached again. Harriet glanced over at him and let him clear our bowls away and replace them with the next course, small plates of broiled ocean fish.

"So, he came into the bar," I prompted when Harriet didn't pick up the story right away. I'd never spent much time thinking about why Harriet and my dad had gotten together—it was a romance I couldn't even begin to imagine, even though my curiosity had always been there in the background, the same as it had been with those strange patterns I'd picked up in some of her holos.

"He did. This is damn good fish, by the way." Harriet put down her fork. "He sat down at the best table and ordered a drink. We were all staring at him, trying to figure out what the hell was going on. Why the head honcho was in the merc ship. But nobody wanted to go ask him."

"Except for you," I said, and I thought of all the things I refused to ask my father, things that were more important than why he was drinking in a bar. Like what had happened to Isabel on Catequil. My cheeks turned hot with embarrassment, and I took a long drink of water.

"Except for me." She laughed. "I went right up to him, sat down, told him he was going to pay for my drink."

I smiled. "What did he say to that?"

"Nothing. He just looked at me." Harriet gestured between her eyes and mine. "Just stared at me. I stared right back. We were both waiting to see who blinked first." Harriet grinned, jabbed her thumb toward herself. "It wasn't me."

A woman who beat Dad at something, even if it was as stupid as a staring contest. I wouldn't have expected that to be an attraction for him.

"We started talking after that. Turned out he'd come to the ship 'cause he wanted a drink. Said merc ships have the best bars. At least, that's what he told me." Harriet shrugged. "He was probably spying on us; that was my guess. I didn't much care at the time. We talked a bit about the mission." She stirred her fish around on her plate, and I wondered again what exactly that mission had been. I could look it up in the files, if she wasn't going to tell me. She was probably contracted into silence, anyway. "Then he invited me to spend the evening at Star's End. Rest is history."

"And you actually said yes?" I said.

Harriet laughed at that. "Hell yeah, I said yes! I told you he was handsome. I'd been off my birth control—I made the mistake of thinking he was fixed, which was damn stupid of me. Six weeks later, I was puking as we flew out of the Coromina system." She looked up at me, and there was a sadness waiting behind her eyes. "I couldn't bring myself to have an abortion—here was my one chance to bring in a life; I didn't want to give that up. But I couldn't keep you with me, either. They don't let us raise merc babies anymore."

I stared at her. I didn't have words.

She rubbed at her forehead. "And that's probably for the best. Mercing's a hard life. A violent life. And you can't just leave once you're in it. Not a lot of job options for you outside of fighting. That's why I had to give you up. There just wasn't any other choice." She sighed. "I'd gotten a taste of what Philip's life was like, what it was *going* to be like, a big orgo-built house in this tropical paradise he was creating. And I thought—*Shit*, I thought, *this won't be so bad for her, will it?* But some days, I wish I'd said *fuck it* to the whole system. Some days—" She looked away from me, out in the jungle. "Some days, I wish I'd kept you with me. That maybe—" She shook her head. "That maybe it would have been better."

Tears prickled at the corners of my eyes. All the china and silverware laid out on the table blurred. I wiped at my face, trying to be discreet. I didn't know if Harriet noticed or not. She was staring out the window, out at the jungle. The rain had stopped and the windows steamed up, blurring everything into streaks of green.

"Are you happy?" she asked me. "Here? Are you happy?"

Under the table, I twisted my napkin up into knots. She was still staring out the window, and her expression was so mournful that I couldn't tell the truth.

"Yes," I whispered. "I'm happy."

After lunch, I asked John to drop Harriet off at the base. It was burrowed even deeper into the woods than the Veiled Garden was, although it was guarded not by a holographic facade but by soldiers with light rifles. It had been erected only two weeks before by the same terraforming technology that had built the Coromina Group offices. And so it had an eerie, organic look to it, like the buildings might start breathing, like their doors might open up into cavernous jaws and eat you alive.

The car drove under a sensor to confirm our identities, and I shivered as that imposing light passed over me and through me, digging down deep into my cells. It was unnerving, like finding a patch of cold water in a warm ocean.

John glanced over his shoulder at us as we made our way into the interior of the base; I hadn't bothered activating the privacy screen in the car. "Where should I drop off Sergeant Oxbow, Ms. Coromina?"

"The loading zone will be fine," I said, feeling awkward that he had asked me instead of Harriet, as if I were Harriet's keeper. But she only leaned back in her seat like she didn't care.

"That was quite a meal," she said. "I hope we can do it again."

I wondered if that would actually happen. Maybe, before the war started. But nobody knew when the war was going to start—nobody but Dad, anyway, Dad and his inner circle. And I wasn't a part of that.

"Once the war gets going, we'll be on lockdown. Hell, I'll probably be up in the black most of the time. Usually the way it goes with these things."

I hated how calm she was about that fact, like she didn't even care that she could die out there. It felt like our roles had switched; like I was the mother, and she was the daughter.

"If nothing else, we should be able to talk on CG's Connectivity." I glanced at her sideways. "If you wouldn't mind, I mean."

"Of course not!" Harriet beamed at me. "I was going to suggest the same thing myself."

The car arrived at the loading zone, pulling up behind an unmarked transport vehicle I recognized as a Coromina design. Harriet unlocked her seat belt and reached out for the car handle. It was happening too fast. One lunch wasn't enough to ask her everything I wanted, and CG's Connectivity wasn't the same, especially during wartime, when it would be monitored and recorded and sifted through for signs of treason.

"Wait," I said, just as Harriet pushed open the door. She glanced over at me, eyes bright. Kind.

"I'm sorry, I just—I had one last question. Before you go."

"What is it, sweetheart?"

The *sweetheart* stung me. I wondered if she said that to everyone. She didn't seem the type, but then, I didn't really know her, did I? Maybe I was the only sweetheart in her life. I took a deep breath.

"Your holos," I said. "The ones you sent me when I was a little girl."

Harriet's kind expression didn't flicker.

"I saw something in them," I said. "Or thought I did. A pattern." I laughed a little. "I was always too afraid to ask about it. Afraid it would get me in trouble."

"Well, isn't that odd." Harriet laughed. "Must be space static or something."

I smiled, even though I burned with embarrassment. Space static. Just like I'd thought. But part of me had stayed convinced that I'd found something about her, this tiny clue that she was leaving behind just for me. And it was nothing. Just a bit of debris caught in the transmission.

"Would you mind helping me with my trunk?" Harriet said. "Not sure I'm going to be able to lug it out of there after that big meal."

She was looking at me, not John, and so I nodded and slipped out of the car into the muggy, damp air. Harriet walked around to the trunk of the car and I followed her. I felt silly. I shouldn't have asked about the pattern. All children have overactive imaginations. I wasn't any different.

I reached in alongside Harriet and tugged on her trunk. It hardly weighed anything. She didn't need my help. But I was touched, too, that she had asked.

The trunk thudded on the ground and Harriet looked at me. "Can I give you a hug?" she asked.

My heart fluttered, and I nodded. Harriet wrapped her arms around me and pulled me in close—it was a real hug, a mom's hug, and I sank into it. For half a second, I felt like a little kid again.

And then Harriet's breath was tickling my ear, and she was speaking, low and throaty, and my whole body went rigid at what she had to say.

"The patterns weren't your imagination," she murmured. "I wanted to tell you the truth. But I can't say anything more. Look again."

She pulled away and grinned. "See you on the Connectivity," she said, and the transition from the frantic whispering was so seamless, I almost though I had imagined it.

"You'll do what I said, yeah?" she said, and something in her eyes glinted, and I knew she wasn't talking about the Connectivity at all.

"Yes," I said. "I will."

She picked up her trunk and studied me. "I'm proud of you," she said. "Proud of what you've become."

I didn't know how to respond to that. So, I ignored it.

"Stay safe," I said.

She smiled at that. Inside my head, I thought of the pattern, the *slow slow slow quick quick slow* rhythms that had thumped behind her voice all those years before. And then I thought of her riding in a shuttle up into the black to go to war.

"I'll be fine," she said, and I hoped it was true.

I told John to take me back to Star's End instead of the office. I didn't have any meetings scheduled for the afternoon, and the rest of my work I could do from home. But there was one thing I wanted to do first, and I couldn't do it anywhere near the Coromina Group headquarters.

I went straight up to my suite and shut the door behind me. My heart was fluttering fast inside my chest. The exchange with Harriet had happened so quickly. *Keep looking.* But for what? And *how*? And what was the truth? About Dad? About me? Or was it larger than that—about OCI? The war? The company?

The patterns had been a game when I was kid, and a way for me to find a connection with my mother. Now they felt serious. Life or death.

I dragged the lockbox out of my closet and flipped it open. The datachips gleamed up at me, and the holocube was nestled in the corner of the box. I picked it up first and switched it on. My mother flickered into view, shockingly young—she almost didn't seem like the same person I had just eaten lunch with. I held the cube to my ear and listened beyond her words.

The pattern was still there, faint but steady, the rhythm the same as I had remembered. I tapped it out on my thigh.

When the holo looped, I paused it and grabbed a handful of the datachips. I plugged them one by one into my lightbox, listening for the pattern. The ones that didn't have it, I set back inside the box—but the ones that did, I piled up neatly on my sofa. There were thirteen holos total that contained the pattern, including the big holocube.

I played the holocube again, this time with my lightbox screen lit up in front of me so I could scribble out the pattern. *Slow slow slow quick quick slow quick*, on and on, a system of binary that should have been easy for me to work out. All my childhood notes had been lost, but bits and pieces of them came back to me as I worked. I had thought it might be Morse code, from Earth, which the militaries still used from time to time, but it wasn't. It wasn't digital binary, either.

I played through each of the datachips. It was the same pattern every time. Thirteen separate patterns, repeated. I counted the number of occurrences in the pattern before it repeated itself—seven. I briefly considered taking the pattern to my assistant Miguel, to see if he could have it analyzed by some of the experts employed by the Coromina Group, but I dismissed the idea almost immediately. This wasn't my PM secret projects. This tied back to Harriet, and this was a *warning*.

I switched off the currently playing holo and slumped down on my sofa. I suspected the key to breaking the code was in the numbers, thirteen and seven. As a kid, I'd assumed the pattern hadn't been in every single holo because Harriet couldn't put it in every time. Now, I was starting to think it was on purpose.

The breakthrough should have made me excited, but instead it left me frustrated. Harriet had sent this to me when I was a child, and yet I couldn't even solve it as an adult. I rolled the two numbers around in my head. Seven and thirteen, seven and thirteen. Both odd numbers. Both numbers that couldn't be divided evenly. Easy math. Math that a kid could do.

I stood up and paced around my room. The rain had cleared and I shuffled up to my window to look down at the garden. Everything sparkled in the sunlight. A figure moved in the distance—one of the soldiers walking the perimeter.

I froze.

This whole time, as I struggled to figure out the pattern, I'd missed the most obvious clue: Harriet herself. Harriet, and her whole reason for giving me up. She didn't want me to become a war child. Because Harriet was a soldier. And all the militaries had their own methods of communication, their own secret codes so that they could communicate with each other and *only* each other.

"Holy shit," I whispered, and then I grabbed my lightbox and opened up the scribbled pattern again. This was an Andromeda Corps code, specific to that military. Something the Coromina Group was contractually obligated to ignore. Which meant I couldn't take it to the Andromeda Corps CO and demand to have it translated. They would never agree. It was a breach of contract. But it did give me a lead on how to crack it.

I paced across my room, pressing the holocube between my two palms, like I could squeeze its secrets out. I could go to the Star's End soldiers, but this wasn't exactly like the favors I'd asked of them when I was younger, sneaking out to the beach to see my friends. And this close to wartime, I shouldn't ask them to keep secrets from Dad and the company anyway. Adrienne might be able to help; out of all of us, she'd been the best at computer science. But I was hesitant to involve one of my sisters, not just because of the security issue but because my mother was one of those topics we never discussed.

I sighed, slumped down on my couch, and sifted idly through the notes on my lightbox. I was getting nowhere with this. I needed someone else.

I didn't want to burden Adrienne. I didn't want to burden any of my sisters. But surely, Adrienne could understand why I wanted to break a code from my mother.

I grabbed the lightbox and the holocube and slipped out of my room and down the hallway. Adrienne's door was cracked open. Not a surprise there; most of the internships had been cancelled in preparation for the war.

I knocked on the door lightly and called out her name.

"Yes?" she sang out. "Daphne, if this is you, I told you, I'm too busy—"

"It's me," I said, and slipped through the doorway. She was sitting in front of her own lightbox, the holoscreen shining. Whatever she was doing, she looked completely absorbed.

"Don't tell me you're working," I said. "You aren't a fulltime employee yet. This should be a vacation for you."

"I was reading the newsfeeds." She turned off her holoscreen and looked over at me. She frowned when she saw the holocube. "What's going on?"

I shut the door behind me and moved quickly across the room. "I need your help," I said. "I have a code here. I can't break it."

Adrienne's eyes widened "Is it related to the war?" She snatched the holocube away from me and turned it around in her head. "My God, Esme, this thing's ancient."

"No. It's personal." I pulled a chair over to her desk and sat down beside her. She kept puzzling over the holocube. "You have to promise not to tell anyone about this, though."

"Wait, what?" She looked up at me. "What's going on?" Her eyes narrowed. "This isn't about Isabel, is it?"

Isabel. I felt a pang in my heart at the memory of her refusing to call me her sister. I shook my head. "It's something from my mother. It's a code, hidden in with her holos from when I was a little girl. I tried to figure it out as a kid but I never could."

"Your mother?" Adrienne looked down at the holocube, her expression flat. "Your mother left you a secret message."

"She's military, remember?" I said it quietly, thinking how my mother and Adrienne's mother couldn't be more different. "She's planetside. Because of the war. And she told me—apparently the code means something. But that was all she told me."

Adrienne looked up at me. Her eyes were like dark pools. I couldn't see anything in them. "Oh, Esme," she said. "This really is important, isn't it?"

For a moment, I was breathless. Of course it was. But to hear Adrienne say so aloud caught me by surprise.

"Yeah," I said. "It really is."

"Well, then I have to keep it secret, don't I?" She smiled brightly. "If you thought you could trust me with it."

"Of course I could trust you with it." I returned her smile. "You're my sister."

A beat passed, a moment of something shared. Then I took a deep breath and said, "Here, just listen to it."

I activated the holocube first. As soon as it began to play, my mother's voice drifting through the room, I felt a surge of dizziness. I'd never shown these holos to anyone else before.

Adrienne listened, her head tilted. My mother's familiar words filled up the room.

When the holo shuddered and began repeating, Adrienne said, "The pattern was in there three times."

I nodded.

"Can you play the others?"

I did, one at a time, in the order that Harriet had sent them to me. I sat at Adrienne's desk and relived my childhood thirteen times over. Each holo brought with it a memory. Meeting Laila for the first time. Swimming in the ocean during one of the hottest, driest dry seasons I could remember. The flu sweeping across the Four Sisters.

Adrienne, though, just took notes on her lightbox. She was counting—I could see the numbers floating on her holoscreen. These holos didn't mean anything to her. She hadn't even existed when most of them were recorded.

The pattern repeated itself in clumps of threes and fours. Adrienne drummed her fingers against the desk.

"I think the code is specific to the Andromeda Corps," I said. "Mr. Garcia talked to you about military codes, right?"

Adrienne gave me an exasperated look. "Of course he did. We even practiced breaking some of them. I was the best at it." She laughed at herself, tossed her hair over her shoulder. I'd never done that, but then, my tutoring had been different. Much more business-focused. I had been groomed in a way my sisters hadn't. "We didn't do any AC codes, but I think I can see the pattern."

I sat up straight, my blood rushing. "Really? What does it say?"

Adrienne's brow furrowed. White light from her holoscreen washed over her features. "It's super vague. I don't—I don't know why she would send this to you. It doesn't even make sense, really."

"What does it say?"

Adrienne looked at me through the glare of her holoscreen. There was something in her expression I couldn't place. A kind of sadness.

"Adrienne," I said. "Please."

She kept looking at me. Her eyes never left mine. "I could be wrong," she said, "but if I've organized the numbers correctly, then it should say, it should—"

She hesitated and I shrieked in frustration. "Just tell me!"

Her eyes burned into me. The holoscreen light turned them golden.

"'Something was here first.'"

My body was humming with adrenaline. All these years, and I had finally uncovered the secret my mother had been trying to tell me— the secret I'd given up on as I grew up, as I started to turn cynical.

Except I didn't know what the secret *meant*.

Night had fallen, and the house was dark and silent. Red planet-light flooded through my suite, turning everything sordid and eerie. I tumbled Harriet's message around in my head, trying to make sense of it. Adrienne didn't want to talk about it—"This sounds like a company secret," she'd said, and despite what had happened with Isabel, she still trusted the company to do what was best. And I knew what I thought it said, but I couldn't bring myself to believe it. For one, how would she even *know*? Unless she'd seen something when she was stationed here—

I paced around my room, fingering the edge of my blouse, trying to fit together all the pieces. Humanity had never encountered other life-forms—at least not intelligent ones, and I doubted Harriet would encode a message about bacteria wriggling in the unlivable soil of a pre-terraformed Ekkeko. My whole life, I'd grown up with the idea that aliens were a silly myth, a child's story. If they existed, people said, they existed so far away from us that we'd never find them. Adrienne said the same thing, after the silence that followed her decoding the message. It *had* to be something else. A code within a code. A company cipher we had no right to crack.

And part of me believed her. Because it would have been the scientific discovery of the *millennium* if the Coromina Group's scanners had uncovered alien life on the Four Sisters. The credibility alone would have soared the company to new heights of notoriety, and I was certain Dad would have found a way to transform the discovery into profit.

I stopped pacing. I was next to my window, the red light spilling across my feet. If there had been something living there, Dad would have lost the Four Sisters. There would have been no place to set up his corpocracy. He would have had to start over from scratch.

I felt sick to my stomach. I gripped the window frame and peered out into the reddish night and thought about what this world had looked like before terraforming. I'd seen pictures as a child, learning about the process in tutoring. The air had been toxic, the soil rocky and barren. It seemed impossible for anything to live here. But maybe something had. Maybe Dad had wiped them all out and lied about the terraforming.

And maybe he'd gathered up the life-forms first; maybe he had done something with them. Experiments. Like the experiment on Isabel—

I pressed myself against the wall and took a deep, shuddery breath. If these were the questions I was supposed to be asking, no wonder I hadn't found any answers through my usual channels. A secret like forced terraforming and a genocide was something you couldn't risk letting out. It was a secret you would kill for.

I wasn't afraid, though. Not for myself. If this was Dad's big secret, he was going to have to tell me eventually. He would hold onto it as long as he could, because he liked his power, but I was going to be his heir.

I wanted my answers. And I knew the only way to get them was to go to Dad directly.

That, more than anything else, was what frightened me. Dad frightened me. But then I thought about Harriet, my mother, encoding this horrible secret in a holo she recorded for her infant daughter. She had to have known Dad would watch it. But she did it anyway.

My mother's bravery, her refusal to fear my father, was the whole reason I existed. She had been the only one willing to speak to him in that bar. And I had more at stake than she did. My questions were more important. Isabel had been hurt. She'd probably never had Lasely fever.

I wanted to know everything.

So, I went upstairs and followed the hallway to the western wing. Went to his office first, even though it was so late. But no one answered when I knocked.

I pushed the door open anyway.

The lights were out. With the windows drawn, it was too dark to see anything, but I peered in anyway, making out the unfamiliar shapes in the shadows. My fear turned to an anger that simmered deep down in my chest. Dad's lies and obfuscation had forced me to hurt Isabel. I wondered how many others I'd hurt inadvertently. I didn't want to think about it.

I stalked out of Dad's office, slamming the door shut. And then I did something I'd never done before.

I went to his bedroom suite.

No one had ever forbidden me from going to Dad's suite. But the threat was always there, embedded in the walls of Star's End: *you are allowed to visit his office, but you may not go any farther.*

But I was an adult, and I would not let my father tell me what to do. Not anymore. From now on, I was going to be more like my mother.

My heart pounded as I marched down the hall, thumping in time with the rhythm of my footsteps. Twice I considered turning around and going back to the eastern wing and forgetting all of this had happened. But I didn't. I kept moving toward the double doors at the end of the hall. I'd never been to Dad's bedroom suite before, but I still knew where it was. It existed in the house like a heart. You always knew it was there.

I stood an arm's reach from the doors.

The doors were mahogany, stained the color of Coromina I's storm, inlaid with a greenstone carving of a planet flowering with life. My anger flared at the sight of it. *Liar.*

I curled my hand into a fist and set it against the center of that planet. The stone was cool to the touch.

I took a deep breath.

And then I pounded on the door.

It felt like the ultimate transgression, like I was breaking every rule I'd ever learned since I was a little girl. But once I realized what I had done, I didn't stop. I only pounded harder, so hard that the doors rattled on their hinges. "Open up!" I shouted. "I know you're in there! Get the hell up!"

I kept beating against the door, taking out all my rage and frustration, all my fear about the war and about Isabel and about who I was becoming. My bones rattled inside my hand. My knuckles began to hurt. I didn't stop.

The door opened.

I tumbled forward, I'd been beating against the door so hard. But I caught myself and looked up, and I found Dad gazing back at me with a cold expression.

"What the fuck do you think you're doing?" he said.

That sharp edge in his voice might have been enough to stop me before, but it wasn't enough to stop me today. I shoved past him and stepped into his suite without permission. A floating lamp was switched on, hovering next to a potted spider plant. The lamp cast just enough light to see how cavernous Dad's sitting room was. Tall, arching ceilings, a long stretch of hardwood floors covered in rugs from the Kiran system.

"I learned something interesting tonight," I said, "about Ekkeko's history." I didn't look at him but in the direction of the door that led into his bedroom proper. It hung slightly ajar, although I couldn't see into it. And I was glad. That was too much of a deep look into my father's life. I didn't want it.

The double doors clicked shut.

I jumped in surprise. He was letting me stay—or he was locking me in there with him.

I turned around. Dad stood with his arms crossed. I couldn't see his expression in the dim light.

"Did you, now?" he said. "And you thought it was so important that you had to wake me up?"

I hesitated. I'd been propelled here by my rage, but now I didn't know if I still had the strength to face him. He wore his nightclothes and slippers, but even without his impressive tailored suits, his presence was enough to generate fear.

"It was a shock," I finally said. "And I didn't think you should keep this particular information from me, given that I'm set to inherit the company."

He didn't say anything, just watched me through the darkness. I pressed on.

"Something lived here," I said. "Before you terraformed. This world wasn't abandoned."

Dad's expression gave nothing away, but that didn't mean anything. He was practiced in this sort of thing. "That's not Ninety information," he said. Then, speaking to the room: "Lights up! No use standing around in the dark."

The floating light blinked off and the overhead lights brightened in a careful, calculated way. The light was warm and diffuse like sunlight, a much softer, much more expensive version of the golden lights we had the other rooms of the house.

It made Dad look like a king.

"I don't give a damn if it's Ninety information or not. I figured it out. And I think it has to do with Isabel's surgery." I took a deep breath, drawing up my courage. "I know she didn't have fucking Lasely fever. You made her lie to me and Daphne and Adrienne. I want answers."

Dad lifted his chin and gazed at me from under heavy lids.

"But you're a Ninety," he said.

"Fuck being a Ninety!" I shouted. "Fuck your whole stupid system. If you don't tell me what the hell is going on, I'm taking this information public."

Dad laughed. I glared at him.

"I'm taking it to the Connectivity Underground," I hissed. "I know my way in. And they'll—"

"You *knew* your way in," Dad said. "When you were a girl. They won't listen to you now that you work for the company and you don't have your trashy village friends to vouch for you."

Something snapped inside my chest. I hadn't let myself think about Laila and Paco in years. Their memories were too painful. "Don't you dare talk about them like that."

Dad laughed again.

My anger was burning up inside me. I kept curling and uncurling my hands into fists. Dad looked at me, looked at my hands. And then he smiled, small and knowing.

"Calm down," he said. "Tell me, how'd you find all this out. Do you even have proof?"

I hesitated. As soon as I did it, I knew I'd made a mistake.

"I can find it," I said. "I have my own channels in the company. I know how to get information."

Dad smiled at that. He ambled toward me. "I know you do. You think I hadn't noticed you trying to fix all the system's shithole villages?"

The air was sucked out of me.

"I know about you looking into Isabel's surgery, too, even after you *saw* her on Catequil. I guess that wasn't enough for you." Dad tapped the side of his temple, as if his ranking was a measure of his intelligence. "It always impressed me. I'll say that much. You certainly are the most tenacious of my daughters. I do think you're the one best suited to taking my position."

"No," I said. "Don't you dare. You are not going to pit us against each other."

Dad nodded. He turned away from me and strolled across the room, his hands tucked into the pockets of his nightclothes. I didn't move, just listened to my heart beating too fast, felt my chest growing tighter and tighter and tighter.

Dad sat down on his sofa. He crossed one leg across his knee, stretched out his arms along the back cushions.

"See?" he said. "You really are the best suited. I'm sure Adrienne would have fallen for that. She's so competitive."

I glared at him.

Dad settled back further into the cushions. He tapped out a rhythm with his fingers.

"So, you caught me," he said. "You went snooping and caught me."

I wanted to tear around his suite, ripping the light paintings from the wall and hurling them against the ground so that their energy flowed across the wooden panels. I wanted to break the glass in his windows. I wanted to smash down the door to his bedroom.

I wanted destruction.

"I find it impressive," he went on. "I don't like being defied, but your determination at undermining me is almost admirable."

I didn't say anything to that. This conversation was a web drawing tight around me. I knew I wasn't leaving there with any answers.

"Look at me, Esme."

I did, but only out of the periphery of my vision. I couldn't help myself.

"Look at me."

The air was as thick as smoke. I couldn't breathe. He'd sit there in that sofa forever. I'd never known anything as certain as I knew that, in that moment.

So, I looked at him.

His mouth curved up into a smile crueler than anything I could muster.

"You're my daughter, and I've every intention of you inheriting the company after I die."

If you'll ever die, I thought.

"Not just because you're the oldest. You really are the best option out of your sisters. Daphne's a lost cause. Isabel doesn't give a shit about her studies, and she's useful to me in—other ways besides."

"How?" I felt cold. I felt sick. My suspicions had been right. "How is she useful to you?"

He just grinned at that and wagged his finger at me, like I was a little girl being told I couldn't have a puppy. "Adrienne's too pretentious, too focused on appearances. You, my dear, are my best choice. I always thought a son would be easier to groom to take my place, but you came along quite nicely." Another smile. It made my skin crawl. "These secret projects show a good corporacratic attitude, they really do. That's why I admire them so much."

"What if I just leave?" I said. "It's wartime; once I jump out of the system, they'll never let me back in—"

"You're not going to do that." Dad rolled his eyes like he was bored.

"You don't think so?" I glared at him. "You think I want to be the CEO of a company that killed an entire species just so they could have a planet to themselves?"

"Oh, is that what you think? That they're dead?"

He was toying with me, trying to trick me somehow. I fumbled for a response.

"I'll defect to OCI—"

"Oh, stop it." Dad sighed. "This posturing is exhausting. How about I raise your clearance level? All the way to Ninety-Nine. Then you can find out my deep, dark secret."

"What?" I gaped at him. This was certainly a trick. What else could it be?

"What can I say? Your little investigation has impressed me. Besides, I've been meaning to upgrade you. You need to know how to run a war."

Silence. Dad was grinning. I wanted to storm out of the room like I was still a teenager, capable of throwing tantrums, but I didn't. I just took steps backward until I bumped up against the closed doors. The soft light of the room seemed to choke me. Dad kept grinning. My anger was seeping out of me a little at a time. And why wouldn't it? My anger was impotent. It had always been impotent.

"How about I change your clearance level now?" Dad turned his gaze upward. "Bring up CG Connectivity."

A panel slid out of the end table beside the sofa. Dad tapped it and a holo appeared, filling up the entire room. All I could see was the sweep of a mountain vista, but Dad said, "Full view," and the vista melted away, replaced by a floating cluster of unfamiliar icons. Through the murky haze of the holo, Dad tapped an icon shaped like a DNA strand, and the screen blossomed into something like a wild, windswept tree. It looked like art.

"All the clearance levels in the company," Dad said. "Lovely, isn't it?"

I was swept up in a riptide. I was being dragged out to sea. I came up there thinking I'd rage and scream into the wind, but instead, Dad was giving me the answers I'd always wanted.

Shame was just like heat. I couldn't escape it. So, instead I said, "I didn't think getting a Ninety-Nine clearance was so easy."

"It is when you're my daughter." Dad tapped out a pattern on the holo that sent it raveling and unraveling through those branches of security levels. I couldn't make any sense of it.

"Esme Coromina," Dad said.

The holo stopped. My full-body image appeared, dressed in a gray suit, my hair pinned back away from my face. I looked harsh and unfamiliar.

"All your information is contained in that image," Dad said. "Just like how your own body contains all of *your* information. Code and DNA. Clever, isn't it? I still think about the woman who designed all this, back when we first started the company. Brilliant woman, simply brilliant. Refused to take rejuvenation treatments." Dad looked at me through the image of myself. "Clearance level change requested."

It was as if I were watching my own surgery. My image on the holo flowered open, and in the stream of visual information was a number. Ninety.

"Don't," I whispered, but I knew I didn't really mean it, I knew that I wanted this. The thought turned my blood cold.

Dad touched the number twice. It glowed golden.

"Ninety-Nine," Dad said.

The number changed. I expected to feel different, to feel my skin tingling over my bones like when you passed through a scanner, but I didn't.

"Security lock, shut down."

A pause, the images pulsing. And then the holo disappeared.

I closed my eyes and dropped my head back against the wall. I thought of my mother's message. *Something was here first.*

"Now you can know all the secrets," Dad said.

I opened my eyes. He was staring at me, his arms still stretched out across the sofa.

"I hate you," I said.

"You don't hate me enough," he said. "Tomorrow, I'll take you to the Hawley Lab. It's brand-new." He lifted his chin. "Inner circle only. You want to know what happened to the creatures who lived on this planet first? You want to know what Isabel's surgery was really for? You'll find out tomorrow."

My whole body trembled.

"Get some sleep." Dad turned away from me, moving toward his bedroom. Over the corner of his shoulder he said, "Tomorrow's probably going to be difficult for you."

I woke up the next morning sprawled across the sofa in my suite. For a few seconds, before I fully woke up and remembered, everything was peaceful. Sunlight and the scent of seaweed poured in through my open windows. I rolled onto my back and blinked up at the ceiling, where dots of light chased each other across the room. I dug the heel of my palm into my eye socket. Light burst against darkness. Last night almost felt like a dream. Had I really confronted my father? Had I really stormed into his personal suite? It didn't seem real.

The Connectivity chimed.

"Ms. Coromina! There's a car waiting for you downstairs."

And with that, everything came back. Harriet's hidden message. Aliens. My being a Ninety-Nine.

"Ms. Coromina? Are you awake?"

"Thank you," I choked out. "I'll be down in a moment." My voice wavered, but I doubted Grace heard it. The sunlight suddenly seemed too bright. Out of place. I marched across my room and yanked the curtains shut, hoping the darkness would calm me. It didn't.

I was going to the lab today. That was what Dad wanted, and so that was what was going to happen. What I wanted didn't matter.

But part of me was afraid that maybe this all *was* what I wanted. The idea frightened me. What if I wanted this to happen not just because I would learn the truth so I could protect Isabel and Daphne and even Adrienne, but so I would *know*?

My stomach churned, and I dressed, pulling a pressed gray suit out of my closet. I brushed my hair back into a ponytail. I didn't bother with makeup.

Adrienne and Daphne were eating breakfast in the dining room with Grace when I went downstairs. I just stood in the doorway and told Alice to grab me an energy pack to eat on the way. I couldn't stand the thought of actual food.

"Where are you going?" Daphne said with mild interest. She didn't take her eyes away from the glow of her lightbox.

"To work," I said, more curtly than I intended. Adrienne snickered and Daphne glared at her.

Alicia pushed through the kitchen doors with my energy pack. "If you see Isabel," she said, "tell her I'm worried about her."

The sound of Isabel's name sent a sharp bolt of panic through my system. "Why?" I said. "What happened?"

"Nothing," Alicia said. "Just the same old thing. She keeps dragging herself around the estate."

Adrienne looked up at that and frowned. I took the energy pack from Alicia, thanked her, and left the dining room before I could have any more of a conversation with my sisters or the staff. The mention of Isabel stirred up my guilt and confusion even further, and I was afraid if I spoke, I would say something to reveal the kind of damage Dad had done to our family. To Isabel most of all.

The driver waiting in the car wasn't John or any of the other usual drivers. He leaned up against the side of the car, his eyes shrouded in a cap. I could hardly see his face and I wondered if that was on purpose.

"Ms. Coromina," he said, and he looked at me for a second longer than usual. My skin tingled. He was scanning me. Making sure of my identity.

"Good morning," I said, and climbed into the car so I wouldn't have to interact with him further. He waited a beat and then climbed in too and started the engine. I peeled open my energy pack and the car shot out of the drive and onto the highway.

We sped away from the village, toward the east, in the opposite direction of the office. I sucked on my energy pack and stared down at my lap so I wouldn't get even more nauseated than I already was, from the blur of trees on the side of the road. The driver didn't say anything to me. I didn't say anything to him.

We sped through the countryside.

The trip was longer than I expected, far into the lush tropical forests that grew around the shore. I asked the car for the time and discovered we'd been driving for nearly an hour. Dread coiled in my stomach. I had no idea where we were going.

Twenty minutes later, the car slowed down enough that I could see the forest again, towering maneles heavy with flowers. The road twisted through the woods. I didn't recognize any of this. The woods here were wilder, less cultivated than the woods outside of Undirra City, where the Veiled Garden was tucked away behind its facade.

I pressed my face against the glass like I was a little kid flying on a shuttle for the first time, looking out at the stars and the streaks of color on the planets below. Just swap flowers for stars, narrow flat tree leaves for planets. It felt just as foreign to me.

But not nearly as magical.

And then the trees fell away and the car pulled into civilization.

That was the wrong word. Deep down, I knew that. But it was still my first thought upon seeing all those gleaming glass-and-metal buildings reflecting the green of the surrounding forest. We drove through an energy barrier, the faint electronic tingle tickling at my skin. The space behind my eyes hummed. I wondered what would have happened if the scanner had read the wrong DNA. I could ask; Dad had to tell me now that I was a Ninety-Nine.

Not that I was sure I wanted the answers. Not anymore.

The driver pulled the car up to the overhang. The tropical forest crushed in on the building, vines and flowers already growing along the glass. The builders must have activated the terraforming to get all this ready. Even the buildings had that look of being terraformed, the glass melted down from sand and sculpted into place. I could just picture Dad and the rest of his team standing behind a reinforced barrier, watching this little world come into existence.

I stepped out of the car.

The air was soupy and still. I didn't bother saying anything to the driver, no thank-you like I usually did. I doubted he'd care, doubted he'd even respond. He would have been trained not to.

Heat clung to my skin. All around me was the earthy rainy scent of the forest. I went inside, hoping the cold jolt of the climate control would rattle the anxiety out of me. It didn't.

There was a receptionist, an Alvatech soldier with her hair clipped short. My heart stuttered: at first; she looked like my mother. But it was the wrong military, and when she lifted her face, her eyes had an odd reflective sheen that meant she'd been bioengineered for scanning vision. She looked younger than my mother, less hardened by the universe.

She scanned me, that same faint prickle as the energy barrier. "Esme Coromina," she said. "Level Ninety-Nine. You're to go up to the twenty-seventh floor. Ms. DeCrie will be waiting for you."

She turned back to her holo, that swirl of swimming fishes.

Ms. DeCrie. Flor. I took a deep breath, bracing myself.

The elevator was narrow and oddly shaped, nestled into a groove in the wall. Definitely a terraformed building. The little glass pod shot up to the twenty-seventh floor, showing me the progress on a holo installed in the floor. When the doors slid open, they revealed a long, tiled hallway lined with pale white lights. Flor stood waiting for me, her hands clasped behind her back. She smiled like she didn't know this whole trip was just my father's way of torturing me.

"Esme," she said. "It's so good to see you again."

I thought about the wariness behind Isabel's eyes anytime she passed me in the hallway. The sorrow. This woman had helped put it there.

But I only smiled at her and said, "Yes. You too."

"Philip said he recently amped up your security level. I suppose congratulations are in order."

"Yes, thank you." I tried to force an enthusiasm I didn't feel. It worked better than I expected.

Flor turned and gestured with one hand down the hall. "I hear you're interested in the Radiance Project. I must say it's exciting to get to talk with you about it, especially when I couldn't say anything back on Catequil."

My stomach twisted around. "Not Project X?" I was trying to be polite. Professional. Maybe this would be easier if I heard the standard pitch, and not the cold harsh truth.

I stared down the pinpoint of the hall. It seemed to stretch on for longer than it should.

Flor laughed. "No, that's the name the gossip hounds give a top secret project when they don't know the real thing. There have been about twenty Project Xs since the Four Sisters were founded." She winked at me. "You'll get to hear about them all in good time, I'm sure."

I wondered how many of the other Project Xs involved Dad kidnapping his own daughter.

"Anyway," Flor went on. "I thought we'd get straight to the heart of things." She started walking down the hall and I followed her, drawn on a line that had been cast by my father. The lights flooded over us, as thick as water. I could drown in those lights.

"The whole point of the Radiance Project was to perfect our biogenetic soldier program," Flor said cheerfully. "But it started with an unusual discovery Philip made several years ago."

"The aliens?"

I'd been trying to shock Flor into dropping her good corporate facade, but it didn't work. She just glanced at me and laughed. "Philip said you uncovered our big secret." She said *big secret* like it was a joke. "Quite an accomplishment."

I didn't say anything. We kept walking past closed doors, their locks all blinking red. Activated.

"But no, I wasn't referring to the discovery of the Radiance themselves—that happened before my time, during terraforming."

"What?" I stared at her. "He terraformed even though the planet was populated. That—that was illegal. Wasn't it?"

Flor laughed. "If your father cared about legality two hundred years ago, none of us would be here."

I said nothing.

"Besides, the actual discovery of the aliens wasn't the key. I was referring to the connection between the indigenous species and the flu epidemic," Flor said. "Philip discovered it during the outbreak. Well, Philip and a few members of R&D."

The flu epidemic. My skin felt cold and my stomach felt hollow. It was a piece of the puzzle I hadn't even considered.

"He was trying to develop a vaccine, of course. But they realized the flu was—well, nonhuman, for lack of a better word."

"All viruses are nonhuman."

"Yes, of course." Flor laughed. I wasn't trying to be funny. "But we still share a common genetic structure. We're all from the same place originally. That's something that's easy to forget during wartime."

That caught my attention, and I glanced over at her. But she was staring ahead, still chattering along.

"So, this virus," Flor said, "it didn't have the structure we expected to see. It had something completely different, something—alien."

The way she paused made me think she'd practiced this speech in front of a mirror. It wouldn't have surprised me if she had, knowing Flor.

I wondered how many Ninety-Nines there were.

"Philip was ecstatic, of course. The virus provided a safe way to study the Radiance. We'd been trying during the whole life of the company, but we couldn't get at them. Now we could." Flor's voice flushed with pride.

The whole life of the company. Dad had found existence of other life in this universe and then terraformed over them.

"So, Dad killed the aliens off and they left a virus behind." I thought about Dad's taunt from last night, the insinuation that these creatures, these aliens—the Radiance—were still here. Maybe this was what he meant. Their virus was still here, picking us off.

"Anyway," Flor said. "When he realized what he had found, Philip divided up the team in two. Half were looking for the vaccine, the other half—well, they were looking for ways to *apply* this information."

We'd come to the end of the hallway. Flor swiped her hand over the sensor beside a door and the door popped open. She opened it, gestured for me to go through first.

I stepped through the door. The air shimmered. Another energy barrier. I'd passed; my DNA was acceptable. We stood in a stairwell, empty and echoing.

"We're going down again," Flor said. "Sorry about the convoluted path; it was part of the design of the building. Lots of ways of keeping secrets, you know. So, the second R&D team noticed some unusual transformative properties with the flu. It wasn't a flu at all, of course, but that was an easy enough name for the newsfeeds. This was actually a kind of . . . terraforming bug, in a sense, writ small. It did to the human body what our terraforming programs do to planets."

That cold, sickly feeling returned. Every time I stepped down my stomach lurched. We twisted around a couple of turns of a spiral and came to another door, another sensor. Flor swept her hand over it and I stepped through another energy barrier.

This hallway was indistinguishable from the last one. Flor strode along, talking to me over her shoulder.

"The flu's 'terraforming' mostly wreaked havoc on the human body," Flor said. "That's why it was so deadly. We're still not sure why it jumped around the way it did, but we have our theories. Do you want to hear them?"

"No, thank you." I walked past door after closed door. We hadn't passed another human being once.

"You know you can, now that you're a Ninety—"

"I don't want to hear the theories. The flu was the aliens' way of terraforming the human body. Why? To make us suitable for the planet? That makes no sense. This was long after we'd changed the atmosphere." But as soon as I spoke, I knew that wasn't the answer.

Flor stopped in front of a door. It looked like all the other doors. She let out a small cough. "You're right," he said. "We think it was chosen for its destructive power. We think they were trying to kill us off."

I stared at her. "You mean to say they were still around during the epidemic? The Radiance?"

"That's the theory." Flor's expression was easy, friendly, like this information didn't bother her in the slightest. Maybe it didn't. Maybe she'd known it for a long time. Maybe this indifference was what happened when you were a Ninety-Nine.

"Well then, where *are* they?"

"That, we don't know." Flor swiped her hand over another lock. "We think your sister might." The door opened. I half-expected to see a stairwell, but instead I got another hallway, this one much narrower, much more dimly lit. It slanted slightly downward. No doors.

"This lab was built to hold secrets," Flor said, "We'll be there soon."

I didn't give a damn about the lab's architectural structure. "My sister," I said, trying to keep my voice measured. "You think my sister knows where the Radiance are?"

We passed through the doorway. Another energy barrier. My skin was drying out; my hair was charging up with static electricity, strands of it floating away from my head.

"We do. And if you'll let me finish—" Flor tossed her hair over her shoulder. "We learned that the only humans who could survive the violent change brought about by the flu were fetuses, since they were already developing anyway—the bug just worked its way into their system and starting messing with things."

I was numb. The overhead lights flickered. A door waited at the end of the hallway and I knew that I wouldn't like what I saw on the other side.

"Only two infected babies were born," Flor said. "Most of them died when their mothers did. The first belonged to a woman who was already nine months pregnant, and the baby didn't require time in an incubator, as Isabel did."

I felt breathless. There was another baby? Another child my father had tortured? "What happened to it? The other baby?"

"Nothing. She was unaffected except for a case of synesthesia and an aptitude for reading people's expressions. I'm sure she'll go far. Your sister was the important case."

We'd come to the door at the end of the hallway. Flor turned to me. Her features were blurred out by the dim, shadowy lights.

"What I'm trying to say is: your sister is the closest thing we have to an indigenous specimen. Her DNA is not human DNA. If the Radiance are here, hiding, she probably knows where they are."

I took deep, gulping breaths. The hallway seemed to spin around. I pressed one hand against the wall, trying to steady myself. Isabel was an *alien*? I didn't know if I should believe Flor. Maybe this was all a joke. This was Dad fucking with me for demanding answers.

"At the moment, we're not terribly focused on the Radiance themselves. Let them hide—the real threat is OCI. And Isabel is the reason we're going to win this war. That's what the Radiance Project is all about. Defeating OCI and unveiling the best bioengineered soldiers in the galaxy. And your sister helped."

The surgery on Catequil. Isabel on the holo, telling me she was fine. It had never been about Lasely fever, just like we'd suspected. It was something darker. Something crueler.

And I hadn't stopped it.

"You used her DNA without her permission," I said.

Flor turned away from me and swiped her hand over the lock. The door didn't open; instead, a holo sprang up, asking her to solve a word puzzle. She did without looking at it. Then the door slid open.

"It was just her DNA," Flor said.

The other side of the door was not a hallway but a room: a wide room lined with vats. It looked the same as any other bioengineering room on the Four Sisters. I'd been in dozens of them since Dad moved me from PM to Genetics. But I didn't want to go into *this* room. It was a moment of decision. I could step through the doorway and pass under the sensor crackling on the air, or I could turn around and follow our path back to the lobby. I could wash my hands of all of this.

But would that even be possible? Would I get lost inside this organic maze of a building? Could I disown the violence of my father this far into my career?

"Ms. Coromina?" Flor said. "I know I've dumped a lot of overwhelming information on you, but you really will want to see this. It's one of the Coromina Group's greatest achievements."

I didn't want to see it.

I stepped through the threshold anyway.

The sensor washed over my skin. It didn't find me lacking. I still wondered what would happen if it did. In a building like this, all ends were tied up. Dad might have terraformed mazes and puzzles to keep out intruders, but he would have installed weapons, too.

I imagined my cells rupturing beneath the light of the sensor. Imagined my body turning to a smear of blood. Or maybe the sensor would just incapacitate me enough that the company could pack me up on an exile ship. That would certainly be the official story.

The vats bubbled on either side of us. My stomach churned. Flor started to chatter again, explaining the engineering process, how they drew out the alien strands of DNA from the material they collected from Isabel and isolated them and converted them for use in a typical genetic embryo. She was so casual about it, and I kept thinking about that day in the garden, me telling Isabel everything would be fine.

"That was when the really cool stuff started happening," Flor said. "The DNA just *attached* itself and did all the work for us! All we did was kick back and watch the infographics on the holos. It was amazing."

I looked at the embryos in the vats. Holograms flickered across the side of the glass. I'd learned enough about genetics these past few years to know that they were tracking the changes in the embryos' DNA. I walked up to the first one and stared at it through the murky liquid. It was a fetus. They always arranged them that way, the newest at the beginning, the oldest at the end. That way, when they were finally born, they wouldn't have to walk past rows of themselves.

"We have a squad of full-grown R-Company soldiers," Flor said. I jumped; her voice was closer to me than I expected. When I turned around, she was smiling at me. "They're really quite remarkable. I don't get a chance to show them off that often, and they're probably itching to see someone other than me or the rest of the crew. There are only five Ninety-Nines in the company, you know. Six, including you." She smiled. "Any answers to any questions, you can have them now."

I glanced at the fetus one last time. The DNA codes flickered against the water. The fetus floated there, suspended, not moving. It was hard to believe it was something living.

"All right. Show me the soldiers," I said, even though I didn't want to see them. But I was there; I hadn't fled. I'd made my choice.

Flor led me through the dim reddish light. It reminded me of the light of the planet. Everything on the Four Sisters was stained by the color of Coromina I. Even this laboratory in the middle of the jungle.

We went through a doorway—I was shocked there was no sensor—and into a narrow hallway that led down to a door marked TRAINING. Flor took me through. It was like stepping into a completely different building. The light was soft and warm, and there was a woman sitting at a desk, moving files around on a holo screen. She glanced up at us and smiled.

"Is this the new Ninety-Nine?" She stood up and smoothed down her blue Coromina Group suit jacket. "I'd heard there was a new one. It's such a pleasure to meet you. I'm Gabriella Lewen." She held her hand across the desk and I shook it, feeling dazed.

"Esme Coromina," I said.

"I know! I looked you up when I got word that Phillip had made the upgrade. I'm in charge of Interpersonal Development," she said. "For the R-Company. It's so nice to have someone join us from the outside! The R-Company will be delighted to have a new person to show off to." She laughed. I forced out my businesswoman's smile and thought of Isabel the day she had come home from Catequil, her hair lank, her eyes shadowed.

"We train them with stations," she went on. "So, we have a handful resting in the barracks right now, on their break." She touched her holo and said, "Attention, Squad Alpha! You have a visitor."

She beamed up at me. "I think you'll be very impressed, Ms. Coromina." Gabriella bustled out from behind her desk. She pressed her hand against the lock on the door at the back of the room. We filed in, one at a time. Another hall. More closed doors. These were marked with holographic signs: WEAPONS. ESPIE. MESS HALL. HISTORY. FLIGHT. I couldn't see any logical pattern to the signs. Maybe this wasn't the place to look for logic.

The barracks were at the end of the hall, the only double doors there. Gabriella hit a chime before she pulled the doors open.

"Attention!" someone shouted inside the room, and there was the stomping lockstep of soldiers moving into place. I'd seen it plenty of times before.

I crept cautiously into the room, staring at them. The Radiance soldiers stared back, waiting beside their neatly made beds. They weren't all dressed the same—some had on full Coromina Group uniforms, some were in lounge clothes, a few were shirtless—but all of them wore the same face. I recognized it as one of our prototypical soldier models.

"Squad Alpha," Flor said proudly. "I'd like to introduce you to Esme Coromina, the newest addition to the Radiance Project. She's very excited to meet you."

I couldn't stop staring at them.

"At ease," I finally said. The words were dry and scratchy at the back of my throat. There was a sense of loosening, like air going out of a balloon.

"It's very nice to meet you all," I said. "I look forward to seeing what you're capable of."

The Radiance soldiers didn't move.

"Do you have any questions?" Gabriella asked. "Would you like to see what they can do?"

"Aren't they on their break?" I glanced around at them. "I hate to make you work when you don't want to."

One of them seemed to smile. Maybe it was my imagination.

"Well, aren't you in luck, boys." Gabriella laughed.

One spoke. His voice was familiar. How many soldiers had I spoken to, soldiers that looked like him, that shared parts of his DNA?

"Sergeant Michael Woods speaking," he said. "It's very generous of you, Ms. Coromina. But we don't mind."

The others nodded in agreement.

"We discussed it," he added. "Without saying anything. It's something we can do."

Gabriella and Flor looked as delighted as parents, but I felt only a cold shakiness in my core. Telepathy? They had *telepathy*?

Did Isabel?

"Can you discuss things with—with me?" I said. "Without saying anything?'

The Radiance soldiers shuffled, looked at each other. Sergeant Michael Woods smiled. "Sadly, we can't. Only with those who share our DNA."

I wondered if they could speak with Isabel. If I could bring one of those soldiers back to Star's End and give him to her as a protector, as a friend. Someone she could talk to about what had happened.

"What would you like to demonstrate?" Gabriella asked Sergeant Michael Woods. "The flight simulators would be impressive, I think."

Sergeant Michael Woods nodded. "Yes, that's what we were thinking."

The other soldiers nodded in agreement, their heads bobbing up and down in unison. I shivered.

"And they're available," Sergeant Michael Woods went on. "Squad Gamma has finished their training."

"Even I didn't know that." Gabriella looked over at me. "It's just astonishing, isn't it? They're all connected on an energy level that we can't experience. Works a bit like the lightbox linking but completely natural. No mechanical augmentation required."

"It's simply brilliant," Flor said. "Phillip is simply brilliant."

Squad Alpha were already changing their clothes in front of us, wriggling into flight suits, flashes of lean bodies snapping on the edge of my vision. I wrapped my arms around my chest and squeezed. I kept thinking about Isabel. I couldn't see any connection between her and these soldiers, but I knew it was there.

"Let's take you up to the observation deck," Flor said. "Let the squad get ready."

We left the barracks. My thoughts hummed when we stepped back out into the hallway, as if the sound of the air had been muffled when I was standing in front of the Radiance soldiers. Maybe it had. That wave of energy Gabriella had talked about, the one keeping them all linked together. Maybe we ordinary humans could notice it if we tried hard enough.

I followed Flor and Gabriella into the elevator. That humming in my head didn't stop. Maybe it wasn't the wave of energy after all; maybe it was something about this cold, labyrinthine building.

The observation deck was a small round room shielded with glass windows and veils of transparent energy. It was elegantly furnished with expensive brocade furniture, and a flat paper painting of a jacaranda tree, no doubt unimaginably expensive, hung on one wall like a centerpiece.

"Watercolor," Flor said. The word had no meaning to me. "One of Phillip's favorites. He bought it from a dealer on Ryta. Lovely, isn't it?"

To my eyes, accustomed to light paintings and holos, it looked flat and lifeless. Which explained why my father would have wanted it so badly.

"Usually, we set out a buffet," Gabriella said, "But Mr. Coromina announced your visit at the last minute—"

"It's fine. I'm not hungry." I walked over to the window, close enough to feel the prickle of the energy shield. The flight simulator waited down below, its lights glowing steadily. I'd seen plenty of flight simulators since joining the company, but I didn't recognize this one. They generally used actual starships that had been grounded, but this didn't even look like a starship command deck. It could have been a living room in a stylish house. Twenty chairs arranged in two concentric circles, all padded and covered in shiny fabric that reflected the overhead lights. No lightboxes. No holos. Just those twenty chairs.

"It's something, isn't it?" Gabriella sided up alongside me.

"I've never seen anything like this." My voice came out flat and uninterested. I wasn't interested; I was horrified. I just didn't know why.

"That's because only Ninety-Nines get to see it. These are the newest model of starships, our secret weapon against OCI. We'll unveil them during the war, and once the rest of the systems see what we've been working on—well, let's just say this war's going to be profitable." Gabriella nodded, her gaze fixed on the chairs waiting down below.

A green light switched on.

"Here they come!" she cried, and leaned forward, close to the glass. Flor rushed over to join us. The walls parted like curtains, velvety and unsettling to watch, and Squad Alpha marched in, divided into two equal lines. They sat down on the chairs in movements as choreographed as those in a dance troupe.

"The ships and the soldiers go together, all part of Project Radiance. When we start selling them, we have a whole show planned out for how to prove that the R-Company are doing this all on their own." Flor's eyes shone with the shiplights. "Holos showing the live ship engines and all that. Unfortunately, we don't have it set up completely yet."

"You'll have to take our word for it." Gabriella laughed.

I didn't answer, just watched the Radiance soldiers. They sank deep into their seats, and the dark shiny fabric oozed up between the legs, around their waists. My stomach twisted but I couldn't look away.

The ship lights dimmed, flared, and then the flight simulator began to shake and tremble. The Radiance soldiers kept sinking into the oily darkness of their seats. They didn't seem bothered by it, just kept staring straight ahead with their eyes open. Staring at each other? It was impossible for me tell.

The flight simulator lights blinked off. A beam of blue light shot out of the middle of the circle of chairs. The Radiance soldiers didn't even move. That blue light filled up the flight simulator. It rattled harder and harder, then went still. My eyes burned, and I lifted one hand to my brow to try to shield them from the light. It didn't work.

"The light's a kind of radiation," Flor said. "We don't fully understand it yet, although it does affect humans. Not the R-Company, though."

"That's why we have the shields over the glass," Gabriella added. "You're perfectly safe."

My eyes watered, tears streaking out of my eyes. I turned down to the floor and tried to blink the burning away. When I looked back up, the Radiance soldiers had been completely subsumed into their seats. Only their faces remained, those faces that were also the faces of hundreds of other soldiers, all washed out with the blue light.

My stomach twisted. I gasped and stumbled backward, my breath strangling in my throat.

"I don't understand," I said. "This—this is inhumane."

Gabriella and Flor looked at each other, then roared with laughter.

I stared at them, stricken, terrified, angry. This was what they tortured my sister for?

Gabriella strode over to the opposite wall and activated the building's Connectivity. "That's enough," she said. "Ms. Coromina's finding your flight system upsetting."

The blue light vanished. The seats receded and I let out a sign of relief. The soldiers were all still there.

Sergeant Michael Woods stood up. "Nothing to worry about, Ms. Coromina," he said, his voice distorted through the speaker. "It's as natural to us as swimming is to you. Or running, walking. Take your pick."

"Yes, thank you," I said.

Gabriella dismissed the soldiers and they stood up from their seats as if nothing had happened and filed one after another out of the flight simulator. I collapsed on one of the brocaded sofas. My body sank in deep. *Just like the soldiers*. A faint hint of my reflection appeared in the glass, shimmering with the energy shield.

Gabriella and Flor sat across from me.

"Spectacular, wasn't it?" Flor said. "All bioengineered."

"Even the ship," Gabriella added.

Spectacular wasn't the word I'd have chosen. "They were being *consumed*."

Flor laughed. "Well, yes, we designed it that way. The new ships are completely organic, designed like a machine but grown and cultured like the soldiers themselves. It's the next step in operator-machine linking."

"Organic?" I stared out at the flight simulator. "I didn't think the terraforming system worked for machines. Just static buildings."

"It wasn't created through the same process as the orgobuildings," Gabriella said. "And we use different starting material. We actually extrapolated out from the alien DNA in the sample."

"The sample you forced from my sister." I was still looking down at the flight simulator. It didn't look organic, with its overhead lights and cushiony chairs. Although the lights did cast a strange, phosphorescent glow, like a firefly. I hadn't noticed that until now.

"The ship is jump-capable," Flor went on, and I noticed that neither of them acknowledged my comment. "We had to augment it with a few computer parts. But we wanted to have all our bases covered once we go public with these. Militaries are always looking for jump-capable fighter ships."

Gabriella nodded like she hadn't heard this before.

"You're lucky you got to see them when you did," Flor added. "They're about to be deployed."

"What?" I whipped my head over to her. "Deployed? Sent off to war?"

"Well, yes, that's why we made them." She laughed.

"That's not what I meant," I snapped. "We haven't gone to war yet."

Flor and Gabriella exchanged glances. They both looked amused. There was a streak of cruelty in Flor's expression that I didn't like.

"What?" I hissed.

"You were only just promoted," Gabriella said. "So, you wouldn't know. But the start date for the war has been decided. Tomorrow."

"Tomorrow," I whispered, and I thought about my mother stepping off the shuttle. The way she smiled at me like I was everything. Tomorrow and she'd be up in the black, gone from me again.

"The first battle of a war is perfect for bringing out the R-Company." Gabriella smiled again. "We'll get the attention of every military in the galaxy."

"That's the hope, anyway," Flor said.

I listened to this with a dull throbbing ache in my chest. It was all happening at once. War. My sister's alien DNA. My mother leaving me at Star's End for the second time in my life.

I stared at the organic lights of the flight simulator and I was empty.

When I left the Radiance lab, the sky was heavy with rainclouds. It fit my mood. I told my driver to take me to the Starfish Lounge, down on the beach. The tourist roads were empty, but whether that was because of the impending war or the impending storm, I didn't know.

Less than a day of peace. The thought made me numb.

I contacted my mother on the drive to the beach. Her face flickered in the light of my portable holo, and she smiled grimly at me. "I guess you heard," she said.

Of course. The soldiers would know they were shipping out. I nodded.

"I'll be fine," she said. "It's nothing I haven't done before."

"I know. I just—" My eyes were heavy. I didn't want to cry in front of her. "I just wanted to wish you good luck."

I cringed when I said it, because I knew it wasn't a military thing to say. But she smiled, and I thought she looked too sad for a soldier. "Thank you. That means a lot to me."

A light blinked in the corner; she had to disconnect. I wanted to scream that I was a Ninety-Nine, that she had to stay on the line with me, but was the point? She was going out to fight regardless.

"I'll contact you when we get back," she said, and then she was gone, and I slumped back in my seat, the holo resting in my lap. The privacy barrier glittered between me and the driver. I took a deep breath, like the air didn't have enough oxygen.

Not long after that, we arrived at the Starfish Lounge. It was a diver's bar, one I used to sneak to as a teenager, back when I still harbored a few streaks of teenage rebellion. The divers were out today, storm or no; from my table I could see a pair of them stretched out on the pier, sorting out their haul. Their boats flashed on the horizon. It was dangerous, diving during a storm. But most of them would do it anyway. You had to enjoy danger in order to become a diver. It was a bit like being a cog in the corpocratic wheel.

The waitress brought me a rum-and-lime. "Odd choice for a suit," she said as she set it down. "This is a diver's drink."

"It's a diver's bar." I didn't tell her I used to drink these one after another when I came there with Laila and Paco. I took a long drink, the rum burning my throat. The waitress gave an approving nod and went back to the bar. I set my drink down and watched the divers on the pier. Two women, around my age or maybe younger, with tanned, lean bodies. Coromina employees same as me, serving that dual purpose of drawing tourists to the village and collecting the pearls and coral that went into making Coromina-specific electronics. That was the real trick to running a corpocracy. I'd learned it in my time running secret PM projects. Never let something do one thing when it can do two. Or more.

Like Isabel's DNA. Or Isabel herself. Was she dual-purpose, like those divers? A dual-purpose daughter, instead of a dual-purpose employee? I thought back through the last fourteen years, trying to find the clues to Isabel's secret origins. But all I saw was my sister.

I finished my rum-and-lime. The waitress came over just as I set my empty glass down. "You want another?"

I was the only person in the bar. It would fill up when the diving hours were over, or when the storm blew in with its full force, whichever came first. But until then, it was just me and the waitress and the bottles of liquor stacked up behind the counter.

"Sure." I slid the glass toward her and she picked it up and set it on her tray. "Wait," I said.

She glanced at me. She was older but she had the look of having been a diver herself once. The usual ropy arms, the hair cropped short against her skull.

"Do you know someone named Laila Zubiri?"

The waitress blinked at me. Then she shook her head. "No, I don't think so. Was she a diver?"

"No." I turned back to the window. The ocean was as dark as the storm clouds.

"Well, this is a diver's bar, like you said."

"She had diver friends. How about Paco Lang?" I glanced at her again. "Does he ever come in here?"

The waitress frowned. A line formed between her eyes. "You knew him?"

The past tense in her question made me shiver. "Knew? What happened?"

She sighed and put her free hand on her hip. My empty tumbler caught the lights and tossed them over my table. "He died. Two years ago, maybe."

My head rushed like the ocean. "Accident?"

"Yeah." The waitress hesitated. "Stayed out during a storm like this one." She tilted her head toward the window. "Got caught in the riptide. Sad thing, but—" She turned away from me and went back to the counter. I couldn't move. Paco was dead. The first boy I ever kissed, drowned trying to get pearls and coral for the Coromina Group.

I wondered if I would have known about it if I had still worked in PM. If I hadn't been distracted with all the secrecy of Genetics. I reached over and grabbed the sanitizer light they kept on all the tables and fiddled with the switch, the way I used to do when I came there with Paco, watching him move beneath the dim lights, his bare shoulders gleaming. I couldn't stand the memory. He'd died and I didn't even know it.

"Got your drink." The waitress set my refreshed tumbler down on the table. "I really am sorry I had to tell you about that. I— You must not get village news, being—" She gestured at my suit.

"No." I took a long drink. "He was my first boyfriend. More or less; you know how it is."

The waitress smiled, although she looked sad. I slumped back in my chair. The waves slammed up against the pier, throwing high arcs of foam.

"Boats are starting to come in," the waitress said. "It's gonna get crowded in here."

"They don't like having suits around, do they?"

"Not really." She tilted her head. "They'll wonder about you drinking that, though."

I laughed. "Probably, yeah."

I expected her to go back to the counter, but she stayed at my side. The waves crashed into the shore. Every now and then, one of them was dotted with a diver's boat, the lights flashing wildly in the darkening light.

"I'll tell 'em you knew Paco," she said. "If anybody gives me shit."

I looked at her. She was still staring at the window. "Thanks."

"Not a problem."

Silence fell over the bar. Thunder rumbled overhead, closer now. The light fixtures rattled. By this time tomorrow, Alvatech and the Andromeda Corps and a squad of soldiers created from my sister's DNA would intercept the OCI military in an abandoned expanse of space on the edge of the solar system. Mercenaries would kill each other on our behalf; my mother might be among them. They would burn up in the heat of sun bombs; they would be dragged into the vacuum to suffocate. And when it was all over, the newsfeeds would activate and they would tell everyone in the Four Sisters, me and Isabel, the waitress and the divers riding into shore and Laila, wherever she was, that those horrors had been done to protect us. And maybe some of us would accept it.

But I was a Ninety-Nine now, and I knew what was true, and I knew what was a lie.

"You want to hear a secret?" I sipped at my rum-and-lime. The waitress looked down at me.

"What kind of secret?"

"Company secret."

Her expression collapsed in on itself. "I don't—"

"Don't tell anybody, you'll be fine. And everyone in the system's going to know by tomorrow night anyway."

She went quiet and I knew that I didn't actually have to say it out loud.

"Tomorrow?" she whispered. "It's starting tomorrow?"

I nodded, drank, stared out the window. Divers dragged their boats across the sand. Light forked in the sky.

"Who are you?" she said. "You have to be—*high up* if you know that. And you knew Paco?"

I drained the last of my drink.

"Yes," I said, and in true Coromina Group fashion, I never specified which question I was answering.

I walked home. I made it to the edge of the estate just as the sky opened up, water falling in shining gray curtains. I slipped off my shoes and walked barefoot through the lawn, mud squelching between my toes. I still felt numb from what I'd learned about Isabel's surgery. It was like a nightmare I had just woken up from, and I turned the memories of it around inside my head, trying to make sense of them.

Dad had known the perfect lie to spin to me. She was sick with an embarrassing disease, we could fix it with a single surgery and no one has to know, just tell everyone she's got an internship—I'd sat trembling in my chair as he spoke, knowing I had to protect my sister. I just wished I hadn't been so blind, that I'd given her the kind of protection she really needed. That internship had always felt wrong to me, and yet I did nothing to stop it. Nothing.

I stepped onto the back porch, out of the rain. Thunder rumbled through the clouds. I suppose I should have been more shocked at the idea that my sister was some kind of part-alien, but the truth was, the idea was so bizarre that I couldn't grasp it. All I could think about were my own failings as her sister. All I could think about was that day she was born, when I promised myself I would protect her. But I couldn't protect her, because I didn't know anything about her. Dad had kept that all from me.

I went inside and tossed my shoes aside. I was dripping across the floor, leaving a snail's trail behind me. Easy to track. I didn't care. I walked up the main stairs, heading toward Isabel's room.

The hallway was dark; the lights had been switched off, and any sunlight had been swallowed whole by the storm clouds. But there was a glow around Isabel's door, as if her room was enchanted. I walked up to it, lifted my fist to knock. But then I hesitated, wondering again if she could read my mind the way the soldiers could read one another's. No, probably not—they said they couldn't read the minds of anyone unlike them. But Isabel was different. She wasn't manufactured. And maybe she knew I was standing here, trying to decide what I wanted to stay.

I closed my eyes and knocked.

She didn't answer. I felt a swell of fear: I was right. She could read my mind. And she wasn't going to answer.

I knocked again, harder this time. "Isabel!" I called out. "I need to talk to you."

Something shuffled inside her room. Footsteps pattering across hardwood floors. I knocked again. "Isabel," I said, and I pressed against the door and dropped my voice low. "I—I know. What you are."

My heart was beating much too fast. My throat tingled from saying the words aloud. And then the door swung open, and there was Isabel, skin ashy, hair tangled, eyes sparking.

"What did you say?" she hissed.

"Dad told me everything," I said. "About you. About—Catequil."

I expected her to slam the door in my face. But she just stared at me, her knuckles turning white from squeezing the edge of the door.

"I'm sorry," I said, voice raspy.

She narrowed her eyes at me. "You knew before. And you didn't bring me home."

"What?" I shook my head. "Look—can I come inside? I don't want to talk about this out in the—"

"No," she snapped, and she braced herself in the doorway, stretching out her arms and legs to take up space. "You knew what they were going to do to me in Catequil and you let me go anyway." She leaned forward. "I *saw* it. In your head. I can do that; did Dad tell you?"

"You misunderstood," I stammered, but I knew it wasn't convincing—I was stunned at the thought that she had seen inside my head. Hearing her say it aloud was a sharp, harsh reminder that she wasn't human. Not all the way.

Shame washed over me. Could she see all that, too? But she hadn't reacted at all. Just kept glaring at me.

"You misunderstood," I said, my voice clearer this time. "I didn't know what Dad was really doing. He told me you had Lasely fever—*you* told me you had Lasely fever."

She shook her head, her eyes burning. "I told you it was possible. But you knew something was *wrong*. You knew he was *lying*."

I gasped. Shook my head.

"You let him hurt me," she said.

I shook my head, but even I knew that was a lie. All my time at the company, I'd tried to fight back against Dad. I'd fixed roads and tried to uncover his secrets. But it had all been bullshit. He'd tortured my own sister and I had let that happen. It was a secret I hadn't bothered looking for until it was too late.

"I'm *sorry*," I said, and I reached out to her, to put a hand on her shoulder. She jerked away.

"I don't want to See you," she said.

"What?"

She pulled the door shut. I jumped back so that my fingers wouldn't be caught. I stood in the hallway, the gloomy shadows oozing around me. The one thing I wanted to make right before this war started, and I couldn't do it.

I realized my cheeks were wet.

The next day, I ate an early lunch in the kitchen, fish soup and a hunk of the bread that Mrs. Davesa had baked. The staff scurried around, preparing the day's meals for my sisters and ignoring me. I wondered if they knew the war was starting. Probably not. The tension in the room didn't feel right.

I thought I'd throw my food up as soon as I took a bite, but instead I kept eating like there was a black hole inside of me.

When I finished my soup, I slipped out the staff entrance and walked around to the front driveway. The wind had been roaring all day, bringing in the scent of rainstorms. Dark clouds lurked over the ocean. It wasn't quite noon yet, but a car was already waiting for me, a different driver linked in behind the wheel. I had received word late last night, as I lay in bed and agonized over what Isabel had told me. At 2 p.m. Ekkeko time, the war would begin, and my presence was requested to watch the first battle.

I knew that was a lie. I knew my presence was required, now that I was a Ninety-Nine.

I hesitated for a moment, watching the car. The wind whipped at my hair. No point in delaying. I climbed in.

"Good evening," the driver said. The engine hummed to life.

"Good evening." Then, because I hated the heavy silence: "Storm's coming."

"Yes, ma'am."

But he had nothing else to add, and neither did I.

The car zipped down the road. I closed my eyes and listened to the whine of its movement. My thoughts drifted away from Isabel, to my mother. She was probably already converging up in the black, moving into her assigned space. Last night, I learned I had lost Isabel—I didn't want to lose her, too.

Raindrops splattered across the windows and sluiced in lines down the side of the glass, glowing with the road lights. We were in the jungle already, and the driver had slowed down enough that I could see square lights floating among the trees, lighting our way.

The lab was a beacon in the rainy shadows.

The building itself glowed with a pale green phosphorescence, an old terraforming trick to limit the use of electricity when the planet was only half-done. I didn't know why Dad had chosen to use it there, but the organic lines of the building were even eerier when they glowed like a firefly's abdomen.

"Thank you for driving in the rain," I said when we pulled into the driveway. The driver didn't respond, and I climbed out. Damp wind lashed across my bare legs. For a moment, I just stared at the doors leading inside. The soldier at the reference desk stared down at his holo. Otherwise, the lobby was empty.

I took a deep breath.

I wished I was anywhere but there.

I went inside.

The pale electric lights were stained green from the phosphorescence. The soldier looked up at me, but I walked over to him before he had a chance to respond and offered my thumb for the sensor.

"Top floor, Ms. Coromina," he said. "You can take the main elevator."

I didn't bother thanking him. My shoes clicked against the tile, echoing with a faint reverberating shiver. The sound made me feel more trapped. I rode the elevator alone to the top floor, my arms wrapped around my chest. Already this felt like a routine—offering my blood, riding the elevator. And I hated it.

The elevator doors slid open.

They didn't open into a hallway, as I expected, but rather a large, airy room with big windows lit by the building's glow. Twenty people stood in the room, most of them in military uniforms: green and blue for Alvatech, red and black for the Andromeda Corps. A handful were in gray Coromina suits. Dad stood at the center of the room, sipping at a tumbler that glowed golden in his hand. A few faces, curious, turned toward me.

"There she is." Dad's voice boomed through the room, drawing all the attention. "My *lovely* daughter."

He said *lovely* like he expected people to disagree. Of course, everyone only smiled politely.

"Someone get Esme a drink. This is her first battle."

A couple of the Coromina suits chuckled at that. The Alvatech general frowned, though. I didn't blame him. This wasn't my first battle. I'd never go to battle.

Flor strolled up to me, smiling like we were friends. "What would you like?" she said. "We've got bourbon, whisky, vodka—"

"Bourbon." I swept my eyes around the room. Gabriella was there, chatting with a pair of military men, one hand fluttering next to her throat. She looked excited. But other than Dad and Major Water, I didn't recognize any of these people. I assumed the ones in Coromina suits were the rest of the Ninety-Nines.

Flor reappeared at my side with the bourbon. "You're just in time," she said. "The holo will be coming on anytime now. This is *very* exciting, to get to see the R-Troops in action. I've been looking forward to it since the first one came out of the vats—since we first looked at the sample of alien DNA, really. It's pretty much a dream come true."

I sipped at my drink as she spoke. Her words rushed over me like the alcohol, and made me just as dizzy.

"Esme!" Dad called out. Flor and I both looked over at him, and he gestured for me. He was standing next to those anonymous men in the gray suits.

"Daddy's calling," Flor said sweetly. I glared at her.

I wove through the room, taking wide loops to avoid running into anyone. It was easy, given how few people were there, how big the room was. Most of them were clumped together near the center, satellites clinging to Dad's gravitational pull. And I was being pulled in too.

I tossed back the rest of my bourbon. I needed the strength. I didn't even bother tasting it. I'm sure it was expensive. I'm sure it was smoky and sweet with a vibrant finish. But the taste wasn't why I wanted it.

"These are the people you'll be working with," Dad said, gesturing out at those gray-suited strangers. "Now that you're a Ninety-Nine. It's time to get you ready."

"Well, not too ready," one of the men said, laughing. "I don't imagine you'll be retiring anytime soon."

They all laughed, even Dad. I smiled politely because I knew it would not be in my best interests to make these men angry. Not if I was going to undo what had been done to Isabel.

The storm had picked up and rain slammed up against the windows, smearing them with green liquid light. We were high up enough that the building seemed to sway with the wind. I thought of the storm crashing through the building, taking us all down, swallowing us up. The planet's revenge.

A chime sounded, three notes one after another like a symphony. The lights flickered.

"The squads are approaching Sector 894." The speaker was with Alvatech, and he sat off to the side surrounded by tablets and controls. "Everyone take their positions, please. Holos will be activating in thirty seconds."

A rush of excitement rippled through the room. It made me sick to my stomach.

"I have a seat reserved for you," Dad said. "Right here beside me." He lifted his glass in a toast. "To your first battle."

I lifted my empty tumbler in response.

The lights dimmed. All the Ninety-Nines and the military officers became silhouettes. I slid into my seat beside Dad. The holo formed a U around its audience, hemming us in. The images were vibrant and crystal clear, as if we were floating in space ourselves. Off to the left, one holo showed a list of soldiers' designations, their vitals blinking in a row alongside them.

A hand brushed my shoulder. It was Gabriella, leaning forward. In a low whisper she said, "I know how overwhelming it is. But the battles don't tend to last long."

Dad glanced over at us and Gabriella pulled away, falling into silence. I stared straight ahead and watched those empty stars.

A ship surged through, blinking into existence in the second holo, then speeding its way through the next five. It came to a stop in the sixth holo and stayed there, dark against dark. I didn't know if it was one of ours; I didn't recognize the design, and it was free of any logos.

"That's the R-Troop ship," Dad whispered. "Watch." He held up three fingers and curled them down in a countdown: *three, two, one.*

The ship disappeared.

There was some scattered applause from the Ninety-Nines.

"So, it space-jumped," I said. "Brilliant." My anxiety was making me surly.

The Ninety-Nine sitting beside me laughed. "No, it just turned off its heat signatures. The holorecorders can't pick up on it anymore, but, more important, neither can the OCI ships." He held up his glass. "Coromina ingenuity."

I thought of Isabel, alone and terrified in a hospital bed on Cate-quil.

We watched the stars shimmering on the screen. Every now and then, a blue-white light would blink, distantly, at too regular an interval to be a faraway sun. It was the OCI holorecorder, hovering in its designated quadrant, watching us watch it. Everything was so very genteel, two corpocracies whirling through space, waiting for their employees, their contractors, their creations, to kill one another.

"They've got no idea," one of the Ninety-Nines said, and the room rippled with throaty chuckles. My head didn't feel like it belonged to me.

"Probably didn't even realize they got intercepted." It was one of the Andromeda Corps officers. I wondered if he knew my mother. If he cared she might die out there. "Think they're out on perimeter check. Routine."

More laughter. It was as if we were watching one of Adrienne's dramas. It was as if those vitals on the last holo didn't mean anything.

I moved to sit up, intending to go refill my glass. But then a line of light shot across the holos. Dad grabbed my arm and pulled me back down. "It's starting!" he hissed. "You don't want to miss this."

It happened so fast that at first, my brain didn't comprehend what my eyes were seeing: an eruption of light out of the darkness, the silhouette of the R-Troop ship against the line of light, a sudden spiraling twist of some unfamiliar spacecraft, narrow and thin—no, not unfamiliar, just OCI. I recognized it from the debriefings.

"Got 'em!" someone shouted, and the room erupted into applause. The Ninety-Nines leaned forward in their chairs, speaking to one another in low murmurs. Dad still had my arm in his grip, and he stared smiling at the screen, the light from the explosions flashing across his features.

The vitals were blinking, changing, moving up and down. I forced myself not to look at them but at the confused maelstrom onscreen. Lights flared and flashed. After a few moments, I was able to locate the R-Troop ship amid the storm of lightfire, and it zipped back and forth with the quick, graceful arcs I associated more with animals than with machinery. There was no way the OCI ship could keep up with it. OCI moved like the past; the R-Troop ship moved like the future.

A loud, persistent beeping came from the speakers. Fires spread out across screen.

"The enemy craft is down," said the announcer. "Repeat, the enemy craft is down."

Everyone jumped to their feet. The Ninety-Nine on my left

dragged me up with him, and the sudden movement made me woozy and disconnected. The R-Troop ship blinked off the screen. Dad wasn't celebrating like the others but listening with his head tilted to the Alvatech General, nodding every now and then, looking utterly pleased with himself. The Andromeda Corps hadn't been deployed yet. My mother was still all right.

"Picking up heat signatures," the announcer said. "OCI has provided backup, repeat, OCI has provided backup."

I wondered why he kept repeating his statements. We weren't out there in space, fighting. We didn't need to be told twice.

Still, his pronouncement drew some of the good mood out of the audience. Sickness surged in my stomach and I slumped back down in my seat. I looked over at the vitals, curiosity burning me up. All of them were still there. Everyone was alive. It didn't appear that any of them were harmed.

More streaks of light filled the screen. There was darkness and then there was the sleek, contemporary design of the OCI ships' tails, tracing across the inky backdrop like a fabric pattern on a formal gown. I counted them in my head: *one two three four five six*. Six ships barreling toward the R-Troop ship.

From my vantage point in a room on the top floor of CG's latest laboratory, it looked as if the R-Troop ship shot straight up. I knew it probably wasn't so simple, but with that one movement, it confused the OCI ships and the lights braided over one another and looped back around, slow and lazy. By then, the R-Troop ship was already firing and the screen became a mass of light again. I watched it and felt as if I should be horrified but wasn't—maybe the bourbon had numbed me. I thought of a light painting I had seen at the museum in Undirra City once, on a wine-and-dine trip with some potential investors. It had filled an entire wall and the light had moved and undulated in bursts and starts. At the time, I thought it was beautiful. Now I wondered if it was just a representation of war.

There was no sound in the room save the occasional tinkle of ice against glass, the periodic groan of a chair leg. The battle was silent. I wondered what it sounded like to the R-Troops. My thoughts kept wandering away from the battle, away, away, to the realization that one of the soldiers I'd seen the other day was in that ship on the screen, strapped into an organic chair, evading fire from OCI. A real person existed in that swirl of light.

I couldn't follow the battle. I slumped back in my chair and let the lights wash over me. I thought I could feel them on my skin. Every now and then, the screen would blink and the announcer would tell us that another OCI ship had fallen. The screen grew dimmer. *Beep beep beep* went the speakers. I stared at the vitals. They didn't make sense to me anymore. Just strings of numbers representing a human being. We all had them, those vitals. The Ninety-Nines tightened their fingers around their glasses, calculating how high their profit margin would be when they went public with the R-Troops.

One last light streaked across the expanse of stars, and then, with a suddenness that made me jump, exploded. The speakers *beep beep beep*ed and everyone leapt to their feet in a riotous joy. Even Dad stood up, although he stayed calm, his expression unreadable.

The R-Troops ship blinked away again.

"—destroyed," the announcer was saying. "Repeat, all enemy craft destroyed. Do not currently note any heat signatures. R-Troops are advised to stay in hiding in case of—"

But no one was listening to him. The Ninety-Nines spilled out over their seats, chattering about marketing plans and business contacts. The military officers, Alvatech and Andromeda Corps both, looked impressed. I stood up too. It had finally happened. We had finally gone to war.

The Alvatech general was talking to Dad, animatedly, and Dad nodded along, sipping at his drink. I didn't understand why they were celebrating already, when the R-Troops were still on alert, lurking amid the stars. What did they know? Should I know it too, being a Ninety-Nine?

That thought brought with it a flood of shame. I wanted to know, deep down. Wanted to know everything they did. It wasn't just about running secret operations for PM. I was a Ninety-Nine. I had reached the top. I got to know everything.

The holo still showed nothing but stars. Dad and the general made their way to the back of the room, and I glanced away from the holo just as they passed. That movement was enough for Dad to look over at me, for me to lock eyes with Dad.

What I saw there was as cold and deep as space.

The Coromina Group newsfeeds reported our victory that evening, running it through every Connectivity system in the Four Sisters. I didn't get home until late, long after the sun had gone down—Dad had kept me at the Coromina Group offices to observe as he and the commanding officers analyzed the battle and devised strategies for the next one. But even as I walked across the courtyard, I could hear the distant boom of the public speakers in the village, telling the story of that afternoon's battle. The words were too distorted by distance for me to understand them, but I suspected I knew the gist of it.

After that, the war became a part of our lives. It happened in a way that felt both organic and catastrophic, as if all the storms of Coromina I went still. War hadn't been a part of our lives, and now it was. Things shifted as simply as that.

I'm not sure it affected my sisters as much as it affected me. The war was happening out in the black, away from any clusters of humanity. It was the only civilized way to wage war. I'd learned that years before from Mr. Garcia, and for the first time in my life, I was experiencing it. OCI and the Coromina Group pushed back and forth against each other, winning one battle, losing another, and not a single innocent person died.

But *innocent* was a relative term. For me, every battle was a long stretch of terror. The R-Troops didn't always fight; it was part of the CG strategy. "Don't want to show too much of our hand," Dad had told me in his office one day, the sun shining brightly outside. But if the R-Troops didn't fight, that meant the Andromeda Corps troops went in instead. I had spoken to my mother briefly the day after the war started, a quick conversation in my office that I was sure was being monitored. Neither of us said anything we shouldn't. When her holo faded away, I'd wiped at my eyes and told myself she hadn't died yet.

People weren't supposed to feel this way during wars anymore.

That was why companies hired professionals. But to me, it still felt like there was a crack in the universe.

Maybe it would have been different if Dad hadn't promoted me, if I hadn't had to spend so much of my time at the office, away from the estate. I imagined that it was easy there, or in the village or in Undirra City or anywhere in the Four Sisters, to pretend the war was an Amanan drama. But on the CG campus, Alvatech and Andromeda Corps soldiers were a common sight, standing around the office with their light rifles. Many of the assistants were let go and replaced with bioengineered soldiers who had been produced by Genetics. I didn't think this was fair, but I understood the theory: assistants have less invested in the company, as they hold low security levels and aren't eligible for enclave housing, not even the flimsy apartments. In normal times, it was a chance for those outside the sphere of the company's influence to prove themselves, to have a chance to rise up the ranks, but that sort of thing needed to be limited during war. And so, unfamiliar faces appeared by the receptionist's desk, men and women in mercenary uniforms. They didn't smile, they didn't say hello. Their loyalty was bought, a package with their fighting brethren, and so it was guaranteed.

Those new assistants, their DNA designed and crafted and copyrighted by the Coromina Group, came in the day the war started. After that, though, it was clear my workday routines were completely demolished. I barely spent any time in Genetics anymore, and I had to delegate most of my work to Miguel. The PM projects had to be put on hold, and not just because Dad knew about them—I didn't give a damn about that. I just didn't have *time*. I spent hours either at the office or at the new lab, working with commanding officers to help strategize for the war. When I went home, I slept. I didn't see my sisters. Not Daphne or Adrienne. Not Isabel. The real world slipped away. I started talking like Dad, using the word *assets* to describe the R-Troops. Every day was cloaked in an insomniac haze. I could feel myself falling deeper and deeper into Dad's world. I hated it.

I hated it, but I didn't stop. What I wanted more than anything was for this war to end. I wanted my mother to be safe. I wanted the company to move on from the R-Troops, move on from Isabel's alien DNA—once Dad made his billions off the R-Troops, we could move onto something else. Something that did not exploit my sister.

I worked, and worked, and worked. And the battles raged overhead and out of sight.

One evening after I had lost track of the days, I entered the wrong set of coordinates into the big company lightbox. The lightbox caught the mistake immediately, wailing and shrieking, but Dad pulled me aside and told me, in a sharp, clear voice, to go home early.

"I'm fine," I told him, heat rising in my cheeks.

"It happens to the best of us," said the Andromeda Corps general, who had taken a liking to me early on. "You'll get used to it."

Dad gave me a dark look. "Go home, Esme. Before you make things worse."

This time, I didn't question. I should have felt ashamed and embarrassed, but I was too tired. It was a relief, really. As soon as I arrived back at the estate, I crawled into my bed and closed my eyes, and then I was asleep.

Knocking intruded into my dreams.

I opened my eyes, confused. Something with the war? But no, war messages would be chiming on my lightbox, not pounding on my door.

I rolled onto my side. I had no sense of what time it was. My room was tinted with reddish light from Coromina I; the sun had set.

"Who is it?" I called out, when the knocking didn't subside.

"It's Grace, ma'am. I need to speak with you."

I sat up, my heart racing. "Come in." A million scenarios flashed through my head: The war was coming landside. My mother had been killed. Something had happened to my sisters—

Grace walked in. I always thought of her as young, wide-eyed and frightened, the way she looked when Dad announced she would be taking Rena's place. But she'd gotten older in the intervening years, older than Rena was when she had died.

A sharp pang of grief twisted in my chest. "What's going on?" I slid out of bed, trying to hide my nervousness.

"I'm sorry to bother you," Grace stammered. "You've been gone so much lately, and I know you have a lot to worry about—" She looked away from me. "I just had to tell someone."

"What is it?"

"It's Isabel," Grace said.

My insides went cold. "Has something happened to her?"

"I don't know." Grace smoothed down her uniform. Her hands shook. "She's gone."

"What?" I sat up, cold terror crawling over my skin. "God, not again."

Grace sighed. "She's not in her room," she said. "At least, I don't think she is. She keeps the door locked, you know."

I didn't.

"She always answers when the staff brings her meals or when I go by to check on her. But this evening, I came by with her dinner, and there was no answer." Grace spread her hands hopelessly. "I set the tray beside her door—I thought she might be sleeping. But it's still there, untouched."

I nodded, my stomach queasy. "Show me."

Grace and I left together and walked through the twisting hallways until we came to Isabel's room. The tray sat on the floor, the scent of pungent spices wafting off it. This was Dad's fault. My fault. In the endless bureaucracy of the war, I'd let her slip away.

I thought about the last conversation we'd had, the way she'd slammed this door, the wood carved with a baroque swan, in the face of my apology.

I put my fingers on the doorknob and turned but it didn't move. The lock blinked red at me.

"Get the soldiers," I told Grace. "They should be able to open the lock." My heart pounded. Blood rushed in my ear. "Hurry!"

It was a pointless command; she was already halfway down the hallway. I leaned up against the far wall and stared at Isabel's door. A war in the sky and a catastrophe down below. I lunged forward and pounded on the door. I screamed Isabel's name.

Nothing but silence.

Grace came back quickly, a soldier at her side. I remembered his name was Private Water.

Please be safe, I thought. *Please be safe.*

To Private Water, I said, "Open the door."

He nodded, then pulled out the disruptor that would break the electrolock. It worked easily, a flash of white light and we were in. He ducked inside first, light rifle up.

"Don't shoot her," I hissed, which I knew was pointless. An engineered soldier never killed the wrong target.

"Clear," Private Water called out from inside the room.

I glanced over at Grace. She had her hands clasped together and she gazed up at me with worry. "Go wake Daphne and Adrienne," I said. "See if they know anything."

"Yes, Ms. Coromina." She scurried away, and I stepped into Isabel's room. Nothing was disturbed—her furniture wasn't askew, and her lightbox glowed softly on the desk. But the window hung open, the sea breeze stirring up the curtains.

I walked over to the window and looked down at the pineapple garden. Coromina I turned everything red. It was full tonight, storms surging. I wondered if they had something to do with her disappearance. She'd always loved astrology.

"How'd she get down?" I asked, and felt a quiver in my chest—what if this was her DNA working somehow?

Private Water slid up alongside me. "Maybe some kind of hoverboard." He sounded like he was talking about a criminal. "The kids in the city use 'em to get around. Probably lets her coast down."

Did Isabel even have a hoverboard? I'd never seen her with one. But there was so much about Isabel I had been blind to.

Private Water scanned the windowsill with a DNA sensor. I gazed around the room. It didn't seem likely that OCI would commit a war crime of this magnitude. Even I, with only a little wartime experience, understood that much about the rules of engagement.

But Dad could have taken her. He'd taken her before.

"Private Sky is on her way to the cemetery," Private Water said suddenly. "And Privates Sky-2 and Wind are checking the holorecordings." He turned back to his scans, a light beeping in his ear. The soundpiece.

I needed to contact Dad. Let him know about a possible security breach. Assuming he hadn't kidnapped her himself again.

I heard soft voices out in hallway, and then Grace stepped back into the room. Daphne and Adrienne trailed in after her.

"Did you know about a hoverboard?" I asked them.

Daphne and Adrienne frowned at each other. Daphne shook her head. "But you know Isabel; I haven't seen much of her lately—" Her voice trailed off and her eyes went to the windows. "God, why does this keep happening with her?"

Silence. Private Water finished his scans and folded the scanner back up and slid it into his belt. "No residue," he said. "At least none that I would ex—" He paused, his ear blinking. "She's not at the cemetery."

"Shit," I said softly. Then, louder: "Well, keep looking for her." I turned to Adrienne and Daphne. "You two, stay at the house in case she comes back. Do you understand?"

They nodded, their expressions serious and scared.

"I'm going to help look," I said.

"Ms. Coromina, you know the soldiers are better equipped for that." Grace stepped toward me. "You should stay here too."

"No!" My voice echoed around Isabel's empty room. I took a deep breath. "No. I want to help. The last time this happened, I was the one to find her. Grace, send word to Mr. Coromina that Isabel is missing. Tell him he needs to contact me immediately about this. Remind him I'm a Ninety-Nine now. Use Mr. Whittaker's encrypted channel."

All of them, Grace and the twins and Private Sky, were staring at me like they expected me to have all the answers. But I didn't have any answers. Only a blank place where Isabel had been.

I scoured the garden and the woods for nearly two hours, calling out Isabel's name until my voice went hoarse. Dad didn't have her. The message had come through almost immediately: *No, we don't have her. I'm sending a liaison to find out if OCI broke the rules of engagement. If she's on the estate, you need to find her.* The night was hot and damp, and everywhere I walked I could smell the rot-sweet scent of the pineapples. Coromina I shed that awful light over everything, confusing my search. All my thoughts were stained red: Isabel's empty bedroom and her open window. The hollow look in her eyes the day she came from Catequil. The way she lurched through the house, trying not to look at me.

The soldier's holocameras zoomed by periodically, sweeping the area, looking for life signs. Whenever I ran into one of the soldiers, I demanded to know what they'd found. "Nothing, Ms. Coromina," they always answered, mostly business but with a faint layer of empathy.

By the time I'd worked my way around the house, I was soaked in sweat from the humid air. I trudged up to the porch and slumped down in one of the garden chairs there. I knew I should go back inside and contact the company to see what my next action should be. I'd gotten the confirmation, halfway through my search, that OCI wasn't officially claiming her disappearance, but the sense of assurance from that claim had evaporated in the night heat. She wasn't just Philip Coromina's daughter. She was Philip Coromina's secret weapon, and OCI might very well risk the treaties to snatch her up into the black for their own cruel experiments.

The woods loomed in the distance, bloody from the planetlight, and I was sick with worry. "Isabel!" I screamed. My voice echoed over the garden and was answered with silence.

I was too antsy to sit there, despite the heat. OCI could be lying. I knew that; Dad knew that. I knew he was already putting the machinations in place to recover Isabel and save face. OCI stealing his greatest intellectual property in the form of a daughter would be humiliating to him—they'd breached the estate's security; they'd pulled her out of the safety of her bedroom. Dad wasn't going to let that stand. But I wanted desperately to find her tucked away in the woods, like she had been as a child. I wanted this to be nothing. Bad enough the war might take my mother. I didn't want it taking my sister, too.

I stood up, knocking my chair away. If she was still out there—

hurt, scared—I was going to find her. I bounded back into the yard, fists clenched in determination. I would go deeper into the woods this time. The soldiers' holorecorders couldn't see everything, not at night, not with Coromina I burning so brightly, you could almost imagine yourself trapped inside its storms. Red rain, red lightning, red winds. All of them toxic. Just as Ekkeko had been before the terraforming.

And yet something had lived here anyway.

I cut across the lawn until I came to the start of the woods. The trees rustled in the hot wind. The air coated my skin with moisture.

And then something moved in the planetlight.

I froze. Sucked in my breath. I willed my heart to stop beating, afraid the sound of it would give me away.

A figure darted across the lawn, clear of the trees.

I didn't quite grasp what I was seeing. The figure, a shadow in the red light. Too tall, too thin to be human. Isabel, her face a pale oval in those eerie, liquid shadows. She didn't look at me. She didn't see me.

She stepped into a bright shaft of planetlight, and then she was gone.

"What?" I whispered. I needed to call Private Water, have the soldiers bring their heat sensors out here, look for her that way. But instead, I kept staring at that beam of planetlight like it would give me an explanation. I had seen Isabel, and then I hadn't seen her.

I took a hesitant step forward, moving by some force beyond myself. I crept out in the open yard. My clothes stuck to my skin. The wind had gone still. In the red light, everything felt dead.

I had seen this before. Years ago. I'd mostly forgotten it. When Isabel was a little girl, she had stepped out of nothing in the middle of a rainstorm.

I felt a flood of relief. Maybe this was like the first time she'd vanished, after all.

"Isabel?" I called out. "Are you hurt?"

Something snapped in the woods. A branch breaking, a foot crossing an old path. I didn't even stop to think, just ran, tearing off in the direction of that snap. I heard another one, and another, a kind of symphony of panicked flailing.

"Isabel!" I shouted. I was at the wood's edge and I grabbed on to one of the trees while I steadied my breath. "Isabel, I saw you! I promise I won't tell Dad—"

More sounds of broken branches, off to my left. I looked and saw leaves shining through the forest like raindrops, emerald and thick, and for a moment I thought I saw a figure, a shimmer of Isabel's outline.

I didn't call out her name this time. I just followed. My feet pounded against the damp ground of the forest, and the falling leaves stuck to my hair and to my skin. The trees rustled and I gasped for breath and I could hear someone else gasping for breath—Isabel. The harder I ran, the more clearly I was able to see her. She became a silhouette, became a shadow. She was outlined by the leaves.

"Isabel!" I screamed, one last time. I was almost to her. I reached out my hand and my chest burned and Isabel's silhouette turned and all I saw were her eyes, two eyes floating without a face, staring wide and frightened.

All I saw were those eyes. No woods, no shadows, no moonlight, no Isabel.

Those eyes. Her eyes.

And then I realized I wasn't in the forest anymore.

I skidded to a stop, stumbling over my own feet. I didn't know how to explain it, because my brain itself couldn't grasp the concept. I wasn't in the forest. I was in a *room*, a big, cavernous room lined with cubes of white light. And yet I kept thinking I saw the trees, ghosts of them, off in the distant, shivering and shedding leaves—

"Get out!" Isabel's voice was shrill and sharp and frightened. "Get out before you cause any damage!"

Someone grabbed my wrist. I screamed and jerked away and then Isabel flickered into focus. Her hair was windblown and tangled up with leaves, but she was dressed in the dark red-black that soldiers wore when they went out under cover of night.

"What are you *doing*?" she hissed. She pulled on my arm, hard enough that pain rippled down my shoulder

"Where are we?" I was too dazed to demand any other answers. "Where did the forest go?"

"Out!" she shrieked. She pushed at me but I braced my feet against the ground—the hard, level, reflective ground, like the surface of a mirror. This wasn't right; the ground was supposed to be lumpy in the woods, uneven, *natural*.

"How did you find this place?" I whispered, tilting my gaze up. It wasn't like any room I'd ever been in, not even the museum in Undirra City, with its high, vaulted ceilings and echoing space. This reminded me of that museum, but I felt an unease from being inside it as well, a sense that I didn't belong, that the room didn't want me.

"It's not one of the old terraforming stations, is it?" I whispered. "Those are toxic, you know. We shouldn't—"

"It's not a terraforming station." Isabel's voice hitched. She was crying. Her eyes smeared with tears that sparkled in the eerie, flat light. I moved toward her immediately, struck by my sisterly duties, but Isabel moved away from my embrace.

"It's dangerous!" she shouted. "I'm trying to protect you! They'll kill you like they did Rena!"

"What!" I stumbled away from her. Rena's death. We'd never solved it, never found an answer for why she had been slaughtered in our back yard. "What are you talking about?"

Her eyes glowed with tears. She shook her head. "Rena was an accident," she murmured. "But I'm afraid—"

She was interrupted by sounds I knew I'd heard before, although I couldn't say where. Hissing sounds, low and steamy like old pipes.

Isabel whirled around and said something in the same hissing voice, and that's when the recognition registered: her language. Her stupid made-up language she used to speak with Daphne and Adrienne.

"Oh God," I whispered. "Oh God, they really are here."

The hissings welled again. Isabel wasn't the one speaking. She was staring at empty space, her head tilted. Listening.

I couldn't move. Her face grew paler and paler and she trembled in her dark clothes.

"Isabel," I said softly, timorously. "You won't get in trouble. I just want to—"

"Shhhhhhhh!" She glared at me. The hissing fell silent and Isabel's eyes went wide. She called out something herself. It sounded more like a human language when she spoke it.

My whole body felt cold.

There was a long pause, and even in the darkness I could make out the rise and fall of Isabel's chest. She was breathing hard. The hissing started again, low and insidious. In that moment I was a child again, hiding under my blankets because I thought a monster was lurking out in the garden, convinced that if I moved even a centimeter it would leap through the window and devour me.

I had stopped believing in monsters a long time ago. Maybe that had been wrong of me.

"You have to leave now!" Isabel said. She shoved me and I went stumbling through the underbrush. "Get out of the woods. I can explain everything, but—*God,* just get out of here, okay?"

Her voice shook, vibrating with urgency and anger.

"I know about them," I said in a rush. "I know about you. Isabel, please, if you're in danger—"

"I'm not in fucking danger!"

The profanity was a shock, the word rattling between us, but it wasn't enough to propel me into motion. My fear kept me latched into place.

"You are!" she screamed. "You're the one in danger!"

A shape rose up behind her, a shadow dappled by the leaves of the trees. Isabel turned around and said something in that language, and the thing flickered once, just as Isabel had, and for a split second, I saw it.

A monster.

Tall, thin, covered in shining, scaly feathers.

Sharp teeth.

Curving claws.

A face long and pointed like a snout. A face that wasn't human. But it was intelligent.

And then it disappeared.

I cried out, my voice strangled and sparse. Isabel looked back to me and her face was unreadable. The leaves had mostly fallen away from her, a few still stuck in her hair, and in that moment she seemed so inhuman that she had more in common with that shadow flickering on the edges of my memory than she ever did with me.

"Go," she whispered.

And finally, I listened.

I was hardly aware of myself as I raced through the woods. Branches lashed out at me and my shins ached from the impact and my chest was tight and constricted but I didn't notice any of that until I cleared the tree line and collapsed in the damp grass. It was like I'd been underwater. I gasped for air and thought about what I'd just seen in the woods. Isabel's pale face, flickering in front of me. Darkness. Darkness darker than shadows. Light that refracted at the wrong angle.

A monster whose eyes glittered with intelligence.

The ground swirled around me. I couldn't catch my breath.

Dad and Flor had both told me the Radiance were still here, lurking in the shadows, but I hadn't really believed them. Part of me had thought they were toying with me, in good corpocratic style. Instead, they'd just been telling the truth, and I'd been too stupid to be terrified.

"Esme! Are you all right!"

My eyes flew open. My thoughts scattered like the stars.

Isabel knelt beside me, her hair falling around her shoulders. She wasn't out of breath. Although my face burned from where branches had struck me, her skin was smooth and unbroken. She hadn't run out of the woods. She hadn't been afraid.

I sat up and my head spun and I braced myself against the ground.

"You saw, didn't you?"

I curled my knees up to my chest. The air was thick with humidity and it settled over us both. For a moment, I thought I smelled rain on the distance, and it was such a normal, familiar scent that I didn't know how to answer.

"Just tell me." Isabel peered at me. "I know what you saw. But I don't know if you're going to admit to it."

"Why wouldn't I?"

"You haven't yet."

I took a deep breath. My lungs burned. Isabel settled back in the grass. She kept staring at me.

"The Radiance," I finally said, my voice raspy. "I didn't really believe they were still here."

Isabel shook her head. "That's Dad's name for them. They call themselves the Divested. That's translated from their own language." And then she hissed from someplace deep in the back of her throat. "It's hard to say properly. But I used my lightbox to find the right word in Corominan. *Divested*."

My dizziness came back to me. "They were kicked out," I whispered. "Divested of their home. By us. By—by Dad."

Isabel stared at me. Her eyes were big and dark, just like her mother's had been. She was going to look like her mother when she grew up.

"Not kicked out," Isabel said. "Just—displaced. In theory."

"In theory?"

The wind gusted, knocking the trees around. I jumped and looked over my shoulder, expecting to see that *creature* come barreling toward us. But the woods were empty.

"That was what—" Isabel hesitated. "What the Coromina Group expected to happen to them, yes."

I kept staring at the woods. My head filled with a fierce, insistent buzzing. *What the Coromina Group expected to happen.*

And like that, my mother's hidden message became clear. She had seen them, the Divested. She might have even helped remove them—displace them. All these years, and she had known that I was living on an inhabited planet, that my whole life existed at the expense of someone else.

Except I'd always known that. To live at the expense of someone else—that was what it meant to be the daughter of a corpocratic CEO. I slumped backward in the grass.

"You told me to run," I said to the sky. "I thought you were angry with me."

"I *am* angry with you," Isabel said. Her voice was small, strained. I looked over at where she sat in the grass. "But that doesn't mean I want you to die."

Horror struck me hard in the chest. "You said they killed Rena." Bile rose in my throat. "And you—you didn't tell us? Didn't tell me?"

Isabel looked away, her hair like a dark curtain. I resisted the urge to crawl away from her, to scream for the soldiers. She was my *sister*. And she wasn't afraid of those things in the woods.

"They killed Rena accidentally," she said softly. "When one of them emerged out of the place where they live—it's like another dimension, side by side with ours. It was a horrible mistake. But they want their home back. I went to them tonight—to stop them. To tell them not to hurt anyone at the house."

Blood pounded in my head. "They're going to kill us," I said flatly.

"No." Isabel looked at me then, and shook her head furiously. "No, I convinced them not to. We'll find some other way."

"How do you *know*?"

Her expression hardened. "They are my family. They listen to me."

My throat dried out. I couldn't speak. *I'm your family*, I thought. But I only stared at her, trying to make sense of what she'd just said.

Isabel stood up and brushed the dew from her clothes. "Are you going to tell Dad what you saw?"

I scrabbled for my voice. "I have to. This is an emergency situation, Isabel. Dad's prepared to accuse OCI of breaking the rules of engagement—"

"Tell everybody I snuck out to meet some friends in the village. They'll accept that." Isabel peered down at me. "Just don't tell Dad about the Divested."

"These things are trying to kill us!"

"They aren't things," she murmured. "And I told you, I stopped them." She looked up at me, eyes pleading. "Don't tell Dad about them. Please. He'll only make it worse."

She wants to save us all, I thought, and my heart twisted, and I was terrified but at the same time swollen with love for my sister, and I knew I believed her.

"Doesn't he already know about them?" I said carefully.

She stared at me for a long time. Then she said, "He only knows pieces. He doesn't know about their home. He can't get to them. He's tried, but it never works."

Despite the wash of fear, I felt a little thrill inside my chest: I knew something Dad didn't.

"I'll do what I can," I said.

The war continued for the next week, a series of battles I watched, tense and shaking, from a locked room inside the laboratory. It was easier when the Andromeda Corps wasn't fighting.

I did not tell Dad about the alien or its home.

I thought about the alien constantly: the sharp, cold, inhuman face, the flicker of movement on the air. And Isabel. *I don't want you to die.* In the moment, sitting out there in the balmy night, I'd believed her, but in the days since she had not spoken to me once, only given me fitful, frightened glances as we passed each other in the hallway. And every time, I was reminded that a part of her was like that creature I had seen in the shadows. A creature that was willing to kill us to get its home back.

One morning while I was working in the office, I thought suddenly of Rena, her body sprawled out on the lawn, blood soaking into the grass. Dad had passed her death off as anti-corporactic terrorists, but no one actually believed that. But now there was an answer. An answer that Isabel said was her *family*.

It made me sick to think about.

I kept my promise to Isabel and did not tell Dad what I'd seen. But I didn't sit by and do nothing, either. I asked the other Ninety-Nines about the aliens, if there were any still alive for us to study. And I learned that were no aliens in captivity at the Coromina Group. "We've never been able to catch one," Flor told me over lunch, her eyes glittering, "but that would be a coup, wouldn't it?" She sighed and gazed dreamily off into the distance. "We just don't know where they're hiding. That sister of yours knows. And maybe after the war—"

Her voice trailed off, and I picked at my salad, trying to look nonchalant. Ignorant. Uninterested.

"They're a danger, you know," Flor said carefully. "To the Four Sisters."

I looked up at her, perhaps too sharply. She smiled, took a sip of her drink. Of course they were a danger. They had unleashed a virus that had wiped out entire villages. Even Isabel knew they were dangerous, and it occurred to me that even though I wasn't going to reveal Isabel's secret to the company, I would have to find a way to keep the people of the Four Sisters safe. The thought made my stomach twist around, because what options were there?

I gathered any information I could about the aliens and kept it close to my chest. I worked on my assignments preparing for the war. But I did not try to speak to Isabel. I couldn't bring myself to do it. I would protect her from Dad; I would keep the promise I had made all those years before. But whenever I saw her, I got a flash of the alien in my head, and I didn't know what to think.

It wasn't long after I'd learned all I could about the aliens from the other Ninety-Nines that the Coromina Group scored another major victory with the R-Troops, a near-annihilation of the OCI battalion sent to fight them. They were getting better—adapting, I had learned, to the OCI's training tactics.

The post-battle meeting was as exuberant as I expected, with bottles of expensive whiskey being passed around among the Ninety-Nines. I sat in my usual place, behind Dad and to his left, and folded my hands demurely in my lap as the celebration unfolded. I wasn't stupid enough to get drunk in a room full of Ninety-Nines, especially when I had the threat of the aliens locked away inside my head. Liquor made it easier to break promises.

Dad, too, sat at his usual seat, and while he sipped at his whiskey and clinked his glass against the toasts of others, he didn't join in with their excited CG chants. Father and daughter, observing the party. I suspected it was for different reasons.

"Order!" Dad called out after half an hour of revelry. The Ninety-Nines quieted down and slid into their seats, although they still leaned over and whispered excitedly to each other, whiskey sloshing in the glasses.

Dad stood up, and I felt a tension at the back of my throat. Something was different here. This wasn't an ordinary post-battle meeting.

"That was incredible to watch," Dad said, and he paced around the table, moving in a wide, slow circle. The Ninety-Nines' gazes followed him around the room. "Your work has surpassed my expectations."

A delighted murmur rose up from the Ninety-Nines. I didn't move. *What's coming, what's coming.* I had learned to hate surprises.

Dad stopped beside a big window that looked out over the jungle. During the day, you could see the tops of trees swaying in the wind, but it was nighttime now, and the glass was a black mirror. Dad gazed out across the table, taking in all the Ninety-Nines. My heart pumped.

"It's time," he said.

A gasp rose up from the table, and then, immediately, excited chatter. I didn't understand. Time for what? Why hadn't I been informed? Was this some attempt to undermine me?

Dad lifted his hands to quiet down the Ninety-Nines. "I want us to go public as soon as possible. I knew we talked about waiting until the war was over, but I think the Four Sisters will do well with the added morale. Too many citizens are still attempting to get offworld, even with the danger of travel." Dad shook his head. "We need to show them what the Coromina Group can do."

"But won't it open us up to espionage?" Flor tossed her hair back over her shoulder. "That was how this whole thing started."

"Let them try," Dad said. "That data's protected by the R-Troops themselves."

The Ninety-Nines murmured to each other. I couldn't see Flor's expression from where I sat, but I imagined her frowning, mouth pinched like she'd bitten into a lemon.

"We're winning the war," Dad went on. "I've already been getting calls from unaffiliated militaries asking how we're doing it. Let people *see* the R-Troops. Let them *understand*. That way, there will be no way for them to dismiss the R-Troop's victories as some Alvatech fluke."

Dad let the words settle over the room. Excitement buzzed on the air. And I only felt relieved. This was an expected maneuver—I would never have thought Dad would keep the R-Troops to himself until after the war. The risk of this was the real beauty of it. I knew Dad didn't give a shit about civilian morale, and the idea that the R-Troops could be mistaken for even the most elaborate engineered military was absurd. But Dad knew if he could reveal the troops *before* we'd won, he was showing faith in his product. It was one thing to reveal a new super soldier after the war was finished and OCI had either slunk off to lick its wounds or been incorporated into the CG. It was another to do it now, when a total victory wasn't assured.

"The newsfeeds will be talking about this battle for weeks," Dad said. "And we want to capitalize on that chatter."

"How do you want to do it?" It was one of the older Ninety-Nines, Frank. "And where?"

Dad grinned. "Bait and switch," he said. "A party celebrating the battle's win—that'll get the gossipfeeds in a frenzy. And then we march out the soldiers." He gestured widely with one hand. "They'll be talking about it in every inhabited system within four hours; I guarantee it. The jump-ships won't be able to jump the news fast enough."

The Ninety-Nines were excited again. Their voices rang out around the room. I watched Dad over the tops of their heads as they leaned across the table to speak to each other. He caught my eye and smiled.

The next day, I did not go to the office but instead told John that I would be working from home. This wasn't an unusual occurrence, certainly not since the war started—it was safer to work from the estate, since it housed civilians, who could not legally be killed by OCI bombs. The main Coromina Group campus was perhaps not the most ethical target, but it wasn't banned completely, and during times of high security, it was better for me to work from my suite at home. Except I wasn't going to be working, either.

I had been waiting for a message from my mother for over a week, ever since I saw the aliens. She had been the first person I contacted after I had my encounter, when I was confused and terrified and had no idea what to do. *I need to speak with you,* I'd said, the holorecorder set so that it only recorded my face and shoulder. Out of view, my hands were fidgeting with anxiety. *It's important. Let me know when you're back planetside.*

Alone, the message was innocuous enough, even during wartime. One search of the files would reveal her to be my mother, and messages like this were monitored by Alvatech, not the Ninety-Nines. No one should make any connections between this and my questions about aliens. I hoped.

My mother's response had finally come the previous night. It had been almost three in the morning when my lightbox woke me up with its bright holographic light, a mechanized voice chirping that I had a message coming through the CG Connectivity. "Esme?" Harriet had said when I'd answered. Behind her I could see the barracks of the Ekkeko military compound. She was planetside, one of the squadrons who would be attending the party in three days' time. Most important, though, she was *safe*. That had been my first thought. Nothing about aliens or about questions. Just that my mother was alive.

I didn't dare ask her about the aliens over the Connectivity, so we arranged to meet on the public beach, down in the village. I pulled on hiking boots and civilian clothes and slipped out of my room and went downstairs. The staff were cleaning house, as if everything were normal and we were not at war. I smiled at Alicia, who was running a duster over the banister.

"I'm going for a walk," I told her. "I need to clear my head. If there's an emergency, you can contact me. Otherwise, I don't want to be disturbed."

"I'll pass the word along," she said, and the banister gleamed.

I forced myself to stay calm as I stepped outside and into the bright sun, already hot for the day. I strode over the lawn, arms swinging, head high, like I had every right to be there. And why didn't I? Star's End was my home. We did not have a battle today. The preparations for the unveiling of the R-Troops weren't yet in full force. I could have this moment.

I followed the main road down to the beach. As it wound closer to the woods, my chest tightened. The trees swayed in the wind, the rustle of their leaves a sweeping, majestic sound. And I saw nothing unusual. No long-limbed figures moving through the shadows. No secret rooms that should not exist.

Still, once I was clear of the woods, I breathed a deep sigh of relief.

It took me fifteen minutes to get down to the public beach, and although I hadn't walked this way in some time, the path came back to me easily. I thought about all those trips to see Laila and Paco, and a string of sadness wrapped itself around my heart. Paco was gone, and whoever Laila was now didn't matter. I had become the sort of person she loathed.

I felt the ocean before I saw it, a salty dampness coating my skin. The path crested up over the dunes and there was the beach, a long, empty strip of pale sand. The water glittered. A single figure was out there, sitting right at the shoreline, her short gray hair ruffling in the wind.

I took a deep breath. I wished I had some better reason to see my mother. Something that didn't terrify me to my very core.

I picked my way across the sand until I was standing beside her. The waves rolled in, casting pale foam over the toes of my boots.

"What's up?" Harriet said, still gazing out at the water.

I didn't know how to start, and so I didn't answer. Harriet tilted her face toward me, shading her eyes against the sun's glare with one hand. "You brought me all the way out here; it's gotta be something important." She paused. "Something you don't want the company knowing."

I sighed. I should have known someone like her, an old merc who'd been in the business since before I was born, would know the tricks. I sat down in the sand beside her. The waves rushed up to greet me.

"Your mission," I said. "When you first met Dad. What was it?"

"You know I can't tell you that."

"I'm a Ninety-Nine now."

It still felt strange to say it aloud, as if I were lying. Harriet swung her head around and gaped.

"Are you shitting me?" she said.

I shook my head. "You can scan me if you want, although I'd prefer you didn't. You're right. I don't want Dad knowing we're talking about this."

Harriet turned her gaze back to the sea. "Don't have a scanner, anyway."

I waited, but she didn't offer anything more. The waves splashed around my thighs, dampening my clothes. It took a few moments before I realized she really wasn't going to tell me. *Soldier first*, I thought. *Mother second.*

"I saw something," I said. "In the woods. The night I messaged you. I—I think you might have seen the same thing when you were here."

Harriet closed her eyes. She looked very old in the sunlight, her skin crinkly and thin.

"You can't imagine what I saw," she said softly.

My face got hot. This wasn't how I imagined this conversation to go—except I realized, with a start, that I hadn't actually known how this conversation would go. I had contacted Harriet out of desperation, before I'd had the chance to fully consider what I'd seen. It was a gut reaction. A little girl reaching out to her mother.

"Something lived here before we did," I said, pitching my voice low so that it would be covered up by the wind. I kept my gaze on Harriet, prepared to shift my tactic if she gave anything away. She sat perfectly still. "And they still live here. I saw one."

Harriet's spine straightened.

"You were helping get rid of them, weren't you?" I whispered. "That was your mission."

Harriet blinked. Not just a blink—she was crying. I could see the tears shimmering on her skin. My stomach flopped around. I couldn't imagine a woman like Harriet crying.

She wiped the tears away with the back of her hand, a quick, furious motion. "Shit," she said, and shook her head. "Shit."

"I just want to know what happened," I said. "I just—" I was too ashamed to bring up Isabel. "There's this whole civilization on the estate and I had no concept of it until a week ago. And I don't know what to do with this." I waved my hand around. "This information."

Harriet gave a sharp laugh. "Philip's got you trained in the business; that's for damn sure."

Her words stung.

"You mean you aren't taking it to the newsfeeds?" she said. "That's what anyone else would do. It's the fucking scientific discovery of the millennium, and we're talking about it in whispers on a beach."

I glared at her. "You don't tell anyone either."

"I was under orders." She looked at me. "And I wasn't supposed to see them, anyway. I was part of the support crew. Didn't go into the field. But a whole squad got killed and the sergeant sent me in as backup. They weren't at Star's End. I'm guessing that's where you saw the thing."

I nodded, my skin cold.

"We fought 'em on the Awa Islands. It was impossible to get a good look at 'em. They were practically invisible. Stuff of nightmares." She stared out at the ocean. "They'd been hiding; that was the theory. Talk among the soldiers, you know. Hiding since the terraforming two hundred years ago. Finally starting to peek their way out."

I felt cold. "You mean they didn't attack?"

Harriet shook her head. "The company wanted them contained. Looked bad. Plus, it was illegal, him terraforming a planet that already had life. We all had to sign a nondisclosure clause before we took the job, a more elaborate one than they usually do." Harriet glanced over at me. "Your father was up to something back then. You bet your ass he'd known about those things from the beginning. He would have gone on landing missions during the terraforming. He saw that shit up close. And he terraformed anyway."

Harriet's voice turned hard and cold on that last sentence.

"I was young," she said. "I didn't want to do any of it. But I knew I had to follow orders if I wanted a career in the militaries." She laughed, short and bitter. "I found out what he was up to after I fucked him. When I learned about you—God, it made me sick, but I didn't have a choice, did I?" She pinched her forehead, her gaze cast down at the sand. "I should have left the military and raised you myself. I should have stopped him. Should have taken the intel public."

Sadness swelled up inside me. He'd done the same thing to her. He'd let her carry the weight of his guilt.

"It wasn't your fault," I said, and I put my hand on her shoulder. She shook her head. "It *wasn't*. He made the decision, not you."

Hesitantly, I pushed my arm along Harriet's shoulder until I had her embraced in an awkward half-hug. This was what my father did. He left a trail of misery in his wake.

"I'm glad they're still there," Harriet whispered. "How fucked is that?"

"Not fucked at all," I said, but I thought of Isabel telling me that she didn't want me to die.

Dad had always hated parties, but he and the rest of the Ninety-Nines were able to pull one together in three days. One afternoon, Mr. Whittaker simply announced to the staff and to my sisters that Star's End would be hosting a party.

The announcement was met with baffled consternation, the staff murmuring together in low voices. Some of them cast confused looks in my direction. Dad had instructed me to be there for the announcement in case anyone had questions; but of course, the questions people did ask were ones I couldn't answer honestly. *Why* was the most common.

"To celebrate the war swinging in our favor," I said primly. I'd rehearsed the line in Dad's office.

"We'll be bringing in outside help," Mr. Whittaker told the staff. "You'll be expected to assist but won't need to participate in any of the planning."

This earned a sigh of relief, although the quiet murmuring didn't stop. No one believed this was about the Coromina Group winning the war. Who celebrates victory before a final battle?

Mr. Whittaker dismissed the staff and then turned to my sisters, who were sitting together on the sofa. Adrienne looked excited; Daphne looked bored. Isabel sat sulking with tangled hair and a tired expression, staring at him if she wanted to burn him down. She didn't even look at me, although I looked at her—studying her, the way I did now, trying to see traces of the alien in her features. But all I saw was the elder Isabel. I barely even saw our father.

"You will, of course," Mr. Whittaker said, "be required to attend."

Daphne rolled her eyes.

"This is a very important moment for your father, and it's imperative that his daughters be present." He gave them a steely look. "It's also imperative that you look your best. Esme will accompany you to Undirra City the day of the party to have dresses prepared and to have your hair and makeup styled. It will be a bit of a rush, of course, but it was the earliest we could have the appointments made."

The twins swiveled their heads toward me, waiting for confirmation. Isabel picked at her shirt, her head tilted down.

"It'll be fun," I said, even though I didn't mean it.

"Whatever you say, sis," Daphne said, and she flopped back on the sofa. Adrienne hit her in the shoulder.

"It will be," she said. "You're the one complaining nothing ever happens."

The next two days were a whirlwind of preparation. I was put in charge of the arriving mercenary troops, which meant I spent the time at the estate, watching the decorations go up on the lawn. Floating lights and flowered garlands and round cocktail tables. A stage, too, supposedly for the orchestra. I knew better.

The troops arrived at staggered intervals, and I directed them to different stations set up around the estate. The officers were placed in the guest rooms in the house, unused since the first Isabel's death; the others set up camp along the perimeter of the woods. I hated going near the woods. I hated the green shadows, the sweetly rotting scent of undergrowth. Nothing strange ever happened out there during the preparations, though. I never saw any flickers of moment, much less tall, feathered monsters or a room full of lights.

When my mother's troop arrived the day before the party, I placed them along the path to the beach, away from the woods. I didn't have a chance to speak to Harriet that day; everything was too hectic. But I saw her unroll her tent with a trio of other soldiers, their movements quick and professional and familiar, and for one shivery moment, I thought about how this could have been my life instead, following her footsteps and fighting for the mercenaries instead of keeping all my father's secrets.

The morning of the party, I woke up early, just as the sun was rising up over the tree line. I leaned out my window and breathed in the balmy sea breeze and looked at the lawn, all the decorations shimmering with dew. It was like a party for ghosts.

As Mr. Whittaker had promised, I gathered up my sisters and took us all down to Undirra City. It wasn't a pleasant trip. Isabel kept slinking off, disappearing out of the dress shop while the dressmakers were busy with Adrienne or Daphne or me. I'd look up and she'd be gone; fifteen minutes later, I'd step out of the dressing room and she'd be standing up on the pedestal while the dressmaker scanned her for sizing. I wondered if the Radiance were here in the city, too, if she was vanishing off to go meet with them. At one point, when Daphne and Adrienne were busy in the changing rooms, I sidled up to her. She glared at me from behind her hair.

"Where are you going?" I asked.

"Nowhere," she said, and walked away before I could ask any more questions. After that, she avoided me completely.

Of course, my sisters weren't the only ones who had to get ready for the party. Dad expected me to look resplendent, an heir to him in every way possible. So, I tried to set my worries about Isabel and aliens out of my mind, and I swiped through the holos of the different dresses, unhappy with each of their cuts or styles. Nothing looked right on me. My body owed too much to my mother.

"The tailor bot can alter these," the dressmaker said. I turned around on the pedestal, gazing at myself in the mirrors. The dress was a long, slinky champagne thing, but it didn't hang right on me. Every time I moved, the holo flickered and you could see snatches of my bare skin and my underwear.

"The color is an excellent one for you and the detailing at the shoulders really flatters your décolleté." The dressmaker sounded bored, and I was vaguely aware that I was at the root of it. By that point, my sisters had all picked their own dresses and were in the waiting area while the tailor bots spun them out. But my dress was more important than theirs, since I was to be part of the unveiling ceremony tonight.

"I don't like how it looks at my hips," I said.

The dressmaker sighed. "What about this?" She tapped her screen and the dress shimmered and was replaced by one from earlier. Dark green and with a wider cut through the hips. "We can combine the two." A few more taps on the screen. The dress turned champagne and the sleeves slipped away to reveal my bare shoulders. I stared at my reflection, standing still so that the holo wouldn't flicker. I imagined myself in this dress, standing up on the stage, lights twinkling around me as the R-Troops marched in front of Dad's investors.

"It's perfect," I said.

The dressmaker sighed. *Finally*, that sigh said, and I gave her a dark look that she ignored.

Afterward, John corralled all of us to the salon. We sat in a square, wearing the holos of our dresses so that stylists would know how best to pretty us up. This was easier: no decisions to be made. Isabel sat across from me, and she sulked as the stylist pulled and combed out her hair.

Hair, makeup, clothes. Adrienne picked out jewelry as well, a shimmering silver necklace that flowed like water down the front of her chest. I'd forgotten about jewelry, and when the car brought us back to Star's End, a couple of hours before the party was to start, I rooted through my lockbox until I found a thin chain I'd bought years before. My champagne dress was waiting for me, laid out on my bed by one of the staff, having been delivered while we were still at the salon, and I draped the chain across it to see how it would work. I thought it looked nice, even though it'd been so long since I'd worn anything except Coromina Groups suits, I wasn't sure.

The house Connectivity chimed, and Mr. Whittaker's dry voice spilled into my room. "Ms. Coromina, Mr. Coromina would like to speak with you. He's in his suite."

I sighed and stepped away from my bed. "Right now?" I caught a glimpse of my reflection in the mirror: my hair had been pulled away from my face in a low ponytail, my eyes lined and smudged so that they stood out against my skin. For one breathless second, I didn't recognize myself.

"Yes," Mr. Whittaker said. "Right now."

I clomped up to Dad's suite. The halls were more flurried than usual, with contract staff, on loan from the company enclave, scurrying back and forth carrying stacks of platters and armfuls of lights and other party accouterment that had been dug out of storage. I breezed past the staff, feeling like I wasn't even in my own house.

Dad's door was shut. I stopped in the hallway and looked at it. He'd actually called me up here, to his own personal space. I didn't know what to make of it.

I knocked once. No answer. I lifted my hand to knock again when Dad's voice drifted out to the hallway—"If this is Esme, you can come in. Anyone else, take it to Mr. Whittaker."

I took a deep breath and stepped inside. The sitting room was empty.

"I'm here!" I called out. "I was getting ready; what do you want?"

Silence. I peered around the room, taking in the expensive furniture, the view of the forest from the window. Then the bedroom door swung open and Dad stepped out. He wore a tuxedo cut in the Coromina Group style, narrow lapels and a long waist.

"Well," he said, hardly glancing at me. "I'm glad to see you took my request seriously."

"What request?"

"To make yourself presentable." He lifted his head. "The salon did a nice job with your hair. None of those ridiculous styles I see coming in from Amana."

That was the closest he came to a compliment.

"I need to get dressed," I said.

"Yes, I know. You took longer than I expected down in Undirra City." He fiddled with sleeves, smoothed one hand over the side of his hair.

"Well, we only had three days. I'm shocked anyone's actually going to show up at this thing at late notice."

Dad gave me a half smile that made me feel like I was being

mocked. "They're company folk. They know to drop everything for something like this. Plus the soldiers. We'll have a good crowd."

I rolled my eyes.

"The party's necessary to get people watching," Dad said, fiddling with his shining cuff links. "On the newsfeeds. A big society event like this grabs people's attention. They might even be watching on the OCI planets." His eyes glittered.

I sighed. I'd never been good at this kind of PR machinations. I worked better behind the scenes. I supposed that made me a good Ninety-Nine.

"I wanted to make sure you understand your part in all this."

"Introducing the R-Troops. A prewritten Formal Two ceremony." We'd been over all this already.

"Have you been practicing?" he peered up at me, his expression sharp.

"I thought that was the whole point of having preplanned ceremonies," I said. "So you can work them in at the last moment."

He grinned, and I felt like I'd passed some kind of test. Either way, the steps for the Formal Two ceremony were fairly simple. A few quick words, a few strikes of a gong. Maybe I'd laugh about it later with Adrienne and Daphne. Isabel didn't do much laughing anymore.

"I still want you to look over the steps," he said. "I don't want you embarrassing me."

"I won't embarrass you," I said as sweetly as I could. Then I left his room before he could say anything else.

Back in my own suite, I activated my lightbox and drew up the Formal Two ceremony recording so that the holo would play in the background as I got dressed. I dabbed scent on the back of my ears and watched the actors go through the motions. The familiarity of it was a slow dawning in the back of my mind. I'd first learned these steps when I was a teenager, attending tutoring every day with Mr. Garcia. He'd taught me all the ceremonies.

I watched through the recording two more times until I was certain that I had it. Then I went downstairs, ready to face the evening.

I floated toward the party. The closer I got to the gardens, the

more tumultuous the house became; in the hallways, I passed scut-
tling contract staff, but downstairs was a whirlwind of people, some
familiar, some not, all of them dressed in Coromina Group uniforms. I threaded my way through, wondering if I might pass by
Harriet in the maelstrom. But I didn't see any soldiers down there.
Not the guests, and certainly not the R-Troops. They were probably
going to drive them in, a whole convoy of miracle soldiers.

Outside, in the garden, things were much calmer. The ordinary
soldiers were milling around in their uniforms—I looked for Harriet but couldn't find her. The decorations that had seemed so dead
earlier were illuminated as if they'd been infused with some sort of
magic. The otherworldliness of it caught in my throat, and I thought
of the place I'd gone in the woods, the place with the monsters.
I wavered, harsh whispers threading through my thoughts. I saw
teeth, sharp claws, scaly skin.

And then I saw nothing but a party. I took a deep breath. The
Radiance had never come slinking out of the woods before; the
night I had gone to them, I had found their hiding place. They were
not going to crash the party tonight.

I drifted over to a table set up in the grass and draped myself
in one of the chairs. The lights glimmered around me, bathing the
pineapple gardens in that soft, icy glow. The woods were a dark
boundary in the distance. I didn't want to turn my back to them.

I stayed at that table and watched the Four Sisters come out. All
of them were present today, in various states of undress: Amana was
full, a bright blue-green disc against the inky sky. Catequil a sliver
like a frown. Quilla half-waned. All of them danced around Coromina I. I held my hand up to the sky and closed one eye and counted
the finger's width between the Sisters and their anchor. Three, two,
four. Crimson storms surged across Coromina I's surface.

"How long have you been out here?"

I jerked my gaze away from the planets. Daphne was striding
across the lawn in her little blue cocktail dress. The salon had curled
her hair and swept it over her shoulder, and it fell down the side of
her face like a dark waterfall.

"You look lovely," I said.

"Oh, please. You already saw me."

"That was a holo."

Daphne rolled her eyes and sat down beside me. "Staring up at the planets, huh?" She hooked her ankle around a nearby chair and dragged it over so she could prop her feet up on it. She sat like that, lounging, leaning back in her chair.

I shrugged.

Daphne dropped her head back. The red light of Coromina I fell across her face. "Doesn't it mean something when they're all ringed around C-One like that? Some astrological thing?"

"I don't know."

"Of course not." Daphne grinned at me. "You're too smart to go in for that sort of thing."

My cheeks burned. "That's not what I—"

But Daphne just looked back up at Coromina I. "Oh, I wish I could remember! Isabel would know, but she's been so gloomy lately, I don't know if she'll want to talk about it."

My heart twisted.

Then Daphne sat up and snapped her fingers. "Oh, I got it now! It's impending doom."

I gave her an annoyed glare, I couldn't help it. She laughed.

"No, really. Well, not that dramatic. But it means something's coming." She gestured with one hand. "All the Sisters crowding around C-One like that, that's the sign for a violent change. It's an attack, get it? The Sisters attacking the anchor?" Then she pointed at Catequil. "And when Catequil frowns, that always means unhappiness." She spread out her hands. "Impending doom."

The wind gusted. It knocked the lanterns around, and for a moment, they were blown out of their magnetic patterns, scattershot across the yard.

"Impending doom?" I said. "More like impending rain." I tried not to think about the Radiance in the forest. "I don't know what Dad was thinking, throwing an outdoor party so close to the start of the rainy season."

Daphne didn't have an answer to that. We sat side by side and watched the staff spill out of the house, readying themselves for the first guests. Adrienne stood up on the porch, shining in a long white-silver gown that was like an extension of her pale skin. She and Daphne might be identical, but this evening, they couldn't look more different.

The door jerked open behind Adrienne; it was Dad, striding out in his stupid Coromina Group tuxedo. The Alvatech and Andromeda Corps generals walked with him. The buckles on their dress uniforms shone in the lights.

"Where's Isabel?" I said, still thinking about the Radiance, about her strange disappearances.

"Who the hell knows." Daphne sat up and put her feet back on the ground. "Grace is probably dragging her down— Oh, there she is."

Isabel stepped through the doorway, stoop-shouldered and shuffling but breathtakingly beautiful anyway. She wore a dark red gown with a long train—it hadn't looked so dramatic as a holo. The fabric smeared like a trail of blood behind her as she walked. The stylist had twisted her hair up into a knot to reveal the curve of her long, elegant neck rising out of the drape of her gown. She was as beautiful as her mother had been.

And she looked like she wanted to be anywhere else.

Daphne lifted one hand. "Isabel! Over here!"

Isabel's head turned toward us and I could feel her taking us in. Her expression didn't change.

"Come on!" Daphne shouted. "Before the old people start showing up!"

A pause. But then Isabel glided toward us, her gown rippling in the dark. Guilt twisted around me. And maybe it wasn't just guilt, either. She had something in common with that monster in the woods.

So did the soldiers I was going to be introducing in a few hours' time.

I stood up. "I'm going to see Dad about preparing for the ceremony," I said, and walked away. Isabel and I passed each another on the path. She glanced at me, slightly, turning her head at an angle.

Our gazes caught. Just for a second, but it was enough.

I walked around the side of the house until I came to the staff courtyard. It was frenzied with activity, but I stayed on the edge, lurking in the shadows and watching contract staff bustle back and forth with trays and drinks and platters of food. Voices rose up in a shout: "They're starting to arrive! Faster, faster, we're running late with those cocktails—"

It was an odd thing to see, like splitting open a lightbox and looking at the light-wires running through its innards. Here's how a party worked. Lots of invisible people shouting at each other in a courtyard set away from the guests.

"Ms. Coromina!" It was Alicia. She rushed past with two bottles of Amanan brandy. "What are you doing here? The first guests have arrived and I'm sure Mr. Coromina needs you greeting them."

"I didn't know," I said.

"Go on!" She pointed at the gardens and then slipped back into the crowd before I could thank her. Not that I was thankful. This whole party was a sham, like so much of the work we did at the Coromina Group. I didn't want to talk to Coromina Group employees. I didn't want to act gracious when I was congratulated on becoming a Ninety-Nine. I just wanted to introduce the R-Troops and maybe see my mother. I wanted the war to be over so I could go back to making this company what it should be. Although I didn't know what that was anymore. I couldn't stop thinking about the idea that I needed to protect the people of the Four Sisters from the aliens, not put them in danger so that the Coromina Group could more easily win its wars. But the realities of how I would do such a thing—I felt like there was only one choice. Like my mother dropping me at Star's End as a baby. If I wanted to protect my citizen-employees from danger, then I had to get rid of the danger. I had to prevent the danger from coming into our worlds.

I had to get rid of the Divested.

Except that was too much like what my father had done, two hundred years ago, and it disgusted me that I was skirting so close to him. I only knew that I wanted to be the one to decide, that maybe I could find a different way. Maybe not destroy them, only lock them up in that place where they seemed to live, that place that both was and wasn't my world.

And so, I walked around the side of the house, because I knew doing my job at this party was the only way I could do what needed to be done.

It was like a sunset, the way light and sound faded from the clamor of the courtyard to the gentle whisper of the party. The band hadn't started playing yet, and I could spot a few non-military guests weaving their way through the soldiers. Voices drifted across the garden. I stopped on the periphery and scanned. I still didn't see Harriet. Dad was standing up on the patio along with Adrienne; it seemed Daphne and Isabel had disappeared somewhere.

The woods. My heart went cold. No. They didn't go into the woods. They didn't go to the monsters.

My skin prickled. When I looked up, Dad was glaring at me from across the pineapples. Adrienne was busy entertaining the Koziaras, listening attentively as Mr. Koziara spoke and gestured. I gathered the hem of my skirt away from the ground and picked my way across the grass.

"Esme!" Mrs. Cho Koziara cried. "I was wondering where you'd run off to. I heard"—and here she dipped her voice down to a conspiratorial whisper—"I heard you had a promotion a few months ago."

"I'm not allowed to talk about it," I said with mock gravity, and everyone laughed at the joke. Even Dad. I smiled at them like this made me happy.

"Well, it *is* wartime." Mrs. Cho Koziara fanned at herself. "I wouldn't want to say anything that could ruin the effort."

Dad laughed again. "That's simply not possible, Hye-jin."

More laughter. It grated on me. At last, the Koziaras drifted off to join the party proper. Dad put his hand on my shoulder.

"Glad you didn't disappear on me," he said in a low whisper.

"You know I wouldn't."

A chime twinkled—more guests were threading through the house.

"Of course not," Dad said. Silhouettes approached the doorway, and Adrienne was eavesdropping while trying to seem interested only in the bangles around her wrist. "This is your job. This is what you'll be doing when I'm gone."

No, it won't, I thought. *I'll be better than you.*

The new guests stepped out onto the patio. Mrs. Okadigbo and her wife. There was an eruption of excitement as Dad pretended he cared about them. I held out my hand; I asked how their son was doing.

This went on for the next half hour.

I'd always found this sort of thing dull, even if I understood the necessity of it. Adrienne, though, was beside herself with delight—she was always complaining at dinner how we had these lovely gardens and never made use of them. But I was too distracted by everything that had happened to really put in the effort. I smiled, pleasantly but not brightly enough to invite a more in-depth conversation. I welcomed our guests to Star's End. I invited them to try the dessert wine. I accepted their congratulations for my promotion. After a while, every face bled into the next. All just filler, to get the newsfeeds focused on us. As much decorations as the lights floating among the trees.

At some point, the band started to play, and shimmering music twinkled through the nighttime. A few brave couples took to dancing, Quillian style. All quite conventional. The arriving guests became more sporadic and I stood beside Adrienne and watched the dancers gliding across the lawn like bits of dandelion. In the floating lights, everything was ephemeral.

"It's beautiful, isn't it?" Adrienne said.

"It's a party." The last party Dad had thrown had been when he announced his engagement to the first Isabel, years before. I looked at him as he spoke with Mr. Dolega from PM. He didn't look like he intended to get married tonight. I wondered what it meant, that he never married anyone after the first Isabel. I refused to believe it meant he had a heart.

A tall, lean Andromeda Corps soldier, younger and far more handsome than most mercenaries, came up to Adrienne. She stiffened as he approached, her eyes wide and delighted, and I could almost hear her heart fluttering inside her chest with adolescent anticipation.

"Ms. Coromina," he said holding out his hand in the formal style. "Would you care to dance?"

She glanced over at me, as if asking permission. I shrugged.

"Of course!" she said, and she took his hand and fell into place beside him in one liquid movement. "Tell me more about yourself."

She'd been practicing for this moment her entire life, I imagined. Waiting for the estate to open so she could fall into her birthright as a princess.

Someone tapped on my shoulder.

"The ceremony will be starting soon." It was Dad, looking genial and determined. "I want to get it over with early on so that the guests will have a chance to speak with the R-Troops before they're too drunk."

"The guests or the R-Troops?"

Dad rolled his eyes. "The guests. The R-Troops don't get intoxicated." He jerked his head back toward the house. "Go inside and let Mr. Whittaker know we'll be starting in about five minutes."

"Five minutes?" I pointed out at the dancers. It was impossible to pick out Adrienne. "Adrienne'll be disappointed; she's out there acting like a character on one of her dramas."

"Five minutes," Dad said. "Go. I need to be out here in case any more guests arrive."

I was grateful to have something to do other than entertain, and so I did as he asked, moving away from the glamour of the party and into the chaos of the house. Staff rushed back and forth, shouting at each other, flinging around trays and towels and empty glasses. I crept along the side wall, my skirt bunched up around my hips so I wouldn't trip over the hem. The staff ignored me. They were only required to tend to us outside, in the soft light of the floating lanterns.

I slid through the crowd until I found Mr. Whittaker in the foyer beside the stairwell, berating some poor contract girl. By the time I walked up, the exact nature of her crime had been explored; Mr. Whittaker was just slamming her with generic invective, trying to make her cry. She wasn't, though, and she stood up straight with her shoulders square and looked him right in the eye.

"Mr. Whittaker," I said sharply, and with that, the hierarchy shifted. Mr. Whittaker turned to me and his features softened.

"Ms. Coromina," he said.

The contract girl stared at me with wide eyes. Her earlier confidence had turned to trembling. She was scared of me, more scared of me than she was of Mr. Whittaker.

I shifted my weight uneasily.

"Go back to your duties," I told her, and she nodded and scurried away.

"She broke one of the glass cruets—" Mr. Whittaker began.

"Something's bound to get broken at a party like this." It was a weird exercise of power, to not care about the cruet when Mr. Whittaker did. "My father sent me to let you know that we'll be starting the ceremony soon."

"Yes, of course, everything's ready." Mr. Whittaker gave me one of his oily smiles. "Come, I'll take you over to the dais. We have it set up in the western garden. The band will let the guests know to begin moving that way any moment now."

We walked side by side down the hallway. It was nearly empty, most of the staff out in the front rooms. Music drifted up from the gardens, lovely and modern. I didn't say anything, and so neither did Mr. Whittaker. I knew he wanted to. But my mere presence was enough to keep him silent.

Finally, we stepped out into the western garden. Staff stood stationed at regular intervals around the lawn, waiting with empty trays. The dais rose out of the grass. It was bathed in white light stained pinkish-gray from Coromina I. And it was empty. None of the R-Troops anywhere. They were probably waiting off in the woods—a thought that made me queasy. The Formal Two ceremony required some formal marching, though, and Dad would want the troops to make an entrance.

Off in the distant, the music stopped. The staff shifted their weight, glanced at one another, straightened their spines. Applause rippled through the dewy night air.

"You'll want to take your position," Mr. Whittaker said.

I felt alone in that moment, despite the staff in the garden and the sound of the party around the bend of the house. There were more people at Star's End than I could ever remember, and yet I was alone, walking up the steps to an empty dais, where I turned and looked out over an empty garden.

"Do you know what you're to do?" Mr. Whittaker said.

"Yes! I memorized all these speeches years ago." He was staring at me coldly. He'd had enough of my insolence in the manor house, I supposed. I sighed. "Dad's going to bring the party around, where they'll find me waiting on stage. I'll say, 'Welcome to Star's End!' and give that stupid speech about the glory of victory. Then the R-Troops will come in." I paused. "You know they're called that, don't you? The big surprise Dad has planned?"

Mr. Whittaker bobbed his head.

"That's Ninety-Nine information," I said.

"Not for long," Mr. Whittaker said.

I watched him walk away, shuffle over the grass and disappear into the gloomy darkness. And then Dad's voice boomed into the night.

"Thank you all for attending tonight." His words echoed around the woods. I felt dizzy, hearing them. I wondered if the Radiance could hear them too. If they understood them. Perhaps Isabel had taught them Coromina Standard.

The wind picked up and a chill ran over me. I wrapped my arms around my chest and squeezed.

"—incredible victory in Sector 894 three nights ago, one of a string of victories the Coromina Group has had in this war. However, we haven't been *entirely* honest with you—"

Laughter rippled up on the wind. I sighed and smoothed my hands down the side of my dress. All that pretty fabric felt too heavy, like it was trying to drag me down through the dais. My makeup was sticky against my skin. The wind rustled through the trees and I looked out in the darkness, waiting for a flash of teeth or shining eyes.

Nothing.

"—secret weapon. Yes, we had a secret weapon! Would you expect anything less from us? And it's my great honor to formally unveil for you the latest project from the Coromina Group—"

I stiffened. The wind blew cold against my skin. Dad's words transformed into buzzing inside my head, and then that buzzing transformed to thundering applause, and for a moment, I was afraid I had forgotten the steps of the Formal Two ceremony—there was a wide, empty expanse where the memory should go. And then the first few guests came into the garden, the women's dresses sparkling beneath the lights, and it flooded back to me, every step and motion and word. It was part of my DNA. I was the daughter of Philip Coromina. The Coromina Group was part of me.

The crowd surged into the garden. Coromina Group employees drifted toward the front; the soldiers hung back. Everyone stared up at me, but their faces blurred together in the planetlight. I waited until the garden was full and the fluttering camera drones had activated, recording the ceremony for the newsfeeds. No signs from Dad or Mr. Whittaker about when to begin. I was on my own. I was a Ninety-Nine.

"Welcome to Star's End," I said, and my voice rang out, magnified by the microphones embedded in the dais. Feedback rattled inside my head. "We come together tonight to celebrate a victory of no small significance, a glorious moment up among the stars." I didn't think about the words as I spoke them; they were meaningless, written fifty years before by some hired scriptwriter. Who knew which battle they thought of as they came up with the speech? One of Dad's, from the old days, from when all he did was sell weapons?

I droned out the rest of the speech. The crowded shifted and stirred, picking up drinks from the staff, leaning into each other. Adrienne was near the front of the crowd, standing with her arm looped in the soldier's, gazing up at the stage, enthralled. In the blur of faces I thought for a moment I spotted my mother.

"It's my pleasure to unveil to you to the source of our victory." A staff member rolled out the big Coromina Group gong, dull burnished bronze glowing in the floating lights. She handed me the mallet and then darted offstage. I held the mallet overhead. "May we win this war."

It was such a weird speech, ancient-sounding without being ancient at all, and far too formal for a party. But the crowd applauded and cheered and I struck the gong, feeling like an idiot.

The sound rumbled through the gardens. I'm sure it reached all the way into the woods. I struck the gong again. My ears hurt. I struck it again, one last time. I thought I could feel its reverberations in my bones.

I was trapped inside my head, my hearing muffled by the gong's thick and sonorous voice, but I still saw movement out in the crowd, people turning toward the woods. For a moment, I thought of the Radiance, and my heart shuddered.

Sharp teeth, sharp claws.

But no, it wasn't the Radiance. It was the R-Troops, marching two by two out of the woods. Lights floated near them, illuminating their way, along with buzzing camera drones that flashed and hummed and took in everything. I dropped the mallet next to my side and watched, as breathless as our party guests. The R-Troops wore their uniforms, dark liquidy blue with the Coromina Group logo emblazoned on their right shoulders. They turned sharply in the garden and made their way up to the stage before fanning out in front of me on the stage, blocking the lights. I remembered the rest of the ceremony—it wasn't just speeches and gongs. I dropped the mallet on the stage and shuffled around to the front. The crowd gaped up at the R-Troops, and a murmur rose up from the garden, thrumming with excitement and confusion.

As I'd first memorized ten years ago, I let the last of the R-Troops arrange themselves into place before speaking.

"We welcome this—product—into the Coromina Group family." I stumbled over *product*, feeling like I should change it, not knowing what to change it to. That's what this ceremony was, the unveiling of a new product. A new weapon. "It will bring us much success."

God, everything was so stilted. But I paused and the crowd picked up on the pause and applauded, just like they were expected to do.

"And now, here's—" I was supposed to say *designer* or *engineer*, but I was about to introduce my father, and I doubted he'd want either of those titles attached to his name. "The CEO of the Coromina Group, Philip Coromina."

More applause. I stepped off the stage, my job done, and Dad took my place, grinning and waving. I didn't leave the garden. Part of me wanted to; part of me didn't want to listen to Dad's speech about the R-Troops and all their strengths and specifications. I snatched a glass of wine off its tray when one of the staff drifted by.

"We're calling them the R-Troops," Dad said, gesturing across the stage. "They may look like typical bioengineered soldiers, but they are far from typical."

In one stomping motion, every single soldier stepped backward except for one.

"Allow me to introduce Private Will Woods."

Private Woods lifted one hand in formal greeting.

"He possess the same features and benefits as all the R-Troops. Using the latest simulation technology, we were able to create effects never before seen in any bioengineered soldier." Dad winked at one of the camera drones. "I know you're intercepting this, OCI. You've already seen what we're capable of. Now I want you to know how we got there. Maybe we can work up a treaty instead; what do you say?"

The crowd laughed, but I knew it wasn't a joke. A treaty—really, a takeover of OCI's assets—would be more profitable in the long run than the war could ever be. And that's what all this was about in the end. Profit.

Dad ran through all the peculiarities of the R-Troops—their psychic link, their superior strength and senses, a brief overview of their connection to the orgoships they fought in. All around me, the crowd was expressing its approval and its interest. I kept my gaze on the soldiers, who stood perfectly still, as they'd been trained to do. Designed to do.

I drained my wine and listened to the wind so I wouldn't have to listen to Dad. That soldier looked away from me. But I found I couldn't look away from him.

I escaped the crush of the party and stumbled over to the plumeria maze, a glass of wine in one hand. People were still knotted around the stage, talking to the R-Troops, but the initial frenzy had died down. I just wanted to be alone, to get my thoughts in order.

After Dad had finished his speech, the crowd erupted, surging forward, guests shouting questions up at the stage while Dad gazed over them with an expression of calm, chilling benevolence.

He owned all of them. He owned every single thing, living or otherwise, in this system. And in that moment, I could see just how thoroughly he understood his power.

I fielded questions of my own: I was the second choice, for people who couldn't get up to Dad. The R-Troops filed off the stage so that the guests could speak to them directly and, in Dad's words, "get a sense of how they operate." I stood beside the stage, spitting out generic non-answers to the breathless questions of the crowd. The R-Troops had broken ranks to mingle. An old businesswoman spoke with the one closest to me, eyeing him up shrewdly, and I wondered if he was the one who had looked at me during Dad's speech. But then a man in an Amana-style caftan stole him away and handed him one of the glasses from the trays. I couldn't tell any of the R-Troops apart.

It was dizzying, overwhelming, but I did what I'd been trained to do since I was a child. I was glad to be free of the mess now, though, and no one was going to bother with the plumeria maze when there were other wonders at the party.

I walked along the path, the blossoms tinting everything with a silvery lavender sheen. They were bright enough to drown out the light from Coromina I. My dress rippled over my legs. The fabric was slick and cool like water, a syn-fabric from the Talu system that was perfect for the climate here. The damp breeze blowing through the window also blew straight through my dress, cooling my skin.

"Esme."

It was still strange to hear her voice without the distortion of the holorecordings. It always took me a moment to place it. I turned around and Harriet leaned up against the plumeria bushes, looking handsome in her black-and-reds.

"Some show your father put on for us." She pushed away from the plumeria and ambled toward me, her hands shoved in her pockets. She kicked at the ground with her big black boot. I had come out there to be alone, but I realized I was happy to see her.

"It's a typical strategy," I said. "Get the word out to as many planets as you can. Stirs up buyer interest."

Harriet looked up at me, half-smiling in the hazy light. "You sound like him."

My cheeks flushed hot, and I looked away.

"No, that's not what I mean, exactly." She moved toward me and put a hand on my shoulder. Just for a second. Then she snatched it away like she'd done something wrong. "It's just, seeing my daughter standing up there, announcing this new type of soldier—" She stopped, locked up at the sky. "When I first found out I was pregnant, I couldn't fucking believe I'd been so stupid. I was more reckless then. Hadn't expected anything to happen with your father."

The wind gusted hard, knocking the plumeria around. There was a chemical afterscent on it, a sharpness that made my throat itch. A military starship flying too close to the ozone, maybe.

"I remember standing in medical, the test results blinking on the holo, and knowing I was going to have to send you away. I told myself at least you were his eldest. That was the thing that reassured me. He wouldn't be cruel to his eldest." She looked over at me. The wind billowed my dress out beside me, and I felt disoriented and strange. Pulled apart. A long time before, Rena had warned me not to become too much like my father, and here was my mother, trying not to tell me that it had happened anyway.

"I cried the day I left you with your father, and mercs don't cry. They beat it out of us. But I cried that day." She shook her head, eyes gleaming as she looked at me. "Did I do the right thing, Esme?"

My mouth was too dry to speak. The wind howled. A rainstorm was blowing in. All those guests were going to be running for shelter soon.

"I don't know," I finally said, and fixed my gaze on the plumeria plants. Their light seemed to pulse. My mother was right to ask that question, and she didn't even know the whole story. I was only there, a Ninety-Nine, because I had betrayed my sister. Because I did what Dad demanded of me. I told myself I wanted to run the company my own way, wanted to turn the focus on PM, but what did that really mean now? There were dangers there that I hadn't even known about until a few weeks before. Dangers, a voice whispered in the back of my head, a voice that sounded like Isabel, that had more of a right to be here than I did—and yet I couldn't think that way. It was my job to protect the people of the Four Sisters.

"We all do things we regret," Harriet said. She took a step closer to me, cautious. "God knows I have. But please don't let those things consume you."

I blinked away tears. *Mercs don't cry.* But I wasn't a merc.

Harriet lunged forward, her movement sudden and surprising, and pulled me into an embrace. It was awkward. Hesitant. Uncertain. "Don't let him change you," she whispered fiercely.

Her words cut at me—I was afraid it was too late for that, because he'd been changing me since I was a child. But I didn't say anything, only squeezed back, my eyes closed as I tried to stave back the tears. The wind roared through the plumeria, and there was that chemical scent again, stronger than before. I pulled away, wiped at my eyes. And finally I found my voice, and I said, "I won't, I promise," even though I wasn't sure it was a promise I could keep.

There was a sound like the earth breaking into two.

I shouted and clamped my hands over my ears even though it did nothing to stop it; I could feel the sound inside my bones, vibrating every part of my body. Harriet was in a fighting stance, a knife out, head whipping around—the knife had come from nowhere; she must have had it tucked away under her uniform because the mercenaries weren't supposed to have weapons as part of their formal uniforms.

And then a horrible, sickly yellow light spread across the maze, drowning out the light from the flowers. I stumbled back, tripped on the heel of my shoe, and landed hard in the dirt.

Harriet's mouth moved, but I couldn't hear her, only that horrible roaring. She was looking at me. Pointing at the ground.

"I can't hear you!" I screamed.

She slammed down on the ground beside me and shouted in my ear. "Stay here! It's hostiles! Stay here!"

Hostiles? OCI?

Harriet scrambled away from me and disappeared in the turn of the path up ahead. I craned my head back, looking up at the sky. The yellow light burned at my eyes, and that chemical scent was everywhere. I blinked, scanning the sky for an OCI ship—they were violating a million treaties, attacking like this. What the fuck were they thinking?

I struggled to my feet. The thrumming noise was fading away, but sound was muffled. Distantly, I thought I heard screaming. I stumbled forward, one hand braced against the plumeria, head tilted back to take in the sky. It wasn't a ship light, I realized. The sky was veined, as if it were an egg cracking into pieces.

A bolt of dread shot straight through my heart.

This isn't OCI.

I kicked off my shoes and ran barefoot. I cut through the plumeria branches and sweet-smelling glossy leaves slapping me across the face. The screams grew louder and clearer. A few seconds later, I shot out into the lawn.

The party had turned to chaos.

I sucked in a deep breath of air, trying to steady myself. The yellow light made everything look washed out and alien. Guests streamed around the house, fighting to get to their cars. Everyone was looking up, twisting their necks around at odd angles, terror shining on their faces. The soldiers ran wildly, crisscrossing the yard, trying to get back to their camps—to their weapons. Their holos shrilled and beeped and blinked in wild, incongruous patterns.

My breaths grew deeper and deeper, turning to panic. I stepped out into the grass and peered up at the sky. The yellow veins were wider now.

"The sky's coming apart," I gasped, and it sounded absurd but it was the only thing I could think. The sky was coming apart and the sun was shining through.

A hand clamped on my arm.

"Ms. Coromina?" It was one of the estate soldiers. Private Water. "You shouldn't be here. You need to get to the safety shelter."

"Do you know what's happening?" I drew myself up, tried to will the tremor out of my voice.

"Ma'am, with all due respect, none of us knows what the fuck is going on." She glanced at her holo and her eyes went wide. "Fuck! Where's Private Sky-4? Tell me what's going on!"

A crackle of voices from her holo. I moved away from her, toward the house. I needed to find my sisters. I needed to get us to safety. But as I raced toward the house and the roiling crowd of party guests, my time at PM came back to me—these were my citizen-employees, and it was my job to care for them.

I jumped on the stage where the band had been playing and grabbed the amplifier. "Attention!" I said, and a few heads actually turned toward me. "Everyone move into the house. Head to the staff stairs! That will take you into the cellar! It's the safest place. Go! Go!"

My voice boomed out across the yard, echoing the booms of the sky as it fell to pieces. I jumped off the stage and raced toward the house. Some of the guests had listened to me, and they crammed themselves into the doors. Someone threw a floating light through the windows, shattering the glass. By now, some of the Alvatech soldiers had returned with light rifles, and they herded the guests, shouting for order. I stayed on the stage, scanning the crowd for my sisters. The yellow light made everything hard to see. It was getting brighter. I glanced at the sky. Those cracks weren't cracks anymore. The starry darkness was being consumed by ugly yellow light. I choked back a scream of fear and felt it strangle in my throat.

"Adrienne!" I shouted, although my voice was lost in the riot. "Daphne! Isabel!"

I jumped off the stage. Adrienne and Daphne I had seen during the presentation, but Isabel I'd only seen before the party started and not after—

God. Isabel.

I ran through the yard, pushing through Alvatech and Andromeda Corps soldiers, spinning around in my dress, the skirt tangling in my legs. My feet were coated in mud. *The R-Troops,* I thought. If they could connect with each other, maybe they could connect with Isabel.

I grabbed the arm of a passing soldier, jerking her to attention. "The R-Troops," I said. "Where did they go?"

She glared at me. "You think I care about Coromina's—"

"I'm Esme Coromina!" I shouted, drawing myself up. "Where did they go?"

Her eyes widened with recognition. "Toward the woods." And then she raced off, shouting instructions into her holo.

I whirled around, heart pounding. The woods loomed up ahead, a black hole that swallowed the light from the sky. But what other choices did I have? Finding the R-Troops was my link to finding Isabel, and she was my best shot at finding the twins. I glanced over at the house. Guests were still scrambling to get inside. Everything was stained yellow. It turned my stomach.

I took a deep breath and ran toward the woods. I didn't let myself think about my decision; I just plunged forward, arms pumping. Distantly, screaming started again, panicked and shrill. I looked up at the sky.

Something dropped down to the earth.

I slowed my pace, unsure of what I'd seen. My panicked imagination? No—there was another, a dark bullet careering toward the ground. Another, this one closer. It landed in the grass with a cloud of sulfuric smoke and then unfurled itself, too-long limbs and glossy black feathers.

For a moment, I was back in the woods on a balmy night, the light red instead of yellow, and I knew exactly what was dropping out of the skies.

Screams erupted in the distance. I turned and ran as hard as I could, zigzagging toward the tree line. I screamed out Isabel's name. No answer. The wind blew hot and chemical. Pain radiated out from my chest. Just a little farther and I would be at the forest, and I'd find the R-Troops and I'd find Isabel and I'd find a way to stop this.

A blast of hot wind billowed out from the direction of the house. I slammed into the woods and slowed, gasping for breath. I whirled around. Star's End was glowing. That yellow light burned my retinas.

"Esme! I told you to stay put!"

For a moment, I thought my mother was a hallucination. I jerked around and there she was, stalking toward me with a light rifle strapped across her chest.

"Mom," I whispered without thinking. It felt right on my tongue, more right than *Harriet*. But I didn't think she heard me.

"I've been looking for you, goddammit." She grabbed my arm and pulled me away from the trees. I shook my head.

"No, I'm trying to find the R-Troops. They're linked to my sister—"

"Your sisters are with your father." Her eyes gleamed with focused intensity. "There's an escape ship set up on the beach. First thing I found out." She stopped, jerked up her gun, head cocked like she was listening. I tried to slow my breathing but I couldn't. Sweat dripped down my spine. "It's a damned invasion. Not OCI." She looked over at me. Our eyes caught. "It's them."

I nodded.

She closed her eyes. Took a deep breath. "Let's get you off this planet."

I gazed over at the house. Was it burning, or was it just the light? I couldn't tell. But here I was, leaving again. Just like I'd done during the flu outbreak. This was what the Coromina family did. We fled during times of terror.

"No," I said. "I'm not going. It's not fair. All those people—"

"Those people are already dead." Harriet pushed her hair away from her forehead. "This isn't your fault, Esme. It's your father's. He should never have terraformed this place. Come *on*."

She started weaving through the trees. My sisters were safe, she'd said, but I was certain she only meant Adrienne and Daphne. Isabel was out there. She was a part of this, somehow.

I wavered in place. The yellow light filtered through the tree leaves, creating long unusual shadows. Harriet stomped through the underbrush up head. "I'm not letting you die here!" she shouted at me over her shoulder.

The wind blew through the tree's branches, and the light shifted, and I saw patterns in it. Spots of negative space. That night, I hadn't just seen the Radiance; I had seen their home. And I knew, caught in the prism of yellow light, I was seeing it again.

"Wait!" I screamed.

Harriet stopped and turned to me in exasperation.

"I want to stop this," I said. "This attack. Please."

She frowned. "What the hell are you talking about?"

I looked at her, pleading. "Just wait for me, please. Just wait."

She rubbed her hand along the grip of her gun. I focused on the visions in the light.

And then I stepped through them.

It was easy, easier than it had been that night a week ago. The forest vanished in a blink; the yellow light turned cool and pale. Blood pounded in my ears. I stepped forward, and my bare feet slid across smooth, slick stone.

"Isabel?" I called out. My voice echoed.

I lifted my gaze around the room. The ceiling rose up so high, it almost vanished from view. The cubes of light drifted through the air. I listened for hissing, but there was nothing, only a deep, thudding silence.

"Isabel!" I shouted again, and I realized I'd been wrong, that she wasn't here after all.

And then I heard the echo of a single footstep.

I whipped around, my mud-stained dress swirling around me. "Isabel?" I said.

She appeared out of the shadows in increments: her eyes, her hair, hands, her mouth.

"You shouldn't be here," she said.

Here here here, said the echo in the room.

"Isabel." I gasped with happiness and jogged toward her. She let me. She let me grab her by the shoulders and pull her into a hug, although she didn't return it.

"Please," she said, her breath hot against my ear. "Leave. Get away. Offworld. Out of the system."

Her voice was jagged. I looked at her and saw that her eyes were red with tears.

"Please," she said.

"What the hell is going on?" And then, without thinking, I said, "What have you done?"

Isabel's face twisted and it was then that I realized what I'd said. I slapped my hand over my mouth, shook my head. "No, Isabel, I didn't mean—"

"You think I want this?" she screamed. Her hands were balled up into tiny, inconsequential fists, but her eyes raged. "You think I want to choose between two families?"

"You don't," I said, moving toward her, holding out one hand. She jerked away before I could touch her. "They aren't your family," I said. "We are."

Tears streamed down Isabel's cheeks. "You have no idea what they are!" she shouted. "You look at them and you just see a monster, right? Is that how you see me?"

"No," I said. My hand was still stretched out toward her, hanging stupidly in the empty space. "God, no, Isabel—"

"I told them it wasn't right," she hissed, "to kill innocent people. That it wasn't our fault—" Her voice hitched. "There aren't many of them, you know. Only about a hundred. And they don't deserve to die either."

She knelt down on the floor and covered her face with her hands. I didn't know what to do. I moved closer to her. I wanted to scoop her up, drag her to the escape ship. Make her come with her family. I didn't understand how she could look at those creatures out there and see herself in them.

"Isabel," I said softly, and then her hand lashed out, and she was pressing her fingers to my chest, her eyes boring into mine. Her face flushed red and she let out a scream and jumped away from me and I knew she had peered inside my head. I knew she had Seen me.

"How can you expect me to see myself in *you*?" she spat, pressing herself against the wall. "The Divested are taking back their home, and you—you just went along with everything Dad said. You didn't care!"

"Isabel," I whispered. My face was wet with tears. "That's not what I meant."

She just glared at me. Her body was flickering in and out of visibility. "Get out," she said, and then she said something in her language, hissing and deep. It shot straight through me.

"Isabel, I didn't *know*," I said.

"You do now. And you still didn't stop it."

And then she winked out of my sight. The big, hollow room wavered around me. I could see the forest in the distance, hear the muffled *boom* of artillery fire. But I couldn't move. I could only stand there, weeping.

Isabel was gone.

I trembled, my bones vibrating inside my body. The Radiance's empty room dissolved away from me, and I was standing in the woods. Acrid air and hot wind slammed against me and made my eyes water.

"What the fuck happened? Where did you go?" Harriet lunged over to me, light rifle out. "You just vanished!" She stopped, frowning. "Are you crying?"

"I can't explain." I wiped my eyes. Isabel had chosen the Radiance. I had gone to her and I said the wrong thing and she had chosen the Radiance. "Get me to the beach."

"I thought you'd been fucking snatched out from under me." Harriet jerked her head to the side and started stomping through the forest. I followed. My muscles moved on some separate impulse of their own, distinct from my mind. Star's End was burning. I could see the light through the trees. I could hear the gunfire, the shouts of soldiers.

"This way!" Harriet shouted up ahead. I stumbled forward, weaving through the trees. Sometimes, Harriet stopped me and went a few paces ahead, then gestured for me to follow. Sweat beaded over my skin. The air was thick with smoke and I wondered if this was the end of our world, if Dad's cruelty had finally undone something larger than himself.

We were clear of the woods now. The yellow light had faded into a burnished orange as it blended with the light from Coromina I. I didn't know what that meant, what that signified. *Isabel,* I thought, and I knew I should go back for her. I should beg her for forgiveness.

But then I heard the sound of the ocean, rushing in and rushing out. "Almost there," Harriet said, glancing back at me. She reached out with one hand and grabbed me and pulled me forward over the sand. Instead of smoke, I smelled the briny fish scent of the sea. The ship was down the shore from us, lights blinking. Harriet shouted, waved her hands above her head. A figure bounded toward us. Another soldier, his light rifle bouncing. For a moment, I could only stare at him, numb with fear, with guilt, with horror at myself.

Then an explosion ripped across the sky, dry hot toxic heat blistering through the woods. Harriet's hand slipped out of mine and then I was flying, hair streaming around me. I landed hard in the thick tangle of grass. All I could hear was the ringing of bells. I lay on my back, panic choking around me. Beyond the forest, Star's End burned.

But the sky—the sky was normal again. I caught twinkles of stars.

"Isabel," I whispered.

"What the fuck was that?" Harriet materialized beside me. She was shouting but her voice was still muffled. "Is this OCI after all?" She peered up at the sky, frowning.

"Ms. Coromina!" It was the soldier. He peeled himself off the sound. "Get in the ship now!"

I sat up. The movement was too much at once and the pain erupted in my side and my head swum. I cried out and tilted forward. Someone caught me. Daphne. Where had she come from? I realized the soldier must have been shouting at her, not me. But it didn't matter. I was grateful for her. At least I didn't deserve her hatred.

She knelt at my side, sand streaking the side of her dress. The makeup around her eyes was blurred.

"We don't have time," the soldier said. "The ship's about to leave."

Daphne nodded. She scooped her arm around my shoulder and helped me, staggering under my weight. Harriet rushed over to my side, threw her arm around my waist. Together, the two of them dragged me over the sand. Off to our right, embers flared up from the fire at Star's End. I turned my head and watched the burning with a dull fury waiting inside my chest. I didn't even cry. There was no point, and crying didn't reflect how I felt in that moment, anyway. The fire did. The fire, raging and devouring and furious.

"Isabel," Daphne whispered in a low voice. "They couldn't find Isabel. I think they're going to leave without her."

"She's gone," I said.

Daphne blinked at me. Tears shimmered on her eyes, catching in the firelight. The ocean rolled in as if nothing had changed.

"Not dead," I said. "Just—gone." Was this true? I didn't know. I only wanted it to be.

Daphne frowned. "What do you mean?"

"She knew," I whispered. "She knew this was going to happen."

Daphne shook her head. "No, that's not possible." The tears dripped over her cheeks. Something was wrong with me, that I wasn't crying too, that I only felt fire. "How could she—" Daphne turned away.

"Don't think on it," Harriet said, her voice hard. "Not right now."

We had made it to the ship, small and sleek and CG-built, glowing with the faint outline of the light-shields. Its engine was so quiet that I could still hear the ocean.

Dad's face appeared in the entrance. When he saw me, he jumped out to the sand. I felt Harriet stiffen beside me.

"Sir," the soldier said, "you need to get back on the ship."

"Where is she?" Dad strolled toward me. I felt like he would walk right through me. "She chose them, didn't she?"

"Leave her alone, Philip," Harriet said. Dad glared at her.

"Who can blame her?" I shot back.

The soldier coughed. "It is imperative that you all get on the ship—"

He stopped. His jaw dropped and his gaze shifted, beyond us. Daphne glanced over her shoulder. Then she screamed and leapt away from me, kicking up a spray of sand. Harriet whirled around, leaving me wobbling on my own, her gun up, ready to fire.

Dad's face was as hard as stone.

"Move," Harriet whispered. "Now."

No one did. I knew what they seeing, what they were staring at with such horror.

Slowly, I turned around.

The alien.

I didn't know if it was the same one that I had seen that night I became a Ninety-Nine. Maybe. Maybe not. Maybe it didn't matter.

But this one, I saw all the way through. Not in snatches through the shadows.

It stood on two legs.

It was taller than any of us on the beach.

Its claws gleamed in the firelight.

And it was staring at Dad.

"Move!" Harriet shouted, and she grabbed me and Daphne by the arm and dragged us toward the escape ship stirring up sand. I let her do it. I was limp with grief; all I wanted was a mother to take care of me.

Not that the alien was attacking. I looked over my shoulder as we approached the whine of the escape ship. It stared at Dad, and Dad stared back at it. He didn't shake; he didn't tremble.

"Philip, you stupid piece of shit!" Harriet shouted, and the soldier who had run out to greet us grabbed Dad and yanked him back.

The alien vanished.

Dad screamed and blood pooled across the sand, oil-slick and almost black in the shadows.

Harriet and the soldier opened fire, streaks of lights lighting up the beach. The image of the alien flickered. Someone yanked me into the escape ship—Adrienne, it was Adrienne, her face pale, her expression unreadable. Daphne threw up in the corner.

And then Dad was shoved in after me. Harriet leapt aboard, screaming, "Go, go, go!" The other soldier was still firing his gun. Blood splattered across the opening of the ship, sprinkling across Dad and Harriet and dropping three spots on my dress, one after another, like a memorial.

The escape ship lifted up off the sand without the soldier.

I heard his screams as we were carried away to safety.

We went to the space station. Where else would the Coromina family go in a time of horror?

My sisters and Harriet and I were corralled into a common area and told, by a soldier in an Alvatech uniform, that we were to stay there, that Harriet's assignment was to guard us—I knew this really meant she was to keep us tucked away. I drew myself up and demanded to see my father. "I'm ranked Ninety-Nine," I told the soldier, who remained stone-faced. "I have a right to know what's going on."

"Your father fears you're emotionally unstable right now," the soldier said calmly. "He thinks it would be better if you stayed here."

"What's happening?" shouted Daphne, who stalked over to us, her eyes rimmed in red. She had wept the entire trip here. "Where's my sister? Where's Isabel?"

The soldier looked at her but said nothing, only turned and stalked out of the room. Daphne lunged after him, and Harriet caught her, gently, by the arm, and pulled her back. "It's not worth it," she murmured.

"Get off me!" Daphne wrenched her arm away from Harriet. "Don't tell me what to do." Daphne turned to me. "What's happening? How could we leave Isabel behind? You said she wasn't dead!"

"She's not." I hoped this was true. I hoped the Radiance really were a second family to her, that they had gathered her up and taken her into that strange echoing realm of theirs. But the truth was I didn't know, and my chest felt hollow.

"Then where is she?" Daphne shouted. She flung herself away from me and stalked across the room to where Adrienne sat, curled up tight like a snail. She hadn't said a word on the trip there, only stared out the window as we blasted through the atmosphere, her face pale in the light of burning oxygen. She still hadn't spoken, in fact, but now she turned to me, her eyes hard and bitter. She did not look like herself.

"You know more than you're telling us," she said in a voice so quiet it frightened me.

I looked at them, Daphne and Adrienne, staring at me from across the room. There was so much space between us. Harriet stood near the door, fulfilling her assignment, keeping us away from Dad and whatever decisions he was making in my absence.

"Yes," I said.

I expected Daphne to start shouting again, but she only slumped down on the faded sofa beside her sister. The walls of the space station thrummed. I glanced over at Harriet, and she nodded at me, just once. It wasn't her place to give permission, but she did it anyway. I needed that from her right now.

"Tell us," said Adrienne, still speaking in that quiet, dangerous voice, "what you know."

I was suddenly exhausted. All the adrenaline had fled my system. I collapsed in a chair across from the sofa and dug the heels of my hands into my eye sockets. "Isabel," I said, my throat dry. "Isabel— there's something about her—she's different."

I looked up at them. The room seemed to constrict upon us, and for a moment, I was aware of the precariousness of the space station, the way one punch through the wall would kill all of us.

"She isn't completely human," I said.

And with that, everything else flooded out. I told them all of it: I told them about the Radiance; I told them about the flu and the way it shaped Isabel in their mother's womb. I told them about the surgery, and I admitted to them, tears trembling in my lashes, that I hadn't been able to stop it.

Daphne leapt to her feet, her face red, her hands curled into fists. "I don't fucking believe this!" she shouted. She grabbed a statue from the end table and flung it across the room. It bounced off the wall and shattered when it hit the floor. Harriet didn't try to stop her; I suspected she understood her anger. "Why didn't you fucking tell us this earlier!"

"I couldn't." My voice came out too small. "It was Level Ninety-Nine information." I regretted saying this as soon as the words were out.

"Are you kidding me?" Daphne whirled around, her eyes blazing with fury. "We're fucking *family*. We had a right to know what the company was doing to her!"

"I'm sorry." It didn't feel like enough. Daphne scowled at me and then sank back down on the sofa, her hands covering her face.

Through all of this, Adrienne had watched quietly, her hands folded in her lap. But now she turned to me, and I saw in her expression a glitter of betrayal, of something like hatred. My stomach felt as if it were filled with lead.

"That surgery happened months ago," she said, her eyes fixed on mine. I couldn't move. "How can you still be working for the company?"

Her question took my breath away. Defection was an option I had never even considered. How could I? The company had been promised to me since my birth. My entire life I had been shaped to take it over.

"I would have left," she said, her eyes burning. "It's not like we don't have the money or the connections. You could have disappeared. You could have taken us with you. You could have taken *Isabel* with you."

I shook my head. I was cold all over. "It wasn't—I wanted to change things from the inside. I was trying to *help* her, Adrienne, you have to—"

"You didn't give a shit about Isabel," she said.

I trembled. A weight pressed into my shoulder—it was Harriet, who had left her post at the door, who was trying to comfort me.

"Don't speak to her like that," Harriet said.

"You stay out of this," snapped Adrienne. "You aren't part of this family."

"Yes, she is," I said. "She's my mother."

Adrienne rolled her eyes. "Yes, and you could talk to her anytime you wanted, couldn't you? Send her your little holos? All we had was a plot of flowers in a cemetery. That was all *Isabel* had. That's the real reason you didn't take Isabel away, wasn't it?" She stood up. Her face was incandescent with fury. And I knew, in that moment, her fury was really for our father, for his company. But she couldn't abuse him like she could abuse me. He wasn't there.

Harriet stayed her ground, her hand still on my shoulder, but it wasn't enough.

"You had your family!" Adrienne screamed. "You had a mother and so why should you care about us?"

"Is that true?" Daphne said, looking at me. "Is that why you didn't take us away?"

I was crying, tears streaming down my cheeks. I couldn't even look at Harriet. I didn't know why I hadn't taken them away. It had never occurred to me as an option. I had been so focused on changing the company from the inside that I hadn't thought I could just leave it all behind.

Because I didn't *want* to leave it behind. That was the truth.

"You're my sisters," I said, tasting the salt of tears on my tongue. "I love you."

"But you didn't protect her," Daphne said.

"I didn't know!"

"You found out!" Adrienne screamed. "You found out and you still didn't protect her!"

My tears fell harder. The room blurred. I had no answer for the twins, and so I stood up, shaking, and collapsed into my mother's arms. Maybe it was the wrong thing to do, going to my mother when their mother was dead, but she was the only ally I had in that moment.

She wrapped her arms around me, squeezing me tight.

And I could feel my sisters' rage like a fire.

A few hours later, someone knocked on the door. I was curled up in the corner, away from Adrienne and Daphne, who had fallen asleep on the sofa. The room was thick with anger. No one had spoken much, because what was there to say?

Harriet answered the door and conferred with whoever was on the other side in a low voice. I sat up, watched her, wondering what was going on. I was vaguely aware of one of the twins stirring, but I didn't look over at them.

Harriet nodded and turned to us. "Your father has called a meeting," she said. "All of us have to attend."

"No," said Adrienne. I glanced over at her in spite of myself. She was shaking Daphne awake. "No, we're not going."

Harriet stepped aside and an Andromeda Corps soldier stepped inside. His light rifle glowed with its charge. Adrienne's eyes widened.

"You don't have a choice," he said.

I stood up, my limbs shaky. Maybe this would help them understand that things weren't so easy. That I couldn't just pack them all up and fly to some other system.

"No," Adrienne said again.

The Andromeda Corps soldier lunged forward, shoving past me. He yanked Adrienne up by her arm. She let out a yelp of surprise and then strained against him. Daphne, still bleary-eyed, shouted protests.

"Let her go," I said, nausea rising in my throat. "This really isn't necessary."

"Sorry, ma'am." The soldier glanced at me as he dragged Adrienne off the bed. "All of you need to be in the meeting."

He wrenched Adrienne to her feet. Daphne stood up on her own, sullen. "Are you going to come without trouble?" he said.

Neither of my sisters answered. But when he pulled on Adrienne's arm, she shuffled forward, and Daphne followed. I let them go ahead because I wanted to keep my eye on them. Not that they cared. Adrienne glared at me as she passed.

"This meeting isn't going to be anything good," Harriet said in a low voice.

I knew she was right.

We followed the soldier out into the narrow corridor. The lights were midmorning bright, the same as they would be down at Star's End. *Star's End.* It was probably gone now, destroyed in the fighting. And all those people—

I hoped Isabel was safe.

We arrived at a room at the end of the hallway. The windows were darkened and thrumming with security shields; when we stepped into the room, the shield prickled over my skin. Dad was already there, along with Flor and Gabriella and all the rest of the Ninety-Nines. They'd all gotten out of Star's End safely. Maybe the destruction wasn't as bad as I feared.

No, I knew better. They got out of Star's End because they were top priority. In all likelihood, they'd been escorted by the R-Troops.

"I'm glad you're finally letting me join you," I said to Dad.

The door slammed behind me. Adrienne and Daphne cowered together, their hands linked. Of course they didn't lash out at Dad. They would only do that to me.

"I wanted to give you time to clear your head," Dad said. "But we also need to move fast on this. Most of the plans have already been set into motion. I just need to brief you." His eyes flicked away from me, over to Harriet, to the twins. "All of you."

"What's going on?" Daphne said, jutting out her chin. "Where's Isabel?"

"Isabel is gone," Dad said flatly. "According to the R-Troops, she's still alive, but they don't have a handle on her exact location."

Adrienne made a choking noise, covered her mouth with her hand.

"I told them everything," I said, staring at Dad.

He gave me a thin smile. "Well, that just saves us a step, doesn't it? Please, sit down."

I stumbled forward. My thoughts felt thin and wispy, like dry-season clouds. Isabel was alive. That was the one thing I could hold on to. Isabel was still alive.

I sank down in my chair. Harriet sat beside me. The twins didn't move. Dad didn't protest.

"Star's End is lost," Dad said, leaning forward over the table. I slumped back in my seat. *Isabel is alive.* It repeated in my head like a refrain. *Isabel is alive.* "The Radiance." Here Dad glanced at the twins. "Did Esme explain that much to you?"

Adrienne fixed him with an icy gaze. "Esme told us everything that you did." Her words dripped poison. Dad just smiled.

"Good," he said, unfazed. I hated him in that moment. "The Radiance destroyed the estate, but with the help of the R-Troops and—" He stopped and looked at me. His face was unreadable. "—and Isabel, they have been permanently sealed in their dimension."

One of the Ninety-Nines snorted. "Let's hope it's more permanent than the last time you said that."

Dad looked at him coolly. "We went over this. It's permanent. We had a weapon we didn't have last time."

I felt dizzy. Who was the weapon? The R-Troops? Isabel?

"Are you sure you don't know where Isabel is?" I demanded.

"Trust me," Flor said, turning to me, smiling cruelly, "if we knew where she was, we'd have her up here with us."

"You better not be lying to me," I snarled.

"Esme, stop." Dad's voice sliced through the room. "Isabel is gone. As a Ninety-Nine, you have the right to know, and I'm telling you: We don't know where she is. She aided the R-Troops in sealing off the Radiance's dimension. She was able to make it back into our world and then she vanished. We lost six R-Troop soldiers tonight, but we didn't lose her."

"You can't expect me to believe that," I said. "People don't just vanish in the Four Sisters."

Dad looked down at his hands. "They can when the world slips into chaos. Which it did last night."

He lifted his gaze. I glanced over at Daphne and Adrienne. They had both sunk down to the floor, still holding hands. Daphne's face was wet with tears.

"Because we were able to secure the Radiance," Dad continued, and that was how I knew the discussion about Isabel was over, "we are not going to evacuate Ekkeko."

"What?" Harriet leaned forward. "Don't be an idiot, Phillip. Again."

Dad glared at her. "This is not your decision to make, Sergeant Oxbow." He paused, gathering himself up. "Evacuation is costly. It's dangerous. We are still in the middle of a war with OCI, and we have been working overtime to ensure they don't find out the truth about the destruction. We have begun seeding out reports that the attack was the result of anti-corpocracy rebels, which will, if anything, engender some sympathy for us from OCI, at least from their populace. It might serve useful for us in the long term."

He smiled. I wrapped my arms around my chest. It made sense, actually. Secure the Radiance. Hide the truth so there wouldn't be panic or riots. Let people keep living their lives while we worked to protect them.

This was exactly what I had wanted.

"You can't do this," Adrienne said, standing up, her face flushed with anger. "You can't lie to the people—"

"We lie to the people all the time," Dad said. "You and your sisters lap those lies up every time you turn on one of your precious Amanan dramas."

Adrienne recoiled, just for a second. The fury twisted her face again. "You won't get away with this. People will find out—"

"People don't want to know," Dad said. "People want to feel that they are safe." His face hardened, and he switched on his lightbox and set the projector to glow above the table. I sank back in my chair. I didn't know what he was doing. I was sure it couldn't be anything good.

A holorecording began to play. A man wearing prisoner's clothes, sitting in the cell of an exile ship.

"What is this?" Adrienne demanded. "Are you saying you would exile us if we try to tell the truth?"

"No," Dad said.

A woman stepped into the recording. She wore a gray Coromina suit and carried a slim briefcase, and I knew, suddenly and with a sick lurching in my belly, what Dad was showing us. What he was threatening my sisters with.

The woman strode forward. The prisoner sat up. Said something we couldn't hear. Sound was unimportant. The woman set down her briefcase, opened it, pulled out a long, thin hypodermic needle. The man stopped talking. Stared at her. Through the flicker of the holo, I could see my sisters' faces growing paler and paler. I could hardly breathe.

The woman, in one quick graceful motion, slid the needle into the man's throat. He didn't even have time to fight back. He just slumped down on the bed and lay there, unmoving, as the woman gathered her briefcase and left.

Dad let the holo play for a few moments longer. Daphne covered her mouth with her hand. Adrienne's features had gone slack with fear.

"You are my daughters," Dad said, switching off the holo. "But if you break the silence of this meeting, I will have you killed."

The word *kill* hung on the air, sharp and glittering.

"You're all monsters," said Adrienne. "All of you." She looked at me. I looked away. Under the table, Harriet grabbed my hand and squeezed, but it wasn't enough.

"Sometimes, you have to be," said Dad. "Better you learn that now." He stood up. "Our official story is that the rebels attacked

Star's End with a bioweapon. That gives us an excuse to seal off the area completely, which the surviving R-Troops are doing as we speak. They're also evacuating the village, just to reduce the likelihood of anyone snooping around. However, Coromina headquarters will stay in place, as will the company enclave. I'm having a house prepared for us right now. We should be able to return planetside in a few hours."

"You can't do this!" Adrienne said. "You can't just pretend like nothing has happened." She looked over at me. "Esme, you can fight this! You're a Ninety-Nine! You can tell people the truth!"

For a moment, I was stunned: had she forgiven me? But I also knew I couldn't help her. I knew I would fly down to the planet and I would keep up Dad's lies, because if the truth came out, Ekkeko would be consumed with fear. We'd be weakened enough that OCI would destroy us, assuming we didn't destroy ourselves in the panic first.

And if we lied, if we set everything back to normal, I would be able to engender change in the company. The only way to do it was from within. I wished Adrienne could understand that.

And maybe I'd be able to find Isabel, too.

"Adrienne," I whispered. "I'm sorry." I felt the burn of tears. I'd cried too much tonight.

"See!" she screamed. "See! You never really cared about us! You never really cared about Isabel!"

The Ninety-Nines shifted in their seats, looked to Dad for guidance. He just pressed a button on the table, and the door flew open, and a pair of station medics rushed in. Daphne jumped in front of her sister, shouting, fighting them off as best she could. I leapt to her feet.

"I won't let you kill her," I said.

"I'm not killing her," Dad said. "Calm down, Esme."

The medics slid a needle into Daphne's arm, then Adrienne's. They immediately calmed, and the medics guided them down to sitting. They weren't dead, just dulled. They looked out at the room with glassy eyes. Daphne laid her head on Adrienne's shoulder.

"It'll wear off in a few hours," Dad said. "We'll need to keep them under close observation, at least until they understand why we're doing what we're doing."

I trembled. I wondered if I should protest. If I should scream like my sisters had, and fight, and demand the change they wanted. But it wasn't the change I wanted, was it?

My change was smaller, safer, more likely to succeed. My sisters might hate me for the rest of my life, but at least I could shape the company the way Dad had shaped me. I could make it in my image.

I slid back into my chair. Everyone was staring at me. I hoped Harriet understood what I was doing.

"I think this sounds like an excellent plan," I said.

NOW

When Esme stepped off the shuttle after her trip to Amana, her thoughts were fuzzy, from space travel and from the conversation with Adrienne, and she knew she couldn't handle the board right now, or anyone at the company. She had contacted Will when she landed, and he agreed to meet her at his house in the village, claiming he could sneak away from the office early. He didn't live in the enclave, and Esme had never asked him why. She was afraid the answer would be that he wasn't allowed.

The house was in a shabby little neighborhood surrounded by trees. Esme didn't know if it was the same neighborhood where Laila had lived all those years before, but it was how she had always imagined Laila's home. The houses were painted in bright colors to match the flowers blooming in the yards. Will's house was a bright, lemony yellow, like the sun.

For once, Esme was grateful Will lived there and not in the enclave. No one in these houses would know about her decision yet. They were pearl divers, retail workers. Even the rumors wouldn't have reached them. When they looked at her through the curtains of their windows, they wouldn't see past her suit. And that, she was used to.

Esme rapped on Will's door and then crossed her arms over her chest. A breeze blew in from the direction of the sea. The door opened.

"Hey." Will smiled at her. "Glad to hear the trip went well."

Esme nodded and slipped inside. Light paintings blinked on the walls, out of sync with one another. She stretched on his shabby sofa and slipped off her shoes, dropping them on the floor.

"I'm exhausted," she said. "I can't believe both of them agreed to come back."

Will sat down on the floor beside her, one arm draped over the cushion beside her head. "It's because you went to them," he said. "They don't hate you as much as you think."

Esme snorted. They did, and she understood why. But she didn't say anything.

For a moment, the two of them sat in silence. Esme listened to the wind rustling the hibiscus bushes outside the windows. Will cleared his throat, and she dropped her head to look at him. She expected him to say something about her sisters, or about her father, but instead he said, "I wanted to thank you, by the way."

"What?" She propped herself up on one arm and studied him. He picked at a loose thread on the sofa. This wasn't like him, not making eye contact, exposing his nervous tics.

"For shutting down weapons manufacture," he said.

"You heard about that." It wasn't a question. "I wanted to tell you myself, but I had to rush off to Amana—"

"It's fine." He looked up at her, his eyes clear. "I just—I wanted to thank you."

Esme's cheeks warmed. She smiled at him, felt that easy comfort she always did when they were together. "I'm giving the engineered soldiers full citizenship, too," she said. "I don't know if you heard that part."

He stared at her for a long moment, and she knew he hadn't. Her heart fluttered. Yes, Will had it easier than most of the soldiers, because he was one of the first batch of R-Troops, because during the rebuilding period, the company had decided he would serve them best as a liaison while they rolled out the next wave of

R-Troop soldiers. He had this house, he had his light paintings on the walls. But that didn't make him a true citizen.

"Thank you," he said, his voice rough.

"I'll have to fight the board about it," Esme said. She rolled onto her back and stared up at the ceiling; she was afraid if she looked at the brightness in Will's expression any longer, she would start crying. "So, it may be a while. But I'm changing this company from the inside, just like I always wanted." She spoke to the ceiling fan turning in its slow lazy circles. "No more exploitation. No more war." She sighed, twisting her hands together, and tried not to think about what Adrienne had told her, about corpocracy all being exploitation in the end. No. She didn't believe that. It was like when she was younger, when she worked for PM. It was the company's job to provide for the citizen-employees, not the other way around.

"You brought your sisters home," Will said. She felt a weight on her hand—it was Will, scooping it up in his own. She looked at him, smiled. "You can do this."

"I didn't bring all of them home."

Will didn't let go of her hand, and she didn't pull away. It wasn't supposed to be appropriate, a company CEO and an engineered soldier. A citizen-employee and a product. But the company didn't work that way anymore, did it?

"About that," Will said. "I have an idea."

Esme sat up, sharply enough that her head spun. Will dropped her hand; she could still feel the warmth of his touch. "An idea?" she said.

Will took a deep breath. He put his hands on her shoulders and looked her straight in the eye. "Yeah," he said. "But you'll need to promise me your silence."

Esme frowned. She felt a tightening in her stomach. "Will," she said slowly, "what are you involved in?"

He stared at her for a long time. His hands dropped away from her shoulders, like he was afraid he shouldn't be touching her anymore.

"Will?" Esme said.

"I know who's responsible for the security breaches," he said.

"I've known for a long time. But they're the ones who can help you find your sister."

They couldn't take a driver, and Will told Esme to change out of her suit—it would be uncomfortable, he said, and now Esme understood why. They had left Will's house and walked down to the place where the woods grew in thick and heavy. Esme was dressed in some of Will's old clothes, everything clinging to her in the wrong ways, baggy where it should be fitted, tight where it should be loose.

When she saw the woods, Esme stumbled back.

"You recognize them," Will said.

Of course she recognized them. For two thirds of her life, she had lived within walking distance of these woods. She had crept through them to get to the beach when she was a teenager; later, she had torn through them, terrified, when the Radiance broke their restraints and burned Star's End to the ground.

"I told you it may be hard for you," Will said in a soft voice.

Esme squared her shoulders. "It's fine," she said, her voice clearer than she expected. "I'll be fine."

They pushed through the underbrush. Will led the way, hacking at the vines with a clearing-blade, the electricity humming as he swiped it through the air. Already Esme was sweating, and tiny insects buzzed around her head. Had the woods been this dense when she was younger? Or had one of the staff gone out in the cool mornings to clear the underbrush so she and her sisters could pretend to be explorers in the wild?

Will and Esme worked their way through the woods. The path was unfamiliar, but Esme knew where they were going: the ruins of Star's End. Will had told her that much, when he explained why they had to go on foot. It buzzed around in her head: *Star's End.*

She took deep breaths, sucking in the hot, humid air. The clearing-blade sang. Branches rained down around them, the ends singed and still smoking from the blade. She wondered if they would pass the cemetery where the first Isabel was buried. If she would even recognize it, if the flowers they had planted on Isabel's grave would have grown until they were part of the jungle.

Will stopped and then held out one hand to stop her. Up ahead was just more forest, thick and impenetrable, but Esme knew Will could See things she couldn't. He could hear the voices of the others in his head, calling out to him.

Another deep breath. She didn't feel like the CEO of the Coromina Group in that moment. If the board found out about this, she would be exiled from the planet immediately. Well, if they found out about it without the right spin, she told herself. She could work this to her advantage. Make it part of the new direction of the company. Bring these outsiders into the fold instead of kicking them out into the black. She already knew a place for them in her version of the Coromina Group.

"They're ready for us." Will turned to Esme. Sweat beaded above his eyes. His hair was soaked with sweat. "Are you ready for them?"

For them, yes. For Star's End? She didn't know. But she nodded anyway.

"Stay behind me," Will said. "Keep your hands in the open."

Anxiety buzzed in Esme's brain. She did what he said, holding her hands up as if she were prisoner. Will led her forward, swinging the clearing-blade with an easy grace.

And then they were at the house.

Esme let out a strangled gasp and threw one hand over her mouth. *House* was the wrong word. It was the ghost of a house. She could see the framework, and part of the roof was still standing. But the rest of it had been reduced to a pile of charred rubble already half-overgrown with vines. The gardens were gone. The plumeria maze had been subsumed into the forest.

There was nothing of her childhood here.

Someone emerged from the rubble—a soldier, identical to Will. He raised one hand in greeting, let out a shout. Immediately, five more soldiers materialized out of the trees. They all had Will's face. All of them, Esme had last seen thirteen years ago, when she announced their existence to the world.

The six soldiers who had been lost in the attack. They hadn't died at all. They had simply settled here, in the palace her father had built to his own success.

She pressed herself against Will, her hands up in the air, and tried to control her trembling. Will shut off the clearing-blade and slipped it into his belt. He lifted his hands, too. "You know why we're here!" he called out.

"Still need to secure the perimeter," the first soldier said. The others crept around the woods, light rifles out. The first soldier, though, walked toward Esme and Will. His gun wasn't pointed at them, but Esme still couldn't take her eyes off it.

These were the six soldiers who had been inside the Radiance's dimension when the boundaries were sealed up, securing the breach to keep the people of Ekkeko and the rest of the Four Sisters safe. But they hadn't died, Will had told her, sitting on his sofa, keeping his voice soft and soothing as she listened to him with a growing sense of horror and excitement. They had forged an alliance with the Radiance—except he called them the Divested, the way Isabel had—and found a way out of the Radiance's dimension. Five years ago, during the first round of security breaches. It hadn't been the Radiance trying to take over at all, just aftereffects that the Coromina Group misread. This latest round of security breaches had been more of the same—nothing sinister, just these six original R-Troops staying in contact with the Radiance.

No wonder Sergeant Woods had told her to speak to the Radiance herself. She was starting to see that she and the company did not understand them at all.

The soldiers there weren't exactly rebels hoping to take the company down. But their loyalties lay with the Radiance. Just as Isabel's had.

And just as Will's did, he'd confessed, his head bowed down, not looking her in the eye. "I just wanted to keep them safe," he said. "I didn't want to let the company hurt them. But I wasn't going to let them hurt anyone on the worlds, either." He peered up at her. "I wouldn't let them hurt you."

Esme had looked away, her cheeks burning. All these years, he'd been playing his own game, trying to make his own changes from within the company, same as her. He fought for the Radiance, she for her citizen-employees. And the winner was still the upper eche-lons of the Coromina Group. It always had been.

But not anymore. For the first time, she saw something like the truth: if her Coromina Group wasn't going to exploit its people, then it couldn't exploit the Radiance anymore, either. They would have to become like Will. Protecting all their citizen-employees, and all the other denizens of the Four Sisters, too. The first soldier stopped a few feet away from Esme. He looked her up and down. His hair was long, pulled back in a ponytail, and a shadow of a beard had grown in. It was like looking at another version of Will.

"So, this is the new CEO," he said.

Will didn't say anything, at least not out loud. Esme took a deep breath and held out her hand. "I'm Esme," she said.

The soldier stared down at her hand. Esme didn't drop it, didn't let herself think she had made some kind of mistake.

Then he laughed. "Esme, I'm Aiden." He grabbed her hand and shook.

"Aiden," she said, trying to remember if that had been a name given to him by Flor and the rest of Radiance Project team, or if it was one he had chosen for himself. Then she realized it didn't matter.

"I hear you're setting us free," he said, taking a step back.

"Sector three clear!" one of the other soldiers shouted.

"I'm changing the focus of the company." Esme drew herself up. "No more weapons manufacture."

"So, you won't be making any more of us," Aiden said.

Esme shook her head. "No more human products."

Aiden tilted his head at her. A few strands of dark hair loosed themselves and stuck to his cheek. "We aren't human."

"Sector four clear!" called out another soldier.

"We're both," Will said. Esme glanced at him; his expression was hard, his eyes glinting, and she knew he'd told the truth, when he said he wanted to protect the citizen-employees of the Four Sisters, too.

Aiden grinned. "Fine. We're both."

"Sector one clear!"

"It seems Will was telling the truth," Aiden said, turning back to Esme. "You didn't bring any CG goons with you."

Esme shook her head.

"Good." He jerked his head back toward the rubble. "Let's talk. Will says you need a favor."

"Sector five clear!" And then, layered over it, the last "Sector two clear!" The other soldiers started moving toward them.

"We're not, of course, in the practice of giving favors to the CEO of the Coromina Group," Aiden said as he led her toward the ruins.

"We'll make an exchange." Esme kept her gaze fixed on the ruins. *It's not Star's End,* she told herself. Memories kept flashing through her head. Adrienne and Daphne as toddlers, chasing each other through the garden as Isabel, their mother, watched on, draped lazily in a chair. Sneaking through the woods so she could go to parties on the beach. Finding Isabel that day in the rain. Her whole life, burned up and left to the devices of the forest.

Aiden glanced at Will. "You told her, didn't you? That we can still speak with the Divested?" He didn't sound angry. More— amused, almost.

"I had to," Will said. "It's part of the exchange."

They were talking about the security breaches. Esme closed her eyes. All those interviews. That investigation she had called upon Eleanora Dixon. And she still hadn't come close to the source of the breach. It had been these lost soldiers living in the wreckage of her home. They had been opening the channels, communicating with the Radiance. Communicating, she knew, with their family.

Aiden led Esme and Will up to the wreckage of the house. The two of them walked on, but Esme had to stop. She gazed at the wall, unrecognizable up close. She tried to connect this burned, crumbling, vine-covered structure with the home she had known as a child.

"Are you coming, CEO?" Aiden called out. Esme jerked herself out of her reverie and stepped in among the rubble. Grass had grown up in the ruins, dragging them down into the dirt.

Aiden and Will stood beneath the half-roof, and when Esme stepped into the shadow with them, she realized, with a jolt, that she was standing in her father's library. The stones and vials of sand had disappeared, and the ground sparkled with the shards of broken memory glass squares. The glass in the windows was gone; the curtains lay in a moldy pile on the ground. Esme felt tears prickle at her the edges of her eyes, and for a half a second, she saw the library as it had been—always so dark, from the curtains, always full of shadows.

A hand pressed against the flat of her back. "We need to make the arrangement," Will said, his breath brushing across her ear. "We need to find Isabel."

Esme nodded, wiped at her eyes. Aiden just watched her. He was sitting in one of the old wooden chairs, his rifle leaned up against his knee. Esme breathed in deep. She walked toward him. Her tears were still there, right on the verge of falling, but she wouldn't let them.

She had to find Isabel.

"Please," Aiden said. "Have a seat." He gestured at another chair, metal and simple. Had this been somewhere in the house? It didn't seem familiar. Esme slid into it, keeping her back straight. She heard Will's footsteps as he came to stand behind her. The other soldiers waited outside the ruins—she could see one, his hair shorn to the scalp, standing out on the grass.

"Will told me the situation," Aiden said. "About your sister."

"Isabel," she whispered.

"Yeah, Isabel." Aiden squinted off at something in the corner. Esme didn't dare take her eyes off of him. "I remember her, you know. She talked to us that night. The night this happened." He gestured out at the house.

Esme's heart clenched up. "She talked to you?" She leaned forward, greedy for knowledge. "What did she say?"

"Nothing. Small talk." Aiden turned back to her. His eyes were dark and piercing. They weren't Will's eyes at all. "I'm going to be frank with you. I have no fucking idea where your sister is."

Disappointment swallowed Esme whole. And then it was replaced, quickly enough, with a vast flood of fear. She jerked around to look at Will, suddenly afraid she had misread him completely, that this whole thing was a set up to have her assassinated.

Aiden laughed. Will looked at her and said, "He's playing with you."

"What?" She looked back at Aiden. Curled her hands into fists. "What the hell are you saying?"

"Apparently, Will didn't tell you everything." Aiden leaned back in his seat. He was enjoying this, Esme realized. Enjoyed watching her squirm. "We don't know where your sister is, but the Divested do."

Esme's heart pounded so fast she could hear it echo inside her head. She stared at Aiden and gripped the armrests of her chair. "You're not going to ask them for me, are you?" She already knew the answer.

"Of course not. You want your sister, you can go in there and ask them yourself."

Esme whipped her head around at Will. "Did you know this?" she demanded. "You didn't warn me—"

"I said it would be hard for you." His voice so quiet, it was like the breeze.

"We'll take you over to their world," Aiden said. "We'll offer some measure of protection. Not that you'll probably need it—after what happened with your sister, they aren't keen on wiping humans off the planets anymore."

"What?" Esme whispered.

Aiden shrugged. "She refuses to live with them. If they try anything, it could kill her. Us, too. So, they won't try anything." He paused. "If we help you, though, you've got to do something for us. Will said this was an exchange."

Esme took a deep breath. *Isabel. Isabel. Isabel.* As long as she repeated her sister's name, she wasn't afraid. This wasn't about her father anymore, and she had never given a damn about ensuring her inheritance. Her sisters weren't going to take over the company. All she wanted was to see Isabel one more time. All she wanted was to apologize. "I can grant you amnesty," she said, watching Aiden as she spoke. "You aren't supposed to be living here. I could have you arrested. Deported."

Aiden said nothing.

"But if you help me, I'll give you amnesty, and the chance to make our world safe for humans and the Rad—the Divested."

Aiden's eyes narrowed. "What are you saying?"

Esme took a deep breath. She glanced at Will, who gave her an encouraging smile. "I want to work with the Divested. I want to find a way to share our world. But I need help communicating with them." She nodded at Aiden. "I'm willing to give you amnesty for your help, no strings attached. But I also want to create a position for you, to help broker an arrangement. You'll work alongside Will. You would be full citizen-employees, of course, with all the benefits that entails."

"You want us to be your soldiers again?" Aiden leaned back, crossing his arms over his chest.

Esme shook her head quickly. "No, not at all. I want you to be— to be diplomats. Liaisons."

Aiden studied her. Then he closed his eyes. Dropped his head back against the chair. The sounds of the forest echoed around them. Insects chirping, birds screaming. Esme felt utterly alone in the world.

Aiden's eyes snapped open. "The others agree to your terms," he said. "But if you show any sign of exploiting us or the Divested—"

"I won't," Esme interrupted. "I'm not my father. If they can change, so can the company."

"You'll never see us again." Aiden's eyes glinted. "Let's hope you're not your father. Come with me." He stood up. Esme did too, although her legs were shaking. She thought he'd lead her into the woods, but instead he led her deeper into the ruins of the house. She stared at the grimy, vine-covered walls and recognized vestiges of her childhood.

"You don't have to do this," Will said, suddenly appearing at her side. He put a hand on her arm.

"Yes, I do." Up ahead, Aiden pushed aside a rotting brocade curtain, a curtain she remembered because it had hung in the sitting room, always pushed open to let in the view of the garden. "You know that."

Will didn't answer.

Aiden turned toward her, holding the curtain open. "Here," he said. "This'll take you into their world."

Esme's heart thudded. "They live in the house now."

"No." Aiden's eyes narrowed. "They live in the dimension you and your people trapped them in. We opened the connection when we came back seven years ago. The boundaries have always been thin here." His mouth stretched into a grin. "Because of your sister."

Esme took a deep breath. She glanced over at Will, and he nodded once. She wondered what he saw, what he heard, in that connected head of his. If there was a danger he wasn't telling her about. Not to betray her, but because he knew she would fight him on it.

"They're waiting," Aiden said.

Esme walked up to the entrance. Past the curtain, everything was dark.

Isabel, she thought.

And then she stepped through.

It happened as instantaneously as it had thirteen years ago, when she had stepped through the boundary in the woods. She was not in the ruins of her childhood home anymore. She was in that space she remembered from the day Star's End burned. Shining stone floors, floating cubes of white light. An enormous, cavernous space. Another world.

It wasn't empty.

She felt them more than she saw them. They flickered in and out of the edge of her vision, shadows shuddering so that when she turned her head, they appeared to be nothing. But she could feel them regarding her. The back of her neck tingled.

"Hello?" she called out. Her voiced echoed timorously and rang out, just for a second, like a bell. But then a noise started, off to her side, a *shh shh shh* that reminded her of ocean waves. It rose up around her, a wall of sound. She was too petrified to move.

Up ahead, the air glimmered.

"Hello?" Esme whispered, and then she swallowed, hard, and raised her voice. "Hello? I'm here about my sister. About Isabel."

The glimmer in the air darkened, solidified. Esme knew what she would see in the seconds before it appeared.

The creature on the beach.

It unfurled itself before her, glossy black feathers cascading down its back. Its limbs were too long, its body too thin. It had a face that didn't look human enough, and its teeth were long, jagged knives. For one second, Esme fell backward through time, and she was standing on that escape ship, the engines pouring hot air, as the soldier fell beneath the Radiance's claws.

"Issssssssabel," the Radiance said, its mouth stretching wide to reveal its teeth.

"Yes." Esme's voice shook. Her knees buckled but she didn't fall. At least the Radiance did not come any closer. "Isabel. She's my sister, and she's missing. I want to find her."

"Ssssiiiisssssssster," the Radiance said, drawing the word out into a long hiss. It had not occurred to Esme until now that she might not even be able to communicate with them. But perhaps those R-Troop defectors had taught them Corominan.

Or perhaps Isabel had.

"I'm trying to find her," Esme said again, speaking slowly. To her side, those flickers in her vision grew stronger, and she caught glimpses of other aliens crowding together around her. She dug her nails into her palm to keep herself steady. "She went away. A long time ago. And I need to find her again."

The Radiance took a step toward Esme, and Esme did not let herself recoil. It bent down. Studying her? Its eyes looked like galaxies, empty space filled with a million tiny lights, and Esme didn't know what it saw when it looked at her.

"Why?" The word scraped in the Radiance's voice, harsh and unfamiliar.

Esme stuttered. "W—why do I need to find her? Or why did she leave?"

"Why ssssshe left."

"She was angry with me," Esme said. "Angry about what I had let happen to her, and what I had done—" She looked off to her left, to her right, at both groups of Radiance pressing together. Their faces loomed out of the darkness, their bodies half-invisible. "What I had done to you," she said.

The main Radiance, the queen Radiance, lifted one too-long arm. "Cooome," it said.

"What?" Esme trembled.

"Come," it said. "Let me Sssssseee you."

Esme thought of Isabel saying that, using *See* like it meant something else to her. Esme had decided, in the months after Isabel left, that it was her way of talking about the telepathy she shared with the R-Troops. With these creatures.

"Please," Esme said. "I don't want to hurt you."

"Hurt," the Radiance said, all in one voice. "We have hurt already."

"I know." Esme drew herself up. She pictured Isabel's face clearly in her mind. "And I'm sorry. I'm deeply, truly sorry. I didn't understand everything that was happening, but that was no excuse." She took a deep breath. "I want to make things right. Aiden told me how you've stopped trying to attack our world because of Isabel. I want to do the same for you. I have an arrangement with him and the others—we want to create a way for all of us to live together. For everyone to be safe."

"Aideeennn," the queen Radiance said softly. "Like Issssabel. Wouldn't stay heeeere. With ussssss."

Esme choked back a gasp. "Please," she said, her voice stuttering. "Please, I want to work with you. I want to make things better." She wondered if she could explain about her father, about inheritances, if these creatures would understand.

But then the queen Radiance said, "Come." Was that an urgency in its voice, an insistence? Or was Esme only imagining it?

"Do you think that's fair?" Esme asked. "For us to work together?"

"Perhapsssssss." The Radiance still held out its arm, its long hand turned palm up. The arm, the hand, were all covered in something like snake scales. "Now let us Seeeeee. To find Issssabel."

Esme was numb with fear, but for a moment, it blinked away. "You're going to help me find her?" she whispered.

The queen Radiance said nothing, only continued to hold out its hand.

Esme moved forward, her steps small and stumbling. The queen Radiance stared at her with its black eyes, the other Radiance watching her from the sidelines. When she was close enough, the queen Radiance whipped out her arm and pressed her hand against Esme's face. Esme cried out and jerked back, but something stopped her—it was the other Radiance, half-invisible, holding her in place. A surge of panic washed over her. She thrashed, trying to move away. *Will*, she screamed in her head, as if he could help her.

"Think of Issssabel," the queen Radiance said.

At the sound of her sister's name, even in that hissing, scratching voice, her panic slid away. And she did think of Isabel. Seeing Isabel as a baby for the very first time, and the promise she had made. Isabel in the hospital bed, staring at her through the holo. Isabel lurking in the hallways, sullen and quiet and Esme not knowing what had happened to her. Not understanding. And she wasn't afraid anymore because she was swollen with guilt, with sorrow. Eighteen years ago, she had looked down at her sister and promised to protect her. And she had failed.

Her face was wet when the queen Radiance slid her hand away.

"Sssssissster," the queen Radiance said.

Esme nodded, sucking in deep, choking breaths of air. The Radiance were still pressed in a crush around her, their slick skin cool through the layers of her damp clothes. "My sister," she said. "I just want to find her."

"Hurt," it said. "You hurt her."

"Yes." Tears streamed down Isabel's face. "I didn't do it on purpose, but I hurt her. Please. I just want to make it right."

"I Sssssaw." The queen Radiance stepped back, and the others parted from her, shimmering into invisibility. "You hurt usssssssss. Make that right?"

Bile rose in Esme's throat. "Yes," she choked out, worried that her whole plan was falling apart. They didn't understand her. She didn't understand them. "That was what I was saying. I'll work with Aiden and the others, and Isabel, if I can find her. We won't keep you trapped here." She tried to gesture at the room, wound up knocking against one of the other Radiance. They were so close.

"But we'll have to work together. Because you hurt my people, too. You killed us."

The queen Radiance said nothing. A few seconds later, a sound rose up through the crowd of Radiance.

Esme swooned. She swayed to the side, stumbling. One of the Radiance caught her and shoved her upright.

"Hurt ussss firsssssst," the queen Radiance said.

"I know." Esme wished she could sit down. The room felt too big and too small, both at the same time. "But we can stop hurting each other. Please."

The queen Radiance said nothing. Esme stared up at her, weeping. Her vision blurred. She could taste the tears on her lips.

"Please," Esme whispered.

"If you lie," the queen Radiance said, "we kill you."

"I'm not lying."

The queen Radiance lashed out with her arm again, pressing her hand to Esme's face. The scales felt like water that didn't leave a wetness behind. "I Seeee that," it said.

"Please," Esme said. "Please. Just tell me where my sister is."

And in one voice, the Radiance told her.

The shuttle landed on a frozen tarmac, icy wind slashing across the windows. Esme stared out at the unfamiliar landscape of Quilla. No trees, no vegetation. Just endless stretches of white. The only break in the whiteout was the lights of Watchet, the largest city on the planet. They glimmered in the distance, looking like candles through the snow.

"Your driver is waiting for you, Ms. Coromina." The steward smiled at her from above his jaunty blue scarf. He'd put it on as they descended into the atmosphere. The terraforming on Quilla had been damaged mid-process, presumably by the Radiance. But the planet's climates existed only in the extreme. Unbearable heat at the equator; frozen wastelands at the poles. The cities here were all self-contained, like old moon colonies in the days before terraforming.

Esme stood up and stretched. The steward held out a thick, full-length coat and a scarf of the same cut and color as his—a part of the Coromina Group uniforms, a new piece updated from the days when Esme traveled the Four Sisters for Planet Maintenance.

"Thank you." She infused her voice with chilled professionalism. Anxiety gnawed at her insides, but she wasn't going to let anyone, not the steward, not the driver waiting for her in the cold, and certainly not Isabel, know about it.

The steward nodded politely and helped her into the coat. It was bulky and uncomfortable and Esme wasn't used to wearing layers. She twisted the scarf around her throat.

"Gloves are in the pockets," the steward said. "You're certainly going to want them."

Esme slipped them on. The voice of the Radiance kept bouncing around her head. *The top of the smallest world*, they had told her. And a string of numbers that Will had recognized as coordinates. Not the sort used by the Coromina Group. He had fought with Aiden until Aiden translated them: an apartment building in Watchet called the Lacheta. It had not taken much for Esme to pull a list of residents, to find the name *Christina Sulka*. She had been a minor character on *The Intensity of Days* nearly ten years ago. And Esme knew: there was Isabel.

"Are you ready?" The steward picked up her suitcase—a small one, as she didn't plan on staying there long. He grinned at her. "Brace yourself."

Esme didn't respond, but when the steward pulled the door open, she realized that his warnings weren't a joke. The wind was as sharp as a knife, slicing across her features, cutting her face to shreds. Her eyes watered. She turned away and pulled the scarf up over her mouth and nose.

"Driver's just down there." The steward pointed. The air glinted with dried snow, but Esme was able to make out the dark shadow of a car waiting for her. "Follow me. Keep your head down."

Esme did as he said. The wind howled and shrieked, sounding like a woman's screams. The steward scurried over the tarmac. Esme couldn't walk as quickly. The ice was too slick, and she had to hold out her hands to her side and concentrate with each step.

"May I help you?" The voice next to her ear was soft and female and unfamiliar. "It's difficult if you're not used to it." She took Esme's hand, and Esme glanced up, caught a glimpse of glowing blue eyes. The driver.

"Thank you," Esme said.

The driver smiled. The steward was already at the car, loading the suitcase in the back. Esme and the driver walked in tandem across the tarmac. Esme felt as if she were learning how to dance. Her steps were so clumsy.

The driver helped her into the car, which was, mercifully, filled with heat, a dry manufactured heat that was nothing like the sun-heat Esme knew. The door closed and Esme pulled her scarf away. She shivered violently, her skin burning. The wind was muffled but she could still hear it howling and shrieking.

This was the place Isabel came, of all the places in the universe. In a way, it made sense. It was one of their father's few failures, this unlivable planet.

The driver climbed in, bringing with her a blast of cold air. Esme shivered. The door shut but the cold air lingered, fighting with the heat. The driver hooked into the car without saying a word. Esme had scheduled her itinerary on the shuttle. They were to go straight to the Lacheta.

The driver glanced up in the rear-view mirror. Her eyes glinted. "Are you certain about this?" she said.

Esme frowned. "Certain about what?"

"The Lacheta. It's not—well, it's not a good part of town—"

"It's not your job to ask questions." Esme didn't mean to sound so sharp, but sharpness was easier than kindness right now.

"Just trying to warn you." The driver seemed nonchalant about the whole experience. "Don't want you getting into something you can't handle."

"I can handle it," Esme said. She had negotiated with the Radiance. She could speak with her sister.

The car lurched forward through the snow. The engine had a faint humming whine to it, and a red glow wrapped around the car as it glided forward. A heat wave. Melting the snow until they came to Watchet.

Esme leaned back in her seat. Melted snow splashed across the windows, smearing her view. That was fine. Nothing to look at, anyway.

It took longer than she would have expected to get to the city—the car couldn't go as fast as it could in warmer climates. The drive gave her time to think, to practice what she was going to say. *I spoke with the Radiance.* She shook her head. The Divested. She needed to call them the Divested, to think of them as the Divested. *I spoke with the Divested. We are going to find a way to live together in peace. No more weapons manufacture. No more exploitation. You can help.*

Come home, Isabel.

Esme didn't know if it would be enough. It had barely been enough for Adrienne and Daphne, and they had been human. Their DNA had never been used against them. But it was all Esme had to offer. Their father was dying, and she was CEO. She could shape a new future.

The city's lights grew brighter. Outlines of buildings appeared in the snowy haze, all of them that twisting organic shape of terra-formed architecture. They were like extensions of the ice, jutting out at odd angles, sparkling from the surrounding lights. It didn't look like a human city. But of course it was. That war had been won twice over. Everything on the Four Sisters was a human city.

Did Esme want to change that? She thought maybe she did, if it meant she could bring her sister back.

Soon, they came to the boundaries of the city. One minute they were out in the wilderness, and the next the car flooded with light as they passed through the shields keeping the cold at bay. Ice and snow vanished from the landscape, and the car picked up speed, winging through the narrow streets. Esme dropped her head back against the seat. There was no point in looking out the windows anymore. Everything blurred together.

She closed her eyes.

She thought about what she was going to say.

She thought about the Divested pressing around her. About the queen, the leader, laying her hand on Esme's face and Seeing something inside her mind.

She thought about Isabel.

The car slowed to a stop.

Esme's eyes fluttered open. She straightened up. The driver looked over at her, the glow in her eyes dimming.

"We're here," she said. "I'll wait if you want me to, but I'd appreciate it if you didn't. This is a bad area for a Coromina car."

Esme looked past the driver, through the window. All she could see was an apartment building streaked with dark smears, like soot or ash.

"I don't know how long it'll take," she said. "I'll send a holo when I'm done."

The driver smiled. Her eyes faded to their former dull blue. "Headquarters set you up at the Grand Watchet Hotel," she said. "It's a lot nicer than anything you can find around here."

"I'm sure it is. I'll leave my bags in the trunk."

The driver's smile flickered. "I expected you would."

Esme took a deep breath and stepped out of the car. The city slammed into her: a smell like mold, a buzzing from the shields, a blast of freezing air. Esme pulled her coat tighter around her shoulders and rearranged her scarf so she didn't have to breathe that rotten air. The apartments rose up around her. They were shoved up close to another, so close you could stretch out a hand from the window of one building and touch the windowsill of another.

The car sped off, its electric whine echoing through the buildings. The street was hardly wide enough to accommodate it. Esme turned to watch its bright blur disappear around the corner. Then she turned back to the apartment.

WELCOME TO THE LACHETA, read the sign hanging above the door. The letters flickered and popped. Esme went up to the entrance. The door didn't close all the way. She nudged it open with her foot. Apartment number 4903, that was where the resident list said Christina Sulka lived.

The foyer was as small and cramped as the road outside. A few squares of dirty tile, a wall with a flickering holo flashing weather reports, a narrow elevator. That was it.

Esme pressed the call button for the elevator, grateful she was wearing gloves. The elevator creaked open immediately. It smelled of must and damp and an odd salinity, like the sea. Esme stepped on. The floors went all the way up to 75. She pressed the 49 button.

The elevator groaned upward.

It took a long time. This was not like the elevators at the office, sleek and modern and designed to take people where they needed to go as quickly as possible. Esme stood in the center of the elevator, her arms wrapped tight around her chest, watching the numbers go up. She didn't know what she would do if someone climbed on the elevator with her. The CEO announcement still hadn't gone public. But if there was anti-corpocracy sentiment—and of course there was, there always was where the poor lived—they might already know.

As it turned out, it didn't matter. The elevator reached the forty-ninth floor and expelled Esme without her seeing another soul. But the floor itself showed signs of life—voices filtered through the walls, shouting, laughing. Music. Footsteps. Esme drew herself into her coat and marched down the center of the hallway until she came to 4903. She knocked.

No answer.

Esme closed her eyes. The sounds of the apartment swam around her like they were trying to draw her in. She had a key, of course. She'd gotten it from PM. Secretly, shamefully, without telling Will. She was CEO, and she could get keys to cheap apartments.

A few doors down, there was the sound of breaking glass and then a chorus of screams. Esme fumbled in her pocket, yanked out the key, and swiped it across Isabel's lock.

The door popped open.

Esme let out a long breath. She knew she shouldn't go in. All her careful planning would be for nothing if she violated Isabel's privacy. But the screams continued, and the driver wasn't waiting, and Esme was a coward.

She went in.

The lights were switched off. Esme closed the door behind her and made sure it was locked. "Lights," she said, but nothing happened, so she slid her hand over the wall until her fingers hit a switch. A single bare bulb flicked on.

The apartment was a room, with a bed in one corner and a sink and a toilet and a hotplate in the other. It wasn't very warm, either, but Esme slid off her coat and scarf and draped them across the bed. She looked around the room. There was nothing of the Isabel she remembered in it, and she wondered if her suspicions were wrong, if Christina Sulka wasn't Isabel after all. The walls were bare, and clothes lay in piles around the floor. There was a single window above the sink that looked into a window across the way. Something hung next to the glass, glittering a little, and when Esme moved closer to examine it, she saw it was a teardrop crystal exactly like the crystals hanging from *The Intensity of Days* chandelier in Adrienne's dining room.

This was Isabel's apartment after all.

Esme sat down on the bed. She felt numb. Thirteen years ago, Isabel had lived in a private estate on the Coromina peninsula, with a pineapple garden and a beach and an entire suite of rooms to call her own. Now she lived in one room that was smaller than any one part of that suite.

Esme closed her eyes so that she wouldn't cry. This was her fault. Her father's fault, too. They had done this.

Something plinked against the window, startling Esme. But it was only snow. It left dirty streaks against the glass. Esme stood up. She shouldn't be there. But she wasn't going to leave. Not until she saw Isabel.

She began folding Isabel's clothes.

It was simple, mindless work; it distracted her from the waiting. Dishes were stacked in the sink as well, and Esme could wash those once she finished the clothes. It was a nice gesture: *I entered your apartment without permission to ask you to see a father you hate, but at least I folded the clothes.*

Yes, it was stupid. But Esme wasn't going to sit there, either.

She plucked each item of clothing off the floor and folded it over itself, her movement clumsy and unsure—Esme had never lived in a place where she had to fold her own clothes, because there had always been staff or the auto-cleaners on hand. But she had done more difficult things than fold clothes in her life.

She picked up a flimsy little dress, more like a slip, and something fell out.

Esme stopped. It was a cheap cloth bag, the sort of thing they sold in historical amusement parks. She knew she shouldn't look at it—clothes were one thing, mysterious bags were another. But she was overwhelmed with a wave of curiosity. All she wanted was insight into her who sister had become. Maybe it was selfishness; maybe she wanted to know that she hadn't fucked Isabel up too irrevocably. Or maybe she didn't want to know, so she could do her penance.

Esme leaned down and picked up the bag. It was heavy. For a moment, she just let it sit in her hand, a dead weight. She ought to tuck it back into the dress and leave the dress lying on the floor. But she didn't. She upended the bag and dumped its contents on her empty palm.

A glass vial, filled with a pale white liquid.

A self-heating metal slab.

A dropper.

Esme stared at it for a long time. She'd seen this sort of thing on holos, and she had a vague idea of how it worked: you dropped the liquid on the slab, and heated it, and held the slab under your nose to take in the fumes. They called it Salamander. It was a low-class drug, and on the rare occasions that Esme went to company parties, she'd find her people doing the higher-class version in the bathrooms sometimes, dropping it straight onto the tongue or into their eyes, depending. She'd turned a blind eye, the way her father had instructed her to do. *People have to have their fun,* he'd said.

Esme dropped the metal slab and the dropper on the bed. She held the vial up to the light, where it glowed a sickly yellow. This is what Isabel had become, breathing Salamander in this box of an apartment in the coldest part of the system.

Her chest was so tight, she could hardly breathe. Blood rushed through her eyes. Without thinking, Esme walked over to the sink. She unscrewed the vial. She dumped its contents down the drain.

Outside, the lock beeped.

Esme whirled around, dropping the vial so that it shattered across the tile floor. The door opened.

Isabel stepped in.

She didn't look like herself. Beneath the bulky coat, she was much thinner than Esme remembered, and she wore her hair swept up in a way that revealed the too-sharp lines of her cheekbones. For a moment, she only stood in the doorway, and that sallow light shone straight through her skin.

"What the fuck are you doing here?" she said.

"You've been breathing Salamander."

It was the first thing Esme could think to say. Isabel's expression didn't change. She stepped inside, closed the door. This was more than Esme expected, for her to close the door. Isabel scanned the room. Her eyes settled on the folded clothes on the bed, then Esme by the sink, then the glass sparkling across the floor.

"What did you do?" she said.

"I got rid of it. You shouldn't be doing that stuff."

Esme braced herself for the addict's howling she always saw on holos, shrieking and clawing and gnashing of teeth, but Isabel only dropped her bag on the floor and said, "I can get more of it, you know."

Esme did not know how to respond. Isabel peeled away her coat and scarf. She seemed too frail to move, but she did, albeit with slow, shuffling strides. She walked over to her bed and knocked the folded clothes onto the floor.

"You had no right to come into my apartment," she said, not looking at Esme.

Esme did have that right. She was CEO of the Coromina Group. But she said nothing.

Isabel looked over at her. "Why are you here?" Her voice had a husky quality that Esme didn't remember, a roughness like the last thirteen years had rubbed over her like sandpaper. "Need more of my blood?" She pushed up the sleeve of her sweater to reveal her arm. Her veins stood out pale blue against the white of her skin. "Didn't you assholes learn your lesson the first time?"

"We don't need your blood anymore."

Isabel laughed, a sharp, harsh bark. "Yes, well, I do watch the newsfeeds now and then, down at the cafe." She pressed an indentation on the wall and a clunky old auto-cleaner creaked out, jerking sideways back and forth across the floor, heading toward the broken glass. "Once you had the R-Troops going, you didn't need me anymore. Is that it?"

Esme's face flushed hot. "You ran away."

Isabel glared at her. "What choice did I have?"

Esme felt a stab through her chest. The auto-cleaner buzzed around her feet. "I didn't know," she whispered.

"You didn't know," Isabel said. "Until you did." She draped herself across the bed, as if standing required too much effort. Esme braced one hand against the counter to steady herself. When the auto-cleaner finished, that was when she'd tell her. It was a good deadline.

Neither of them spoke. Isabel pressed her hand over her eyes. The auto-cleaner made one last circle around Esme's feet and then trundled off back to its storage unit. The floor was clean.

"It did a good job," Esme said.

"Why are you here?"

Esme looked away, over at the window. Snow had piled up a few inches on the outside sill.

"Dad's dying," she said.

"Good," said Isabel.

"You don't mean that."

Isabel shrugged. "He caused a lot of harm, didn't he? To the Divested, to the people living here." She gave Esme a hard look. "To all the guests at the party that night."

"You're right," Esme said. "I won't deny that."

Isabel kicked at the floor. Shrugged.

"He wants to see you," Esme said. The room was too tight, too small. How could Isabel live like this, in this closet in a frozen wasteland? "He wants to see all of you. I know you know that Adrienne and Daphne left after you did."

"Well, we always shared a connection," Isabel said. "We had the same mother."

Esme's cheeks burned. She thought back to the other things her sisters had shared that she been cut out of. The secret language of the Divested. The tea parties in the garden. An entire childhood. "We all had the same father, and he's dying. He wants to see you."

"Why?"

Esme knew it wasn't worth lying. "He's handed the company over to me, and he needs all three of you to cede any claim to the company. You have to do it in person."

Isabel laughed. "I thought for sure you'd try to tell me he wanted to apologize." She stretched her legs out on the bed, pressing her back against the far wall. Esme moved toward her, warily, the way she would approach a wild animal. The way she had approached the Divested leader.

"He tried to claim that, actually. But he didn't mean it."

Another laugh. It almost felt easy, being here with Isabel. Easier than it had with the twins, at least.

"Are you worried about me stealing your inheritance?" Isabel asked.

Esme stopped. "No."

"Good. You didn't need to be." Isabel toyed with the end of her hair. "Why do you think I should go see him? Really? Since you're not worried about the inheritance."

Esme stopped. She considered all the answers to the question. Only one was true.

"To watch him die," she said.

Isabel stared at her for a long moment. Then she laughed, tossing her head back, her thin hair fanning out above the bed.

"That's why Adrienne's going," Esme said.

Isabel pulled her knees up to her chest. She studied Esme for a long time. Esme shifted her weight, ran her hands over the counter.

"I knew you were coming," Isabel said suddenly.

"What?" This statement was like a slap. "How?" But as soon as she asked the question, Esme knew.

"The Divested," Isabel said. "They told me. I can speak to them if I go outside the city limits. I can cross over to their world. I don't do it much anymore." She shrugged.

"Why not?" Esme leaned against the counter. She could barely stand.

"They don't have anything for me either." Isabel picked at her bedspread.

Esme felt hollow. "Come home," she blurted. "Please. Not for Dad. Not for me, either. Just—"

But Isabel acted as if she hadn't heard. She rubbed her fist over the bedspread, as if she were trying to smooth it down. "They told me you made an arrangement with them. With Aiden." Isabel peered up at her. "They told me about Aiden, about the R-Troops, the ones who got stuck in their dimension. They wanted me to come back and live with them. But I didn't want to."

"Why not?" Esme asked, her voice barely a whisper.

"It wasn't my home." Isabel shrugged. "After the surgery, I thought it would be better, living with them. That they would understand, you know? But they didn't. I'm too human. It wasn't until I tried to live there I finally realized it." She looked up. "So, keep that in mind, if you want to make this work. To find a way for us all to live together."

"I know it'll be difficult," Esme said. "But I have to try. We'll have to designate certain areas for the Divested. Star's End will be the first. They can change the landscape, make it safe for them to live—I'll get Psych involved. Maybe Aiden and the other R-Troops, too. Show the worlds that it's possible to be both."

Isabel nodded. "And you'll be able to do it all, too. Since Dad's dying. You're going to be CEO."

"I am CEO."

Isabel's head jerked up. She stared at Esme for a long time. Esme didn't dare speak. She knew she'd probably already said the wrong thing. "But he hasn't died yet."

"He gave me the position a few weeks ago. We're still working on the public announcement."

Isabel's expression was blank. Esme moved toward her again, her footsteps echoing off the tile floors. When she reached the bed, she put out one hand, tentative, and pressed it against the mattress. Isabel didn't protest, didn't move away. Esme slid onto the bed and tucked her legs up underneath her. She and Isabel looked at each other.

"I've already shut down weapons manufacture," Esme finally

said. "I'm granting all engineered soldiers full citizenship, including the R-Troops. They can do anything they want."

Isabel's eyes shimmered, and Esme felt her own sorrow welling up inside of her.

"I promise," she said, in a husky voice, "things are going to be different. I promise."

A tear slid down Isabel's cheek.

"I promise," Esme said. "I promise. I promise." She wrapped her arms around Isabel and pulled her in close, and when Isabel let her, then Esme's tears came too. She wept into Isabel's hair. "I promise," she whispered. "I promise. I promise." It became a chant. It became a prayer. Nearly twenty years before, she had made that first promise to Isabel, and she had broken it.

She would not break this one.

When Esme left the Lacheta, stepping out of the shabby lobby and into the freezing, choking street, Isabel was at her side.

It was the first thing that had felt right to her in years, that she and her sister could walk together to the Coromina car Esme had called earlier, a backpack full of clothes hanging from Isabel's right shoulder, or that they would ride in the back seat to the shuttle that would take them back to Ekkeko. Isabel was quiet, and she stared out the window at the inky black of the stars.

"Are you all right?" Esme asked her, when they were surrounded by the pitch of space.

"I'm not sure." Isabel turned away from the window. Her eyes were huge in the drawn lines of her face, but she smiled, thin and wan. "Thank you, though."

"For what?"

"For coming to look for me."

And with that, Esme felt a pang in her chest. All the things she wanted to say were trapped inside her. She had tried to find Isabel in those days after Star's End's destruction. Those months. Those years. But Isabel was unfindable. She had wiped herself clean. For a long time, Isabel had thought she had wanted it that way. Maybe she hadn't after all.

When they arrived at their father's house, Daphne and Adrienne were already there, alerted by the holos Esme had sent on the last drive through Watchet. They waited outside, in the bright tropical sun. Daphne in her windfarmer's clothes, Adrienne in a dress the same colors as the hibiscus growing around the porch. When Esme stepped out of the car, they said nothing. But when Isabel stepped out, looking even frailer in the sunlight, Adrienne stood up, her hands hanging at her side.

"It's been too long," she said.

"Two years." Isabel floated over the lawn.

"You stopped answering my holos."

"Yeah," said Daphne. "Mine, too."

Isabel stopped. She looked up at the house. Esme kept her distance, afraid that if she crowded them, they would scatter, that she would lose all three of them again.

Isabel shrugged. "I had to hightail it out of Isera City. I'm fine now."

Isera City. Another town on Quilla, frozen into the landscape.

"I told you if you had trouble, you could stay with me." Adrienne swooped down on Isabel and pulled her into an embrace, an easy one, as if they hadn't been separated for years.

"And you were always welcome on the farm," Daphne added.

You were always welcome here, Esme thought, but she said nothing. She knew it wasn't completely true. Although it was now.

"You didn't need to worry about me." Isabel stepped back. She glanced over at Esme. "I guess we should get this taken care of, shouldn't we?"

For the first time, the twins acknowledged Esme's existence. Adrienne's gaze flicked over as quick as lightning. Daphne studied her like a painting. And Esme's stomach twisted into knots. She wanted to tell them that things were going to be different. She wanted to tell them that because they came back, she knew she was no longer in any danger of becoming her father.

But she only smiled. "Yeah. We should."

They went inside the house, one at a time, Esme leading the way. Their father was no longer in his bedroom but in a clean chamber that had been installed in the house's parlor. A doctor waited for them outside and handed them clean suits.

"Any contagion could kill him at this point," the doctor explained.

The twins looked at each other. Isabel ran a shaking hand through her hair. None of them said the obvious, that he was dying, who cared if he was contaminated?

But then Esme grabbed the suit and pulled it on, and the others followed.

When Esme and the others stepped inside the clean chamber, the walls hummed with light and then faded. They were contagions, but acceptable ones.

Their father was curled up on his bed. The vitals monitor blinked at this temple, and he was far gone enough to require breathing aids, and so wires bled out of his mouth, spilling around his chest. This was the first time Esme had seen him since he moved into the clean chamber. She had avoided him so assiduously after shutting down weapons manufacture, and she had been preoccupied, too—with the breaches, with her new role of CEO, with finding her sisters. Now that she was here, she was struck by how small he seemed, how insignificant. This was the man who had lived for three hundred years; this was the man who had tried to mold her into another version of himself.

But he had failed. Her sisters were here, and he had failed.

"You found them all," he said, his voice raspy. He tilted his head, turning it toward Daphne, toward Adrienne. Toward Isabel. Esme's body tensed. But Isabel looked away from him first, her hair falling into her eyes. He said nothing.

"They're here to cede their claims to the company," Esme said. "That's all."

Her father laughed, then coughed, then choked. Blood sprayed across his pillow. He nodded. "I figured as much."

One scrawny hand crawled across his bed, toward a lightbox affixed to the frame. He swatted at it, the movement almost too much for him. The lightscreen illuminated beside the bed, revealing Daphne's files. Already, they had been changed to reflect that she no longer had any legal claim to the company.

"Walk through," Esme said. "It needs your DNA to confirm."

Daphne did. The words in the file rearranged themselves. Daphne no longer had her claim.

Isabel went next, stepping through, her head ducked down. She smiled shyly at Esme when she finished. "Good luck," she said.

And then, finally, Adrienne, who studied her file for a long time. She studied it long enough that Esme was almost afraid she would refuse, that they would have to fight each other, that there would never be a connection between them again. But then Adrienne sighed and looked over her shoulder at Esme.

"Don't fuck it up," she said, and stepped through.

Afterward, they stood in an awkward clump. Their father looked at the holos and nodded once. "It's all yours," he said, not looking at Esme, although she knew he was speaking to her. "Let's hope that bullshit decision of yours pays off."

"I've been working on it for the past five years," Esme said. "I know what I'm doing."

He laughed, coughed, shook his head. "Won't have me around if you screw up."

"Stop it," Isabel said. "She's done more good in the last few weeks than you ever did in the last three hundred years."

Esme expected him to lash out at her, one last cruelty before he went. But instead, he fell silent, his eyes fixed on the ceiling. Esme edged over closer to her sisters.

"Well," he said, after a time. "She brought you here. So, I suppose you're right." He tilted his head toward them. He was a ghost of the man Esme remembered. "One last time for me to see all of you." A fractured, trembling smile. "Isabel."

Her face hardened, and her body went very still. Esme braced herself, ready to whisk Isabel out of the room if she needed to.

But all her father said was "You always looked the most like your mother."

Silence, except for Daphne, who made a scoffing noise under her breath.

"I suppose I just wanted to keep a part of her," he sighed.

"Really?" Adrienne said. "That's your excuse? Everything you did"—she gestured at Isabel, at Esme, at all of them—"and you're going to try to blame it on our dead mother?"

He didn't answer, only closed his eyes.

"It's not worth it," Esme said softly. "Let's go."

And so, they left their father after that. They all knew that was the closest he'd come to an apology. They went back outside, the sun bright after the dimness of the clean chamber. Esme blinked her eyes against the light.

"So, there it is," Adrienne said, turning to her. "You brought us home. You secured your claim."

"I got to see you again," Esme said.

Adrienne frowned at this, pretended to look down the street. She brushed one hand over her hair. Daphne kicked at the grass. All four of them stood in silence, the hot sun beating down on them. And then Isabel spoke.

"I'm not going to stay on Quilla anymore."

Esme closed her eyes. Her chest constricted. They had talked about it, of course, but Isabel had still been undecided. Still been unsure.

"Good," said Daphne.

"I'm coming back to Ekkeko."

Esme forced herself to open her eyes, to look at Isabel. She seemed transparent in the sunlight.

"Why?" asked Adrienne.

"I'm going to help Esme." Isabel crossed her arms, shifted her weight. "We're going to find a way to help the Divested. Together."

Esme smiled. Her heart was beating too fast. She looked at her sisters, at Daphne and Adrienne, and Isabel. As adults, they felt like strangers. But they were still her strength.

"Thank you," she said.

Isabel shrugged.

Daphne was the first to react. She nodded, shoved a lock of hair out of her face. "Just be careful."

"I'm not Dad," Esme said. "Not anymore."

Daphne looked up at her, and maybe there was something like

a smile in her expression. And Adrienne, squinting into the sun, almost seemed to approve too.

Esme took a deep breath. She didn't quite allow herself to feel happy. But the sunlight seemed to cut right through her, revealing all her truths. No more secrets. No more shadows.

Everything was new again.

ACKNOWLEDGMENTS

On the first day of January in 2013, I wrote the first five hundred words of *Star's End*—then called *Four Sisters*—as part of a New Year's resolution to up my daily word count. Now, four years later, the manuscript has gone through countless revisions and been made all the better for it. Two people in particular guided me through the grueling editorial process, and they deserve my utmost gratitude. This book would not be the book it is without them. So to my agent, Stacia Decker, and my editor, Navah Wolfe: thank you, thank you, thank you!

Special thanks also goes out to the members of my (still nameless) critique group for reading through the earliest draft of this book: David Young, Chrissa Sandlin, Kevin O'Neill, and Chun Lee. Thanks, guys.

And as always, thank you to the friends and family who have supported me in my writing career: Elizabeth White-Olsen, Layla Al-Bedawi, Holly Walrath, and the rest of the Writespace crew; Amanda Cole; Alexandre Maki; Bobby Mathews; Bonnie Jo Stufflebeam; Ross Andrews; and, of course, my parents. Thank you all!

HOPE CITY, ANTARCTICA.

The southernmost city in the world, with only
a glass dome and a faltering infrastructure
to protect its citizens from the freezing,
ceaseless winds of the Antarctic wilderness.

A female PI
looking for a way to the mainland . . .

The right-hand man to the gangster
who controls the city's food come winter . . .

An aristocrat
with a dangerous secret . . .

An android
that has begun to
evolve . . .

But the city is evolving
too, and in the heart of
the perilous Antarctic
winter, factions will clash,
dreams will shatter, and
that frozen metropolis
just might boil over. . . .

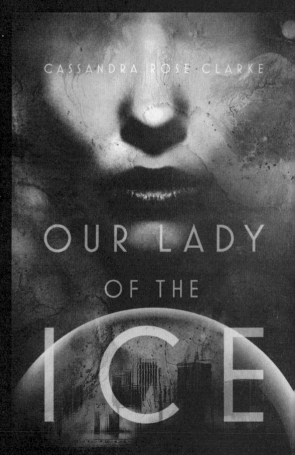

CASSANDRA ROSE CLARKE

OUR LADY
OF THE
ICE

"THE MAD SCIENTIST'S DAUGHTER IS A DEEPLY
ENGAGING TALE BEAUTIFULLY TOLD. CASSANDRA
ROSE CLARKE IS A SUPERB WRITER AND THIS
SPELLBINDING NOVEL SHOULD APPEAL TO GENRE
AND MAINSTREAM READERS EQUALLY."
—GRAHAM JOYCE, AUTHOR OF THE SILENT LAND

CASSANDRA ROSE CLARKE
FINALIST FOR THE PHILIP K. DICK AWARD

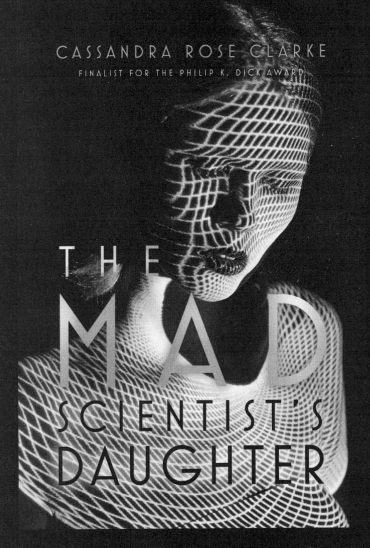

THE
MAD
SCIENTIST'S
DAUGHTER

PRINT AND EBOOK EDITIONS AVAILABLE
SAGAPRESS.COM

STARRING:

Mary Jekyll, Diana Hyde, Catherine Moreau, Beatrice Rappaccini, and Justine Frankenstein!

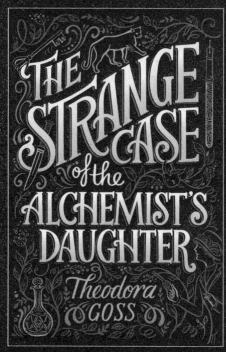

The daughters of literature's most famous mad scientists must come together to stop a murderer—and solve the mystery of their own creation.

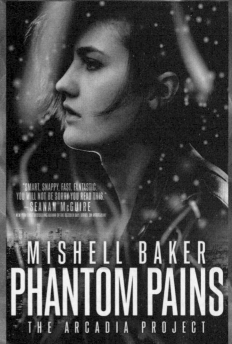